LOOKING FOR TROUBLE

LOOKING FOR TROUBLE

THE EROTIC FICTION OF R.J. MARCH

MANUFACTURED IN THE UNITED STATES OF AMERICA.

THIS TRADE PAPERBACK ORIGINAL IS PUBLISHED
BY ALYSON PUBLICATIONS INC.,
P.O. BOX 4371, LOS ANGELES, CALIFORNIA 90078-4371.
DISTRIBUTION IN THE UNITED KINGDOM
BY TURNAROUND PUBLISHER SERVICES LTD.,
UNIT 3 OLYMPIA TRADING ESTATE, COBURG ROAD, WOOD GREEN,
LONDON N22 6TZ ENGLAND.

FIRST EDITION: MAY 1999

99 00 01 02 03 a 10 9 8 7 6 5 4 3 2 1

ISBN 1-55583-455-8

LIBRARY OF CONGRESS CATALOGING-IN-PUBLICATION DATA
MARCH, R.J.
LOOKING FOR TROUBLE : THE EROTIC FICTION OF R.J. MARCH.
—1ST ED
ISBN 1-55583-455-8
1. GAY MEN—SECUAL BEHAVIOR—FICTION. 2. EROTIC STORIES, AMERICAN. I. TITLE.
PS3563.A6342L66 1999
813'.54—DC21 98-52511 CIP

COVER ILLUSTRATION BY BEAU.

Contents

INTRODUCTION

My father was my first erotic fiction. He was a story I wrote and rewrote in my head, and he figures in one way or another in most of the stories that are included in this collection. He exuded sexuality for me before I had the vocabulary to express what it was he called up in me. He rarely spoke, leastwise not to me, and that added to his allure. He was unachievable morally and emotionally, giving him a stony godlike status that made me adore him—although quietly, secretly, and wrongly.

What I remember about him back then, back when I was 12 and seeing things through changing eyes, is that he rarely wore a shirt. He was a laborer and well-muscled from hard work, and he had a tattoo of a heart on one of his arms with the word MOM written in it. I remember also that he didn't like underwear—and wore none more often than not—and that his jeans sometimes hung low on his hips, baring his bones and the hair on his lower belly, which seemed to thicken as it went down. He was covered with the stuff, and it grew in like a spade from a point between his clavicles, around his pectoral muscles, fringing his nipples, narrowing again at his sternum and spreading, as I said, on his belly. In the winter he would grow a beard, and then his naked chin would surprise me every spring.

He ignored me for the most part. I think he discovered early on that I was not going to be the son he'd expected. I would not kill cats or set fires or smoke at an early age. I would not fight or end up in reform school. I think he looked at me when I was 4 or 5 and decided I would live to embarrass him. And I think I had decided the same thing of him, so I ignored him as well. But I watched him—how could I not? I studied him, his bare torso, my own so much like a birdcage. I was slight, invisible, see-through. And he was formidable, monumental, and in a way heroic, although he was mean to dogs and my mother, foul-mouthed, pathologically antisocial. And, as far as I could tell, he liked the neighbor boys far better than he would ever like me.

There was one day, maybe it was an odd Saturday when he didn't work and we were alone in the house together. He'd taken a shower and went to his room to lie down—he wore this little thing my mother bought him at Kmart, a little terry wrap that buttoned at the waist like a skirt. I went in there when he was asleep to look at him facedown, that towel-wrap high on the back of his pale spread thighs, able to see clearly the hair-choked split of his ass, the huge twin orbs of his testicles, the wrinkles of his sack pressed out and about ready to burst, or so I thought then. My heart knocked about in my bony chest, pressing up into my throat, touching my esophagus like a finger. He didn't move. There was the soft and even rise and fall of his shoulders, reddish-brown from outdoor work, and the channel that ran down his back, splitting him, and his long, haired-up legs, and then the grayish-white soles of his feet.

At that moment he became a character for me, more useful to me this way than as a parent. He was to become every dark-haired man, every obsession.

I grew up on a lake in upstate New York, a fact that figures in my work almost as often, I think, as my dad. We lived down the road from the lake called Oneida in a one-story house built on a cement slab. It was flat-roofed and asbestos-shingled, but my father turned it into something different. I got home from school one day and part of the roof was gone. He did things like that.

But the lake...

My father's brother took us down to the lake every day one summer. He was back from Vietnam and not talking about it. He wasn't looking for work, living out of a little camper my parents parked in our driveway close to the house. I could see it through my bedroom window if I stood on the bed because I had those high windows that were close to the ceiling, like the ones people have in their basements, only I wasn't in a basement. My uncle stuck in my head like a thorn.

He wasn't much like my father. First of all, he was light-haired and funny. He was always talking, always kidding. He played games with my sister and me. I liked him best, though, because he would change with me in my room when we came back from the lake, stripping ourselves out of wet bathing suits, the air on my wet bare flesh extraordinary—was it like that for him? I was afraid to look, though, until he stepped into his briefs and I heard the snap of his waistband. He was as hairy as my dad but not as trim.

The thing about the lake was that it invited all this near-nakedness. Sylvia from up the street, brown as an African with lighter skin glinting between her breasts; her skinny husband in tight trunks, waxing his boat, shaking his long hair out of his face; those boys my father liked so much, smoking and swearing in fringed cutoffs, whooping on the diving platform that all the fathers had worked on together, even my own; and the hippies who lived on the Point, who swam naked and played loud music, infuriating our parents but delighting me, one of them a substitute teacher I had once in fifth grade. Imagine my thrill—a naked one-time substitute teacher!

When we were old enough to be allowed down at the lake unattended, my friends and I would go swimming. One of us would invariably slip out of his shorts and throw them at one of the others—an invitation for the rest of us to follow suit. It was scary to lose purchase of your shorts, though, because there was no guarantee you'd get them back. I would take mine off and hold them, giddily treading water with one hand. We were for the most part covert, keeping everything under cover of water, except for the occasional flash of fanny, and sometimes the bravest of us would do a back flip, rising up out of the water, arching, bringing his crotch up out of the water and into full sight for a split second. And it was daring and exciting and puzzling to swim between the legs of your friends and fish-kiss their privates.

I found a book in the camper, snooping when my uncle wasn't around. It was a paperback titled *The Men's Room*. I don't remember much about it except that one of the characters was gay and in love with his roommate, who was straight, and the gay one would have sex in men's rooms, thinking about the man he loved. I thought it was very sad and very exciting. I read the thing for a week, jacking off like crazy, still unable to come. I learned a lot from the book and put my newfound knowledge to practice with Johnny A., who was accommodating, asking me days later "Does this make us fags?"

The book was my introduction to a world I had hoped existed, where men did things to men—and loved them too. It was like a bonus. I also thought later that I could do that, write that kind of stuff. *Aw, that doesn't seem so hard*, I thought, and I gave it a shot. It was years later, though, when I was in my 20s. My uncle was fat then, and there was something reprehensible about him, something I couldn't put my finger on. And I had by that time stopped talking to my dad. I had other inspirations, but I was drawn to my first ones. They are indelible, inexorable. They are the basest base of my sexuality, this longing that cannot be assuaged, not ever. And the stories, these stories, are the vented hisses of a desire that is dark and terrible and wonderful, a wanting that is crazy and compelling.

It all seemed to happen in one summer, although I know it didn't. It couldn't have. However long it took, it was the beginning of something lifelong—and the beginning of all this, the seeds of many stories. My answer to Johnny A. was "No." But the die was already cast for me—it was a done deal, and I think I knew it then. I wanted Johnny and I wanted his father and I wanted my father and I wanted my uncle. I wanted the boy who stuck up for me on the bus when I was in first grade and the boy whose father was a DJ at radio station WNDR and the boy who wanted to beat me up for going out with Jackie DonVito. I wanted Tommy and Butchie and the other Tommy and his brother Kevin and little monkey-faced Jerry. But not Ralph; I never wanted Ralph.

* * *

I want to take this opportunity to thank Fred Goss, my first full-fledged editor and thereafter my friend, who championed my work from the start and made me feel as though I were doing something worthwhile and creative.

R.J. March
December 1998

Looking for Trouble

Ron jumped when he heard the doorbell. He'd been standing naked by his bedroom window, endeavoring to check out his new neighbors, a pair of college boys who still hadn't put up curtains and who also disdained all but the most worn, brief, and (to Ron) provocative clothing. The sound of the doorbell sent Ron scrambling for something to put on and deflated his self-induced excitement—his neighbors, for some reason, had been fully dressed. He bounded down the stairs, carrying a pair of basketball shorts. There was someone big out there. He flicked on the porch light and looked outside once again.

He shook his head and touched the doorknob, stopping himself from actually opening the door. What was Matt McCaffrey doing here? Ron hadn't heard otherwise, so it was quite feasible that Matt—a onetime juvenile offender and one of Ron's former "students" at Whitcomb Hall for Boys, a detention home tucked away in the Pocono Mountains of eastern Pennsylvania—had left the Navy, in which he'd been "placed" by a judge who had decided that all Matt needed was some good old-fashioned kick-ass discipline. Matt had originally been placed in Whitcomb Hall for his part in a series of burglaries in his parents' affluent New Jersey neighborhood masterminded by an older tough who seemed to Ron to out-Svengali Svengali. Ron had suspected the older man of a certain kind of coercion, of manipulating the big, good-looking boy by his dick strings.

Matt McCaffrey adopted a homeboy swagger at Whitcomb, shuffling around in jeans that hovered just below his hips and clung tenuously to the boxers he wore beneath them. Ron never realized what the kid did on his own time, but he found out one night when he filled in for someone on vacation and had the bathroom shift just prior to lights-out, making sure the little kiddies hadn't set any toilet fires or murdered a peer in one of the stalls. He'd taken advantage of the empty quiet and was taking a quick piss when Matt ambled in wearing just a towel. Ron caught himself staring, openmouthed. Matt caught Ron's eyes and ducked his head to hide his own mean, self-satisfied smile. Ron regained his composure enough to warn the boy that he had only a couple of minutes before lights-out. Matt made a face and unknotted his towel and turned quickly, allowing only a teasing glimpse of his cock and dark bush but a long, lingering view of his pretty white ass. Ron shook his cock and zipped up. "I always thought you were fat," Ron said. "When'd you start working out?" The water squealed, and Matt stepped into it, his ass still to Ron, and he shrugged his shoulders. "Well, hurry it up," Ron said, turning away from that skin, the hairs going straight on his bowed legs. Ron walked away, hands in his pockets, wondering why 16-year-old boys had to look 22 nowadays.

Matt was 18 now and looking for someplace to sit down in Ron's sparsely furnished living room. The homeboy strut lingered, but his jeans were belt-bound, and his T-shirt was tight, betraying the evident continuation of the boy's workouts. Ron crossed his arms over his chest and wished for a shirt and some underwear. The shorts offered but scant coverage, and every step he took made his cock bob and bounce. He noticed that Matt noticed.

"Used to call you Mr. Morecock," Matt said, smiling at Ron's crotch. Ron scowled, feeling his face going red. "You could always see it, man, like when you'd walk past our desks. Kids said you'd had a black-dick transplant."

Matt sat on a chair, his legs spread wide. He wore high-top brown leather work boots that were unlaced and held the cuffs of his jeans. He put his hands between his legs.

"You got something to drink? Like a beer, maybe?"

There was a shirt hanging over a chair in the kitchen, one of his dress shirts. Ron put it on. It fell past the hem of his shorts, making it look as if it was all he had on. He carried two beers back to the living room. Matt was toeing off his boots. He looked up.

"They're new," he said. "I just got them yesterday, and they're tearing my feet up. Do you mind?" He took a beer from Ron and touched his stomach, grimacing. "Didn't eat dinner," he said. Ron went into the kitchen and warmed up his leftover lo mein, trying to remember where he'd left his wallet. He came back into the living room with a plate of the microwaved Chinese food.

Matt was stripped down to his underwear.

Ron stopped dead.

The boy's chest was smooth and defined, with wide, dark nipples the size of half-dollars. His belly button protruded, a sexy knot surrounded by black fur. His legs were still spread but covered now with hair instead of denim. Ron stared at Matt's white briefs.

"Is it, uh, hot in here?" he asked the near-naked boy. Matt shrugged and began to eat and didn't speak until he was finished, although he looked up from time to time to stare at Ron and make him squirm.

Finally the boy put the plate down, belching softly.

"Excuse me," he said.

He stood then and walked around the room. "You

didn't just move in, right? I mean, you've lived here a while, haven't you?" Ron shook his head, then nodded, then threw up his hands.

"You don't have a lot of stuff," Matt said. "You want some stuff?"

"Stuff?"

Matt scratched himself through his shorts. "Stereo equipment, big-screen TV, computer?" He smiled. "My dad—you know," he said, and Ron remembered McCaffrey's Electronics of eastern Pennsylvania and New Jersey.

He walked in front of the big bay window, holding open the curtains. Ron looked at the boy's covered ass, remembering his first encounter with the bared version. "Where's that girlfriend of yours?" he heard Matt ask. "That one you always used to talk about."

Caught off-guard, Ron stammered, trying to concoct a simple but believable lie. Matt turned around and faced the man. "I had a feeling about that," he said, nodding knowingly.

He stood at ease in front of the window. "You used to rule that classroom," he said. "You can hardly speak now." He gave Ron a long, hard look. "You're not afraid of me, are you?"

Ron blinked. He looked at the beer bottle in his hand as if it had just materialized there. What are you supposed to say to a former student standing uninvited and undressed in your living room?

"No, not afraid," Ron said finally. "Just a little confused, I suppose."

"Am I confusing you?" A smile moved his lips. He took a few steps toward Ron. He looked exceedingly good in underpants, and Ron guessed the boy knew it. Ron took a few swigs of beer, keeping his eye on the half-naked boy.

"Are you confused, Mr. Wilcox?"

He took a few more steps. The coffee table was between them, an arm's length of distance.

He had never had any trouble with Matt. At Whitcomb, Ron had had his share of assholes, punks who wanted to kick his ass because he made them do homework or tried to break through their tough facades. He was able to physically restrain the biggest, strongest boys. He'd earned a grudging respect from most of them and a cool disregard from a few like Matt. But right now he couldn't read the situation. The plain facts of the matter were too plain to be true—Matt was trying to seduce him? There had to be some underlying reason for all of this, Ron was thinking, but what? Had he come looking for trouble?

"I guess I need to be a little more straightforward," Matt said, as if he had heard Ron's thoughts. He stroked himself through his shorts, rousing his dick. It began to thicken noticeably, growing downward, filling the pouch. The head of it sneaked out the side.

Ron was beginning to feel a little straightforward himself. He tried to disguise the burgeoning rise of his own cock under his shirttails, but to no avail. He sat very still, barely breathing, eyeing the mushroom head of Matt's prick. Fully extended, Matt's cock now resembled a fat, blunt redheaded cannon. He dragged his briefs down his thick thighs, and his pecker thwacked against his stomach, making him smile proudly. He hefted his balls, big and low-hanging, and looked at Ron.

"Does this surprise you?" he said, wagging his stuff.

"Your penis?" Ron said.

"Yeah," Matt said, shaking it again. "My penis, my cock. The fact that it's out and in your face."

"It's a surprise," Ron answered, swallowing an enormous amount of saliva that had suddenly formed in his mouth.

Hadn't he always wondered what it would be like to kiss one of those boys? Any one of them? Carlos, Billy Post, Johnny Meyers, that big asshole from Trenton? Hadn't he wondered how it would be to hold one naked and hard, to have him kiss back? Matt opened his mouth, and Ron, now standing, sucked his tongue. The boy groaned and pushed Ron back against the chair, fumbling with the buttons of his shirt. He grabbed hold of Ron's chest and smeared his mouth over the man's cheek and tongued into his ear. He pushed Ron's shorts down, baring the man's clublike cock. He stopped to look at it.

"Oh, shit," he said.

"Are *you* surprised?" Ron asked.

Matt shook his head.

"Suck it," Ron said.

Matt hesitated, ducking his head, shaking it again. "No way," he said.

He was pretending he didn't know what to do with it, Ron realized, watching the boy hold the veiny thing delicately with his thumb and fingertips. "You look like a lady at a tea party," Ron said, sneering. Matt flicked his tongue at the big-ended cock and looked up, doe-eyed and innocent. He opened his mouth, and Ron watched the head disappear, followed by much of the thick white shaft, past the dark ring that marked his cock's halfway point.

Ron held the boy's head and worked himself in and out of the hard-sucking hole. Matt cupped Ron's balls with one hand and grabbed a handful of ass cheek with the other. He worked on the long log, bruising his throat with the round, buttery head. He smoothed his tongue up and down the tender underside.

Ron tugged on the kid's ear. "Upstairs," he said, and he followed Matt up to his bedroom, groping the smooth white ass he'd first seen two years ago, directing it gruffly where to go. He pushed Matt down on the bed and grabbed his ankles, splitting him like a wishbone, revealing his dark crack. He put his hands on the boy's cool cheeks, spreading them and putting his face into that dark, musty split. He rubbed his hands along the backs of Matt's thighs and down to his ankles, which he grabbed again and pushed forward, getting the boy up on his knees. He got hold of Matt's ample package, pulling the handful back between his legs.

Matt moaned loudly. "Oh, yeah," Ron heard him breathe as Matt lifted his head and looked over his shoulder at his former teacher. Ron smiled sardonically and tightened his grip on the kid's nuts, making Matt's eyes squeeze shut. *If it's trouble he came looking for,* Ron thought, *he's found it, big-time.*

Ron pulled on Matt's dick, making it greasy, and brought his open hand down, raking his fingernails across the pale left buttock. Matt grunted and pushed his face back into the mattress.

Matt's bung hole pulsed. Ron ran his thumb over it, pushing into it as if it were a hot, overripe melon. His thumb disappeared into Matt, and the boy made a muffled noise. He fucked Matt this way, thumbing into him, enjoying the boy's newfound acquiescence. Matt's heavy joint trembled and dripped with anticipation.

Ron got himself up on the bed, slapping his dick against his open hand like a cop with a nightstick. Matt lifted his head, looking back.

"You gotta be kidding," he said, trying to smile.

Ron shook his head.

"I don't think I can take that, man," Matt said, moving slowly and carefully away from Ron, eyeing the thick-shafted monster that hung from Ron's groin. "I've never done that. It's too fucking big." Ron followed him across the mattress, chasing the boy up against the far wall. He jammed his legs between Matt's, pressing his big, big cock against the haired-up crack of his ass.

"Let me suck you off, man," Matt debated halfheartedly. "I suck cock real good, Ron."

"Well," Ron said, gently butting the back of Matt's head with his own forehead. "You suck cock well, and I won't begrudge you that. But right now we're going to try something else."

Ron noticed that Matt was no longer squirming but was pushing rhythmically backward, actually creating a pleasant friction for Ron's pecker with every movement. Ron pushed himself harder against the furry channel. Matt stopped moving and looked up.

"Promise you'll be gentle?"

Ron nodded.

"All right," Matt said. "Let's do it."

Ron tossed the boy across the bed again but stayed with him, on top of him, holding his wrists gently with one hand. He kept his face behind Matt's ear. "I promise you, this'll go easier if you relax," he told him.

"I am relaxed," Matt said, his voice muffled. "I'm not fighting, man. I want it."

Ron pushed forward, and the tip of his cock breached Matt's hole.

"It hurts," Matt said, and then he laughed. "Of course it fucking hurts—it's too fucking big. How much is in?"

Ron reached in between them and felt around.

"You've got half the head," he said.

"Give me some more," Matt said, and he cried out when Ron pushed in. "When is this gonna feel good?"

"Feels good already," Ron said, starting a little back-and-forth movement that concentrated on the sensitive glans. Each stroke fed Matt a little more dick, loosening him up and getting him used to the new sensations. He was up on his knees and elbows, and Ron had his hands on the boy's hips, smoothing them. Then he slid his hands up the boy's sides and played with his hardened nipples. Ron no longer wanted to ram into Matt, desiring instead only to please his new fuck buddy. A slow, easy fuck to introduce the boy's anus to Ron's big invader was in order.

"That's better," Matt breathed. "Better, yeah." His head was bobbing, and he moved his ass for a better strike on his prostate. Ron leaned over the boy's back, kissed it, and reached under and stroked Matt's balls as the boy jacked hard on himself. It wouldn't be long, he was thinking—an 18-year-old's staying power was whimsical, his recovery time lightning-quick. Ron wasn't sure if he should try to keep up with the boy this time around or let Matt go on his own and wait five minutes for Round 2.

For all of Ron's thinking, it was his dick that made the final decision, and once Matt started heaving and hollering, Ron started doing the same. He pumped hard into the boy, forgetting all about slow and easy, and Matt seemed to enjoy the forcefulness. He straightened up, clenching hard on Ron's joint, and released a spraying load of come all over Ron's pillows and sheets. Ron clenched his teeth, riding the smooth, hot hole, his mind a big black blank. He put his face against the boy's shoulder, biting gently on the muscled flesh there, and burst up inside Matt's cunt, churning up a come butter that the boy would eventually eat off Ron's resuscitating dick, signaling the beginning of Round 2.

Ron was the first one up the next morning. He eased out of bed and looked at the sleeping boy's face. The morning light shone on it, making it angelic and beautiful—a Caravaggio beauty, half saint, half rough trade. He was going to go downstairs and whip up a big breakfast for both of them when he saw his wallet on the nightstand. He glanced at Matt and picked it up, taking it with him.

The Golden Boys

He'd been living in the rented cabin for a week when it was put up for sale. There was something about this place—the cabin and the little town—that suited him, and the asking price for the cabin was ridiculously low, even considering the money it was going to take to refurbish the place and turn it into a year-round residence. So he bought the little cabin and had the contents of his apartment in Rochester moved to Cross Lake.

It wasn't much of a town, really—just a concentration of cabins like his own plus a few newer, sturdier brick homes built in the '50s. There was a square of sorts, around which sat a convenience store, a diner, a drugstore, and two bait shops. The village of Cross Lake sat on the shore of the lake itself, and while fishing wasn't considered an economic concern for the town, it probably was the most popular pastime for its older inhabitants.

Mike Polsen bought himself a little boat. It looked like the ones you see in paintings you can buy at Kmart—an old man and a little girl sitting together, rowing sweetly. It was wide and sun-bleached white with huge, long-handled oars. "You could put a little trolling motor on the back of that—anything bigger'd sink ya," said the old man who'd sold him the boat. "Got one the missus bought me for Christmas some years back. Ain't worth a damn to me, so's you can have it with the boat here. How's that?"

Mike had the summer free for the first time in years. He got himself into a routine of having breakfast at the diner and then going down to the stone beach to read the nearest local paper. There was a small island in the center of the lake, a green float that obscured the view of the other side. Boys went out there, the same pack he always saw floating around town, aimless, handsome. They all looked alike, like brothers, but they weren't, he figured, hearing them call each other by their last names, jostling one another outside the convenience store, leaning against the shining fenders of their cars. There were five or six of them, all roughly the same age, just out of high school, a couple of older ones, and two of the group were brothers, he gathered. Mike got them mixed up until one of them showed up on his doorstep with the trolling motor.

"I'm Kyle Briggs," he said, holding the motor and twirling it on the porch like a cane. "My grandfather said he was giving this to you." He eyed Mike suspiciously, as if Mike had connived the motor away from the old man. The boy peered through the screen into Mike's living room, which he'd outfitted with two linen-covered sofas and a coffee table made out of the door to an outhouse. The apricot-colored walls gave him away, he supposed, but the reflected light was lovely, coming from the candles he had lit as though awaiting a lover. The boy stood and stared, squinting.

"Looks like a magazine," Kyle said. He leaned the motor against the wall beside the door. "You fixed the dump up nice. Shoulda seen what it used to look like." He stopped and looked at Mike, smiling. "Well, I guess you kinda did," he finished.

Mike asked the boy in—being hospitable, he wondered, or testing the lake's waters? The boy was of medium height and had sand-colored hair. He had the thick, freckled arms of a baseball player, but he wasn't a big boy, so to speak. He shoved his hands into the pockets of his denim shorts, long and baggy, the tail end of his braided leather belt pointing in the direction of his groin. He sort of smiled, dallying on the porch until the screen door opened and he stepped inside. Kyle looked around himself before entering, as if being seen were not in his best interests. Mike noted all of this with a small amount of satisfaction.

He showed the boy around the house, reveling in Kyle's exclamations over the changes he'd produced in the shambled cottage.

"The upstairs is next," Mike said with a sigh, the task of it a burden he'd been putting off for a while. "I've got to get it insulated up there."

"My brother'd help you," Kyle said. "He does that kind of stuff. He works with my uncle. You should talk to him. He'd help you."

"Send him over," Mike said. They passed a side table covered with trophies, old ones that Mike had collected, all topped with male figures with wreathed heads, arms upheld in victory. Behind them on the wall was a black-and-white photograph of an old beau, naked and resplendent on a zebra skin, ass up, dark-cracked. The boy looked closely, then away, his face a mortified blank.

"Well, I ought to get g-going," Kyle said, taking on a bit of a stutter. He hurried to the door and stopped short. "Place looks cool," he said, turning to face Mike. "I like your things."

Oh, you do? Mike thought, standing at the door, watching the boy disappear into the dark beyond the light of the porch lamp.

Kyle Briggs lay on his back on Davis's bed, listening to his friend complain the way he always did about the lack of local pussy. The only babes, he said, were on the other side of the lake, like Jenna Krupp. Kyle was only half listening, mesmerized while watching Davis change clothes. Bill Davis had a man's body, more so even than Kyle's brother, Kevin. He stared at the easy hugeness of Davis's biceps, round and smooth as softballs, and his thighs, covered with dark and curling fuzz, the rest of him hairless and white so that he looked almost like a satyr. Down to dingy white briefs and talking about busting his nut, Davis had the swagger and appeal of an older boy.

Kyle was thinking of Mr. Polsen in his pinkish candlelit living room. He didn't look like a fag—more like a gym teacher, with those big tree-trunk legs and furred forearms, short-cropped dark hair silvering a little on the sides, standing at the door in a pair of shorts as tight as briefs and showing everything. Kyle had gone home that night, gotten himself into bed, and fallen asleep, only to dream about the guy, waking up with a boner he could not ignore.

"Pussy," Davis chanted. "Pussy, pussy, pussy."

"Pussy," Kyle rejoined, thinking, *Dick—big, thick, fat dick.* He could see Davis's cock in the yellowed front of his briefs, thumb-size, its covered head inching upward. Davis was a grower; his little uncut wiener grew as fat as a sausage at the state fair. He watched the boy brush at his future hard-on, pushing it down. It would eventually curl down the curve of his tight-bagged balls, trapped in the tightening cotton pouch.

"What do you know about pussy?" Davis said.

"Just your mom's," Kyle returned.

Davis jumped him, getting his armpit over Kyle's face. The boy resisted the strong urge to lick his friend there, the black and stinking beard that lined Davis's underarms. Davis didn't go for that kind of shit, though; none of that ass-grabbing stuff the other guys did so easily, without thinking, it seemed, as if it were all innocent and beyond implication. Davis was always the first to bust on the queer kid at school and on fags they saw on television. But Kyle also felt the bone Davis sported and remembered a time when they'd jerked off together looking at a *Playboy* Kyle had stolen from his brother's room. He liked thinking about the awesomely high arc of Davis's spew, how droplets of it landed on Kyle's arm, droplets he'd discreetly licked off when the other wasn't looking. And he thought about other times, recent times: Davis complaining about the pain of his hard-ons, the pain of needing to get off so bad, and then doing it as if it were a necessary course of nature, allowing, if only for a moment or two, Kyle to put his mouth on the cowled head and tongue into the sleeve of skin and taste the sweetness of his best friend.

"Shit," Davis muttered, rolling off of Kyle, hiding his erection against the mattress. Kyle wanted nothing more than to reach under his friend and squeeze the hell out of the big thing—he would have been entirely happy to jerk Davis off, just to see the thing shoot again. His own come spurted out in thick clots onto his belly, seeping into his bush; it didn't propel itself the way Davis's would. *He must get a face full every time he whacks*, Kyle thought.

Thinking about touching his friend's prick got his own going so that it started leaking, leaving dark, wet spots on the front of his shorts, ones he used to wear in gym class. He hated the way his cock dripped and made a mess of his underwear, betraying any excitement he tried to hide (though there were times when all that extra lube came in handy—like the night before, when he'd had his prong in his hand and Mr. Polsen on his mind).

Davis's white-clothed butt shone in a rectangle of sun that came in from the window beside his bed. Kyle watched the dancing dust motes over it, the suddenly interesting intricate weave of the cloth, the small flexes of Davis's butt muscles—glutes, he recalled his gym teacher calling them—as Davis did a little mattress humping. He had his arms up under his head, and Kyle saw him facing him, closed-eyed.

He wants it, Kyle realized. *He's all horned up, and he wants it. All I have to do is make the first move, so he doesn't feel like he's begging for it.*

He put his hand on his friend's cotton-covered butt.

"Cut it out," Davis complained, making his glutes jump under Kyle's moist palm.

"One more time," Kyle said. "You aren't any closer to the inside of Jenna Krupp's pants," he added meanly.

"You're not a faggot, are you?" Davis asked, opening his eyes and looking into Kyle's.

"Are you?" Kyle asked back.

"Yeah, right," Davis snorted, rolling over and and presenting Kyle with his briefs-encased throb.

Kyle moved himself up so that his head was within range of Davis's sweet-smelling crotch. Davis thumbed his waistband down so that his cock fell out, hard and bareheaded. It landed quite nearly in Kyle's mouth. All he had to do was stick his short stub of a tongue out to touch it, and he did, and Davis put his hand on the back of Kyle's head and drew his mouth down the thick stalk, pressing Kyle's nose into that lush black bush.

"Easy," Davis said, and Kyle raised his eyebrows in surprise—who needed to go easy here? Davis's hand on the back of his head was insistent. It drew Kyle down into that silky, wiry pad of hair again and again.

"Oh, man," Davis breathed, and his fingers went slack and curled against Kyle's scalp, almost a caress. His nuts had tightened even more than they had to begin with, hairy little walnuts that Kyle stroked with his fingers, rolling them around, pressing beyond them toward the soft, furry rut of Davis's ass crack, to lips that went rigid, as hard as a kiss from a maiden aunt.

He took his mouth off of Davis's thrusting bone. "I want to see it," he whispered, taking it in his fist, jacking the slack-skinned thing. He wished for his own forsaken foreskin; the sight of Davis's slipping back and forth over his purple dick head was enough to unleash a flow from his own untouched cock. He rode the mattress, anticipating Davis's blast, and came himself when Davis bulleted a rope of come that fell heavily into Kyle's hair from a thin slit of a piss hole.

Davis got himself up quickly—no lingering for him. "The guys are waiting," he said, not looking at Kyle, who wanted to lie about and enjoy what had just happened between them. But for Davis it had never happened. He started in about pussy again, looking for something to wipe the spit and come from the end of his dick with, and he talked about Jenna Krupp and how hot she was, and Kyle watched the dust dancing in the beam of sunlight falling uninvited through the window.

He was sitting on his porch, combating mosquitoes, wishing he had gone ahead and screened himself in when he'd had the opportunity earlier that year. There were a couple of citronella candles on either side of him and a book on his lap, but he wasn't reading, couldn't read. The darkness surrounded him. He had his bare feet up on the porch rail, flexing his toes until they cracked. Crickets chirruped. His balls dangled, spiked with stiff, straight hairs. He was just about ready to go inside and yank out a fuck film to masturbate with. *Fucking boonies*, he complained to himself, regretting just now his exile in Virginville. Sure, there were good-looking guys floating around, riding by. Stopping by, even, bearing gifts, he thought, recalling the boy with the trolling motor. But where was he now, this Briggs boy? He recalled the boy saying, "I like your things." Not, apparently, "I like your thing." More's the pity. Mike sighed.

There was some rustling in the distance, some panting. *The boys playing a prank?* he wondered. Then there was some faint whistling, something nameless and tuneless that stopped short, and the rattle of keys, or something like it, and then the quick steps of something on four legs. It turned out to be a dog, a golden Lab striding toward him as if it had finally found home.

"Blanket!" he heard whispered sharply. The dog trotted up the steps and pushed its cold nose into Mike's crotch and bared balls.

"*Oof!*" he said, closing his legs fast.

"Blanket!" someone called, a man, a boy. Mike stood up and tried not to squint into the darkness that edged the dim light of his lamps.

"It's Kevin Briggs, Mr. Polsen," he heard. "Kyle's brother. Dan Briggs's grandson."

This Briggs boy was an older twin of his brother. His hair was only slightly darker, impossibly shorter, his frame slightly larger. He was wearing jeans and a shirt shorn of its sleeves, left open and untucked, revealing the soft gold of his torso. He had his brother's stubby freckled nose and light-colored eyes. Green? Blue? Polsen couldn't tell from this distance. His hands in his pockets lowered his jeans so that his pubes were evident, as were the dipping lines that dropped from the boy's hips down to his crotch. He looked at Mike, who got up out of his chair, pulling at the crotch of his shorts to cover himself thoroughly.

"My brother said you needed some help."

Help? Mike thought. "Oh, yeah, the attic," he said, crossing his arms over his chest, squeezing his pecs together and giving himself some awesome cleavage. "There's next to nothing for insulation up there, and I wanted to get things squared away before the cold sets in."

"You planning on making this your home year-round?" the boy asked, making a face.

"I do," Mike answered. "I think it's nice here."

"I guess," Kevin Briggs said.

"Not enough action, huh?" Mike asked.

"Not nearly enough," Kevin affirmed, shaking his head. He drew his hands out of his pockets. Crickets came up singing, and the dog fell to the floor at Mike's feet in a tired heap. "Ain't much to do out here," Kevin said, rolling his shoulder like a pitcher doing seven innings. "No girls to speak of," he added quietly.

"I hadn't really noticed," Mike replied, getting a quick grin from the boy.

Getting the boy into bed was the easy part; getting him to do something there was a different matter. Kevin lay on his back, naked and hard, with his hands behind his head as though ready to take a nap. Mike heard the dog sniffing around the living room. The boy's cock was thick and not very long; sparse blond hairs grew on the shaft, which tapered sharply at its end, taking a left turn. His balls hung low in the V of his legs, resting on the sheets. He seemed very comfortable, looking at Mike through half-closed eyes. There was a shining thread of precome hanging from his dick.

Mike put his hand on Kevin's stomach. It was hard and hot and quivered under his touch.

"I ain't queer, you know," Kevin said. "There just aren't enough girls around."

"You do what you can," Mike said agreeably.

"I got this guy who sucks my dick. Friend of my brother's." He looked at Mike as if awaiting judgment or congratulations. "I want to fuck him, but he won't let me—says it's too big. Is my dick too big for fucking?"

Mike looked at it, thinking nothing was too big for fucking. He took it in his hand, squeezing the shaft, turning the pointed head purple.

"This," he said, "is perfectly suitable for fucking."

"You like getting it up the ass?" Kevin asked.

"Not too much," Mike admitted.

"Does it hurt?"

Mike shook his head. "Depends. You want to find out?"

"Fuck, no," the boy said, almost laughing.

Mike pinched out a droplet of dick honey and licked his sticky fingers. Kevin's eyes slitted. He bent his toes back and cracked them and spread his legs a little.

"When was the last time your little buddy sucked you off?" Mike asked.

"Oh," the boy said, "not too long ago. Sometime last week, I guess."

"You horny now?"

"Dude, I'm always horny."

Still spread-eagled on his back on the too-soft mattress, Kevin looked up at Mike with a mixture of manly lust and boyish impatience clouding his eyes. "I've got an idea. Why don't you just jerk me off?" the boy suggested.

"Is that all you want?" Mike asked. "You could do that yourself."

"Feels good anyway," Kevin said, lifting his head a little. "Spit on it and jerk it off, man."

He did not mind doing the boy's dirty work. He'd gone long enough with his own in his hand, and Kevin's shaft fit in the curling cup of his palm the way Mike's own couldn't. At its base it had the circumference of a zucchini, narrowing to a gumdrop-size head that made Mike salivate. Perfect for fucking, he was thinking, if he were the one to be fucked. It had happened only a few times, countable on one hand, and that was by a Greek monk-to-be with similar-size equipment, though not so anus-stretching, its girth more evenly distributed from top to bottom. He slid his slippery hand over the boy's little head and watched Kevin's legs twitch as he leaked a gob of lube from his tiny piss hole. Mike's grip was good and wet, sloppy-sounding, the noise turning up his own horniness a notch.

"Lick that shit up," Kevin said, his voice deep and manly, dirty and sexy. *If the boy ever learned what to do with his hands, he'd be one hell of a lay*, Mike was thinking, lapping up the salty-sweet seepage from Kevin's tightened nuts. Kevin put his hand on the back of Mike's shaved neck and pressed the man's mouth down the long and thickening pole.

"Suck it, man," Kevin whispered, pumping himself down Mike's constricting throat. Mike's cock was trapped in his pants, aching for some kind of manipulation. He twisted his hips and managed to press himself against Kevin's naked shin, riding the hard bone of it.

He reached both hands under the boy's butt and spread his ass cheeks wide, stretching the hole open and causing the boy to yelp like a puppy lifted by its ears. Mike pressed on and fingered the gulping hole, moist already, as if lubed. He knuckled into the boy, making him squirm, taking the quivering stick into his hot mouth, imagining himself on his feet, dipping into the ankle-grabbing wiseass, fucking the daylights out of the Briggs boy. He found the boy's prostate hardening and felt his ass lips tightening. He finger-fucked Kevin the way he wanted to dick-fuck him: fast and hard.

"I'm gonna shoot!" Kevin shouted suddenly, filling Mike's mouth full of warm, creamy come. Mike got up on his knees, wobbling on the spongy bed, and pulled his cock out of his shorts. He spat out a little of Kevin's jizz onto his buzzing dick head and swallowed the rest, jacking hard on his long pole, thumbing the sensitive head. The boy stared—curious, smug—as Mike pulled on his fat-headed prong. He straddled the boy's thigh and rubbed his balls against it. The boy fingered his own still-hard pecker, pinching out the last drops from his nuts, offering the juice to Mike, who leaned over and took the come-covered fingers into his mouth.

"Oh," he said, squirting a thick, flying line of white all over the surprised boy. His body shook with the last few strokes, and Kevin wiped the come from himself with the corner of a pillowcase.

"Sorry," Mike said.

"S'cool," Kevin said. "I just wasn't expecting it. You always shoot like that?"

"It's been a while," Mike shrugged.

The boy looked up at the ceiling. "We can get on that when the weather breaks." Mike looked up. The attic. He nodded, his dick dripping onto the boy's blond-furred thigh.

Kyle went out to the island by himself. He was supposed to meet Tim and Hal at Bill's house at 10 but came here instead. He felt weird about being with Davis and the other guys, like what they'd done that afternoon was all over his face—he always felt like that after they did stuff together. His penis rolled in his shorts. He sat down on the cool, damp sand; lay back; and looked at the stars. He couldn't get the thought of Bill Davis's prick out of his mind or get the feel and taste of it out of his mouth.

He stood and undid his shorts, letting them fall, feeling the night air between his legs like a caress. He was erect as he stepped into the water, treading carefully over the slippery rocks, small waves licking at his ankles, his shins, and his calves. He brought Bill and Mr. Polsen together in his mind, the two of them making love on Bill's twin bed, fucking and fucking, Polsen sticking his cock deep inside Bill and making the boy wail, Bill choking Polsen with his fat little pud.

The lake covered his cock like a warm mouth, and he felt the suck of it, the flow of it, and he came underwater without touching himself at all. On the shore, toward home, he heard the hoots and hollers of the guys. They were coming looking for him. He dived in and stroked through the black water, out to where he couldn't feel the bottom without going under, and he waited for his friends to come.

Bed Pig

Man was pissed. He came into the cell with a rolled newspaper—no telling what it was wrapped around, something heavy the way it bent his wrist, something hard. He had it with both hands, like

a bat. I watched the newspaper, wondering if it was one that I had read.

"That last one said you were unkind about his size," Man said, pounding out each syllable with a slap of the newspaper against his palm. "I cannot afford to lose a customer.""I need another book," I told him.

"Did you make an unkind remark about his smallishness?" The newspaper swung over my head.

"I only asked if he was in yet." The roll came back and caught me hard on the side of the face. I was not mistaken about its weight, and my jaw felt broken, and he said to me, touching my hair nicely, pushing my face softly to his pant leg, "Hate to do that, hate to, boy," and I could feel him against my cheek, his cock getting hard. I touched it with my fingers, feeling the heat of it. It dropped low and made a slow ascent until it wedged itself, the head of it pressed hard against the thinning dirty cloth. I breathed on it, put my mouth on it. He fingered my ear, and I heard the bell.

"A customer," he said suddenly. He left the cell.

This is now, and things have changed. I read about the past, what things were like in the '90s, from someone's journal that I keep hidden as if it were my own: "May 2, 1992: Saw Scott again. We walked down the boardwalk and got lost in some dunes, ignoring the DO NOT TRESPASS and STAY OUT OF THE DUNES signs to have a little fun. He begged me to put it to him, and I did, with some spit and elbow grease. I fucked him good, and he said my name over and over and that he was in love."

If I had a journal, I would write, "18.12.2014: I had the small one again today, and he didn't leave me anything. I hate him, and it galls me to have him sweat over me, poking me with that pinkie. Man. I want Man."

"Here's my best," Man said, holding open the flimsy curtain that passed for privacy. A man stuck his head in and glanced around the room. *New one*, I was thinking. I was wearing a baseball uniform, one that Man got from a warehouse stash, some old man hoarding memories of the good old days. Man let him come by for free, but all he ever wanted was someone to touch the back of his head where his white hair was greasy and thin. He'd come by and leave me things, whatever he happened to have in his pocket: an inkless ballpoint pen with a lady on the side whose negligee would disappear when the pen was flipped; a silver thimble; a brittle package that held a dried-up condom.

This new customer was a Builder. I could tell by his hands and the heavy boots he was wearing and the look in his eye—a dim sort of intelligence, but intelligence nonetheless. Builders could afford this sort of luxury. Wreckers, whose wages were considerably less, weren't here as often—only on special occasions—but I liked them the best. They were big and stupid, and there was always one who wanted to lie back and lift his legs. Wreckers were kissers; Wreckers would suck cock. A Wrecker would say, "Shoot in my mouth; let me eat your seed." Builders never said much of anything.

This one did not like my costume.

"What would you like?" I asked him. He was a big one—clean-shaven, dark-eyed. He turned his back as I undressed. His pants were tight in the seat and going thin. He flexed his butt cheeks, knowing I was watching.

I had a see-through baby-doll negligee that I hated, but I thought he would like it. It made me humble, and I couldn't look a man in the eye when I had it on. Man said that's what the customers want. I knew that Man liked it fine.

"Do you like this?" I asked him. He turned around. "Will this do?" He looked me over quickly. I felt my cock thickening in the ladylike sheen of sheer panties.

"Take that shit off," he said. He watched me undress this time, lighting a cigarette and squinting into the smoke. He touched his brow, and I saw his roughed-up fingers, blunt-ended and nicked, scarred with dirt. He squatted, resting on his haunches. His thighs strained his work pants, and I could see the beginnings of a splitting seam at his crotch. "You got anything regular?" he said. He had a small space between his two front teeth and lips that tended to stay open. "You got any jeans or something?" His eyes went over my bare body. "Some underwear?"

"Briefs? Bikinis? Boxers?" I offered.

"Put something on," he said.

I could hear Man breathing outside the cell, could see his boots under the sway of curtain.

I put on a pair of old Y-fronts that were a bit small. He wanted a regular boy, I was thinking, less interested in costumes than he was in ritual. This one was operating from some memory, I decided, from an old book or movie he might have got hold of. I was guessing, of course—there was no pinpointing the mind of a Builder—but it was something to do, to think about, like a crossword puzzle. He finished his cigarette and looked for someplace to put it. I waved a hand as if to say "Anyplace."

He stood, wiping his hands on his pants.

"What's your name?" he wanted to know.

"Wilton," I said.

"I'm going to call you Billy," he told me. I looked up at him, nodding, liking the way he towered over me. His belt buckle caught some of the dim light and glittered, a star over his crotch. I wanted to put my hands on him. I found his face, his eyes catching mine. His eyebrows met over the bridge of his nose, his short hair stuck up like brush bristles. I thought I saw him wink.

I was waiting for scenario, a clue about how to make things progress.

And then he said, "Do you love me, Billy?"

I blinked up at him.

"Seriously?" I said. He made a face and looked away.

"You know I do," I told him, catching on.

"Yeah, right," he said, looking into a corner. His profile was suitable for coining. I wanted to press his silhouette between my legs. I moved around in bed so that I was on my back, up on my elbows, legs bent and heels dug in.

"No," I was saying. "I do, I do love you."

He looked at me again, all laid out for him. He said my name, the one he gave me. He got down on his haunches again, putting a finger on the inside of my knee, pushing it out, opening my legs. He stared at the white cover of my crotch, and I felt myself inching about down there, my cock rolling over and waking up. The Builder's eyes, close to black, seemed almost to touch me, and I felt his eyes on my body as he looked me over.

"My name is Geary," he said softly. "But you can call me Brad, right?"

I put my bare foot out and toed the split of his pants. "I love you, Brad," I said, and he laid his hands flat on my thighs. I worked my big toe into the hole and made the hole bigger, and I felt the hairy warmth of skin. "Come lie with me," I said, reaching for one of his hands. He stretched himself out beside me, and I felt the roughness of his clothes and smelled his breath, a blend of whiskey and tobacco and whatever he'd had for lunch. I put my hands on his chest, fingering the buttons of his shirt.

"Kiss me," he said.

"You a Builder?" I asked him. He nodded and pushed his face against mine. He opened his mouth as our lips met, and I felt his tongue swipe across my teeth. He made a noise and pulled me onto him. He laced his fingers over my butt and pulled me closer still, grinding my crotch against the rough front of his pants. I felt all of him, the hardness of him up and down, the rocky muscles of his chest and shoulders, the thick columns of his legs. His chin rested against my cheek for a moment, stubble scratching, as he said things, quiet things, and we rolled over the mattress, his hands going everywhere on me.

He got off me and stood. His mouth was shining with spit. "You can take off my clothes now, Billy," he said, his lips hanging open. He looked dumb and earnest, terrifically sexy. I got to my knees and crawled up to him, unbuttoning his shirt. He wore layers and layers. I stripped him down until I could smell his skin and see it, swirled dark with hair, and I licked the points of his red nipples, the little cave of his navel, the all-but-gone elastic of his boxers hanging low and held up most likely by the stiff prong of his cock.

Brad bent at the waist and put his hands on my shorts. I felt his fingers prodding behind my balls. He poked and probed as I slicked his hairy chest with saliva thick as wallpaper paste, my own cock dancing in my briefs.

"Take it out," he said, looking down at himself, and I uncovered his penis. It stood hard and red and tapered to a pointed, cowl-covered head. Inside the puckered end I could see the glisten of precome. I touched it with my finger and tasted it. "Early dew," Brad said, and he made his prick bob and glisten more. He grasped it at the base, and the tight skin slipped back over the head. He grabbed the back of my head and pushed my face up to his big stick, keeping it just out of mouth's reach. I flicked my tongue at it and drooled over his balls. "Oh, Billy," he said, laughing and wagging his sex playfully before my face, nicking my nose with it from time to time until I was fighting his grip, slobbering for a taste of the Builder's teasing cock.

He pushed my head down to the mattress. He pointed his dick down, dipping it into the well of my mouth. I swirled my tongue along the shaft, feeling the skin give and slide, and tightened my lips to catch the head before he slipped out. I got my hands on his loose sac and palmed his nuts, pressing them back against the thatch of hair that grew around his asshole. I breathed in the strong smell of him down there—piss and shit and sweat—and my crotch roiled, and I humped the mattress as best I could.

Brad stroked the side of my head while I worked on blowing him. I wanted him to fuck my mouth, to jam all of his prick in, to choke and gag me with it. Instead, he caressed my hair. And then he said, "I hope Uncle doesn't catch us."

I choked anyway, but from surprise, and I began to laugh, which was not acceptable behavior. I stifled it quickly, making more choking noises for cover.

"Who?" I said.

"Uncle," Brad said, a little louder, looking perturbed that I had broken character.

"Right," I said. "I hope Uncle doesn't catch us."

"I'm scared," Brad said.

"Me too," I replied, giving his cock knob a long, hard suck, bringing up a mess of goo. Brad folded himself over me and freed my prick from its prison of briefs, and I felt the hot insides of his mouth, a quick and total envelopment of wet heat from piss slit to pubic bone. *Oh my!* I thought, unable to speak, as the Builder began to work his shaft in and out of my face hole.

"What's all this?" I heard and choked again. Brad jumped up and nearly tripped on the tangle of shorts and pants around his ankles. I looked up at Man, who stood over the mattress with his arms folded across his chest.

"So this is what happens when I leave the two of you alone in this hayloft," Man said, fighting a smirk.

"We're going to get it now," Brad said, while I tried to figure out what a hayloft was.

"You bet your ass you're going to get it," Man said, giving his pants front a groping. "Now, one of you better get over here and get Uncle's dick wet."

Brad was pulling on Man's zipper before the words were out of his mouth, and while I was always ready to give Man head, this was Brad's show, and he had first dibs, so to speak, on who did what to whom. I stretched out, satisfied to be a spectator for a change.

Man's pants fell to the floor, his belt buckle clattering on the cement, and Brad began to kiss and peck at Man's long, soft cock. I watched Brad handle the mottled red shaft that was snaked with veins. My mouth watered. Brad licked the nicked rim of the flared head.

"Get it in your fucking mouth, boy," Man said, grabbing Brad's skull and pulling it to his crotch.

"And you," Man barked, winking and wagging a finger at me. Brad looked up from the slowly rising member before him. "That's Billy," he said.

"Shut up and get to work," Man said, knocking his knuckles against the top of Brad's head.

"Billy!" Man shouted.

"Yes," I said, belatedly adding "Uncle." Man's lips curled up. "Get your ass over here and get to work on Brad's butt." Brad, as if on cue, rose from his crouch and spread his legs, making the dark tangle of hair and hole more accessible, not breaking contact with the long suck he had on Man's thick, drooping prick.

I put my hands on Brad's smooth white cheeks and sniffed the stinking ditch of his ass crack. His hole winked and pouted, and I touched it with my tongue. Tensed up, it was like a hard kiss, but then Brad relaxed, and his pinched hole turned to mush. I pushed in and tasted his butt hole. I worked it for a while, listening to the sweet music Brad made with Man's dick.

"Is he all wetted up back there?" I heard Man ask. I nodded. Brad sputtered a bit, and Man pulled away, his club of a cock bouncing heavily in the air.

"On all fours," Man ordered. I was impressed with his performance and got on my hands and knees. "Not you, fool," he said, swatting my head with his big hand.

"Not me," Brad said, on his knees and shaking his head. "Not me."

I saw Man's fists at the ends of his arms. I saw Brad's wide chest swirled dark with hair, his nipples red like cherries.

"You're supposed to do *him*," Brad said.

"But I want you," Man said with a scary grin. "I can have this bed pig any time I want." He had his hand on his cock, rubbing the head with his palm. It shone with Brad's spit.

"You want it too," Man said. "You know you do."

Brad touched his fingers to his brow. His shoulders rounded as he pressed his tits against his thighs, his ass hovering an inch over the floor. "You're supposed to do Billy, and then I'm supposed to do him. That's how I told you I wanted it."

"This ain't about you anymore," Man said, getting Brad by the hair and pulling him up to the fat, split, leaking head. He pushed his crotch into Brad's face. Brad opened up with a groan and sucked down Man's prick, taking it to the bone. I put my hand on the small of Brad's back. It was wet with sweat; I smoothed the dark hairs that grew up from his ass, making them all go in the same direction. I slipped my hand down into the dark crack and felt for his hole. It was burning and open, its pucker gone, smooth now and ready. I slipped a finger in easily; he squirmed a little with two fingers, and with three he fucked himself on Man's giant dick, tears squeezing from his eyes, hands gripping Man's beefy ass and forcing him in again and again.

Man cuffed him.

"Take it easy, or I'll misfire," he growled. He pulled out and held on to his nuts. "This sperm is for your butt, Brad. You want it now, don't you?"

Brad nosed into Man's balls, which had tightened up and were riding close to his body. Brad tongued through the matted hair, worshiping the sac that held the hot load.

"Hands and knees," Man barked, and Brad did as he was told, positioning himself on the mattress. Man stood behind him and squatted, spitting into the cup of his hand and giving his pecker a few loving strokes. He put his hand on Brad's ass and touched the hole with his thumb, pushing in with no fight whatsoever. He fucked Brad like that for a while until Brad started whimpering. Man slapped his back hard and told him to shut the fuck up. He gripped himself and pushed his shaft, red and veined and hard, inside Brad's pretty ass.

Brad cried out. "Wet it," he yelped, "for God's sake."

"You're wet enough," Man said, and he began to pump into the big, muscled butt. I got myself behind him and licked the salty sweat that ran off him. He grabbed me in a headlock, and my face was pressed hard against a massive pec, a big nipple against my lips. I sucked on it and bit it, and Man held me tighter, the stink of his armpit against my cheek.

"It hurts," Brad said, his voice deep and choked. "It hurts, Uncle." I sucked all of Man's tit into my mouth, biting into the huge, hard muscle, and Man chuckled and slapped Brad's reddened butt, getting a leg up and reaming into the man even harder, causing him to curse hotly, his words busted by each ramming stroke, his breath taken away again and again.

I got myself free and stood up, my cock waving hard and dripping. Man looked at it under his nose. He cocked

his eyes up at me, sniffing. His face was all wet, and he licked his lips. I put my pecker end against them, and he put out his tongue again. I saw Brad twisting around to look at us. Man took all of me into his mouth, and I touched his face. I was long and narrow and had my end skin. Man liked to peel it back and lick around inside. He put his tongue in and made his lips hard. I pushed more and more into his mouth. I knew he liked to choke on it, enjoying the feel of it hitting the back of his mouth, his throat closing down around it. He grunted happily, making piggy noises. Brad shook his head, and droplets flew. His back was broad and shining, all muscle, and the knobbed channel of his spine ran down the middle of him, right down to his crack and the gush of hole that Man was filling with dick. I wanted to ride on that back myself, wanted to pump myself into his ass and make him yell and shake his fists and beg for more.

Man gurgled on my come stick, and I felt myself knotting up and getting stony. My nuts sucked up, and I went up on my toes and blasted into Man's mouth. Pearly strings of jism spilled out, and Man rolled his eyes up—they disappeared into their sockets. Meanwhile, he increased his tempo, sliding into Brad's butt with lightning-fast jabs. Brad was very nearly squalling with the fucking he was getting. He hollered for more cock, and Man gave him all he had, bellowing up at the ceiling as he shotgunned into that burning red cunt, firing load after load of oatmeal-thick goo.

"Get down there and take Brad's sperm," Man said, hitting me with the side of his hand. Brad raised himself up and stood on his knees, jacking himself off mightily. I stretched out in front of him, ready for his come, the first of it hot and blinding in my eye. I licked him off my lips as Brad heaved and growled, pumping out more to cover my chest and stomach. He fell over on top of me and kissed the cream from my eyelid, his mouth all over my face until it found my lips. He kissed me deeply. I watched Man dress and leave.

At the end of his time, Brad said good-bye and dug into his pockets for some sort of gratuity. He pulled out lint and something folded up. "It's a picture of me a long time ago," he said. I opened it up gently, looking at an image of him as a very young man. "I was barely 18," he said. He was shirtless, sitting under a tree, smiling. He had yet to pack on the girth and muscle of manhood. I stared at his open crotch where the pale skin of his balls had seeped out from his shorts. I felt myself going hard again.

"You're giving this to me?" I asked him.

"I am," he said, grinning, showing the space between his two front teeth.

It was the nicest thing anyone had ever given me, and I told him so.

He looked down at the picture and then at me again. "My pal Billy took this," he said.

Man came in later, at the end of the night. He stood by the curtained door and looked at me in the strange light cast by the little lamp I read by.

"You did good today," he said. He put his hand up under his shirt and rubbed the fur on his belly, then undid his pants and crawled across my bed. I watched his dark-haired ass tense as he made his way up to me. He put his head on the small of my back and blew kisses over my butt, his hot breath curling around my anus, and then I felt his finger. I could see him humping the mattress.

"Tell me about the old days," I said to him. "What was it like back then?"

Man licked at the hairs that grew in a triangle over my ass—hair oddly golden, when all the rest was dark.

"The '80s?" Man said. "The '90s? It was different."

"Come on, tell me," I insisted.

Man gently pushed a finger into my butt hole. "I love your tight little pussy," he said. "How do you keep it so nice and tight for me?"

I squirmed around under him.

"Shut up and fuck me," I said, and he did.

Spider

Man, I'll tell you, I was fucked-up. One week I'm trying to get Jeannie back from her extended solo vacation, and the next I'm digging my hands into the honey-pot pants of one of my little brother's buddies. I'd thought I had that shit under control, but I was wrong—I was anything but under control.

It had started innocently enough, this shit, a little grab-ass in the locker room after a match, that kind of stuff. The guys on the rugby team were big fuckers, and I was one of them, rock-hard, all man, so maybe that's why I'd go back to my dorm to shower after practices. When the naked towel-flicking began, when Buzz Jaworski started horse-biting every poor bastard's ass who was stupid enough to turn it to him, when Tony the Italian exchange student uncoiled his donkey dick from his cup and started swinging it around to get the kinks out, that's when I hightailed it. It was too much for me. I was dating Jeannie then, but sometimes the sight of this horseplay was enough to make me run for home with my pecker throbbing, pushing up past my navel, the big fucking evil thing. It conspired against me, I swear.

There was this one guy, fucking Bradley William Patterson—he and his crew team; can't walk across the fucking quad without causing neck injuries to every fucking chick he passed, pretty boy—I didn't see his ass on the rugby team. While I limped around with a split brow and three broken fingers, he crewed the Schuylkill and smiled. He'd smile right at me, this big, toothy shit-eating grin that did me right in. I'd see him and whistle through chipped teeth: Fucker was perfect. That's all I could think of. I'd look at him and shake my head—fucking perfect. And he'd stroll by looking like one of those Greek statues you see slides of in Art History. "Hey, Spider," he'd say, because everybody else did, and I was, believe it or not, treasurer of the student senate, so everybody knew Spider Matoukas.

I got married right after graduation—no big surprise there. Everybody knew Jeannie and I would do it eventually—dating ever since second semester of freshman year. Well, no surprise to me, it didn't work out, didn't last a year. "Where are you?" she'd ask me, me sitting right next to her. I just wanted things to be the way they used to be, and it pissed me off that they weren't, that I had to dress in a suit and tie every day and come home after work to watch *Seinfeld* together on the couch, eating take-out Vietnamese if she didn't have a late meeting. I started spending hours at the gym and started feeling a little more normal, but I hated the distraction of the aerobics room, separated from the free weights by a wall of glass, women jumping around in spandex. You'd be talking to some guy about a game or mutual fucking funds, for Christ's sake, and he can't even hear you because his eyes are bouncing in their sockets trying to focus on all them tits.

I had this town house to myself—three bedrooms, a pool table down in the rec room. I roamed around this place like a fucking ghost, stupid and clumsy. My little brother, Demos, kept bugging me to let him move in with me, but there wasn't any way I was going to bring that on myself. He was a little wigger in man-size clothes, a wanna-be homeboy. He hung out a lot, bringing his friends over, and to tell you the truth, I appreciated the company. Some of them weren't bad-looking, not that I did too much looking myself, and they seemed to look up to me as though I knew or had something, but I think it was the cases of beer I had laid in. I'd tell them, "You guys ought to be in school. Fucking 20 years old, and you aren't doing shit." The only one who seemed more interested in me than the beer was this one named Jason, my brother's buddy from way back—kindergarten even. Kid was pretty, man, had a smile that must have made the girlies wet. He started dropping in without Demos, begging booze, offering dope. He'd roll in wearing those gigantic jeans, crotch hanging down around his knees. I started wondering what was holding them up. One night, just the two of us, I decided to find out.

It was a stupid move. *What the hell am I doing?* I asked myself, my hands down this kid's pants. I told myself I was lonely, that I'd had too much to drink. I told myself it would never happen again, and after I dropped a hefty load down the kid's gullet, I kicked his ass out and told him to stay the fuck away. He looked scared, terrified even, and sad too, like I just told him his dog was hit by a car. I felt like a big piece of shit, but I was as scared as he was, I think.

I don't know what happened. One minute I was sitting by myself watching *Seinfeld;* next thing I know, I'm grabbing my brother's best friend and diving into his pants. Kid was always giving me this look, hanging out in those clothes, the plaid of his boxer-covered ass like a red cape to this bull. He walked by to grab us a couple more beers, and I grabbed him. "What's up with this?" I said, pulling on the waistband, baring his ass. "Why bother wearing anything? It's just a fucking tease—you and your homeys teasing each other, right? You all get off showing your asses, get yourselves all excited, and then what do you do? What happens then?"

Kid didn't say shit. He got this sweet look on his face. He looked like a fucking choirboy. I got a boner. I went to hard lickety-split, poking up stiff in my shorts, and I got him on my lap. I told him, "You need to eat more, gain some weight, work out." I was thinking how he'd look in the rags we used to wear to the gym and what 20 pounds of muscle would do for him. *Fucking gorgeous,* I was thinking and hating myself. Gorgeous? Gorgeous. I was turning into a fucking fag. I had my arms around him, and he was sucking on my ear. My prick was bent and aching under him; he squirmed his little ass.

"Demos's dick ain't this big," he said, putting his hand under his rump and grabbing me. "Can't get my hand around it!" he said, and I told him to shut up like I was ashamed of it. Truth is, I am, a little. Big and ugly—at times it's like having another person in my pants, some living thing that doesn't have too much to do with me. Jeannie hadn't liked it, hated to touch it, wanted never to see it. It hurt her, made her cry. I think we fucked no more than five times in the six years we were together. Usually what I did was rub the big old thing between her legs, across her thin pussy hairs, grunting like a pig, making her hate me even more.

Jason said to me, "Your lips are fat." He made it sound like a compliment, though, and turned around and put his mouth on mine. He had a little beard that was as soft as Jeannie's pussy hairs, and he was still working my joint through my shorts.

It wasn't the first time I'd kissed a guy, although I wouldn't have admitted that then, not even to myself. I told myself that I might have been kissed a couple of times, but I never kissed back.

I kissed this one back. I ate his fucking mouth, his hairy little chin, his smooth fucking throat. I wanted him. My shorts were soaked from my leaky pipe, and he was sucking my tongue and hanging on to my shaggy pecs. His pants slid down easily, along with his boxers. He was pale and naked save for the tangle of his jeans around his ankles and the shirt he had pulled up to expose his little titties. He pinched my nipple as though he were trying to remove it, and I told him to stop—not because of the pain, which was slight, but because of the massive wave of guilt the pleasure inspired, making me feel like some kind of evil. I wrestled him as though he were my conscience, right down to the couch.

He had arms like a boy's. I would have had him doing curls. He looked up at me sweetly, the way Jeannie used to a long time ago. He had his hair buzzed to the skin on the sides, and the rest, long and brown, was tucked up under his ball cap, which he wore backward. He had six or seven mud-color hairs around each pink nipple, and his nipples looked frosted, like lipstick. They were pointy little things. I licked one and then the other.

I didn't know what to do next. All I ever had to do with another guy was just stand there, letting whoever and his nice warm mouth suck the come out of me. I wasn't much of a challenge—it didn't take much to make me shoot. I'd just about be zipping up and mumbling my thanks before the guy realized that the hot shit in his mouth was my load. He'd just be getting used to having his mouth stretched like that, doing that boa constrictor thing in order to take the head and another half inch, and I was a goner. *Drink it*, I'd think, emptying my nuts into him.

I started grinding on Jason, gut-fucking his muscle-ribbed stomach. The kid had awesome abs, absolutely no body fat, and this slim, curved pecker that was bothering my thigh. I wanted him. He disappeared under me, but I felt his hands struggling with my boxers, getting them off my big ass and down my legs. His fingers tickled into my crack; he grabbed my butt cheeks and held on.

There was a voice in my brain begging me to stop. I heard it as clearly as I heard the kid moaning under me. I stopped, confused. His eyes were closed, his mouth open. "What did you say?"

He opened his eyes, looking embarrassed. "I want to suck you," he said.

"Sure you do."

He wormed his way out from under me and pushed me around until I was on my back. He sat on the edge of the couch and took my cock in his hands. He held it carefully and with respect. "It's a two-hander," he whispered.

It was a pain in the ass, I told him.

"No shit," he said, shaking his head in awe.

He put his mouth on it, tonguing the big gape of my piss slit, and I passed him some vital fluid—a lot of it.

"Your eyes are bigger than your mouth, man," I said to him, but that wasn't quite true. Kid took the head, opening wide, and worked a little bit and a little bit more of the thick shaft into his mouth. I was fucking dying seeing this shit, this kid, Demos's bud since kindergarten, gnawing on my thwacker in my own fucking living room, and I realized then that nobody'd ever sucked my cock in my own living room, and that alone was nearly enough to pull my trigger.

"Gewgaw," I said, meaning "Here I come," and I started knocking into the kid's pharynx with my sticky knob, drowning him with my nut sauce. *Drink that shit,* I was thinking.

Then I was ashamed. The kid creamed all over my ankles, choking on my bone, and I was all about saying a Hail Mary, beginning my penance. I jumped off of him, skinning my ankle on the coffee table. *Oh, boy,* I said to myself, *you have gone and done it now, smart guy.* And I sneaked a glance at the kid, this horny pony who'd just milked me, and he had my come dribbling down over his tiny goatee.

I slammed my palm against my forehead. "Fucking stupid," I said aloud again and again, pacing the room. I leaned against the pool table and picked up the cue ball; squeezed the fucker, wanting to grind the damn thing to dust.

"Get out," I said quietly. Kid blinked up at me, those fucking hurt eyes. "Get your ass out and don't come back."

I worried he'd spill the beans to Demos, but for all I knew, I thought, Demos was probably getting some from him too. So I processed the shit and got over it—swore I was off dick for good—and I spent a lot of time at the gym staring at all those bouncing tits. But nothing made me hard until I got into the showers of the locker room. I decided I'd be better off driving home and showering there, and I realized I hadn't progressed much since college.

Fucking mortgage was killing me, so I put an ad in the paper: HOUSEMATE WANTED. I weeded out a few of the prospectives over the phone: the guy who lisped, the smoker, the used-car salesman, the lady with the cats. I set up three appointments, the first with a Brad Patterson. The name didn't register until I opened the door and saw him standing there, already grinning.

"I knew it was you," he said, pointing at me. He shook my hand hard. "Good to see you, Spider," he said.

I could only nod, hoping my lips were forming a smile.

"You look good," he said. "You look real good."

I let him in, and he looked the place over. All he had to do was say he was interested, and the place was his. I was ready to make his fucking bed, for Christ's sake.

"The $500 includes everything?" he asked. His eyes were blue, his lashes gold. He had a thin white scar over his right eye, the cause of which I wanted to know. He was wearing a suit. "I work for the mayor," he said.

"Tell him I said hello."

"You know Ed?"

"My dad does," I said. "They went to school together or something." There was a pause. I asked if he wanted a beer.

"Didn't work out with Jeannie?" he said, holding up the beer as if toasting the kitchen. I shrugged.

"I'm still looking myself," he said. He looked me in the eye for such a long time that I began to wonder, you know—*What if?*

"So," he said finally, looking at his wristwatch. "You want me, Matoukas?"

I canceled the other appointments. Yeah, I wanted him.

He didn't make it easy for me. He'd come in from his evening runs and peel his clothes off at the fucking door, right down to his strap. He was in awesome shape, better even than in college. He treated the whole house like it was his fucking locker room. He would shower and wrap a towel around his waist and stay that way for the rest of the night. He'd sit on the couch with me or on the floor, and I'd have to wear my shirts untucked to cover the rise and fall of my crotch. I kept thinking of calling Jason, I was in such a state, except that Patterson was always around. He never dated, hardly went out for anything unless he had to, some city affair, an occasional mayoral function.

He had wide pecs and lats, fat nips, thick golden forearms. One night he laid himself out on the floor, white towel around his waist, knees up in the air, and I could see the fucking waves of muscle in his stomach. I had waves too, but they were hidden under all this fur and an ounce or two of fat. Patterson was built like a gymnast.

He was looking at me this night. "Did you hear me?" he said. He wasn't on the floor anymore but was standing next to me with the cordless. I could see his dick under the towel, the mark it made against the terry cloth. There were twisting vines of hairs that traveled up and into his navel and stayed there. "I think it's your brother," he said.

I took the phone and mumbled into it. It wasn't Demos, though. You know who it was.

He said he was sorry. There was a lot of static. I pictured him on a starry cliff, like in some movie, and he was looking out over the lights of the city, phone in one hand, his dick in the other. "I was thinking..." he said. He was hoping I was going to ask him over. How could I? Not with Patterson in his little towel. I didn't say anything. The static was mean. Patterson stretched himself out on the floor again, the towel coming undone and falling open. He didn't do anything to fix it, just let it lay that way. I was looking and wondering: *Is this guy a fucking nudist or something?* And I heard Jason sigh into the phone, and I went to stone again, my balls sweating, and I was thankful for the untucked T-shirt, but I was still standing tall and proud. The bitch was hard to hide.

"I was wondering," Jason said. "Have you...seen Demos?"

I said no.

"It's just—I thought that was his car I saw in your drive. I was just passing by, and I saw it, and he said he was going to get a new car..." Kid rambled, stumbling over his lame story. Demos was in the market for a car like Patterson's Lexus? The golden curlies of Patterson's thighs fascinated me, and I was wondering how they'd feel against my lips.

"Well, I guess I'll let you go," he said reluctantly, and I was horned-up enough to ask where he was—*Just curious*, I was saying to myself—and he said up the street.

I was this close to finding an excuse to run out for milk to get milked by the kiddo when Patterson decided it was fucking hot in the room and dispensed with the towel altogether. I looked down the length of him laid out on the floor, his dick like a fat cat curled up on that bushy pile of gold, and I was drawn by an instinctual urge to pet the fucker.

I turned off the phone and put it on the floor. I probably hung up on the poor kid, but you can bet I was distracted. I couldn't stop looking at it, at his thing. It was perfect. It was gorgeous. I was turning fruity. I tore my eyes from his crotch and looked at his eyes and said to him, "You got something against clothes, Will?"

"Does it bother you?" he said, getting up, looking concerned and gorgeous. "I mean, I'll put something on if you want me to, shorts or something. It's just that—" He stopped. He looked me over. I watched where his eyes went. They went to my crossed ankles. They went up my shins, between my legs, along my furry thighs. Where was he going? I was getting myself in trouble, losing a battle with my dick. It thickened and pulsed and grew longer and longer, telescoping out of my shorts. "Son of a bitch," I breathed, pulling my shirt down over it. *He's got me*, I was thinking—just like with fucking Jason. I was busted.

Big and red and not much thinner than a man's wrist—though not *my* big, haired-up wrists—my dick uncovered itself. It was veined and fat-headed and ringed around the middle with brown, and it smelled, I swear to God, like a loaf of French bread. Will couldn't stop staring. His mouth was open, and he looked a little sick. "Oh, my," he said.

I couldn't just grab him the way I did Jason. This was Will Patterson, after all. Besides, his dick hadn't moved an inch—it stayed squat and golden and picture-perfect, like the dicks you see in *Playgirl.* Fucking gorgeous. I'd never sucked dick, but I'd never seen anything so suckable.

There was a coffee table between us, and I was considering my options. His little fatty had me salivating, and I'd developed a sudden oral fixation. I got up slowly, putting my knuckles on the table, as though I was planning to run him down, which was sort of on my mind, but I was also thinking, *To suck or not to suck?* I was risking my rep here, an awesome living arrangement, and for what?

Such a pretty helmet, though, a fucking gorgeous knob. I stared at it. And his balls, fuzzed over, big and bobbing. My heart was banging.

"It's your own fucking fault," I told him irrationally right before I lunged at him, catching the soft stogie in my mouth. It was tasty and rolled over my tongue, and he did nothing to stop me—not that he could have, not at that point. I punched my chin against his nuts and breathed hotly into his beautiful bush. He was the perfect shape and fit my mouth perfectly, so when he started going hard, I was almost disappointed. Almost.

"Are you going to fuck me with that thing?" he asked, miles above me. I looked up to see his eyes pinched with worry. His dick swung heavily out of my mouth, and I went pale with embarrassment, looking down to see that my pecker had swooped out again and was dipping into a glass of water that was on the table.

"It's incredible," I heard him say, his own jutting a respectable seven or so inches. It smelled of my spit, and that made me proud. It had a wide-flanged head the size of my grandfather's pocket watch, with a scimitar curve that had it pointing to the rightmost corner of the room. I breathed on it, wanting it.

I climbed over the coffee table and sat my ass down. He stood and fitted himself back into the hole of my face and reached down, affectionately petting my prick. My mind and body were feeling all sorts of tremors. When he took hold of it, I thought I'd squirt then and there and very nearly did, so I swatted his hand away and hoped that sufficed as an explanation. He went for it again, though, and I let him, despite the trouble he'd likely cause. He encircled it with his fingers under the head and jerked it slightly, enough to milk out a load of precome, which he used for lube. I was impaling myself on him, in some kind of heaven, trying hard to keep it together long enough to make it worthwhile. I wasn't counting on anything, though.

He broke our bond and went to his knees. He held the thing with both hands and licked it all over, paying special attention to the glans. He licked me up and down, getting my balls and the soft overhang of my asshole as it dangled from the edge of the table. My hole fluttered in response, and my mouth felt empty. I was ready to get going again when Patterson stood up and said, "Let's go." He turned and started walking, and I followed. What else was there for me to do? I was dick-whipped now, his sex puppy, and I'd have done anything. I followed him up to his room. "Lie down," he said, and he was on the floor reaching for something under the bed. I lay down and waited for him, and when he came up he was holding an amazingly large dildo. He spat on it and waved it at me. "I don't think you'll be too much trouble after this," he said, grinning like a little devil.

He put the rubber monster on the bed and squatted over it. It was slippery with lube and slid right in. I watched and had never seen anything more fascinating, and for some reason I was reminded of horses being born. He eased his ass as far down as he could; to take it all would have been like getting fucked by a drainpipe.

"How does it feel?" I whispered in awe. The golden boy was a butt slut.

"Not anything like the real thing," he said. He held on to the pole and got himself onto his back, lifting his legs in the air. "Work it in and out for me," he told me, and I got hold of it and began to fuck his ass with it.

"Easy, Spider, easy," he said, almost laughing. "Now pull it out," he said, and I did, and his anus was a big, windy cave. "Think you'll be able to squeeze in there?"

"Whenever you're ready," I told him, getting on my knees. I crawled between his legs, aiming my prick at the soft red cunt. He put his hands on my triceps.

"Just take it easy, OK?" he said.

"It's my first—" I said.

He gave me a look.

I nodded.

His hot, wet ass lips kissed my fat head, asking me in. I pushed gently, watching the tip of my prick disappear, sucked up into his insides. It was a smooth ride, and deep, and I was surprised—no, shocked—to find more than half of my shaft gone. He grabbed the other half, gripping it tightly, trying to work the rest of me in. He tried and tried and grimaced the whole time, and I worried about his insides.

He groaned, giving up. "That's all I can take," he complained, writhing on my thickness. "Is that OK?"

I didn't answer but commenced fucking him. I grabbed his ankles and lifted them high. I stroked into him easily, afraid of hurting him, and the suck of his hole was something else, better than anything I'd ever had done to my cock. He took up his rigid dick and was beating it in his fist and looking up at me. I stooped down to lick his collarbone and somehow got his lips instead, and we were kissing, tonguing each other while my big boner slid up into him.

"Come on, Spider," he said, bouncing under me, his ass turning to mush. "Come on, man, give it to me."

"What the fuck do you think I'm doing?" I said, sweating over him. "Ain't it any good?"

"Good? Yeah, it's fucking excellent," Will said, the first time I'd ever heard him use the *f* word, flicking a switch somewhere inside me, and I was thinking, *Fuck, fuck, fuck, fuck,* slamming into him, going as far as he'd allow and getting primed to blow a big load.

I held back, though, grunting through gritted teeth, wanting more than anything for him to shower himself first with his own creamy load. I guessed the location of his prostate and tried to keep the knob of my cock in its general vicinity, you know, trying to catch him up with the Spider, feeling a little like a troubleshooter for the public-works department. I numbed my pecker by thinking of baseballs and the order Sportsworld had placed last Friday, and in my mind I started spending the big fat commission I was due on dildos and lube and dirty movies and cock rings, and I was panting and swearing, holding out just long enough to see the first of his flying drops, and the fucker went as stiff and quiet as a corpse as he covered himself with his hot, funky come.

I scrambled out of his fuck hole and fucked my hand instead and gushed out wads all over Will's pecs. I twitched and sighed and lay on top of him, my face in his neck. I gave him little kisses there, still breathing hard, and I took his earlobe gently between my teeth. I moved my chest around, mixing our dick spit and causing a pleasant buzz around my nipples.

"That was—" Will said, and I nodded. It fucking was, wasn't it?

Now I got my hands full. Patterson turned into a fucking dick junkie, and Jason started stopping by, making himself extremely useful on those late nights when the mayor was up for reelection and Will was being kept busy—not that that kept him from stopping by my bedroom at 7 a.m. to get a little (like you could get "a little" from me). Anyway, just when I was in fuck heaven, what do you think happens? Doesn't Jeannie call and ask—no, she fucking begs—to come back? Now, I don't know how it is with you, but with me, I had some bad fish once and haven't had a bite of the stuff since. Flounder, tuna, perch—I can't eat the shit, just from that one bad experience. So I said to her flat out, "Jeannie, it's like this: I'm a fucking fruit."

"You're too hard on yourself," she said back.

"Not as hard as I was on Will Patterson's ass last night," I said, feeling a little like that girl in *The Exorcist.*

She paused. I heard her not breathing. Then: "Will Patterson? From Temple? On the mayor's committee? *That* Will Patterson?"

"That's the one," I sang into the phone.

"You're telling me—now, this is unbelievable; I must be hearing things—you're telling me you're having"—she paused—"anal sex with Bradley William Patterson? The same Bradley William Patterson we went to school with?"

"The same," I said with pride and glee.

She paused again, and the silence was a huge chasm between us—we were miles apart physically and in every other way. I was the happiest I'd ever been, and all it took was two guys. Who'd have guessed?

"Oh, you're funny, Spider Matoukas," she said, her voice rising. "You're a real fucking comedian. Will Patterson wouldn't let you touch his ass with a ten-foot pole."

No, I was thinking, touching myself into a hard-on, *but he'd let me with a one-foot pole.*

The Man in the Blue Speedo

My brother, Will, was getting married. "Kev," he said early on, "you're my man, man, but Connie Takis practically begged me to be best man." I didn't bother telling him what a relief it was to be freed of the leviathan task of representing my brother in that capacity, and I went a little sad-mouthed for good measure.

"Look," Will said, panicking, "fuck Connie. You're the man. I'll just explain."

"No way, Will. Con's been your bud since Albright. Plus, he wants it so bad."

Will shook his head. "He's a crazy son of a bitch. I can't believe you've never met him."

"He was in Greece that one time I got up to see you at school."

"Yeah, and he busted his leg before spring break and wasn't in Lauderdale with us either. I can't wait for you to meet him—you're gonna love him, man."

He slipped his fingers down the too-tight neck of my tux shirt when we were at the church. "Hey," he said, "hey, hey,

hey." He had too much time on his hands; he needed something to do, something to drink. He'd been following me all day—upstairs, downstairs, all over my parents' house. He was a dog on my heels. I wanted nothing more than to be rid of him and the bothersome erections he was causing me, the way he slipped out of the guest room with a towel around his shoulders when it should have been around his waist, his eyes always on me, his breath suddenly at my ear, surprising me.

I thought I'd escaped him, but he'd found me down by the pond, my glass of gin sweating, the rest of me sweating too.

"You ought to get out of this," he said, talking about the tuxedo I had yet to take off.

"Deb said there were going to be more pictures," I said, eyeing his unbuttoned shirt. Christ knew where his coat had gone to. *Best man*, I was thinking. He was the best man, all right, the best-looking man at the wedding, but that was none of my business. I had a girlfriend somewhere in Africa with the Peace Corps, making muddy huts and fighting off a small case of Ebola. She called herself my girlfriend in her letters, anyway, even though there was very little between us—or maybe a lot between us; a lot of space, I mean—that really linked us in any way.

We were on the edge of an apple orchard, and crows cawed, unseen, hidden among the fruit.

"What are you doing down here by yourself?" he asked, the setting sun on his face making it orange. He was dark-skinned anyway, a Greek. His name was Connie, short for Constantine. He made me feel the way the guy in the Hanes commercial made me feel, the way no girl had ever made me feel, no matter how many chances I gave them or myself.

"I've got this picture of you," he said, making a dopey face, looking at the cattails on the other side of the pond. "You're wearing a blue Speedo, and you're standing with your brother, and you've got a beer can balanced on your head."

I knew the picture and wondered how he'd gotten it.

"I stole it from Will," he said, explaining that little mystery.

You could see the lights of the reception, thousands of twinkling lights in the mimosa trees that surrounded the patio. We were maybe 500 yards from the open doors, through which poured a samba, and I felt as though I were in a movie—a strange version of *The Graduate*. Call it *The Best Man*.

"Wonder if we can swim in this thing," he mused, and I looked at him. His hair was dark and curling. His eyebrows hovered thickly over brown eyes. He was carrying an empty beer bottle by its neck, swinging it out in front of him, back and forth, a hypnotist's dangled watch.

"There are goldfish in there," I said, "and who knows what else. Look at that green stuff floating over there on the side." The notion, though, of Connie's getting undressed in front of me created a very vivid picture. I could sit here very innocently watching this 6-foot-2 Acropolis ornament disrobe and wade into this reflective pool, hoping the water didn't rise past his knees. What I'd seen of him so far—what hadn't I seen so far?—defied description. He was perfect in all sorts of ways, covered with a coarse mat of hair, dark everywhere, even his prick, which hung low and swung seductively the other night when he came naked from the bathroom. I would have blown him there and then, which wasn't something I was taking lightly. I'd been the recipient, of course, of a variety of suck jobs in the men's room of the Park City Mall, but I had yet to take the actual plunge and open my mouth to accept another man's pecker. But seeing Connie's slack sausage wagging heavily had made me lick my lips involuntarily.

He tossed his empty into the pond, an ecological faux pas I was willing to overlook. "I lost my studs," he said, showing me the open front of his shirt. He reminded me of Tom Jones in ill-fitting slacks, and it was then that I noticed an enormous thickness off to the side of his groin, defying biology in its girth and sudden taper, and then I saw the glint of a bottle cap, and Connie pulled another beer from his pocket.

"Wanna take a walk?" he asked.

I looked back at the reception. I could hear the old-fogy band struggling through the hokeypokey.

"What the hell," I said, getting up.

"I was expecting you at Will's bachelor's party," Connie continued.

"Dallas. My boss thought he wanted to buy a racetrack," I said, sipping some gin. I was feeling the need for more, but we were walking away from the source of booze and toward the apple trees I'd seen earlier.

Connie nodded. He seemed distracted, almost pensive. In the twilight he looked foreign, from another land instead of Long Island. He looked to me like the rug sellers I saw in Pakistan. He walked ahead of me, looking down at the grass. He stopped and turned, and I very nearly crashed into him.

"What's up?" I said.

"I want to fuck you," he said simply.

I didn't know what to say or how to react. I stood there with my hands in my pockets, feeling a little stunned and wishing I'd gone back for just a little more gin. My cock nudged my hand through the pocket lining.

"I've been wanting to fuck you since I saw that picture, you in that bathing suit, those brown nipples, the hair on your stomach. I'm hard now," he said, looking down at himself. "Touch it."

My hands stayed in my pockets.

He put his beer bottle under his arm and unzipped his tuxedo pants. He hauled out his long brown boner, loosely circumcised, the glans shaped like an arrowhead. He gripped the shaft with his thumb and forefinger and pinched out a glimmering drop of precome. He fingered it up and touched it to a spot somewhere below my chest. I backed away.

"You're not telling me you don't want it, Kevin," he said softly. "You wouldn't be here if you didn't want it, I know that much." His hands went to the front of my trousers, fumbling with the fly. My own cock was rock-hard, admitting my sin, my attraction. He dug into my boxers, manhandling my prick. He went down on his knees, and his beer bottle dropped to the ground with a dull thud. His mouth closed over the head, and the tip of his tongue burned into the piss slit. His lips slid down the shaft, and his nose burrowed into my wiry patch of pubes. He grabbed my hips and began working the cock in and out of his mouth, humming as he worked, pulling me into him, pushing me away, never letting go, even when he gagged himself.

He unfastened my pants and pushed them down, the cool night air playing on the bare backs of my legs. My white cotton undershorts glowed in the dusk, and he backed off to push my cock back through the fly and pulled them down as well. His hands all over my thighs, he resumed sucking me off, working harder, snorting with the exertion. He slammed my dick against the back of his throat, showing off for me, and I was duly impressed. His hands slid up the cool and pleated front of my shirt and found my nipples, pulling them down. Suddenly I could not stop my hips from bucking, and I pumped my cock into his hot-lipped mouth. I fucked it shallowly, keeping the head just inside his mouth, feeling the roughness of his teeth against the flanged rim. I brought myself close, right up to the teetering edge, and tried to take a step back, but he held me fast, enveloping my bone to the root, his throat constricting around the head and drawing the come up out of my nuts. I grabbed the back of his dark head and shot down his throat, stifling a cry, my knees threatening to go out on me.

Connie looked up at me, his lips fatter and shining, drool running down his chin. "I told you you wanted it, Kev," he said, smiling.

My experiences in the men's room hadn't prepared me for after-sex conversation; the usual routine was a quick shake of the dick and getting the hell out of there. My prick went limp slowly, close to Connie's face. He seemed content enough just watching it deflate, his own pecker untouched and stonily jutting up from his open fly. Was I obligated to reciprocate? I was certainly ready to, though not as ready as I had been before coming. He stayed where he was, though, his hands caressing my nut sac, pulling and stroking the balls gently.

"We ought to get back," he said, getting up and tucking himself away. I must have had an odd look on my face, because he laughed and said, "Hey, you haven't seen the last of it, Kevin. You owe me one, that's all."

The reception didn't end so much as fizzle out, like old coals in a hibachi left out in the rain. Deb's uncle Jameson swore he was having a heart attack—"His fifth this month," Deb said—and demanded he be rushed to the nearest emergency room. And our dad had fallen asleep on the pot in the men's room. The geriatric air had something to do with our moods, I think, and we decided to call it a night even though the band had been hired to play until midnight.

Once home Mom and Dad kissed me good night, smiling sleepily at Connie, who had already changed into his skintight black swim trunks, and made their way to bed. Connie and I went outside to the back lawn, walking through the cool, wet grass to the pool. Paper lanterns hung over the pool, remnants of Mother's last soiree. I turned them on and went into the changing hut for a suit to put on. Connie raided the bar, looking for my father's scotch.

I came out wearing the same Speedo I wore in the snapshot Connie said he had of me. It had faded to a powdery gray-blue from sun and chlorine, and it barely covered my ass cheeks anymore. I joined him at the bar, where he sipped from his glass meditatively. He was a picture: dark-skinned, his hair glossy and curling, looking like a Caravaggio painting. He looked at me over the rim of his glass, his brown eyes sharply attentive all of a sudden, the glass hardly concealing his foxish grin.

"You've changed," he said, his eyes on mine.

"Bathing suit," I said back.

"No," he said, "I mean from that picture—that's the same Speedo, isn't it?"

I nodded.

"You're bigger, wider up here," he said, reaching across the bar and drawing his finger from shoulder to shoulder. He leaned over, looking down at my legs. "And your legs are thicker. It all looks very good. You must live in the gym."

Admittedly, there wasn't much else for me to do after work. I went to the office, to the gym, and back home again, day after day, an endless cycle. I lingered in the showers, enjoying the naked camaraderie and feasting my eyes on the unsuspecting flesh all around me, the dripping, dangling sex, mossy with hair, thick with blood, small and large, hooded and bareheaded.

Connie stepped out from behind the bamboo bar without his trunks, his prick thickening, on the rise. He stood very close to me; I could smell the scotch on his breath, commingled with a mint. His cock head touched my leg, and he fit his face into the crook of my neck, licking me there. He fondled the pouch of my bathing suit, squeezing my pecker, bringing it to life. He put his other hand on the back of my neck, and I went down, bending at the waist, putting my mouth on his pointed head, tasting the salted leak of him. He brushed my hair back with the palm of his hand and let my lips slip down his shaft to nestle in his fragrant black bush.

"You're good down there," I heard him say, and I endeavored to be better. I swallowed him whole, choking but valiant, successful, and I heard him moan, sweet and low. "You belong on your knees," he whispered, his voice catching as I pushed my stubbled chin into his soft ball bag.

"Kiss my hole, man," he said, spreading his legs, opening up his ass to me. I got under him, my hands on his white cheeks, pressing my face into the shadow of his crack. He tasted dark and bitter, and his balls melted over my chin. He grabbed his big prick and began to jack it, his asshole pulsing. "That's good," he said. "I like it, Kevin." He squatted, and his hole opened like a mouth and sucked on my tongue.

My own cock pushed out against the nylon, begging for attention. Connie reached down and pinched the head gently, and I felt the ooze he released spread warmly all over the front of my bathing suit. He pushed his hand inside the suit and played with my balls, cupping them firmly, rolling them under his palm. His fingertips began probing the hard channel that separated balls from asshole, then farther back, dipping into the wrinkled pit of my butt.

His furry stomach held my head fast to his needy prong, kept his thing planted deep in my throat, causing me to breathe through my nose. The lack of oxygen was thrilling, and I humped my dick against his hairy wrist while he dug around in my briefs.

"You ever get it up the ass?" he said.

I shook my head, full of dick, with limited motility.

"This is going to be sweet," I heard him say, and he unplugged his pecker from my slobbering lips and pulled my bathing suit down so that it lay stretched and useless around my ankles, very much as I imagined my asshole after Connie got through with it. He got himself behind me, his hands on my hips. I could feel his bouncing dick head against the hard, smooth crack of my butt. I felt his haired-up thighs scratching against the backs of my thighs as well as the grip he had on me, as though he were afraid I was going to skip out on what I had coming. Then I felt the hot breeze of his mouth, surprising the shit out of me, as he chewed around the pink entrance of my rectum. His tongue came knocking, screwing itself into the tight little opening. He laid swaths of spit down, as thick as honey, as slick as motor oil. I felt his fingers pressing in all around the wrinkled edges of my wet crater, watching ants crawl around my feet, seeing the swinging shadows of the breeze-blown paper lanterns. My long toes cracked as I struggled to keep my balance, and a lone ant ran up my ankle and back down again.

He replaced his tongue with something much thicker. He pressed his dick against my resisting hole, which seemed determined to deny him access. Connie leaned back and dropped a gob of spit that landed directly on my pucker, and he leaned into me again and was denied nothing. He slid in easily, too easily.

Connie put his arms across my back as though leaning on a bar. "This isn't the easiest way to take it at first," he admitted, his voice quiet and businesslike. He worked his cock all the way in and tickled my back with his fuzzy belly. He leaned over even more, so that I felt his tits, hard little pebbles, across my shoulder blades.

"Do you like how it feels?" he asked, making short little stabs into me, humping his dick against my prostate. I nodded.

He pushed me forward. I grabbed for the bar. "Up on the stool," he instructed.

I severed our connection, seeing his cock swollen and swinging, amazed to have had all that inside me. I got myself up on the stool, and he grabbed my legs, hiking them up over his shoulders. His pecker plunged into my asshole, sucked in by my wanting it so much. He went deep, and I gasped, and he smiled, eyeing my boner.

"You gonna do anything about that?" he asked me.

"I'll blow if I touch it," I told him.

"Am I that good?"

"I'm just that horny," I said, secretly admitting that yes, he was that good. He drummed my insides, playing me like a musical instrument. Sweat poured off of us, his legs slick between my legs. He leaned over and tried to lick one of my nipples, and I reached up and grabbed both of his, pulling. He grunted and banged me harder, and my perch squealed under the force of his attack, and my hole opened up even more, taking everything he had to give.

He stopped suddenly. "I can't do this much longer," he said. His planted cock throbbed inside me. I could feel our pulses, the beat of our hearts; his rod was taking root.

He grabbed my dick and squeezed, and I spurted all over myself with a whimper and a wide, wet spray that covered my chest and stomach and face. "Aw, shit," he said, making one final jab, commencing to fill my butt with his gyro sauce.

Connie left, and so did my prospects of a sex life. I wanted something more than what I'd had before I met my brother's best man; I just didn't know how to go about getting it.

I planned my vacation to begin with Will's wedding. I had roughly two weeks of nothing to do, deciding to save some money and stay at my parents' place. They had left on their own vacation, and the place was mine. I hung out by the pool, drinking beer and reading my dad's daily *Wall Street Journal.* The pool, however, was a constant reminder of Constantine, and I thought often of calling him up. He practiced law in New York, lived in Manhattan. It wasn't that much of a drive down to Bucks County. But for some reason I could not bring myself to call him. I stayed put on the chaise and opened one beer after another, jumping into the coldish water when the sweat on me turned to a thin white dust.

There was a pile of notes and instructions from my parents, including a reminder that the lawn would be mowed, and the boys liked to be paid in cash. I was half expecting a couple of kids with old, beat-up push mowers and was surprised to be awakened from a nap one day to the high whine of a pair of power mowers being driven by two muscled men. Hardly boys, these guys were huge and pushing 30. They swung around trees and hit straightaways at a good clip, practically jogging behind their swift-cutting machines. They both wore cutoffs and boots. Their legs were meaty, shining with sweat, and their torsos bare. One was covered with a fine spray of light brown hair that glistened wetly. The other had wide nipples that seemed to hang like dark cherries from his smooth, rounded pecs. I felt ridiculous in my Speedo when one spied me and waved, and I ran to the hut for a pair of trunks that had belonged to Will. Back in my chaise, I had the perfect view of these two sexy grass gods. They zigzagged back and forth across the lawn, and I was thankful for all that acreage. I sipped my beer. The bottle gleamed seductively and caught their eyes. It was a miserably hot day, and they'd probably been at it good and hard since 7 in the morning. I was getting hard just thinking of the two of them getting into their truck together, imagining the cab of their pickup so cramped that they had to sit pushed up against each other, and I imagined the sweetness of being stuck between them.

The smooth one's hair was practically black and cut close to his head. He had the humped-up traps of someone who wrestled or played football. The other's hair was longer, much lighter than the stuff that covered his chest; he'd taken off his baseball cap to wipe his forehead, and it spilled out, covering the shave job he had up over his ears and the back of his neck. His body was lean and cut with muscle everywhere, and his lip was curled into a permanent sneer. He had blue eyes discernible across the lawn. The closer he got, the better he looked. His hips swung with each long stride, and the back of his jeans was dark with sweat. His brown shoulders twitched, and his triceps dimpled.

When they were finished the light-haired one came for the money.

"It's in the house," I told him, keeping my eyes on his, fighting the urge to let them wander over his body. I could smell him, and it was neither unpleasant nor without its effects. My pecker did a little dance in my trunks. He stepped aside and followed me up to the house, hesitating at the back door when I entered.

"Come on in," I said, feeling a little grand, a little pretentious. Apparently, Mother paid him at the door, obviously not sharing the same interests as her son. "You guys do a hell of a job," I said, small-talking my way through the house.

"Yup," he admitted.

The cash was on the kitchen table under a pile of mail. I knew it was there, but I made a show of looking for it, postponing his departure so that I could at least have some decent memories of him for future reference, when the hand would have to make due. *What's his name?* I wondered. *Clint? Deke? Or something softer...Josh?*

"They left it around here someplace," I said, pretending to be confounded by its disappearance. I turned around and caught him staring at my ass and glanced for a while at the front of his shorts, the denim mound of his crotch. He crossed his arms over his chest.

"Why'd you go and change into them trunks?" he wanted to know. He flattened his hand and sent it down into his shorts.

I just shrugged, amazed to be hearing what I was hearing.

"Why don't you go put 'em on again?" he said, his voice softer, more insistent. He stepped forward and got hold of my trunks with his free hand and pulled them down. My half-hard popped out, making him smile.

"What about your partner?" I asked.

"Ain't I good enough?" he asked easily, wrapping his big, dirty fist around my hot dog. "We got an agreement, him and me, and I been carrying around a hard all day. Need to get it off."

We went out back, and I almost laughed at the strangeness of the situation and the fact that I was about to get laid—again—beside my parents' pool. I stepped into the changing hut to put on my Speedo again. When I came out the lawn man was on a chaise, his shorts around his boot tops, gripping a huge, dripping monster of a cock.

"Bring that ass over here," he said.

I walked over to him, sporting my own pouch-buster. His baseball cap, black-rimmed with grime, came off, and his hair fell just below his ears. His mouth opened, and I saw the pink tip of his tongue and knew he wanted to go down on me.

"Sit on my lap," he said, and I paused. "Straddle me frontward," he clarified.

I threw a leg over the chaise, looking him in the eye. He let go of his dick and let me sit on it, moaning under my weight.

"Rub your ass all over my pecker," he said, and I dragged my nylon-encased butt up and down his shaft, digging on the thickness of it against my asshole. I ran my hands across his chest, damp with sweat, and fingered the stiffened knobs of his tits, sitting high and hard on his pecs. I wanted to suck the salty grit off them, nose around in the fine blond hairs that covered him. I wanted to suck my way down his belly and crawl up between his legs. I wanted to lick the son of a bitch clean and have him ride home smelling up the cab with my spit.

He was more than content, though, with the slick smoothness of my Speedo rubbing up his cock, and I wasn't having that bad a time myself. I palmed my own dick through its cloth cover, enjoying the rough ride. He took my nipples and pulled hard, leering up at me, stinking of sweat and gasoline and grass. He dug his heels in and thrust up at me, his big pole slipping sweetly over my begging pussy, petting it and getting it sloppy; he leaked as much as I usually come. Making a mess of the ass of my bathing suit, he flipped me over and simulated the best fuck I'd ever had, rutting against my Speedo-encased ass. He grunted over me, smearing his sweating chest all over my back, licking my shoulder blades, drawing his sharp-stubbled chin down my spine. He freed my dick and beat me off with both hands, humping me with a force that would have done a number to my insides.

"Ah!" he bellowed, shooting up straight. I glanced over my shoulder to see his grimaced face looking skyward, his chest heaving, the wet dots of his dark brown nipples trembling as he hosed my back with his baby-making butter.

He hopped off the end of the chaise and turned me around. "Give it to me," he said, dropping to his knees, and I choked out wad after wad of come across his face and into his open, hungry mouth.

"Sweet," he said afterward, smacking his lips. I was squeezing out the last drops of it and fingering it into his mouth when his partner, the dark brute, appeared by the fence.

"Watching again, Murray, you fuckin' closet case?" my lover said.

"Quitting time was a fuckin' hour ago. Carlene is gonna chew me a new asshole for being late with the paycheck," Murray complained, eyeing the two of us casually.

"I'll chew you a new asshole, Murray, but you'll like it," said the guy who'd just worn out the back of my Speedos. He turned to me, pulling up his shorts. "I'll be back," he said, winking.

"You do that," I said, tucking my cock back into my bathing suit.

The cordless was beside the chaise. It sat there, benign, a little useless for all its utility. I picked it up and dialed Connie Takis's number and left him a message, just a "Hey, bud, how you doing?" kind of message. I figured it could go either way: Either he'll ignore it, or he'll hop a train on Friday and come down and fuck my brains out again. Until then I had the lawn mower and his promised return to look forward to. I picked up a pad I'd brought out earlier, located a pen between the cushions beneath me, and started a note to my "girlfriend" in Africa. "Dear Lorna," I began. "How's the hut building going? Your Ebola getting any better?"

ELECTRICITY

Ben turned over in bed, trying to avoid the hard shaft of early morning light that stabbed through the window. He heard the soft sound of footfalls over his head and the low hum of music. He waited for the sound of water—the boy up there taking his shower. He could see the boy clearly in his mind's eye: dark short hair, eyes the color of slate, a heavy brow, a nose not quite refined. He could almost see the boy standing naked outside of the shower stall, pushing back the plastic curtain, stepping into the streaming water. Ben had not actually ever seen the boy without his clothes, but he had seen him enough times in just shorts so that he knew his smooth torso was muscled but not built up, the tiny dots of nipples that looked like small coral-colored pearls. He had stared once—while the boy pointed out a leaking pipe under the kitchen sink—at those pinkish dots that had also reminded Ben of peas, early peas, new ones, the peas you bought at a farmer's market, the ones you had to shell.

The boy often reminded Ben of food.

Ben was 22 that year, the year of short hair, as he called it, because everyone seemed to have his hair cut to the scalp. Ben would walk into the College Barbers and sit in his favorite chair and tell his barber, "Show me some skin and leave a little on the top." The house Ben was living in was his grandmother's, and she was in Florida year-round. Ben rented the upstairs apartment to students at the state university, where he was taking the long road for a B.A., which for Ben stood for bachelor of anything.

The boy upstairs wasn't much younger than Ben—probably this side of 19, Ben was thinking—but he had a boyish face, a boyish figure. Maybe 5 feet 8 inches, slim-hipped, and smooth, the boy had a long-muscled torso, a killer stomach, and legs that Ben dreamed about wrapped tighter than a belt around his waist. The boy's name was Chris, but Ben, in the privacy of his own bedroom, called him Boy.

Chris was the perfect neighbor, hardly made any noise at all, lived like a monk, and was all wrapped up in his studies. Sometimes Ben would be sitting at his desk with his big fat *Norton Anthology of English Literature* in his hands, and he'd catch himself staring at his ceiling for minutes at a time. Just staring as though he had Superman eyes and could see his little Jimmy Olson padding around upstairs in raggy boxers, eating crackers out of a box, reading about marketing strategies, criminal law, corporate holdings. What he wanted was to be up there with him, stretched out and staring between the V of his two feet at the boy, the boy's pale legs shocked with black hair, cute little butt hidden in the bag of shorts, sweet soft cock knocking at the fly as he walked around the room with a thick and heavy tome of Russian poetry. Just hearing the boy's feet on the floor overhead could give Ben an aching jetson.

What he liked best was the sight of the boy's laundry up on the second floor back porch, a line hung with hand-washed boxers and limp jock straps, pairs of sweat socks—all the intimates of a boy's life. He watched out the window for Chris to come back from his evening runs, red and sweating, as if from athletic sex, and he wanted the boy's hot wet skin against his own.

But he barely acknowledged his neighbor when they passed one another coming and going to class. Chris seemed so self-contained, and Ben was more than just a little unsure of himself. He had had quite a few girlfriends up until Chris moved in, and a couple of really strange sexual encounters with a couple of really strange guys so that he wasn't quite sure what he wanted. Whatever he was feeling about his neighbor, it was strong and seemed to center at Ben's crotch. Thus the sight of the boy's laundry made him twitch in his own shorts, and seeing the boy at school, however distant, could prompt Ben to make a trip to the nearest men's room stall to shoot a load into the white porcelain toilet bowl, not caring much if there was anyone on the next crapper to hear him.

Ben was trying to write a paper for his Art and Cultures class. "Art as Spiritual Participation" was the title of his essay, and that was all he had so far. He stared at his word processor, his face lighted by the screen, the only light he had on in the house. He had just worked out and showered and slipped on a pair of sweats and a T-shirt. Upstairs the boy was playing some new music, the latest by Erasure, and Ben tapped his foot along to the beat that sifted down through the ceiling.

The screen died and the music too, and Ben stood up in the sudden darkness, cursing the ancient electrical system that frequently went on the fritz like this. He went looking for a flashlight, unable to remember where he put it last. For all he knew it could be down in the cellar next to the fuse box from the last mishap. He lighted a candle and listened to the boy, who walked across the ceiling and opened his door and ran down the stairs, skipping steps. Ben heard him at his own door, knocking softly.

Ben opened the door. Chris was barely recognizable in the dark. The boy said hey, and Ben said hey back.

"It's like the whole city or something. It's all black," Chris was saying, standing in the foyer.

"I was just going down to the basement," Ben said. "I thought we blew a mess of fuses."

Chris went to the front door and opened it as if to prove what he was saying, and he did—the sky was pitch black and every house he could see was dark.

"There wasn't a storm, was there?" Ben asked. "I didn't hear any thunder or anything."

"I don't have any candles or anything," Chris was saying as he closed the door and moved closer to Ben's threshold.

"I've just got this one," Ben said, motioning to the one that was burning on table in the living room. "You want a beer or something."

Chris followed him to the kitchen. Ben opened the refrigerator door and was stupidly surprised that the light inside didn't work. He squatted, feeling his dick swing freely in the dark cave of his sweatpants, and grabbed a couple of bottles, handing one to Chris.

"I'm not afraid of the dark or anything," the boy said. Ben heard the twist of the cap and the little gasp the bottle made as it was opened. Re palmed his own cap off. He chugged some beer with Chris. They stood together in the kitchen, and Ben wished like anything that the lights would turn back on right then, so that he could look at the boy, look at him all over.

"Let's go into the living room," Ben said. The kitchen was narrow. He leaned against the refrigerator and Chris was up against the sink, and there was enough room to pass a fist between them. They both turned to exit and knocked shoulders and hips, and Ben realized the boy was shirtless, wearing just a pair of boxers.

"Excuse me, they said together and tried again, and Chris got out first and stood by the sofa. Ben followed.

"Sit down," he said, and the boy sat, and Ben stood looking down at him, seeing him in the candle light that made his skin seem even more pale. He saw the fly of Chris's shorts was open, showing nothing. He eyed the nipples that hung at the outer curve of the boy's pecs. Chris put his bare feet up on the coffee table, his giant boxers hanging wide at his angled thighs, offering another glimpse into nothing.

"I was writing a paper," Ben said.

"I wasn't doing anything," Chris said. He was looking around the room at what he could see by the candle's flame. Ben had the walls painted the color of dijon mustard, hung with prints he found at flea markets. Near the ceiling there was a narrow shelf that went all the round the room, filled with the junk he's collected so far—books, old toy trucks from when he was a little boy, pieces of pottery—a bunch of nothing but for some reason compelling to Ben.

"I was rolling a joint," he said. "That's what I was really doing. I could go get it…if you wanted."

Ben made a face at the paper he was supposed to be writing, and Chris said, "But if you're not into that—"

"It's not that," Ben said. "It's just that I was planning on getting a jump on the paper." He was doing his best to keep his eyes out of the valley the boy's two raised legs made.

"Aw, what the fuck," he said, and he saw Chris smile.

They had a couple more beers and shared the joint Chris had rolled. It was fat and potent, a wicked stogie that made Ben feel buzzed and just a little anxious. "This isn't very mellow, is it?" he said, handing the roach to Chris.

"No, this shit's goofy. I can do some good work on a little bit, you know, papers and shit like that, but..." He trailed off and his face broke into a big stoned grin.

"What?" Ben laughed.

Chris sat up and put his elbows on his knees. "Man, I swear, this weed just goes straight to my dick. Like it's laced with Spanish fly or something."

Ben laughed again, harder this time, the kid was so cute and funny.

"I feel like you're my older brother," Chris said sudden and serious. Ben stopped laughing, but his mouth was still laugh-shaped.

"Do you have one?" he asked, and Chris nodded.

"Yeah, well, sometimes I feel like I'm looking out for you, you know?" Ben said, wishing he hadn't. The boy fell back on the sofa again and his legs fell open. He looked about ready to sack out.

"Am I losing you?" Ben said, regretting that too.

"Huh?"

"I was wondering if you were tired," Ben said.

"No," Chris said. "I was just thinking about how cool it was that this weird shit with the lights happened, like, I've been upstairs for a couple of months and we never hung out. I didn't think you were into it, and now I find out you're totally cool. I figured you were some hyperbrain. I don't even know what you're studying."

"Me either," Ben smirked.

"No girlfriend?"

Ben shook his head.

"Me either," Chris said.

They sat quietly for a long time, listening to each other breathing. They kept looking at one another, and their looks became longer and more meaningful, until finally they were flat out staring at one another, each asking the same silent questions: *Do you? Will you?*

"I've got a fucking boner," Chris said, breaking the long silence. They both began to giggle like kids. "You want to see it?" he asked Ben.

"Sure I do," he said, his mouth feeling cakey. He sipped the rest of his beer and wanted another but couldn't leave his seat, awaiting the unveiling.

Chris worked his dick out the slit of his shorts. It poked up tall and white with a big fat head that kept it from standing on its own. Ben became aware of some action in his own pants. Chris held his cock at its base. He waved it around like a little bat.

"I can take these off," he said, pinching the front of his shorts.

Ben nodded, and the boy pushed at the waistband that curled and rolled down his hips. His pubes were pitch black and thick as a head of hair. He put his fingers into it, scratching himself, his cock lying heavy against his hip bone. "This is kind of cool," Chris said lazily, taking up his rod again. "I like you watching me."

Ben shifted in his chair. He spread his legs wide and his dick, half-hard, pointed at the boy, kept from full ascent by the drum-tight stretch of sweats. Chris gripped his shaft and chucked his fist up and down. With his free hand, he fingered his hard and tiny nipples, those pink sweet peas, and Ben wanted nothing more than to put his mouth on one and then the other. He groaned with the thought, and Chris smiled. His eyes were red and slitted, half-closed with pleasure. He licked his fingers and touched them to his fits again.

"Let me see yours," he said softly, and Ben stood up fast. Stars swirled in his eyes, and he felt a little dizzy, but that passed, and he undid the string that, along with his suddenly jutting cock, held up his pants. He felt 14 years old, reminded of times he and his buddies showed off the wages of puberty—spurts of growth in the dick department, a patch of pubes finally coming in, the quickest shooters. He bared his bone, and Chris said, "Cool." Ben stood, fat but taper-headed prick in a nest of gold-colored hair. The air swirled around his pecker and made it sizzle. He touched it to make its end weep with stickiness. Chris sat up and brought his head close to Ben's cock head.

"Take off your shirt," he said, and Ben complied, lifting the T-shirt over his head. His chest was smooth, twin sheets of muscle with a deep split at the center. His stomach laddered down to his pubes, and his lateral obliques, those funny wing-shaped side muscles, curved, marking the tops of his hips. He put his hands there, and his cock ached to be touched.

"You look good," Chris said. "I like the way your muscles stand out."

Ben watched the boy jack his cock, his own wanting hands, mouth, the tight suck of butt muscle, the boy's ass ring.

"Come here," he said, moving his hips and making his pecker swing.

Chris looked up at him, his mouth just opening. A bit of tongue slipped out and wet his lips.

The candle was beginning to flutter; it sparked and spit, threatening to extinguish at any moment. Ben wanted to see the boy, see him bent over and sucking, bent over and taking the tip of Ben's cock, and then a little more and then a little more. He wanted to see the boy's eyes when his dick got sucked down Ben's throat. The candle sputtered out. The boy sat glowing.

A hand closed around his swinging meat, and then Ben felt the boy's tongue on the under-side of his shaft. He put his hands on the boy's head, curling his fingers against the dark bristles of hair. "Good," he said when he felt the heat of Chris's mouth on his dangling sac, sucking the baggy skin, tenderly chewing, nudging with his tongue Ben's pendulous balls. The boy licked up, kissing the veined kielbasa-sized cock, slipping his mouth over the head swiftly, going down on Ben slowly, surely. Ben came up against the back of Chris's throat, and he pulled back again, the boy's teeth lightly along the top, catching the head and drawing Ben's thick rod in again, lips taut, tongue teasing. He felt Chris's hands now, slipping up Ben's thighs, fingering the curling hairs that grew lightly at the base of his dick. They circled his balls making a tight ring and tugged, and Ben felt his dick dribble, and he heard the boy moan, sucking up the ooze. He backed off.

"What do we do now," Ben heard Chris say.

"Well," Ben said. He wasn't sure what to do next. His experience was limited, but he did not care to divulge this to Chris. This was as far as he had ever gone, getting his joint sucked, shooting his load on the floor with some stranger who milked his own cock as he squatted at Ben's feet.

"Do you want to go to bed?" Ben asked.

"I guess," Chris said.

They walked back to Ben's room, and Ben flipped the light switch, forgetting again that there was no power. He turned quick to say something and Chris knocked into him, and Ben felt the stab of the boy's cock, hard as stone, against his thigh. The boys lips smashed into Ben's shoulder. They grunted together, and Ben slipped his arms around the boy, crushing him into a bear-hug. His hands followed the trail of Chris's backbone to his tailbone, and they grabbed hold of the boy's full ass cheeks, fingers at the rim of the boy's butt pucker.

Chris made some crazy noises and humped himself against Ben's leg. "Man," he said when Ben moved his hands up again to the boy's shoulders. "That's the other thing about this pot—it makes my hole all whacky. I'll tell you, the other night I was so horny for it I used a long-neck beer bottle. I'd just squat on the bottle and jack, then I'd take a break and take a swig from the bottle. I was out of my mind horny."

"You feeling that way now," Ben asked.

"Oh, fuck, man, you know it," he said, turning around and rubbing his ass up against Ben's crotch. Ben dropped to his haunches and started biting the tops of Chris's ass cheeks. He put his hands through the boy's legs and gripped his balls, pulling them back and wetting them with his tongue. He sniffed around the hypersensitive hole that smelled hot and dirty and ready for reaming. He touched it with the tip of his tongue, and the boy whimpered. He pushed the boy over, and Chris sprawled surprised across the dark bed. Ben found the boy's pulsing hole again and started eating it, gnawing with his teeth, probing with his tongue. He fucked into it with spit-slicked fingertips, and the hole seemed to gape. He went deeper with his fingers as Chris fucked against the bedspread, and with his free hand Ben got himself ready with a gob of saliva and a few short strokes on his own fiery rod.

"You want my cock?" he said, and the boy started begging for it, his hips bucking. He flipped over onto his back and lifted his legs high, and Ben took Chris by the heels and leaned into him, feeling the plush hole sigh around his cock head and invite him in.

He never imagined fucking would be so easy. Chris's hole was more than easy—it was a coach, coaxing him in easily, slackly, and then a drill sergeant, tightening up when Ben withdrew. Developing an easy rhythm, he handled his cock the way he handled an oar on the crew team. Stroke, stroke, stroke, nice and easy at first, but slowly and almost imperceptibly picking up speed. He hooked the boy's feet around the back of his neck and fingered the tiny nips. His hips were now slapping against Chris's fanny, and they both grunted. Chris reached up for Ben's head, pulling him down and wrecking his tempo, and he fell into the boy's mouth for an unbelievably hot kiss that very nearly cost him his load.

He crawled up on the bed, still fully engaged with Chris's mouth and asshole. He smeared his lips across the boy's mouth; he whispered wetly into the boy's ear without really thinking: "little brother."

Chris flipped out, turning into a fuck monster. He wrestled and twisted and got himself astride Ben's hips, tripoded on his own two legs and Ben's concrete cock. He rode on Ben like a bronco buster, coming down hard on Ben's hipbones, and Ben wondered what sort of internal damage the boy was causing himself, and then he forgot about the boy's innards save for the heat and the gritty slide, and he felt himself being sucked up, and he felt as though he might just fall up into the red insides of the boy. He pumped his hips and met the boy's ass with sharp slaps, and Chris twisted on Ben's pecs, and Ben felt the heavy whack of Chris's cock against his belly, the hot juicy spray of it as the boy shot and shot with gritted teeth.

"Stay on it," he whispered, "Stay on it, buddy," and Chris continued the ride until Ben's dick burst, and great gobs of milky seed scattered up inside the boy's buttery bun hole.

They were asleep when the lights came on in the morning. It was close to dawn, and they were wrapped around one another. The overhead light shone in their eyes. From upstairs they could hear the music Chris had been playing. They got themselves up and sleepily stumbled around. Ben shut down his computer, his essay title lost in the storm. He went upstairs with Chris to shut off the tape player and the lights left on. With everything black again, they fell into Chris's bed, hard and ready, recharged and eager to generate their own special electricity.

Bones

Hal stood up, holding his cupped hands over his eyes. His long torso was bare and brown, covered with hair that was lighter when it wasn't slicked down with sweat. The shorts he wore weren't his and were too big and hung low on his hips. He turned to Tim, who had himself laid out on a blanket. His shorts were hiked up so that his ass cheeks were showing. His thighs were blown over with dark hairs, and his ass was too, an odd feature that invited some good-natured ribbing from the guys in the locker room. It was something that Hal was fascinated with and thought about often. Tim went up on his elbows, the muscles of his back and shoulders and neck going thick. His black hair was cut close to his scalp and left a little long on top. The white soles of his feet caught Hal's eyes, confounding and irritating him. He looked back over the lake, looking for Briggs and Davis.

"I thought you said they were coming," he said, looking back at the rings of dark hair that fringed Tim's ankles.

"I said they were caddying. They'll be here when they're done," Tim said. He looked down at his clunky black wristwatch.

"Polson's boat's out again," Hal announced. From where he was standing, the dinghy looked empty, calmly unmanned, afloat on the lake, but every once in a while he'd catch sight of Mike Polson's dark head and shoulders. Polson was new to the lake, a renter who'd suddenly decided to buy his cabin and renovate the thing to make it livable year-round. Tim mowed his lawn, what little there was to mow, and said Mike would swing in a hammock he'd hung on the front porch, sipping glasses of water and reading. He'd said he was a writer when Tim asked, but neither one of them saw him doing much writing at all. Besides, he didn't *look* like a writer. The guy looked more like he coached something, reminding Hal of his brusque and muscular gym teacher, Mr. Caldwell, whose cannonlike thighs, shining in the absence of hair, fascinated Hal almost as much as the sight of Tony's naked feet.

Still, there was something about Mike Polson—Hal wasn't able to put his finger on it. Something shifty, shady, even though Tim had said he was the nicest guy. "Cool," he'd said, a pronouncement, but Hal wondered. He'd offered Tim a beer, inviting him to sit. What, and talk about books?

Jealous, Hal chastised himself. He looked back at Tim, whose legs were spread. He pulled up his shorts for the 14th time, feeling again his dick hitch up against his fly, causing a shiver of gooseflesh to run up his belly. He was looking forward to the guys coming over. According to Tim, Briggs had promised a hamper of food, raidings from his mother's refrigerator, and Davis was bringing a bottle of vodka from his old man's liquor cabinet. They'd build a fire and roast hot dogs on a stick and eat Mrs. Briggs's potato salad and mix the Davis vodka with some juice or something. There was a cabin of sorts on the island, built years ago by Tim's father, where they would sleep if they didn't feel like going home.

It was summer, and the boys were finished with high school—finally—and ready to embark in new directions. Hal was going to go to a small liberal arts college in the Catskills; Tim had been accepted at St. Lawrence. Briggs and Davis were staying in Constantia. They talked of getting an apartment together, which made Hal wistful, if not a little jealous. Getting an apartment with Bill and Dave seemed to be much better than going off to school. He could imagine the two of them together—they were both as casual as one could be about nearly everything. Neither one of them was shy about stripping down to nothing to take a swim in the lake. Tim was less bold, and Hal shier still, afraid as he was that he'd be unable to control his hair-trigger erections.

He liked thinking about his friends at night as he stroked himself off, picturing the three of them together, wrestling underwater in an aquarium like the one he'd seen at Niagara Falls. In his mind they cavorted like dolphins, like porpoises, and they were naked and hard and kicking while Hal watched. They would swim together, and Briggs's head would slip into the V of Tim's dark legs, and Davis would slip his cock into Tim's mouth. They would twist slowly, backs arching, pirouetting down and then up. Briggs and Davis pressed together, and Tim swam around them, his erection like a fin fitting into Davis's behind. Hal liked making them come when he was about to come, writhing together like that, mermen. He pulled himself until his cock head burned and his breath quickened. He tried to be quiet because he shared a room with his brother, but Briggs and Davis and Tim were coming too, their jizz jetting into the water, clotting and hanging still and elegant, and then Hal himself would spill, a warm spray all over his belly, his toes popping like firecrackers as he flexed his feet, his whole body shuddering.

Tim announced his need to piss. He stood up and walked over to the bushes that grew sparsely around the island's shore. With his back to Hal, he untied his shorts and dropped them. "Hey, Hal," he shouted, as if Hal hadn't noticed the moon directed at him.

"When are you going to shave that damn thing?" Hal asked him.

"Your mom was too busy last night. She said sometime next week," Tim laughed.

"Right," Hal said, dropping to the blanket where Tim had been lying. He felt an ominous stirring in his groin that signaled future trouble if he didn't start thinking about something other than Tim's butt.

Tim put his hands on his hips and pissed into the bushes. "You know," he said, "my brother was telling me the other day about people who liked getting pissed on, and I thought about you for some reason."

"Fuck off!" Hal said, and Tim turned fast, his yellow stream arching and flying into droplets that landed near Hal, pelting the sand like warm rain.

"Jesus!" he yelled, and Tim laughed hard, turning and showing his soft, fat dripping cock.

"That was stupid," Hal said, getting up from the blanket. He stomped across the sand toward the water. There was a bead of moisture on his lips that he licked at without thinking, and he tasted the bitter salt of his friend's urine. It made him spit, but there was also something about it that made him feel funny, and he looked at Tim, who was taking his time getting his shorts up. It seemed to Hal that Tim's cock looked bigger than usual, that it wasn't its usual dinky little self. He'd never had occasion to see Tim fully pumped up, and he was surprised now to see it in such a radically different state. Normally, he was used to seeing it skinny and thumb-shaped, but now it was swollen, its head flattening as it widened. Tim got his shorts up, replacing his growing dick by hand so that it lay noticeably in the faded blue pouch of his sweats. Hal stepped out into the water, hoping its cruel coldness would help dispel his own growing agitation.

He faced out, his back to his friend, and scanned the shore. He thought he heard the tiny buzz of Davis's little outboard, and he looked for it against the dark green line that was the shore. Polson's little boat dipped and turned in the water. His hand dangled over the edge, slack-fingered. The lake was otherwise empty, at least on this side of the island, and Hal felt alone. He dipped into the water, wetting his torso.

Tim called out to him just as Hal went under. He came back up, the cold water streaming over him, his hair in wet ribbons over his eyes.

"What?" he called back.

"Nothing," Tim said. He was standing by the blanket. The radio was playing loudly a song they both liked. Tim played air guitar, thrashing his head around. "Mosh pit, man," he shouted, stomping around the blanket.

Hal dragged himself through the water. He lurched up over the sand, doing the slow trudge that eventually became the arm-swinging, head-banging, body-bouncing dance of the mosh pit. The two boys collided, trying to keep straight faces. They shouldered and elbowed one another, and Hal accidentally swung his hand into Tim's groin with enough force to make the boy howl in pain. He dropped to his knees, clutching himself.

"You OK?" Hal asked, his hand on the boy's shoulder.

"You broke it, Barkley," he whined, peering into his shorts. "Look! It's all swollen!" He flashed his boner at Hal.

Hal felt his face burn. Tim's dick was fatter now than before, fatter than any Hal had ever seen, fatter even than his dad's, though not quite as long. Tim pulled the top of his shorts down under his balls. He had more hair than any of his friends, a black bush that grew lushly around his cock.

Hal stood awkwardly, using his hands to block the view of his own pants-prop.

"*Boing*," Tim said. He gripped himself hard and smiled up at Hal. A drop of precome sparkled like a diamond set into the deep piss slot of Tim's cock head. Hal felt a terrifying rush chill his stomach. His heart banged, and his tongue dried up in his mouth. The wind whipped up the sand, and it bit at his legs.

"What's up with you today?" he asked. He didn't want to look at Tim's fisted pecker, but how could he not? It was fucking beautiful—and totally annoying. Hal kept his eyes on Tim's face.

"Pete said you liked watching him jerk off," Tim said, letting go of the fat prong that poked up out of all that hair. Hal had never seen anything so dense or glossy. He was thinking about that and not about what he thought he heard Tim say.

"What?" Hal said, looking as though he'd awakened from a dream.

"Pete said you watch him jack all the time," Tim said. "He said you wank him too."

"That's a fuckin' lie," Hal said, his voice rising.

"Don't get pissed off," Tim said, his face changing. He pulled up his shorts, but his erection stuck out like a log under a carpet. He lay back on the blanket. "Doesn't mean anything," he said. "Not really." He rubbed himself through his shorts.

"Well, it's a lie," Hal shouted. He'd never seen Pete do anything like that, although he would have liked to, and that's what made him so mad. He tried to ignore Tim playing with himself. He glanced quickly out at the lake, at Polson's boat doing a lame turn on its own.

"Have you?" Hal asked, getting closer to the blanket, unable now to take his eyes off of the massive mound of Tim's crotch. "Have you ever..."

"Couple of times," Tim said. He squinted up at Hal.

There were several moments of silence that seemed to pull them together, sealing them in a vacuum until Tim rolled over to fiddle with the radio. Hal watched his friend's ass cheeks flex and relax as he humped himself into the blanket-covered sand. It was driving him crazy. His dick throbbed, and he wanted more than anything to touch himself, but even with Tim's back turned, he couldn't do it. He stared at Tim's butt.

Tim jumped up suddenly. "I got to get it off," he said, his horniness like a bee sting or a hair shirt. He ran off into the bushes, and Hal followed, feeling just as compelled.

They both went to their knees in the cool, shaded sand. Tim's dick was out, a fat, fleshy candle that oozed honey. Hal unzipped, and his own pecker flashed in the air, thinner than Tim's but longer by inches, and his bare balls spilled out. He could see Tim eyeing it up and the gentle grip he had on himself. Hal mirrored it.

Tim drew his palm over his sticky head and closed his eyes. Hal spat a thick gob into his open hand. They jacked off in unison, stroke for stroke, swiftly at first and then slowing up as if they both realized that this was something to be savored, something to linger over, a first, never to be repeated. They both let go of themselves when they got too close and looked at one another, panting, not really understanding this strange and new connection between them. It was almost psychic. When Hal looked down at Tim's dripping member, wondering how it tasted, Tim stood up and said, "Try it."

Hal opened his mouth. He'd tasted plenty of his own come, but all of that experience did not prepare him for the sweetness of Tim's cock cream. He licked at the sticky end, sniffing the aroma of Tim's crotch. He widened his mouth to take in the head and managed that much but no more, even when Tim tried to push himself in gently. And while Hal was content for the moment to simply suckle the end of his friend's dick, Tim was itching for some friction. He pulled out of Hal's gaping mouth and slapped Hal's cheeks with his wet prick.

"Did you ever get fucked?" Tim said, his voice sounding terribly loud to Hal.

Hal shook his head. He stared at the red head of Tim's cock, watching him pull on it. A shining drop swung from the piss slit, and Hal stuck his tongue out to catch it. He put his hands on the rich fur of Tim's thighs and rubbed the flexed muscles there, reaching around and grabbing the thick cheeks of his behind.

"Put your finger in me," Hal heard, not quite believing his ears. He slid his fingers into the crack, encountering even more hair, coarser hair. His forefinger found the wrinkled indentation, already slick with sweat. Tim loosened his sphincter, coaxing Hal's finger. He looked down past his fat pecker and into Hal's eyes.

"It's way better than pussy," he said. "Tighter, ain't it?"

"It's tight," Hal said, and he pushed his whole finger up into Tim's hole. It was hot and silky. Tim slid his feet into the sand, spreading his legs, bending his knees. His back arched, and his pecs widened. He was built like a wrestler, small and muscled. He seemed thick all over to Hal, thicker than ever, and Hal put his mouth to the dark dangle of Tim's balls.

"Go deeper," Tim said, squatting on Hal's finger.

"Doesn't it hurt?" he asked, looking up at Tim. His eyes were closed, and his lips parted. He looked to Hal like he was praying. Tim shook his head, working hard on his erection, jacking it off seriously, smacking it juicily. Hal wiggled his finger, making his friend moan, and Hal wondered jealously who else had had his finger up Tim's chute.

"Oh, shit, Hal, that's the place, that hard thing there," Tim said.

"What thing?"

"That knobby thing. There!" Tim said, bobbing on Hal's hand like some kind of finger puppet.

"Holy crap," Hal said, amazed by the sucking pull of the hole. His hand flew to his own cock, which was throbbing and leaking and pulsing. There was an intriguing blue vein that doubled back on itself close to the base; it rolled under his sliding palm.

He ducked his head toward Tim's groin again, but the boy wouldn't let him. "I'll blow," he said simply. He reached back and stopped Hal's finger and pulled it out. He pulled the hand up to his mouth and sucked on the finger, blowing it. It seemed a sophisticated and sexy gesture that struck Hal dumb. When Tim pushed him he fell back easily. He let his shorts be pulled off and his legs spread wide, Tim kneeling between them, holding Hal's prong in one hand and twisting his nuts in the other. He went down on the long pole with a quick thrust that nearly knocked the wind out of Hal. He'd been blown only once before, but it was no preparation for Tim's playful mouth and teasing tongue, the hard suck on his glans, the gentle teething of his flared head. Tim bobbed and choked and grunted, making sloppy noises and drooling puddles of spit into Hal's light-colored pubes. Tim brought him close to coming, then backed off instinctively. Hal's dick jumped and oozed.

Tim crawled up his buddy so that he was straddling Hal's hips. He sat up straight and spat a gob on Hal's gut and pulled Hal's dick through his legs so that it stood up against Tim's pucker. He laid himself flat against Hal and began humping into his own lube, fucking against Hal's flat stomach. He squeezed his legs together, trapping Hal's cock. The friction from the hair and the slickness of Tim's asshole, combined with some spit that Tim added manually, made Hal feel as though he were about to be turned inside out through his pecker. He put his mouth on Tim's chest, licking the stray hairs that had recently begun to grow there, and Tim moved so that his nipple popped into Hal's mouth. He ducked his head, putting his cheek against Hal's almost-blond hair, saying things that Hal had heard in the few porn flicks he'd had the opportunity to see. He put his hands on Tim's hairy butt, the twin cheeks fitting his palms perfectly. Tim rubbed against him more quickly, his thighs clamped on Hal's burning cock.

"Oh, fuck, man," Tim breathed, his strokes becoming erratic, twitchy. He lifted his torso and looked down between them. His log of a dick spat out gobs of white, and he made appreciative grunts with each clotted spurt.

He spun around and threw his mouth down on Hal's quivering bone. The sudden soft heat was what he'd been craving, and while he slobbered on Tim's used, dripping meat, he pumped his own into Tim's mouth, feeling his nuts ascend and ready themselves to pump out the load of Hal's life. The force and amount startled Tim, who was not ready himself for the veritable flood. He stayed the course, swallowing a mouthful and then another before backing off, the white stuff dripping from his grinning lips.

"Christ," he said softly, his voice low with awe.

"Christ," Hal agreed, equally amazed.

Briggs and Davis eventually showed up with the food and the booze, and they built a fire when it got dark and listened to the radio and shot the shit about nothing at all, Hal and Tim all the while sneaking looks at one another. At one point Hal stretched out on a blanket and looked at the stars, and Tim moved next to him. Around midnight, half asleep, he heard Briggs say he was drunk enough to look for another party, and Davis, as always, was in full agreement.

"Mr. Polson said to come by anytime," Briggs said.

"He said to call him Mike," Davis corrected.

"Mike said it was cool, and we saw him at the distributor picking up a case this morning, man," Briggs said, his fair hair glistening somehow. "You guys coming?" he wanted to know, and Hal heard Tim say no.

"We'll probably crash here," Tim said.

"Looks like Barkley's crashed already," said Briggs.

When they heard the little outboard putt out into the lake, they took off their clothes and covered themselves with a sleeping bag. Tim slid in beside Hal, his cock hard again and pressed into his ass crack.

"Is this OK?" Tim wanted to know, and Hal said yes.

"Feel like doing it again?" Tim whispered, his face lit orange in the firelight. "I want to do you this time," he said, putting his lips on Hal's face. Hal nodded.

"You suck me. Get it wet," Tim said, getting up on his knees and crawling his dick up into Hal's mouth. It was fat and burning and as hard as wood; he could not really imagine putting the thing up his ass. And then Tim's fingers stroked Hal's butt, smoothing over the hole, pushing against the taut pucker, coaxing it open. He straddled Hal's head then and lowered his own over Hal's crotch. He blew on Hal's cock and chinned his balls and put his hands on the insides of his thighs and, bringing them up, put his face between Hal's legs, his tongue on Hal's hole. His pussy pinched tight, then blossomed; he gave himself to the sensation, letting out a low moan and wriggling his ass under Tim's tongue's ministrations.

"You're crazy for it," Tim whispered. "I knew you'd be." He blew a wad of spit on his friend's asshole and fingered into it, which made Hal go tight and stiff all over. "Easy, baby," Tim said, pulling out his finger and stroking the pucker, and Hal's legs bent at the knees, and his heels dug into the sand.

He wanted to say, "What are you doing to me?" He wanted to say, "Damn, Tim, I love this." He wanted to grab hold of his cock and shake it empty at the moon that was shining up over them like some kind of voyeur watching their every move. "You're crazy for it," he heard Tim say, and he was. He was crazy for it, and he wanted it now.

He got himself on all fours because that's how he wanted to do it, that's how he'd been thinking of doing it for a long time, on his knees like a dog, like Tim's good dog. He swung his head low and high, like a fretful horse, as Tim positioned himself behind him and pressed his bone against the plush redness. The dick head pushed inside and hurt, and he dropped his head and stared at the glinting sand, which reflected the orange flames of the fire. Tim ran his hands down Hal's sides, bump-bump-bumping along his ribs, and up again, massaging his friend's shoulders, relaxing him and opening him up, making his pussy open like a flower and suck in the shaft and the honey that welled up in the deep-slotted split of Tim's cock head. Hal took it all inside of him and bumped his ass against Tim's hipbones, and the air left them both.

"How about that?" Tim said, and Hal heard the smile in his voice. He turned his head and saw Tim's face and loved the way it looked, half in shadow. He wanted to kiss him, but he couldn't twist any farther, nor could he bend backward the way he needed to. Tim had closed his eyes, and he was deep in his fuck, deep into his strokes, and Hal felt Tim's cock, big and high in his chest, practically up to his sternum, and he reached back to feel how tightly his ass lips were wrapped around the sliding shaft.

"You're a fucking natural," Tim laughed, plugging away. "It's crazy, isn't it? Filling you up like this." He pushed his cock all the way in and pulled hard on Hal's little nipples. "You're my boy," Tim said. "You're my baby. I'm fucking my baby, aren't I? I'm fucking you good." What he said was as good as his fucking, and Hal shook his head, wanting Tim's hand on his dick. And there it went, wrapping wetly around the shaft and stroking swiftly, pulling him closer and closer until Hal felt his coming build in his chest, growing there until he thought he'd split open, and he wailed, "No, oh, no," his pecker squirting here and there, a hot spray of juice that splashed thickly in the sand.

"Oh, jeez!" Tim squealed, and he pulled out and pumped out a high-flying load that fell, among other places, in Hal's hair.

Neither of them felt able to talk coherently for some time. Overhead the stars made a slow crawl across the sky, and that moon hung over them, as pale as bones, and they lay together, watching it watch them.

The Trouble With Trig

His ass was sore from Brandon Moyer's big, bent boner. Nobody had ever fucked him so thoroughly; no one had ever tested his asshole's elasticity the way Brandon had. Getting fucked by Brandon was probably as intense as sex could get—he was relentless with his crooked prick. He had spread Billy's legs wide with his thick, coarse thighs and slammed into the boy furiously. It was awesome.

Billy was sitting in civics class, shifting from one butt cheek to the other, his cunt swollen from the previous night's reaming. He was itching to get to the mall because Brandon had been bragging about the hot guys waiting outside his toilet stall, ready to blow him. And he could see how that was possible, because Brandon Moyer was hot. He played all kinds of sports and had a wicked good body, and his face was thick and dumb-looking even though he was anything but. His jaw was square, and his chin was fanny-split. He had thick lips and big, brown, lazy-dog eyes. He looked dumb and sounded dumber, but he worked hard and was the class president and was being courted by a couple of Ivy League schools.

The reason Billy got to know Brandon so well was because Billy wasn't doing so well in trigonometry—in fact, he was failing. As a last-ditch effort, his stepfather had hired Brandon to tutor the boy. The first time Billy saw his tutor, he didn't think much of him—sure, he was good-looking, but Billy had seen plenty of good-looking guys. What he didn't get a sense of was Brandon's accessibility. There were some guys you knew about right away—Brandon wasn't one of them. So he sat at the dining room table across from this guy and, after an initial appraisal, didn't really consider him. All Billy knew was that Brandon was his stepfather's idea of insurance, a guarantee that the boy would graduate on time.

Brandon went to Catholic High, and Billy was in East High. The first time they met, Brandon was wearing a shirt and tie, his uniform at school. Wednesday was the only night he had free; otherwise he was at football practice or had some civic duty to perform. He sat across from Billy at the dining room table. Outside, Billy's stepfather was mowing the lawn, and you could see him at the end of the yard, walking back and forth in a pair of athletic shorts. He had monster legs: huge, wagging thighs and thick, hairy calves. He had on his boat shoes and no socks, and his T-shirt was draped on top of his head. Billy saw Brandon watching his stepfather's progress with half interest, and he would have been embarrassed if his stepfather weren't so hot. It was just the two of them; his mother left long ago, mysteriously unhappy. Billy saw her every summer, and she was closemouthed about what went wrong. "Incompatible," she would say, shrugging her shoulders.

Billy watched Brandon giving his old man the once-over, and he started giving Brandon the once-over himself. The tutor had loosened his tie and undone a couple of buttons on his shirt. His neck was sunburned and thick, the back of his head freshly shaved, a military cut that was mere shadow on his scalp. He cracked his knuckles and leaned back.

"You play football?" he asked out of the blue.

Billy shook his head.

"Bet your old man played ball," Brandon said, looking out the window again. Billy's stepdad stopped to wipe his face with his T-shirt. Brandon played with his lip thoughtfully.

Billy didn't think anything of Brandon. He sat there thinking his tutor was hot and all, and he wondered what he'd look like without his shirt, stuff like that, but he never thought they'd end up fucking. Brandon hadn't either. Billy knew this because Brandon told him so; he said the first time, mid thrust, "I don't fucking believe this is happening." Billy didn't even think anything about Brandon's checking out his stepdad—seemed like everybody did anyway. Brandon's eyes always seemed so vague and disinterested, an attribute that added to his sexiness: disregard. He seemed at the time more interested in himself.

The next time Billy saw Brandon was the Saturday after their first tutoring session. Brandon had a Mustang convertible, and Billy guessed the boy made good money tutoring. He was wearing khaki shorts and a polo shirt, his bared arms and legs big and suntanned. He stood out on the landing, saying next to nothing through the screen door. Billy was in his underwear just inside the door, standing on one bare foot—he'd been drinking coffee and watching cartoons. "I was just riding around," Brandon said, shrugging, tugging on the front of his shirt. He folded his arms across his chest, putting his face close to the screen. "What're you doing?" he asked.

They were pretty much the same height and weight—6 foot 1, about 180 pounds—and built alike as well: thick-limbed, with powerful chests and backs. They both liked lifting, but neither of them had the inclination to get ripped. Billy watched Brandon through the screen door, looking at the boy's lips: big, fat things that never quite shut. *He's dying to ask me something*, Billy thought. Brandon's eyes shifted here and there, and his tongue tipped out to wet his lips.

"I was going down to the river," he said, finally getting it out. Billy hadn't seen such shyness before, leastwise not from someone so worthy of arrogance. It did something to Billy, and he thought of something his grandmother used to say: *That boy warms my heart.*

He drove fast down to the river, one hand on the wheel, the other out the window, catching air. He didn't say anything, and Billy didn't say anything either, and the radio played Oasis and Bush and Hole, and music blew over their heads. Brandon moved his window hand to the wheel and put his right hand on the back of the passenger seat, close to Billy's shoulder. Billy looked at Brandon's stretched-out legs, their covering of hair. He saw the plaid hem of his boxers and wished for briefs himself because he was starting to get hard. Brandon minded the road and little else.

It was hot, and Billy's ball sac stuck to his thighs as he squirmed in his seat. Dark rings of sweat became apparent under his arms. He lifted his shirt, and the wind played over his stomach, and Brandon's fingertips grazed his shoulder. Brandon apologized, but his fingers remained there.

Brandon tore off the road and onto one that was dirt, and he kicked up a wake of dust and bottomed out a few times, grimacing as the Mustang bounced down the lane. Billy could smell the water in the air, and it was cool in the shade, and Brandon pulled under the cover of trees, through which Billy could see the river.

Brandon turned the car off and turned to his passenger. "I like it here," he said. "I come here a lot." He stretched and seemed to make himself comfortable, as though he had no intention of going anywhere, not down to the water, not even leaving the car. He took off his shoes and brought one bare foot up onto the seat. Billy could see the wide, flattened bulge of Brandon's groin.

Neither of them moved. Suddenly Billy was in agreement with Brandon that there was nowhere else to go. They looked at each other, and Billy leaned against the door and spread his legs, feeling the coolish breeze making contact with his sweating balls. He was sure that they were exposed but did nothing to cover them, wanting to see what the sight of them would do to Brandon.

Brandon's hand dropped off the steering wheel casually and landed on his own crotch innocently enough, but his fingers twitched and played, and his growing cock was plain to see, the tunneling it did between his shorts and skin. Billy looked away to smile, surprised and relieved, happy to have found someone so hot and tough-looking with similar interests. He felt cocky and took off his shirt. The air tightened his nipples, and he felt his shorts blow his cover: He slipped out, the red tip of his head, blunt-ended and good-size, rearing up, throbbing with Billy's pulse.

Brandon glanced away. He looked at the river, he looked at the sky, he looked at his watch, but his eyes kept coming back to Billy's uncovered package, and Billy felt like some kind of king. He scooted his butt toward the handsome boy and watched as Brandon peeled back his pants leg, exposing his cockeyed white-shafted boner. It was hooded, and its foreskin flowered. He slipped back the cover, and the thing drooled. He pushed the extra skin back in place and milked out a clear drop that landed on the vinyl seat.

Billy got hold of himself likewise and jacked, while Brandon pulled on his great hairy balls, which spilled out luxuriously.

He lifted his polo shirt and played with his stomach, fingering his navel. His hand went up and up; Billy watched its progress, his big-knuckled fingers working the tender knobs of his tits. Emboldened, Billy pushed both sets of shorts down to his knees, and his pecker sprang up stiffly, pointing skyward, trailing a sparkling ribbon of precome. He touched his balls, grabbing them and giving them a tug. Sparsely haired and golf-ball–size, they were a pleasant handful, and he'd come to especially like their being handled roughly by callused palms and fingers.

Brandon lifted his shirt and pulled it over his head, throwing it to the backseat.

If they didn't talk and didn't touch, what they were doing was OK, they were OK. It didn't mean anything to either one of them; they were just a couple of guys jerking off; nothing wrong with that. So far it was just good, clean fun.

Brandon spat a thick gob onto his flattened palm, and Billy pushed his shorts down even farther, getting his sneakered feet clear of the tangle. He brought his leg, the left and closest to Brandon, up onto the seat, opening his crotch wide. Brandon's eyes landed on Billy with a thud. He licked his lips and wiped his brow. Billy was feeling pretty much like a whore, the way he was teasing the guy, but he had to be in control, he wanted to be responsible for Brandon's making a creamy mess of himself. *Fuck trig*, he was thinking. *How about you tutor my ass?*

Brandon started moaning. It was low and barely there, but Billy could tell by the way his stomach was caving in under his rib cage. The muscles of his legs began to twitch, and his hips started humping. He thrust up into his white-knuckled fist, his cock head a strangled red. Billy watched Brandon's balls tighten, shrinking up into candied walnuts shaggy with sandy-colored hair.

There were bird noises and leaves fluttering overhead. Billy was close now, and so was Brandon, who started and stopped and started again, bringing himself up to the edge, then backing off, prolonging his agony. Suddenly his legs thrust out stiff, and his butt came up from the seat.

"O-o-oh," he moaned, the drawn-out vowel accompanying his ejaculation. He pumped high and thick, and gobs landed on his sun-dappled torso, across his sternum, between his nipples. He settled down again, breathing hard, his stomach going to hollows, and continued to milk his peter, stringy clots hanging from the head.

Billy scrambled to his knees and aimed his prick at Brandon, who grabbed the thing and stuck it into his mouth, sucking out every last drop, his lips causing Billy convulsions that racked his body, vacuuming the boy until he was empty and quivering, a dried-up wreck.

Billy got a part-time after-school job at a clothing store in the mall. He started on a Wednesday, forgetting all about his tutoring. He sped home, hoping to catch Brandon before he gave up and left. He hadn't seen him since they jacked together, and Billy was embarrassed to admit that he missed him. Brandon's car was still in Billy's driveway when Billy pulled in, and Billy looked in the rearview mirror and saw his own grateful smile. He was hoping Brandon would want to go for a ride again.

The front door was locked. Billy let himself in. Brandon wasn't waiting for him in the dining room, and he wasn't in the kitchen either. He heard voices in the basement, and he figured they were down there shooting their football shit around. Billy slipped off his too-tight dress shoes and walked back to his bedroom to put on some shorts, grabbing a soda before padding downstairs.

He saw Brandon first, stretched out bare-chested on his stepfather's pool table, his eyes closed, his head moving from side to side. He looked, Billy thought, like he was getting fucked. As he crept down the stairs, Billy saw more and more of Brandon's naked torso, his muscled gut, his dirty-blond bush, and his soft cock, straight and long across his hip. And then he saw hands on Brandon's thighs, digging fingers, and then the top of his stepfather's head as he bent over to lick Brandon's stomach. He straightened again and spat on the boy's chest and mauled his tits and leaned over to bite one, making Brandon yelp, his eyes flying open.

"Oh, man," Billy's stepdad said. His big shoulders heaved, and his head rolled back. His eyes were closed, but the boy stepped back anyway. He could see his old man's flat, hairy belly and his fat, veined cock when he pulled out and slapped it against Brandon's balls.

Billy was jealous, sure, but his reasoning, he thought, was fucked. He didn't know what pissed him off more, his stepdad boning what should have been his piece of ass or that it wasn't Billy himself on that pool table getting peckered. Just then Brandon saw him up on the stairs. His dick twitched to life suddenly, and he grabbed his dick and started hammering away. He kept his eyes on Billy, ignoring his stepfather and the battering of his felt-bound fanny.

"That's good," Mr. Dwyer moaned. He took hold of Brandon's ankles and lifted his ass high. He grunted his dick into the boy's rear end, pressing Brandon's thighs against his woolly chest, wreathing his head with the boy's calves and feet. "Good, good," he bellowed, his thrusts increasing in speed and ferocity. Brandon's mouth opened, a manly cry gurgled out, and he spewed come all over himself.

Will Dwyer unplugged his cock from the boy's ass and

banged himself with his fist. He let loose a stream of white that flew past Brandon's head, landing on the green baize, sure to leave a stain, and Billy was awestruck and hard with pride, seeing his old man fuck so well. He crept numbly up the stairs and tiptoed through the kitchen. He had his prong in his hand and was trying very hard to make it to the bathroom before he shot his load.

Billy figured that was the first and the last time Brandon had had his heinie whacked by Will Dwyer. After that Brandon spent his energies working on Billy's ass. He was a ruthless fucker, tutored well. Every time he rammed Billy's ass, Billy felt his stepfather's hand.

One night, come mixed and drying on Billy's stomach, Brandon said, "Your old man's bugging me to come over tomorrow night."

"Figures," Billy said. "I'll be at work."

Brandon shifted his bare ass, and it squealed against the vinyl car seat. "Call in sick," he said. "I'm thinking of boning your old man. You can watch."

He managed to get someone to cover for him. He stayed away until 7, the time his stepdad told Brandon to come by. "I'll get him down in the basement again," Brandon said, cocksure and sexy-mouthed. Billy was to position himself at the basement window over the pool table. He crouched down and looked in and could see the stains from the last time Brandon and his stepfather got together.

Brandon winked up at Billy as he came down the stairs. Billy's stepfather followed in a few minutes. He had a towel wrapped around his waist, and his thigh peeped from the slit of it. He was saying something Billy couldn't catch, but he heard Brandon reply: "It gets me hot down here."

He made his way to the pool table, putting his beer on the edge. "Let's see some skin," Will said, going for Brandon's shirt. "I forget what you look like, it's been so long."

Billy watched his stepdad's butt flex under the towel, and then he was hypnotized by Brandon's buffness. His smooth, mulberry-nippled pecs drove both of them crazy, and Will planted a big kiss on Brandon's left tit and then on the right, and Billy watched him go down to his knees, his towel unknotting. Will smeared his face against Brandon's crotch, his hands pawing the boy's chest. Billy stood up and looked around. It was still pretty light out, but the yard was secluded by trees and hedges. He unbuttoned his chinos and pushed them down. He squatted again, his stiff dick leaking in the cool evening air. His stepfather had Brandon's pants undone by now and was licking up the boy's thigh, up to his skewed shaft. Brandon leaned over and started stroking Will's thick white ass cheeks. When his fingers curled into the hairy crack, Will's head froze. He spat out Brandon's cock.

"You got something on your mind?" he said.

"Maybe," Brandon replied.

"Such as?" Will said, losing his smile.

"Such as your ass, Mr. Dwyer. I'm thinking how good it's going to feel fucking it."

Will shook his head, chuckling. "Time to wake up, Moyer; you're dreaming, boy." He stood up and put his arms around Brandon's, picking him up and lifting him back onto the pool table. He got himself between Brandon's legs and crawled up onto the table with him. All Billy could see of either of them for a while was Brandon's flailing legs and his stepfather's humping butt.

It didn't look good for Brandon's plan. Billy's stepdad was all over him, and Brandon seemed pinned for good, destined for porking. But then his stepfather gave in. Brandon arched and twisted and practically flipped himself over Will, riding his back with his chest and working his legs between Will's, and Will dropped to the felt as Brandon pumped his pecker along the tight seam of the elder man's behind.

Billy felt a little sorry for his stepfather. He yelled when Brandon first stuck him, getting himself up on his knees so that he could play with his own boner. Brandon screwed Will Dwyer like nobody's business, and Billy watched, envious, pud in hand, filling his own butt with a grouping of fingers that approximated Brandon's girth.

It didn't take long for any of them. Will blew first, the tickling of his prostate too much for him to bear. Brandon popped out and directed his spray over Dwyer's back, and Billy fell backward onto the dewy grass and geysered up into the dusky sky.

They shared Brandon for a while, those two, although Billy was pretty sure his stepfather hadn't a clue. Billy failed his math class anyway and ended up in summer school in order to graduate. That's where he is now, squirming in his seat with a hard-on poking up high and mighty in his shorts. The teacher is a good-looking kid, fresh out of college. Billy can practically see the guy's diploma sticking out of his back pocket—not to mention his prick, which is a serious distraction, the way it jiggles around in his pants while he's writing on the board. When class is over Billy's going up to him, looking him right in the eye, and asking him for help.

Shotgun

Billy Pyle took the long way home from work. It was a warm night, and it was spring, and everything that was green was greener, even in the dark, and Billy put his hands in his pockets and walked slower.

He turned onto Locust Street. Tony Palizetti lived on Locust. Tony was dating Billy's best friend, Allison, and she said to Billy the other night that she thought Tony might be gay. Billy kept a poker face and tried to appear only half interested, but he felt a rush ice his veins, and his face went blushing red. They were at Dempsey's, having something to eat after a movie. "How come?" he said, picking at her uneaten fries.

She leaned back on her side of the booth and put an unshod foot on the seat beside him. "Just a feeling," she said, shrugging, and Billy wondered if she'd had a feeling about him too.

"But you guys have done it, right?" he said. "You said you had a pretty good time."

She gave him a look. "As if that means anything," she said with much sophistication. "I tell you too much. Why do I do that?"

"Don't ask me," he said, desperate for a new topic of conversation, and just then some friends from school came in, invading their booth.

Ever since that conversation, though, Tony had been a constant figure in Billy's erotic imagination. He'd seen plenty of Tony, having been lucky enough to have been in every one of Tony's gym classes throughout high school. He'd seen Tony in his underwear often enough to have found the sight familiar if it weren't so awesome. He would catch himself from time to time staring at the dark-haired boy, trying to memorize the thickening curve of Tony's calf or the way his dick lay in the pouch of his briefs, the black wisps that wafted up from under the striped waistband, mental pictures that he brought home with him and reviewed at bedtime like pornographic homework.

Billy had a friend he wouldn't exactly call a friend, some guy he'd met on his way home from work one night. The guy was sitting on a stoop, and Billy smelled the dope he was smoking before he actually saw him. Billy passed him, feigning disinterest, but the pot smelled awesome, and he inhaled deeply. The guy had gotten up and started following Billy down the street. *Shit!* Billy thought, nervous about his tip money and a potential mugging. He walked a little faster. "You've got a nice ass," he heard, even though the man had hardly said it, and Billy almost stopped. Isn't that what he'd been wanting to hear—Jesus!—since he was 16 practically? He slowed up at the corner and let his admirer catch up.

Under a streetlight the guy had a hawkish nose and a self-tailored Harley-Davidson shirt. He wore jeans that were tight and worn to white in some places and holes in others. His hair was short, not much more than a 5-o'clock shadow on the sides and a little longer on top, but not much. He looked like a cross between a biker and a college jock, and Billy didn't feel himself on equal ground with either type. He waited for a parade of late-night cars to pass and tried not to look again at the man standing beside him.

"What's up?" the man said, and Billy had to look again. He was still holding the smoking joint, and the dope smoke smelled sweet; the air was lickable.

"Nothing," Billy said somewhat curtly, keeping things distanced for the time being.

"Awesome night," the guy said. The cars kept flowing by; the light was never going to change. Billy nodded and looked again at the man next to him.

His name was Roger; Billy was going to find that out a little later. Roger was neither a biker nor a jock, at least not in the real sense of either word. He'd certainly been to college, had, in fact, owned at one time a little Honda motorcycle, but now he was just a horny unemployed graphic artist with a dealer who had scored some of the best pot in Lancaster County. He flicked the roach so that it arced into the street.

"More of that," he said, smiling, and when he smiled all trace of menace disappeared.

He had an Ikea apartment and a cat named Whitman. He pointed to a bowl of rolled joints on the glass-topped coffee table and said, "Go ahead, I'm fine for now." He disappeared through a doorway, and Billy heard the strong and steady flow of piss pouring into a toilet bowl somewhere. Billy lit up and smoked some and ignored the cat that wove itself around his ankles. He listened for the man, his nerves coming up through the hard knot of his stomach and buzzing through his arms. *Ain't this crazy?* he was thinking, and *What am I doing here?* went through his brain like a ticker-tape message, but the dope was good and numbing, and the thoughts turned to paper, easily wadded up and thrown away. He wished for music and someone to lick his tits.

"What's he doing?" he said aloud after a good 20 minutes of burning the joint by himself. He stood up and looked around. He thought about leaving, but the idea of getting laid was completely strong now that he was stoned.

"Hey!" he called out. "Where the fuck are you?"

"I'm in the kitchen," he heard Roger whisper loudly, and Billy walked into a dark room that was the dining room. "Back here," the guy said, and Billy followed the sound of his voice.

It was dark in the kitchen too, and Billy didn't know where he was going, so when he bumped into the counter, he let out a yell.

"Man," he heard from somewhere to his left, "you got to be quiet, or you'll wake up the old lady."

"You live with your mother?" he asked, shocked.

"No way. The old lady is *my* old lady—my wife, man."

Back through the kitchen there was a den. Roger lit a candle, and Billy blinked, acclimating his eyes. Roger held the candle high, and Billy saw that he was naked save for a frilly white apron. *Holy shit!* he thought, and he giggled—Roger looked ridiculous, his big, hairy thighs absolutely mocking the starched white cotton, the protrusion of his erection very evident against the stiff fabric.

Roger shrugged. "I don't know what it is about these things, man, but they make me as horny as hell," he said sheepishly.

Despite the apron and the old lady upstairs, Billy felt himself succumbing to the lusty bone in his trousers. "Turn around," he ordered Roger, the weed making him bold, and Roger complied, shaking his ass seductively. Billy undid the zipper of his pants and hauled out his big cock. He saw Roger smiling appreciatively over his shoulder.

"This is my fucking lucky night, man," he said, nodding his head. "Ten fucking inches, I'll bet."

Roger's ass was covered with a fine dark down of hair that appealed to Billy, reminding him of his father's, the sight of which he'd seen plenty. He walked up to the ass and held it in his hands, the silky cheeks going hard, then softening, opening. The crack was dark, and the candle didn't offer enough light to appropriately highlight Roger's pink and pleasant hole. It pouted under Billy's finger, though, and plushly gave in to the pressure of it, allowing the digit entry.

"You've done this before, haven't you?" Roger whispered, turning and putting his hands on the boy's shoulders, pressing him down, down to his knees, where he faced the dainty apron and the sweet press of Roger's hard-on. "Get underneath and clean Mammy up," Roger said.

Billy laughed, but he was serious about eating up Roger's crotch. The mere thought of this straight and studly fuck towering over him in a sissy apron was almost enough to make him tinkle. He licked the long, hard channel between Roger's balls and bung hole, the fine grit of stubble rasping his tongue. He felt the clamp of Roger's thighs on his head, and he was imprisoned, slobbering up the man's bald, silky balls, nosing into his pussy. "Isn't that something?" he heard the man say, and he tried to nod, but he was held fast.

He made noises that sounded something like "Fuckin' right," and continued the laving of Roger's pendulous nuts.

He'd just gotten started on the man's squinting asshole when Roger went tight. Billy was pushed back, sprawling across the linoleum. "The old lady," Roger whispered, his eyes wide. Billy looked up at the ceiling as if he could see her slippered feet scuffling around overhead. He worked quickly to get his hard-on back into his pants, and Roger fumbled with the apron, unable to make his fingers nimble enough to untie the neat little bow he'd made in back.

"Roger?" they both heard. Roger looked at Billy, and Billy at Roger.

"Shit," Roger breathed, his eyes wild. They could hear her at the top of the stairs. Roger held his hand out, directing Billy to stay put, and he left him in the kitchen. Billy heard him call up to his wife.

"What are you doing?" she wanted to know. "When are you coming up to bed? And why do you have that stupid apron on?"

Billy closed his eyes and said a little prayer. "Good luck, dude," he whispered.

"I was making an omelette," Roger said, and Billy stifled a snort. *Oh, the lameness*, he thought.

"Stay away from the peppers," the old lady said, "or you'll stink up the bedroom. And hurry your ass up, 'cause I've got the horns and my period's due in about two seconds."

Roger came back to the kitchen. "You heard her," he said. He grabbed his crotch through the apron. "Gotta save it for the wife."

Billy shrugged. He wasn't much interested anymore himself. He stood up, and they tiptoed to the front door, Roger grabbing a couple of joints for Billy to take along with him. "For the road," he said. Once outside he whispered into Billy's ear hotly. "She's working nights next week. You come back, OK?"

And he did.

He passed Tony's and looked at the lighted upstairs windows. There was a short-clipped yard and a porch that fronted the two-story clapboard house. A low fence bordered the yard, and yellow-headed tulips pushed up through the painted white pickets.

Someone came running up the sidewalk behind him. Billy heard the footfalls first and then the heavy pant of hard breathing. He stepped close to the fence to give the runner room around him, but the runner didn't pass. Instead he slowed and came to a pounding halt, and Billy turned to face a dripping, wheezing Tony Palizetti.

"What's up, Pyle?" he panted, bending over and putting his hands on his knees, his back heaving.

"Not too much," Billy returned, displeased with himself for being found right in front of Tony's house like some sort of lovesick voyeur. "Walking home from work," he added as an alibi.

Tony looked at his watch. Billy watched the boy's lips moving. Tony straightened and walked around Billy with his hands on his waist, kicking his heels back so that they touched his ass.

"I didn't know you ran," Billy said to fill the quiet void.

"Just started, really," Tony answered back. He pulled off his sweat-soaked shirt and mopped his face with it. Billy glanced at the boy's uncovered front.

They were both silent, listening to the night's noise.

"How's Allison?" Tony asked.

"You ought to know," Billy said, making himself smile.

"I guess" was all Tony said. He tossed his T-shirt around his neck and held on to the ends. His dark nipples contrasted sharply with his white skin. He leaned against the fence.

"You get high, don't you?" he said. Billy sort of nodded. "Got any?"

Billy shook his head. His hair was long and center-parted, and he kept pushing it behind his ears. It was brown, the color of chocolate. He wasn't built as well as Tony; Billy was leaner, longer-limbed, and taller, but he was thinking now that Tony Palizetti looked like a man and that he, Billy, was going to look like a boy for a long time still—forever, probably. He looked at Tony's waist, made hard with twisting sit-ups, and wondered how it would feel under his hands.

"I might have a joint left," Tony said, turning and moving up the walkway to his house. He stopped and looked back over his shoulder at Billy, who hadn't budged. "You coming, or what?"

He followed Tony up the stairs. "Nobody's home," Tony informed him. Billy watched Tony's legs as he climbed the stairs—the split of his well-developed calf muscle, the coarse black sprinkling of hair on the backs of his thighs, the silky, fraying hem of his soccer shorts.

Billy looked around Tony's room while Tony rooted through his book bag for the possible joint. Billy scanned a stack of CDs and then a pile of books and recognized a title that was telling, a book he himself had found at the library sale in town. The book was *Numbers* by John Rechy, with so many sexy parts that Billy had read it with his dick in his hand. It was the sexiest book he'd ever read, and the book, dog-eared from many perusals, opened automatically to some of his favorite parts.

He wanted to pull the book out, but he didn't dare. He wanted to say something, but what? He heard Tony say "Found it" and looked over to catch Tony smelling his armpits. Tony smiled and said, "Man, I stink."

They went out to smoke the joint in Mrs. Palizetti's potting shed. Tony turned on a little lamp in the back of the shed, partially covering it with a burlap bag so that there was hardly any light at all. But they could still see each other, and Billy had a hard time not looking at Tony's torso or the front of his shorts. The place smelled like dirt and fertilizer and wet wood. Tony handed Billy the joint to light.

Billy took a deep drag. The dope tasted good, rich compared to what he had been smoking lately. He took another toke and handed the bone back to Tony, holding his breath.

"Don't you have a date with Allison tonight?" Billy asked.

Tony snorted, trying to keep the smoke in his lungs. He shook his head. "She doesn't want to go out with me anymore. Says she doesn't think it's working out." He paused and looked at Billy. "She thinks I'm gay." He passed the joint.

Billy nodded, looking at the orange-embered tip glowing between them and the smoke that wafted up. "Are you?" he asked before sucking on the wet end of the joint. He saw Tony smile as if he'd thought of something funny and watched as Tony scratched his crotch through his shorts. And then he leaned close to Billy.

"Ever got shotgunned?" he whispered.

Billy shrugged, thinking Tony was talking about some kind of sex. He didn't want to seem inexperienced, and he didn't want to miss an opportunity. But he also didn't want to admit to anything—not yet, anyway. He watched as Tony put the hot end of the joint into his mouth. He leaned his face even closer toward Billy's, as if they were about to kiss, and a thin stream of smoke jetted out of the joint's unlit end, and Billy, getting the point now, sucked it up. "Awesome," he said when he finally exhaled.

Tony took another deep drag for himself and put his mouth on Billy's, surprising the boy. The first thing that registered for him was the sharp stubble of Tony's chin, which made him think of his dad and the good-night kiss they'd done away with a long time ago. He felt Tony's hands on his waist, holding him there, pulling Billy closer, so that their bodies touched, and Tony kissed him harder, pushing his tongue through Billy's loose lips. They stood like that forever, it seemed, and Billy felt himself going hard and Tony's own erection against his thigh.

Tony stepped back and pulled his shorts down. His cock was cramped in an old jockstrap, his balls popping out of the sides.

He handled the pouch roughly, looking at Billy with slitted eyes. With his other hand he pulled Billy's shirt up out of his jeans. "Take it off," he said, stepping back to look at Billy in the half-light.

Billy unbuttoned his shirt, and Tony's hands flew to his chest, palming his tits, which were hard, his nipples pointed. His cock was barely covered now, having escaped through the side of the pouch.

"You want to suck me?" he asked Billy. He was grinning still, making Billy uncomfortable. He couldn't help feeling put on somehow, as if this were some kind of a joke Tony was playing on him. Billy looked at the white-skinned shaft between them. He shook his head.

"That's OK," Tony said easily, his voice not much louder than a whisper. He opened Billy's jeans then and pushed down his white briefs. The great prop of his pecker swung out like a catapult.

"You skinny guys get all the dick," Tony said. "Why is that?" Billy's cock was huge, long and thick, a man's meat. Tony grabbed it and squeezed it hard. "This is fucking incredible," he said.

He went to his knees, embracing Billy's pale legs. He mouthed the boy's balls, humming softly, and worked his way up the thick column of flesh, leaving a trail of wet kisses. He swallowed the head, filling his mouth, and Billy arched his back, putting his hands on Tony's shoulders. It felt good, better than good, and it felt right, and Billy shook the fuzzy thoughts that he was doing something bad from his head, and they tumbled like dice into a dark corner of his brain, and he was glad he was stoned. His cock glided into Tony's slippery mouth, and Tony snorted against the assault of it banging against the back of his throat.

He sat back on his haunches, a glistening string of drool hanging from his chin. "Man," he said. "Where have you been, Billy? Where have you been?" He stared at the boy's enormous pecker, the fat, blunt end with its huge piss hole. He stood up and started pulling on his own. He turned around and offered Billy a view of his thick ass cheeks. He pawed himself back there with one hand, fingering up into the dark little hole.

Tony wanted to be fucked, that much was plain to Billy as his friend pushed himself back against Billy's iron prong. *But*, he was thinking, *it couldn't possibly be as easy as that, could it?* Did he only have to stick it in and move it in and out? "Come on," Tony said. "Spit on it and put it in. But do it slow. Don't tear me up." Billy had to wonder then how often Tony had been rear-ended. He looked down at the boy's butt and took aim for the dark split. Tony's hand was down near the hole to guide him in.

"There you go," he said, grunting, complaining then about the girth of the head and the lack of some good lube. Billy was reticent to go all the way in, unwilling to cause Tony any rectal distress, but Tony reached around and then grabbed Billy's butt, bringing his dick deep inside him.

"Holy crap," Billy bleated, some of the wind knocked out of him as he knocked into his new fuck buddy.

"Shut up and screw me," Tony spat, hunching down for optimum impact. This went on for some time, Tony spitting and cursing as he withstood Billy's first, shaky performance as top man. Billy's eyes rolled, and he went into a comalike trance. He fingered the bony knobs of Tony's back as though he were reading Braille. He played with the short dark hairs that grew on the flattened plane over his ass. Tony grunted, grunted and complained, forcing his fanny against the impaling blunt-ended prick, beating it against his prostate, that sweet, crazy button that made him shake and roll his eyes.

"Oh, that's it, man," he moaned. "That's it. Come on, ram me! Ram me hard now!"

Billy did what he could, frustrated that he was not able to go any deeper than his nine-plus inches would allow. He threw himself into Tony's hole again and again while Tony grumbled like a linebacker waiting for the ball to be snapped. He felt himself dragged along into this dirty business by the nasty things Tony was saying, tugged by the dick and the 'nads until he was unable anymore to control himself, and he gave in to the strong suck of the boy's awesome asshole, quite sure that he would never be the same again, convinced that he'd be pulling his dick from Tony's hole like a pencil from a sharpener—not quite what it used to be but all the better for it.

He bent over and put his lips on Tony's back and kept them there as he dumped a cubic yard of come into his buddy's guts. He felt as though his whole body would collapse and that he'd surely be sucked up into Tony's anus like a deflated balloon.

Tony straightened up quickly and blasted the bench before him with glistening drops of slime, yelling the whole time, announcing to the whole neighborhood that he was coming, he was coming, oh, sweet Jesus, he was coming.

Billy shrank into a dark corner of the shed, his dick dripping and stinking of Tony's ass. Amazed by the whole thing, he simply stood limply, staring at Tony, who milked the last drops from his slow-to-deflate cock.

Tony turned the light out, giggling, himself again and not some smoldering porn-flick sex god. He stepped up to Billy and put his arms around him. Billy stayed still as his ear was kissed, then his throat and the center of his chest, and he wondered if it was going to happen again right now. His dick began to inch up again into hardness between them.

"Damn," Tony said, clutching it. "I knew I shouldn't have jacked off after school." He put his other hand on Billy's head and played with his hair.

"You're mine now, Billy," he said. "You know that, don't you?"

Billy shrugged. He didn't feel like he knew anything just at that moment.

"Well, you are," Tony said, putting his mouth very close to Billy's. "And I want you to come back tomorrow. You'll do that, right?"

Billy nodded.

"I can be your pussy. You'd like that, wouldn't you?"

Billy nodded again.

It was late when he finally got home. Tony had somehow been persuaded to pull his ass off Billy's dick, accidentally blowing the boy's brains out in the process. He walked home feeling numb, his cock aching from all of Tony's attention—and teeth. It wasn't exactly ethical, but he found himself dialing Allison's phone number.

"I broke up with Tony," she said. "Scott Atkinson asked me out."

"That's cool," Billy said. Scott was cute, tall, and blond. "He looks like a movie star. Like Robert Redford without the warts."

"His cock's gigantic!" she gasped.

"Why do you tell me these things?" he yelled.

"I don't know! I don't know!" she yelled back. "So what did you do tonight?"

Billy paused and wondered what to say. He decided to say nothing.

"Boring," Allison whispered sexily. "Very boring."

"Oh," Billy said, smiling against the receiver, "it wasn't all that bad."

He hung up with Allison and dialed Roger's number.

"Yup?" Roger hollered into the phone.

"Hey, it's me," Billy said.

"Boy, where are you?" Roger bellowed. "I've had a boner for three hours. I thought you were coming over."

"Got caught up," Billy said, and he slipped a hand into his jeans, fondling his tired and adored prick. It stirred, reliving the memory of Tony Palizetti's awesome ass, the suck and pull of that hot, squinched-up little hair hole.

"Well, I don't know what I'm gonna do with this load, pal," Roger continued. "It's built up so's my nuts are about to burst. You should see my cock, bud, it's fucking pounding in my fist. Head's all red, and precome's just pissing out, man. What am I gonna do without my little-boy mouth?"

"Save it for the old lady," Billy said, hanging up.

WHEN LUDDY GOES

When Luddy got his Camaro, he drove to my house and sat out in front, smoking cigarettes until one of my little brothers saw him there and said, "Jason, your friend's out there." We weren't friends anymore, hadn't been since he started going out with Erin Moyer and we got into a stupid fight over who was going to Darien Lake. All of a sudden we were supposed to be the Three Stooges or something. I didn't even like Erin Moyer—she was pushy and a bitch and talked with her tits. She used her tits the way other people use their hands.

Luddy said, "Hey, Tuck," and I just looked at him. He'd called me "fag" the last time we talked, and Erin was there, and she sort of laughed, making her tits jump just a little for emphasis. There was a split-rail fence around our yard and some flowers my mom had planted. I stepped through them and leaned on the shaky railing, looking at Luddy's new Camaro. I didn't know shit about cars; they were just a means of getting around. Luddy leaned out the window. "Happy birthday," he said, because I'd just had one a couple of weeks ago.

"Me 'n' Erin broke up last night," he said, and I was thinking, *Is that my birthday present?*

"We could go for a ride," he said. He looked through the windshield. He flicked his naked-lady air freshener with his finger. I could hear my mom telling my brothers to knock it off. Luddy had his sleeves rolled up, his arm flexed. I could see his vaccination scar, a little brown crater set into the balled muscle of his shoulder.

"We could go to the driving range," he suggested, because he knew I loved hitting balls around like that.

"Left my clubs in Gossage's car," I said, watching his face. I knew he didn't like Kenny Gossage any more than I liked his girlfriend—his ex-girlfriend. My clubs were actually in the garage.

Luddy kept looking through the windshield, his arms across the steering wheel.

"Get in," he said.

"I've got to tell Mom," I said, running back to the house. "Luddy's here," I yelled through the door. "Be back later!" And I started back for Lud and his car, and I heard my mom yelling for me not to be too late. I got into the Camaro, and Luddy turned to me then, and for a split second I thought he was going to kiss me or something, and in that half second I wanted to hug him and kiss his whole stupid face, his sharp little nose, his foxy mouth. He'd had a haircut—his black hair trimmed down to a mean quarter-inch. He looked, I thought, like a little Marine, and I told him so. He twitched a corner of his mouth and started the car, and we got going.

I had a feeling I knew where he was taking me. I didn't say anything, though—I wasn't sure what I could have said at that moment. I was feeling everything just then, sitting in that bucket seat, listening to the noise the air made and the crickets and the car and Luddy humming something, then saying he was getting a stereo put in over the weekend.

I sat with my back to the door, which seemed a little dangerous and all, but I wanted to look at Luddy. It seemed like I hadn't seen him in months. I wanted to say to him, "Luddy, where have you been?" But I didn't really care to know. The thought of him boning the Moyer chick was enough to tie my stomach in knots, which in turn made me sick of myself for being so queer. I couldn't help it, though—I freaking loved Luddy, and I felt like a freak admitting it to myself, but it was the truth. I never would have told him, or anyone else, for that matter, but I think he knew it anyway.

He was bulking up with weights and protein drinks, and I could see how much he was loving his new body. He put his left hand up under his shirt, touching his belly, and I saw all the hair he'd had there was gone, and I wondered if he'd also trimmed clear around his nipples where it had grown like a dark fringe.

He turned onto Lakeshore Road, then pulled sharply into the Mayflower parking lot, going all the way back to the woods. On the other side of the trees was the Wysockie orchard. He turned off the car,

It was my mom who said Luddy had a foxy mouth. "See him grinning there, the way a little fox does? His lips disappear, and there's just that sneaky little line left." Then she went into her bedroom and pulled out a fox fur stole that had the little head and feet still on it, and we all agreed that Luddy was like a fox, and his face went red, and we all laughed, and under the table Luddy put his bare feet on top of mine.

I followed Luddy through the trees, watching his behind. He wore Levi's, filling them, and an old blue work shirt like my dad used to wear. I was wondering, stepping over a fallen tree, if Luddy had a boner yet. I had a big, aching one that banged the front of my khakis, and I wanted him to turn around and see it and smile the way he smiled, telling me everything was the same. He didn't turn, though, and continued marching through the woods as though we were on some sort of schedule.

He said to me without turning, "Are you going back to school?"

I didn't know. I didn't care at that moment. "My mom wants me to," I told him.

He didn't say anything else, but he slowed up some, and soon we were walking side by side. I could make out the rows of trees up ahead and the fence that marked Wysockie's land. When we were kids we'd hike to the orchard and steal around like spies, climbing the trees and throwing apples at each other. One day, we found a shed in overgrown weeds, for storage or something, in the middle of nowhere. Inside there'd been a moldy stack of dirty magazines. We flipped through the pages, and Luddy suddenly flicked out his cock. It was hard and pinkish, its head like a German soldier's helmet, rounded like that, with this deep split at the top. It wasn't so big then, his cock, not as big as it was now. When puberty hit for Luddy, it pretty much focused on his crotch. It seemed that only recently had his body started catching up with his dick. He stayed short, though, but he was getting broader, thicker. Still, he could go a week without needing to shave.

The last time I was with Luddy was the best time. Used to be, we would just jerk off looking at something—a magazine, a movie he got from his brother. We progressed to jerking each other off, which was nice enough, awesome, actually, having that big thing in my hand. The last time, though, Luddy put his hands on my chest and played with my nipples and stuck his dick between my legs, pushing me back against the wall in his bedroom, dragging his dick in and out of the pussy he made of my thighs, my own dick rubbing up hell against his hard, flat, and hairy belly.

Out in the open, Luddy picked up his pace again, and I straggled behind, my cock wobbling, the sensitive head tingling with every step I took, flickering inside my baggy pants. I looked down and noticed an embarrassing arrangement of wet spots to the left of my fly.

"Luddy," I said, stopping. He kept walking, a man on a mission. "Luddy," I said, louder. He looked over his shoulder. The sun was going down. Crows cawed in the trees. I unzipped my khakis, and my dick popped out.

"What the fuck, Tuck," he said, looking around as though there were actually someone around to see.

I pulled my shirt up over my head and threw it on the grass. I unhooked my pants and let them drop. Sitting on my shirt I got my sneakers off, breathing up the smelly stink of my bare feet. I put my pants out on the grass and got up on my knees, waiting for Luddy, who stayed where he was, hands in his pockets. A flock of blackbirds lifted off a nearby tree, making Luddy flinch. He pulled his hands out of his pockets and swung them around a little, reminding me of a swimmer warming up. He walked slowly over to me.

When he was close enough, I grabbed the front of his jeans.

"I missed you," I said to him. I saw a smirk twist his mouth.

"Missed my dick," he said.

I had. Tall and feverish, it fit the cup of my hand but would not be enclosed by my fingers. The shaft was goose-fleshed, and a few stray black hairs grew halfway up it. His balls were snugly wrapped in a nearly bald bag that did not ever slacken or swing the way mine did when it was warm. His pubes were amazing, though, the richness of black, the sheen, the smell. The hair that surrounded his cock was long and smooth, very nearly straight, looking like you'd want to run a comb through it.

"This ain't right," I heard Luddy say. I pressed my fingers against his hardened cock, knowing I was squeezing out a bunch of precome to mess up his shorts. I wished I leaked like Luddy—he didn't need spit to jack off, his dick supplying all the lube he needed. He wouldn't let me taste it, though, leastwise not by licking it as it sprang from that deep split.

"It's wide open," he said. He hugged himself. I pulled on the tab of his zipper. "Anyone can see," he whispered. His pants came down.

"Nobody's looking, though," I said. His dick appeared like a magician's wand. I slid my fist down it, watching the drool it made. I put my tongue on his thigh, my forehead pressed against his nuts. He bent his legs and lowered his hips, sliding his dick on my cheek. He pushed me back, and I lost my balance, and he stretched himself out on top of me. He lifted up once and shot a gob of spit between us, placing it just over my navel. He put his face on my shoulder and turned away so I couldn't kiss him, but he let me put my hands on him, and I played with his rear end and backside, the new breadth of his shoulders, the silky pit hair under his arms.

My own dick was being roughed up by Luddy's bunched-up jeans. I didn't care—I was blown away by the feel of Luddy's body on mine, the slick drag of his big dick and the noise it made. I felt his mouth open against my shoulder as he sank his teeth gently into the soft flesh there. His hands moved up to cradle my head, and I heard him say my name. He started fucking my gut more quickly, his sticky head knocking against my rib cage. His face turned toward mine, and he sniffed around my ear. He was breathing hard. "Turn over," he said.

I went on my belly and felt a warm drop of spit land between my spread ass cheeks. He slid his fat wiener up against the slippery channel, and he laid himself over me again, pressing his face between my shoulder blades. He humped me, just under my tailbone, while his fingers played in my hair, and I ground my dick against my khakis, against the earth. Every time he slid his pecker against my asshole, I wanted to get him in, but he wasn't going there, and he chugged over it, pile-driving against my fanny, licking up my back, saying my name.

He didn't say he was coming, but I knew it was about to happen. His body went hard, and he seemed to stop breathing, and I felt a sudden warm wetness on the small of my back. I rolled us over so that I was laid out on top of him, on my back, with my legs spread and dick lunging skyward. I buried a finger up my butt and pulled on my sore, rocky prick, tipping my head back and finding his cheek, putting my lips against it, and his hands came around and stroked my belly, digging into my pubes, up and onto my nipples. I dug my heels in the grass, arched my back, and fired off a half-dozen rounds of thick, clotted come.

Luddy disappeared, didn't come home from work one night, and the next day his mom called my mom, wanting to speak with me.

"He didn't say anything to you? Didn't mention taking off with anyone?" I could hear the hysteria that tightened her voice and made her breathless.

"No, Mrs. Ludlow," I said. "He didn't say anything to me about anything."

"Who is this Jay he's been hanging out with?" She sounded ready to cry. I looked at my mother, who was eyeing me like I had something to do with all of this.

"I don't know him," I said, and I really didn't know him, had never heard of him.

Mrs. Ludlow said, "Thank you, Jason" and hung up. I hung up too, and my mother put her hand on my shoulder and said, "Where do you think he'd go, Jason?" and I shrugged because I really didn't have a clue.

Gossage called and said, "What are you doing?" and I said nothing. He said to come on over, then, and I did. We hung out in his garage. He sat on one of his dad's empty beer kegs and said Mrs. Ludlow had called his mom and said she knew Luddy didn't really like Kenny, but did Kenny know where Luddy was or did he have any idea who this Jay person was? He played with the stringy ends of his cutoffs, his thighs flexed and showing the splits of muscle there. He toed the concrete in soccer shoes, no socks, which always made me think of nakedness.

"You don't think he's dead or anything?" Gossage said.

I shook my head—what could kill Luddy?

"And who's this Jay guy?"

"I don't know," I said, leaning against his dad's workbench, my hands getting covered with sawdust. I stretched my arms up over my head, and the dust fell before my eyes like snow.

Gossage said, "You been working out?"

"Some," I said, "I got a weight set for my birthday."

"I got a six-pack from my brother," Kenny said. His birthday was a couple of days after mine. He smiled, showing me his different-colored tooth, the real one lost on a hockey rink last year. It was one of the things I liked best about him.

"Your arms look good, gigantic," he said. He got up off the keg and came up to me, putting his hand on my biceps. I could see the press his dick made in his shorts, the hard downward point. He had always been popping wood in school, sitting behind me in English and whispering, "Hey, Tuck—*boing!*" and I'd have to turn around and look. He'd blame it on some girl, usually, but I had him figured otherwise; I was pretty sure it was me to blame.

"You and Luddy were fucking around, I heard," he said. He was close enough to touch.

"Who said?" I asked. I knew he was fucking with me. Nobody but Kenny would have ever thought about Luddy and me screwing around. The thought had probably come to him when he was wanking off one night, I guessed. His crotch came closer to mine, and I waited for him to touch me again. He didn't, though. He straightened his body and put his hands on his head. I saw his other-colored tooth again.

"Whatever," he said.

We passed his dad asleep on the couch. He was stripped down to his boxers and looked a little like a beached whale, but seeing him there like that gave me a hard-on anyway. Plus I could see the head of his cock poking from the leg of his shorts, and it was the size of a freaking tennis ball. The room smelled of beer and farts, and Kenny said his dad was passed out.

"Awesome piece, though, huh?" he whispered. "Like father, like son."

"You fucking wish," I said back, keeping my voice low.

I followed him to his room. He stood by the door, closing and locking it. I sat on his bed. It was covered with a red, white, and blue afghan his grandmother must have knitted, and some dingy-looking New York Yankee sheets. He turned on his stereo, the volume turned way down. I could still see the lump of his dick in his shorts. He put his thumbs into his pockets and covered his hard-on with curled fingers. He wouldn't look at me, so I could look at him as much as I wanted. He yawned and said it was hot, and he took off his shirt. He had little pink nipples like mosquito bites, and his torso was hairless.

He threw himself suddenly onto the bed with me, bouncing me around. He went up to the head, and I kept to the foot. He toed off his sneakers and threw them into a corner of the room where a pile of clothes lay. I watched him lean over his feet and start picking between his toes, and then he bunched up some pillows behind his back, making himself comfortable, spreading his legs, bending one and resting it against the wall and touching my butt with the other one.

"My brother joined a frat at school," he said. I turned to face him. He still wouldn't look at me, pretending to find something interesting in his belly button. "It was fucked up, man. They made him jerk off with a bunch of other guys. They put them all in a room and gave them five rubbers and said whoever doesn't drop a load into his bag has to suck out everyone else's."

"No way," I said, instantly intrigued. "That is fucking nasty."

"I shit you not," he said back.

"Did he do it?" The idea of it, five guys in a room jacking together, practically made me dizzy, and I was thinking then that even if nothing were to happen between Kenny and me, I'd at least have something to think about when I got home.

"Fuck, yeah, like my brother would drink some guy's come."

"How'd he get it up in front of all those guys?" I wanted to know, not that I considered it much of a problem.

Kenny put one hand down the front of his jeans to scratch or something. "Said he closed his eyes and pretended he was in a room full of chicks watching."

Yeah, right, I thought. *He probably had his eyes wide open and couldn't stop looking at all the other dicks that surrounded him.* I was thinking then that everybody was a little like me, because even Kenny was sitting beside me with his hand down his pants, and then there was Luddy humping me in the middle of the orchard.

It was becoming plainer and plainer that Kenny was wanting to bust a nut. The itch he scratched failed to go away.

"You'd lose, I bet," he said, "if you had to do that."

"Do what?" I said, unable to follow him on account of all the concentrating I was doing on his hand in his shorts.

"What my brother had to do," he answered, and I laughed.

"Think so?" I said.

"Yeah. You're a fucking pussy, man. You wouldn't even be able to get it up, I bet."

I thought at first that he was putting me on, and then I saw what he was really up to, baiting me, trying to initiate a little action and pretending it was just a game, a stupid contest. Whatever, I thought, more than ready to play along.

"You're the fucking softie, man," I said.

"Bullshit," he said.

"Betcha five," I said.

"Sucker bet, and you're going to be the sucker."

"Whatever, asshole," I said. Kenny was grinning like his face would split—I figured he was thinking everything was going his way.

"Tell you what, fucker—I mean Tucker," he said. "Last one to come has to eat the other's load."

I laughed at him for being so fucking eager. "What am I supposed to do, Kenny—hold the shit in my hand until you're finished or what?"

"I just hope you're hungry," he said. He arched his back and undid his shorts, pushing them down. His dick sprang up, looking very hard. It was ruddy and shaped like a torpedo, in between big and small. He didn't touch it—he didn't dare—I could tell he was closer to shooting than he cared to be. He managed to wait until I got undressed, and as I got back on the bed, I accidentally went in-between his legs with my

naked foot and toed his balls.

"Ha, Jesus crap," he said, come fountaining from his pecker. "Goddamn it!"

"Looks like you're the winner," I said. I got up on my knees and crawled unsteadily between his legs.

"You don't have to," he said.

"Bet's a bet," I replied, resigned to sucking up his sweet cream cooling on his belly. I took it up with long licks—it tasted better than anything I'd known and stayed in the back of my throat. I had it all over my face, feeling like a kid with a bowl of batter. I started licking around his balls and across his hip bones, making him shiver. I moved my mouth up to his chest and tickled his nips with my tongue and even pushed his arms up to suck on his pits. He was groaning by now, and his cock, which hadn't bothered getting soft, burned between my pecs, its head all smeared with goo. I decided to lick that off too. I held it at its hairy base and sucked hard on the buttery end. His legs relaxed and spread a little, and his balls dropped down to the afghan, hiding his little brown hole. After being with Luddy, who was so careful not to let me handle him, being with Kenny was like being given a body to play with. I picked up his nuts and squeezed them until he made a noise, and then I poked a finger into his little brownie. I opened my mouth to the whole of his pecker and looked up his long torso to see him playing with his titties, eyes closed, mouth open, head at an odd angle. I swooped up and down on his johnson, dragging my lips up his shaft and pinching them around his slippery end.

I didn't know how much fun he was having until he made me stop. He got up then and started working on my joint, and no wonder he made me stop—I felt as though I was going to blow a hole right through his head. He slurped down to my bush, eating me whole, making little moans that I barely heard, but they rattled the hell out of my bone. He held on to my balls and twisted the sac while he sped his mouth up and down my shaft. He smoothed his tongue over my sensitive cap, making me shudder. My knees shook, and I lifted my hips and forced my way into him until he was nosing my bush again and nearly choking. He backed off, and it was like he hadn't breathed the whole time, and he had drool dripping off his fattened lips, and I saw his cock all red and curving upward, dried come flaking along the rim of its head.

I felt the pressure in my groin and knew I had to unload soon. I grabbed him and pulled his face down to my knob, and while he was down there, he stuck a finger up my ass, making me holler. He pushed me back and kept poking some weird spot that made my legs open and my dick quiver, and I closed my eyes, feeling my cock explode, and he slurped and gurgled over me until I was sucked dry, and he straightened up and shot me an eyeful of jizz like he was shooting a blackbird.

"I think your dad's awake," I said, hearing something crash outside of Kenny's door.

"Probably needs another beer," Kenny said, cuddling down beside me. "We'll be all right." He wiped his

come from my face and covered me with his afghan, and we fell asleep.

Luddy came back and showed up at my door.

"Hey," he said.

"Your mom's going crazy looking for you," I told him.

He looked over his shoulder; there was someone sitting in his Camaro, the smoke of his cigarette swirling up out of the open window.

"Who's that?" I asked him.

"Friend of mine," he said. Kenny stepped up beside me then. He and I were watching my little brothers, my mom gone to her bowling banquet. He was hanging out, waiting for my brothers to go to bed so that he could blow me. He slipped his hand in my back pocket.

"We went to Ocean City," Luddy said.

I nodded, feeling Kenny's fingers move.

"Just thought I'd see what you were up to," he said. He turned around, lifting a hand to say good-bye.

"Good seeing you, Lud," I said, feeling the sudden absence of Kenny's hand. The door closed. Luddy left a smoking patch of rubber.

I'm glad he's back, I said to myself. *I'm glad he's OK.* I went back to the TV room. Kenny's clothes were in a pile on the floor, and he was wrapped up in a blanket on the couch, my brothers sacked out and snoring.

"Come here," he whispered, and I did.

My mom said Luddy was on the phone.

"Hey," he said. "Meet me at Wysockie's."

"I was going to the driving range," I said.

"Your boyfriend going?" I could hear the pissiness in his voice and pictured his face. "I'll see you at 2," he said, hanging up.

I walked to the orchard because my mom was taking the car to work. She said, "You be back soon. I don't want the boys on their own for too long."

I went to the shed where Lud and I first did it, expecting to find him in it. It was empty except for some rabbits that ran wild when I stepped inside. I heard whistling in the distance, though, and stepped out again and saw him down the path that cut through goldenrod and tall grasses, his dark head bobbing along, disembodied. I watched him as he got closer, coming into full view, his pants too big, his shirt a little tight. He was carrying something.

He stopped in front of me, putting his hands behind his back, his chest thrust out.

He said hey, and I said, "Hey, Lud."

"What's up?" he asked.

"Nothing," I said back. His eyes traced my face, and I felt as though he was trying to memorize it.

"I got you something," he said. He held out a little wooden box made out of driftwood. It said Ocean City on the lid. "It's got sand in it and some shells and some sea glass I found," he said, sounding proud and embarrassed all at the same time.

"Cool," I said.

We didn't say anything for the longest time. I tried to think of something, but nothing came to mind. I kept looking at the box, thinking it was the coolest thing anyone had ever gotten me, thinking how much I wanted to kiss him.

I should have done it. I should have grabbed him and put my mouth on his. I should have thrown my arms around him, thrown him to the ground. I thought about Kenny and shook my head a little, and Luddy said, "What?" and I said nothing, and I felt as though I was holding something more than just sand and glass and shells. And then a breeze blew across the field, and the grasses waved and hissed, and Luddy stepped back, and I lost him forever.

Cherry Bomb

Bishop was just getting out of the showers when Digger came into the locker room. Bishop brought his towel up from around his waist and began to rough up his short-haired head, feeling his wet sex dripping and bobbing. He looked past Digger, who was having some trouble with his shirt buttons. "Hey," Dig said as Bishop strutted by. He tightened up his ass cheeks—the left one sporting a little devil, naked and red, holding a big pitchfork—and he felt Digger's stare on his stony butt. He stepped up to his locker and threw his towel over the bench, his back still to Digger. He didn't hear Digger coming up behind him, and he let out a small yelp when Digger pushed him up against the locker, getting Bishop in a neat, quick half nelson. He could feel the full length of Digger's body pressed against his—and something hard against his tightened ass.

"What the fuck?" Bishop grunted thickly, his right arm pinned above his head, his face on cold metal. He felt Digger's breath on his neck. He could smell it—it smelled like milk. "Let me go, asshole," he said.

"You owe me something, Bish," Digger said into the man's ear, his lips on the pink curve that was going red and hot. Digger pushed his hips forward, pressing his chest against Bishop's back.

"Fuck off, man," Bishop said. "Somebody'll come in."

"Two guys having a little disagreement, that's all," Digger replied. He breathed in the aroma of Bishop's hair, placing his cheek against the back of his head.

"Let me go," Bishop said, his voice easing up, going liquid. *I know how to handle Digger*, he was thinking; he knew what he had to do to get the asshole off his back. His left arm was twisted behind him, caught between their hard bodies. He unclenched his fist and touched Digger's bared stomach, banded muscles covered with warm, smooth skin and an amber rope of hairs that rose tangled from under his briefs. He fingered the waistband of Digger's undershorts. His right arm was immediately jolted with renewed pressure, his face smashed against the cold locker door.

"You're real sweet, Bish," Digger said. "But I know your tricks now. And you know what I want."

"I don't know what you're talking about, man."

"You promised me something, pal," Digger said.

"Yeah, well—" Bishop started.

"Well, nothing," Digger finished. "You fucking know you owe me first ride on this sweet ass, and you know you're giving it up."

Digger wasn't expecting much. He was probably going to lose Bishop anyway—not that he ever really had him. With that thought in mind, he gave Bishop one more obligatory shove, then released his grip with a sigh that hinted at the futility he was sensing. But it felt good now letting off a little of that pent-up steam that Bishop had filled Dig with. He turned around, walked back to his locker, and got himself naked. He did nothing to hide the erection he had, even when some of the guys from his hall came in from the racquetball courts. One of them, C.J. it was, said, "Digger's looking to do a little camping again, guys, got his tent pole up."

"Priapism," Digger said. "Can't even help it."

"What the fuck is that?" one of the others laughed, stripping off his jock and tossing it over at Digger, who just grinned, catching the strap with a fast swipe.

"I'm going to have to keep this as evidence," he said easily, throwing the jock into his locker.

"What, your mother stop sending her undies for you to sniff?"

"Hey, Bish, you get those chem notes copied?" C.J. said, walking over to his friend's locker.

"What?" Bishop said.

"Chem notes. I need them back." C.J. looked at Bishop's expressionless face. "What's up with you, man?"

Bishop stuck his bare feet into a pair of loafers and slammed the locker door shut. "Everything is fucking fine, just fucking fine," he said, throwing a look in Digger's direction. "Stop in later—around 3," he added quietly. "OK?"

"OK," C.J. said.

C.J. stopped by Bish's room. He knocked and waited, looking the door over. It was plastered with pictures of pussy and tits ripped from the pages of assorted skin mags. C.J. feigned interest but didn't understand why Bishop went to such extremes—the guy was crazy for boy butt, and there were plenty of boys on campus who knew this firsthand.

What Bishop liked best, though, was cherry boy butt. "I want to be the first," he once said to C.J. "I just want to be your first, baby." *Too bad you've only one cherry to play with*, C.J. was thinking when the door finally swung open, Bishop standing there with a nasty look on his face. "Get in here," he said, and C.J. did what he was told. The door slammed shut.

"Fucking Digger's gunning for me, man," he said. The cords stood out in his neck, and his eyes were mean slits. He was wearing jeans that hung low on his hips and bagged at his ass. His bared pecs hopped as he punched a fist against his open palm. He paced, and C.J. stared, squirming on the bed, wanting to take off his pants and get plowed by the guy who had once shoved the end of his lacrosse stick up C.J.'s ass.

"What's he want?" C.J. asked.

Bishop stopped dead and glared at C.J.

"Fucker wants my ass," he said incredulously, as if he had never heard anything so ridiculous. "That's why I wanted you today, man. I need you to go over there. I need you to get his mind off me. You can do it."

He put a soft hand on C.J.'s face, fingering the boy's ear. "You know," he was saying, being nice to C.J.'s head, "you know, some guys just don't take it. Pitchers and catchers. Know what I mean?"

C.J. nodded and squirmed under Bish's hand. He was ready to play catcher right now.

"You'll do it for me, right? Go in my place?" he said. "I know you will." And he started undoing his jeans.

Standing naked in front of his mirror, Digger splashed a little cologne on his fingers and dabbed it along his jaw. Bish was due in a half hour. He wondered seriously if he should wear underwear, then decided he shouldn't wear anything at all. It had been, after all, his body that had interested Bishop that night at the gym when it was just the two of them, Digger working the desk—but working out—at the fitness center and Bishop lingering after a half-assed run through the weight-machine circuit. Bish wore gym shorts that must have been from his junior high school days, they were so old and worn, a blue that had washed out to gray, tight like skin. Digger could have traced with his finger the outline of Bishop's meaty cock and balls, clearly stuffed into the child-size shorts and straining the limits of the weathered fabric. Digger did his best not to stare. He'd had plenty of opportunity to do this sort of cruising—working at the fitness center afforded him a wealth of crotch shots throughout the day. And sitting behind a desk allowed him to rise and fall without detection. Some days he seemed to stay erect his whole shift and would limp back to his room with aching balls; that is, if he didn't swing by the fourth floor rest room of the university library first for a quick blow job or just jack himself off into a fitness center toilet.

There was a hard knock on his door. Digger went to it bare-assed, opening it a crack to make sure it was Bishop. It was C.J.

"What do you want?" Digger said.

"Let me in, man," C.J. replied, pushing the door. Digger stepped back, and C.J. came in, brushing against Digger's skin. Dig felt his friend's hand slip across his thigh and smelled the liquor that sweetened C.J.'s breath.

"I see you naked more than dressed," C.J. said. "Don't you have any clothes, man, or are you some kind of nudist or something?" He fell onto Digger's bed, which was made up for the first time this semester, with clean sheets even. "I'm depressed, man," C.J. sighed.

Digger stepped into a pair of nylon soccer shorts. "I don't want to hear about it," he said.

"You got any beer?"

"You can't stick around, bud. I got plans," Digger said.

C.J. lifted his head up off the bed and looked at Dig. "I heard," he said. "Give me a beer."

Digger got him a bottle from the little bedside cube and sat on the bed beside him.

"What did you hear?" Digger asked.

"Bish is pissing and moaning about giving up his cherry butt," C.J. said, swilling down some beer, some of it spilling out of his mouth and down his neck, soaking the ribbed rim of his T-shirt.

"He can piss and moan all he wants—the dickhead owes me," Dig said.

"How come?" C.J. said. "Did he pop yours?" He was going to tell of his own popping at the hands and cock of Bishop the Cherry Bomb, but he kept quiet, quickly realizing his bargaining tool and remembering what he had thought of earlier—having another cherry.

"Don't mess up the bed, asswipe," Digger said, getting up and walking to the windows that looked out over the quad. He could see Bishop's dorm, his darkened window.

"I'm going to kick his ass if he doesn't show," Digger said, turning to look at the boy on his bed. "Fucker's dead if he doesn't show," he added, but without much conviction. It was all talk. What could he do? He had come close to simply taking what he thought was coming to him in the locker room today, feeling his pecker slip against the rut of Bish's ass cheeks.

He watched as C.J. tipped his head back to swallow more beer, spilling even more so that his shirtfront was almost completely soaked.

"Fuck," they both said, and C.J. got himself up and out of his shirt, balling it up and wiping himself down with it. He pushed the shirt down his front, rubbing it hard between his nipples, then down his hard white belly. His jeans darkened at the waistband from the spilled beer. He looked at Digger.

"How about me, Dig?" he asked. "Don't you like me?"

Digger looked out the window again. He liked C.J., all right. He liked him enough to fuck him, even. The boy had warm eyes that made Dig feel a little doughy sometimes, like the time they shared a pitcher of beer at the Rock, and C.J. put his elbows on the table and leaned forward, his hair pushed back. That's all he did, and Digger had felt himself go soft inside, and he was feeling that way now.

"You're just drunk, buddy," Digger said finally. "This isn't your kind of thing."

"How would you know?"

Digger shrugged his shoulders, throwing his hands into the air. He saw C.J.'s eyes going over him, taking him all in, and Dig felt a string being pulled, the string that controlled his dick, and it got pulled hard, hard enough to make his dick twitch and fatten. C.J.'s eyes stopped roaming and fixed on Dig's crotch. A smile tilted his lips.

C.J. undid his pants and pushed them down his legs. Dig was always amazed at the size of the kid's thighs, how they seemed to grow like big hairy tree trunks from his white muscled butt. C.J. turned off the lamp and lay down on the bed in a patch of light that fell through the window, the light falling over him like a well-placed sheet. His skin glowed, and the dark-haired parts of him went darker still, and Digger found himself walking over to the bed and falling to his knees.

C.J.'s prick hovered over this thick pubes, its covered-up head hanging over his belly button. Dig had only seen it soft in the showers and had not imagined it so long. He put his lips at its base, into the bush that smelled of soap and crotch, and licked at the boy's tightened-up balls. He felt a hand on the back of his head and heard C.J. say—in a voice he must have picked up from some porno flick—"Come on, buddy, suck it." And Digger put his mouth on the hot head of C.J.'s prick, tonguing the slit, slipping into the meaty cowl of C.J.'s foreskin. He nibbled the frilled end of his friend's cock, pulling hard and stretching it well over the sticky knob. He backed off, watching the spotlit prong stand straight up and vibrate, skin slipping down around the flange of C.J.'s pointed dick head like a turtleneck.

"You've got enough skin for two cocks," Digger said.

C.J. spun himself around on the bed so that his butt was facing Digger. Digger leaned back on his haunches and watched the boy before him bring his heels up on the bed, proffering a funky little hole surrounded by dark hairs. "It's yours, man," C.J. said, "if you want it."

Digger looked at the shadowed pucker.

"It's better than Bish's, I bet," C.J. said.

Digger laughed. "Good or not, fucker still owes me that cherry."

"Why's that?" C.J. asked, just wanting to hear Digger say that he too had had his cherry bombed by Bishop.

Digger leaned close to the bed. He breathed in the smell of the boy's butt. He put his cheek against one of C.J.'s massive thighs, feeling the soft, straight hairs there. He felt C.J.'s hand go through his hair.

"He just owes me," Digger said, and he licked the warm skin of C.J.'s leg and slipped a hand between the boy's thighs before sliding it up his belly, feeling the hard prick that lay along his arm like a hot pipe. He felt his head being pushed toward the split of the boy's ass, and he could see in his mind the way Bishop had looked that night at the fitness center, on his back on a bench in the locker room, his second-skin shorts sliding down his legs, exposing his pale ass cheeks—that fucking little devil!—and the dark split between them, Bishop whispering, "You want this?" licking a finger and pushing it against his tight little pink. Digger had thought he was there, that Bishop's beautiful butt was his, but it wasn't, and somehow—and he still wasn't sure how it happened—Bishop managed to take Dig's own cherry, popping it with ruthless jabs of a dangerously thick dick that left Digger walking funny for a week.

"Fucker owes me," Digger said again, and he moved his hand into the warm crevice of C.J.'s butt, thumbing the pucker, feeling himself aching groinward. His cock was trapped between the cool nylon leg of his shorts and his own hot thigh. He ran his free hand over it and strummed the taut shaft.

"You want this one?" C.J. asked, and Digger groaned. He slipped his thumb into the boy's hole, and C.J. yelped.

"I guess this is going to hurt," C.J. said. "Let me suck you first." Digger got himself up on the bed, his shorts down, his prick hard and ready. He aimed for his friend's mouth, smearing C.J.'s lips with the fat head of his cock. C.J.'s hands went up Digger's thighs to his hips to his furred belly that was hard and scored with muscle. Dig closed his eyes as C.J. fingered his nipples and opened wide to accept Dig's thick piece. He slipped into the wet velvet of the boy's heated insides, filling C.J.'s mouth easily, with uneaten dick to spare. He held it in as far as it would go for as long as C.J. could handle it, until the boy began to choke. Dig eased out and let the boy swallow and breathe a bit before filling his mouth again with his steely prong. He fucked C.J.'s mouth, pretending it was Bishop's, beating his cock knob against the back of the boy's throat, plowing into C.J. the way he wanted to be plowing into that other boy, that fucking bastard. He was blind with it, in some kind of crazy fuck trance. He pulled out of C.J., who gasped and muttered, "No wonder he was afraid to come over here," and Digger grabbed the kid by the hair.

"Hands and knees," he said, his voice hoarse with wanting. When C.J. didn't move fast enough, Dig grabbed him roughly and positioned him with his ass in the air. He pushed C.J.'s face against the mattress. "Don't make too much noise," he whispered. "Don't need the floor knowing my business." And he spat a gob onto the boy's pucker and pushed his finger into the hole.

The first thrust made C.J. cry out. "Motherfuck, you're killing me!" he yelled, struggling to break free, but Dig had him in some kind of half nelson that immobilized the boy and made his asshole prone to more wicked thrusting. Dig slobbered all over the boy's back, pawing at the boy's nipples and pulling on them hard enough for C.J. to forget for a moment the vicious assault on his asshole. Dig pumped away, practically raping the boy, not altogether aware of who was beneath him, so intent was he on the image of Bishop on his knees taking every fucking stroke of cock. Dig slammed himself against C.J.'s butt, feeling the grind of pubes against bone, the boy's ass lips stretched wide at the very base of Dig's huge member.

"Oh, man, oh, man," he heard, feeling C.J. push himself into each stroke, maneuvering his cock between his legs and against Dig's thigh. "You're driving me crazy," C.J. breathed. "Harder, man, fuck my ass harder."

It didn't seem possible to slam into C.J. any harder, but Digger did his level best, feeling his nuts rise. He dug his fingers into the boy's hips and pulled him onto the fat rod that was blubbering already and close to spewing. C.J. pressed his face hard against the mattress, grunting with each stroke. Digger grabbed the boy's hair and pulled C.J. up against him, his mouth rough against the boy's ear. "Ready, buddy?" he breathed. "I am." And he pummeled C.J.'s plush butt, filling his hole with thick jizz pudding. C.J. arched his back, pressing his sphincter against Dig's wiry bush, and shot well over the mattress and onto the floor beside Digger's freshly made bed.

"Holy fuck!" C.J. breathed heavily as Dig pulled out, his still-hard organ red and burning, oozing slightly and stinking of C.J.'s musky butt hole.

Dig got off the bed and stood with shaking legs. His prick hung heavy and long between his thighs, a sight that had C.J. riveted. "All of that in me?" he said, shaking his head. "Fucking amazing."

"You'd better go," Dig said, and C.J. opened his mouth to speak. "Come on," Digger said. "Get the fuck out of here. And you can tell Bish—ah, fuck it, fuck you both." He picked up the kid's clothes and threw them at him. He picked up his own shorts and pulled them on, walking to his door. He stepped out into the hall and headed for the toilets. He went into a stall and closed the door and sat on the shitter, studying his hands. He sniffed up the smell of C.J.'s ass cunt rising up from his prick. He heard the bathroom door open and C.J.'s voice, low and filled with hurt: "Come by my room in an hour. You'll get what's coming to you."

"So, what happened?" Bishop wanted to know. He was lying across C.J.'s bed, arms behind his neck, his T-shirt pulled up, revealing the furred stomach he knew C.J. drooled over. C.J. stood by his desk, pretending to be interested in something there—the chemistry notes Bish had finally returned.

"Am I off the hook or what?" Bish asked, putting his bare feet up on the bed. He couldn't help smiling, and the joint he'd smoked a little while ago didn't hurt either. He stretched his arms over his head, rubbing the balled biceps of one arm. He was already thinking of the next cherry, the cute blond freshman on the track team who had made the mistake of looking twice at Bishop in the showers the other day. *His ass is mine*, he was thinking, smiling again, his dick nudging the front of his sweats. He closed his hands on air and imagined he had the kid's ankles, trim brown things, in his grasp, poking into what had to be a sweet pink pucker. Bishop drew his long legs up onto the bed, looking through the V of them at C.J.

"What's up with you, man?" Bish asked.

C.J. turned from the desk. He shrugged his shoulders.

"Guess I owe you something," Bishop said. He lifted his hips and pushed his sweatpants down his thick and hair-feathered thighs. His dick slapped onto his belly loudly.

C.J. glanced at it and made a face. "My ass is tired, man," he said.

Bishop pushed his fingers into his pubes and against the thick base of his prick, making it stand up straight and tall. It blocked his view of C.J., and this pleased Bishop. In his mind he could see the track boy, his blond hair slicked back with sweat. He could even see the braided string ankle bracelet the kid wore and the dumb little winged-sneaker tattoo he had on his calf. He was going to chew up and down on that kid's ankles like chicken wings, he decided, wagging his stiffer in the air like some kind of magician's wand. He was going to make mush of that kid's butt; he was going to *ruin* that kid's butt. "Why don't you just give me a nice little blow job, and we'll save the good stuff for later," Bish said, touching the end of his prick and making glistening spider web strings with the drops of goo that came seeping out.

"All right," C.J. said, and he turned off the light.

"Hey, don't do that," Bishop said. "I want to see you. That's the best part."

Ignoring Bishop's request, C.J. walked over to him in the dark and found his way between Bishop's muscle-thick thighs.

Bishop knocked his dick knob against C.J.'s nose and wrapped his legs around the boy, holding him tight. C.J. opened his mouth and took the head lightly between his teeth, licking into the leaking slit. He relaxed his jaw and tightened his lips, and Bishop arched his back, slipping deep into C.J.'s mouth. C.J. took it all, the whole fat thing, his nose hard against Bish's pubic bone. "Good Lord," he heard Bish breathe.

Bishop didn't like to fuck around with the guys whose butts he'd ruined. The cherry popping and the work he did to get them to give it up were the best parts, the thing that gave him an aching hard-on, that made him spew like a fire hose into their virgin asses. Usually they didn't want to see him again either, so deep was their shame. He'd see them in the library, and they'd pretend not to see him or say hello sheepishly. *But this kid*, Bish was thinking, *this kid's crazy for my cock, man. He can't get enough of it.*

No sense letting a good cocksucker get away. He squeezed the boy with his legs locked at the ankles. "I'm sorry, bud, but I'm going to have to fuck you now."

He flipped C.J. easily and positioned himself between the kid's thighs, pressing his slobbering cock head against the boy's used hole. The fact that Digger had just emptied himself into the hole made Bishop even hotter, and he pushed into the tight ring and entered a hot and mushy gash slicked up with Dig's come, driving Bishop crazy.

Maybe his eyes were squeezed shut, or maybe he was just too preoccupied with the hard fuck he was giving C.J., but Bishop never noticed the door of C.J.'s dorm room opening, never noticed Digger slipping in. Dig grabbed Bish from behind and locked his arms over his head while C.J. stuffed a handy jockstrap into Bish's gaping mouth to keep him from calling for help. His dick slipped out of C.J.'s hole with a pop, and he fell on top of the boy with a muffled grunt. The three men grappled silently in the dark, wresting the struggling Bishop off C.J. and pinning him prone to the bed. “Cool it,” Digger told Bishop, “or you won’t piss right ever again.”

C.J. kneeled at Bishop’s head, straddling his face and leaning hard on his shoulders. Bish tried his best to bite his assailant but couldn’t, his mouth full of well-worn jockstrap. He wagged his head and breathed in the smell of familiar ass. C.J.’s balls were resting against his chin—he could feel the heat of them and the loose, hair-covered skin that held them. There were hands on his ankles, spreading his legs, and he felt someone’s breath against his own balls. He struggled as best he could, but he was being held too tight and was no match for the men who held him down so purposefully. He gave up.

The first thrust was the worst, and Bishop cried out as his ass was breached, then pummeled again and again. The air became pungent with the smell of sweat and jizz, noisy with the sounds of heavy breathing. Without warning, Bish experienced the sensation of a geyser erupting deep inside him. When C.J. came, shooting a load across Bish’s chest, C.J. and Dig eased themselves off Bishop. Tired from fighting in vain, Bishop lay still, fearful of what they might do next. The lights came on, but Bishop turned his head, not wanting to see who’d humiliated him so mercilessly.

They didn’t speak until the second pitcher had been emptied. Each guy was in his own head, replaying the events of the evening. Neither of them were particularly pleased with themselves, but they couldn’t deny that some sort of justice had been meted out, and no one could say that Bishop hadn’t deserved what he’d gotten. Digger poured himself another beer and topped off the other guys’ mugs. There was some shitty Bob

Seger song playing, and it looked to Digger like C.J. was aching to get the hell out of there. The bartender—a blond boy Dig had seen at the fitness center—came by with another pitcher. He put it on their table, saying, "Here you go, guys."

"Nobody ordered this," Digger said.

The bartender shrugged his shoulders. Digger glanced at the boy's legs—he was wearing khaki shorts—and saw a goofy tattoo—a sneaker with wings. It was the track boy, the one who was all eyes when Dig worked the desk.

"Guy at the bar's got it for you," the blond said, pushing the hair off his forehead.

The boys at the table turned around and looked toward the bar. Bishop was standing there. He winked and saluted them, giving them a smile that was broad and sexy. And then he flipped them off. The blond walked back to the bar, and the four guys followed his ass with their eyes, and C.J. said, "Boom."

"What's that?" Dig said.

C.J. put his elbows on the table and smirked. "Another one of Bishop's cherry bombs, I guess."

BUDDY BOY

The road to the lake, little more than a trail, really, was muddy but passable, and Jim Danzer cursed it every time he bottomed out his Ford Fairlane. He'd long ago shut off the radio in disgust, unable to pick up anything but Holy-Rolling Christian stations with their Bible-thumping bastards pleading with him to repent his evil ways. "I got your repenting right here," he said, grabbing a handful of Jim bone and squeezing. The gesture was lost, though, with no one to see it. He put both hands back on the wheel as the trail took a sudden left into the underbrush, the Fairlane bouncing on squealing springs.

He looked into his rearview mirror—miraculously, actually, because if he hadn't looked, he'd have never seen the kid—and did what he could to make room for the mountain-biking fool. "You're crazy, man," he yelled out the window, causing the boy on the bike to laugh back at him and flip him a good-natured bird, his spandexed butt shining in the sun. Jim watched the boy's bulging calves, sun-browned and feathered with smooth, straight hairs, and he grabbed his crotch again. This time it was a hard handful. He shook his head, not sure what was going on down there. He hadn't had a queer thought in years, and now, all of a sudden…

He was going to the lake to do a little soul-soothing, to get out of the city for a bit. A friend from work told him about this place, this lost little lake, clean and quiet, tucked out of the way, a little to the north, a little to the east. The trail ended, and Jim parked the car in a field of tall grass.

He didn't pull out his gear but instead went walking toward the blue shimmering water he could see through the trees. He passed the mountain bike lying on its side but thought nothing of it. He looked across the lake. From where he stood he could see the whole of it, its edges lined with fir trees, surrounded by the mountains of the Adirondack range. It was long and narrow; he thought he might be able to swim it from end to end without too much trouble. It was then that he noticed the silence, nothing but birdcalls and the noise the wind makes through the trees. He folded his arms across his chest and felt something like redemption.

There was a cabin somewhere nearby. He touched his pockets for the key. The windows would be shuttered, and the place was going to need some serious airing out, he was warned. "It's on the primitive side," Dave had said to him, making a face. Dave's wife was wanting him to sell it, and she thought Dave had found himself a taker with Jim. "Just check it out," Dave had said. "It's going cheap."

Well, so far, so good, he said to himself, finding a path that ran along the shore, heading for a dense cove of trees that seemed a likely spot for a cabin. He heard a small whoop and a splash and saw someone—the mountain-bike boy, he deduced—cutting through the water. *Skinny-dipping?* Jim wondered hopefully, but then he saw the boy climb up out of the water onto a rock that barely broke the lake's surface and saw those fine legs still black-butted in spandex. His upper body was finely developed too, and he stretched his arms up over his head, the water runoff making him shimmer in the midday sun. Jim caught himself staring. Just then the boy appeared to spot him too, looking at Jim with cupped hands over his eyes. He raised a wary hand, as if unsure it would be seen. Jim waved back and got on his way again, talking in his head about how stupid he was, checking this kid out in broad daylight, being so obvious.

As he pushed his body through the tall grass, his bare legs switched by weeds, he thought about the last time he saw Dave, when he was picking up the keys to the cabin. His wife, Connie, was going to be out, and Dave had told Jim to just come around to the back of the house. He found him there, asleep on a hammock on the deck. He was stretched out, his arms thick and akimbo. *The little hairy runt*, Jim had said to himself, looking at his passed-out friend, his legs spread wide, his toes pointed to the sky. He couldn't have been more than 5 foot 6, and he had one of those cocky attitudes common to men of small stature. He worked extra hard in the gym and even harder at work, where Jim had gotten to know him, both of them senior mechanics at Boyle Boys Mufflers. But seeing him there like that, laid out to the sun and half snoring, a little dynamo looking so vulnerable, turned the Danzer dick to marble. He took a moment to scope out the hairy cave of Dave's crotch, dark and hard to make out. Dave shifted suddenly, his hand going down to where Jim's eyes had rested so intently, and plucked out one fuzzy ball and then another, his eyes closed, his mouth pursed, then falling open. He snored for real, and Jim marveled at Dave's bowling bag: *Look at those fuckin' stones!*

Now what? he had wondered. He had a six-pack in one hand. He checked out the yard, looked back at Dave's open legs, the low-hangers that drooped like heavy, overripe fruit on the vine.

He licked his lips and noticed the fine mist of sweat that had formed on his upper lip.

Dave opened his eyes.

"Jimbo," he muttered sleepily.

"What?" Jim barked, startled, almost dropping the beers.

Dave pushed his fists into his eyes, squirming on the hammock, his chest rising and spreading under his T-shirt. "Whoops!" he said, and his hand flew to his crotch, where he pushed his balls up into his shorts again. "Thought I felt a breeze." He grinned. "I'll take one of those," he added, hand out and waiting for a beer.

"I gotta use the toilet," Jim said suddenly, handing the beer over to Dave, who directed him to the one downstairs. By himself, standing in front of the pisser, he pulled out his boner and tried to will it down, but it wasn't going anywhere. A drippy drop of precome peeped up from the pee slot. "Aw, jeez," he complained aloud, resigning himself to the task at hand. He tugged at the loosely circumcised, flat-headed prong a couple of times, half disgusted, half amazed with himself. He looked up at the ceiling and blamed Dave for his problems and dribbled an urgent load into the toilet.

He stepped into the deep shade of firs, the needles slippery under his feet, then the sun was on him again almost as quickly as it had disappeared, and he saw the cabin in the clearing. Pine trees fenced it in and made it secluded, but some were cleared away, allowing for a view of the lake. He ran up to the porch and stood there, and he could see the boy again, the rock being some kind of natural dock. He was tempted to go on down, but the boy being there… He dug into his pockets for the keys.

The place was in much better shape than he'd been led to believe, but he guessed Connie hated it enough to be unable to speak nicely about it even while trying to unload it. He went around unshuttering the windows, getting a good, refreshing breeze going. He took the sheets off the furniture—functional, sturdy. He stepped out on the porch again and started down to the water. He was hot and dusty and decided it was time for a swim. The mountain biker was gone, and he scanned the lake for anyone else and found it empty, so he stripped down to nothing and stepped out onto the half-submerged rocky trail that jutted some 20 feet out into the water.

It was cold but felt good, and he flailed around the way he did when he didn't care who was watching him. He'd had a decent stroke, having taken swimming lessons when he was a kid, but now he was out to cool off. He splashed and kicked and got out and jumped back in again and again. When he'd had enough he lay down on the rock, the water lapping around him, and he was, for the most part, out of it and drying in the sun. He was almost asleep when he heard snapping twigs and a metallic rattle. He opened his eyes and saw the mountain-biking boy parked on his bike at the end of the stone dock.

"Hey," he called out to Jim.

Instead of scrambling for cover—there was nowhere to go but the water, anyway—he decided to tough it out. He sat up and crossed his legs, putting his elbows on his knees. "How you doin'?" he replied, a pained smile on his face as the kid rode out onto the rocks, hopping from one to the next with what looked like great exertion. Jim was amazed that the kid got as far as he did before toppling into the water.

"Shit!" the kid hollered when he resurfaced. "I used to be able to ride out to where you are!"

He got himself and his bike out of the water and, leaving the bike, joined Jim on the last big flat rock.

"Where's Mr. Mazzeo?" he asked.

"Dave?" Jim said, surprised, although there was no reason to be; Dave had owned the cabin for some time now and was bound to be known by whatever locals there happened to be. Up close, he saw the boy wasn't really boyish; the "kid" was probably closer to 30 than 20. Still, he was a good-looking guy, his brown hair looking longer now that it was wet and dripping, plastered to his neck and the sides of his face. He got down on his haunches, his thighs monstrously huge, and Jim saw the crotch of his biking shorts worn to gray, bulging pleasantly. He glanced down at his own wad of cock and balls just to make sure it was all there and not hanging out in plain view. Bike boy stuck his hand out.

"My name's Felix, but nobody calls me that," he said, apparently comfortable enough to shake a nude man's hand.

"So what do they call you?"

"A little bit of everything," the man said, looking out over the water. "They call me Buddy lately." He paused. "Mr. Mazzeo isn't coming up?" He sounded disappointed.

Jim's own discomfort was growing, and he felt he'd better make a run for it before he embarrassed himself. He stood up quickly, seeing his dick had already begun to swell. It was fat and heavy and swayed ponderously. In no time, Jim knew, it would pulse upward. "Uh, Dave's at home. He wants to get rid of the place. He thinks I'm the one to take it off his hands." Jim stepped around the squatting boy and made his way over the rocks. Buddy got up and followed.

He was relieved to get his pants on, but the boy seemed intent on staying. Jim's cock was in that halfway stage; it lay hotly against the top of his thigh and felt good there. He eyed Buddy, whose own dick, trapped in the tight confines of his shorts, was of some prominence, having all the appearances of erection.

"My dad's got the service station up the highway," Buddy was saying, carrying a box of groceries. "We got ourselves a little general store there too, so if you ever need anything, just give us a holler. I'd be happy to run it down to you."

"I'd have to holler pretty loud," Jim said. "No phone."

Buddy laughed. "That's right. I keep forgetting." He set the groceries down and put a hand on a support beam. "I always liked this place," he said. "Mr. Mazzeo used to come out all the time."

"Did he?" Jim said.

"Oh, yeah," Buddy said. "Him and me would swim and hike and stuff, and sometimes he'd send me up to Harley for a bottle, and we'd play poker when I'd come back." He put his forehead against the beam. "You a good friend of his?"

"We work together," Jim said.

Buddy nodded but didn't say anything. He seemed to Jim a little sad. "I'm getting kind of hungry," Jim said. "Got a couple of steaks in the cooler there. Why don't you help me get this shit inside and find a grill and let me feed you?"

Buddy's face broke into a grin. "That'd be nice," he said, still smiling as he picked up the box of groceries and bounded up the steps.

After dinner they went down to the rock again and listened to the fish jumping. The moon was out, along with a million stars. "Me and Dave used to come out here all the time at night like this," Buddy said, his voice soft, as though he didn't want to disturb the peacefulness of the night.

"You really miss him, don't you?" Jim said, feeling the heat of the man's flesh radiate.

"Yeah, but now you're here," Buddy said, and Jim wondered if he was going to have to entertain this big ol' kid for the whole of his vacation. All the noise of the night disappeared then, sucked out as though by a vacuum, and Buddy said, "You want me to suck you off?"

The fumbling hands on his fly; the sudden, hot breath licking his uncovered stomach; the piss-warm water kissing up to his ankles—the combination hoisted up his pecker so that the head peeked out from under the waistband of his pants. Buddy tongued over it, forgetting for the moment to undo Jim's trousers. He put his hands up Jim's shirt, fingers seeking out the tiny, pointed nipples, pinching and pulling them. Jim's fingers tangled confusedly in the boy's hair, and he wondered why he couldn't stop himself and whether he should. He wanted to be a man, and men didn't do this shit, but he also wanted—more than anything else at that moment—to feel the heat of Buddy's mouth enveloping his rock-hard cock. His hands slipped down to the boy's naked shoulders—it was hard not to think of Buddy as some innocent farm boy, simple, eager to please—and massaged his meaty deltoids. He was lean and built, and Jim remembered from the afternoon the brownish hair that grew here and there on his chest—around his nipples, up and out of his black skintight shorts, up to his navel and then over it, fanning out, thinning out over his rolling abs. He felt the boy's hands again on his fly, and his pants fell down to his ankles, into the water, and Buddy bathed Jim's groin with a flood of spit.

"Oh, my," Jim breathed, and he heard his voice echo all over the lake. The dark eyes of the mountain watched him. He closed his own as Buddy took him into his mouth. *What am I doing?* he asked silently, and Buddy's head made a deep plunge, taking all of Jim's burning cock. The seven inches posed no problem to the boy, nor did the circumference; Buddy adjusted his jaw like a snake and took the whole of it with an ease that amazed Jim, who'd never experienced such an awesome blow job. He tipped his head back, looked up at the sky, and marveled at his luck, reminding himself to thank Dave Mazzeo for this cocksucker who seemed to come along with the cabin like the furniture and the view. Then he got to thinking about Dave and his little Buddy. Good old Dave. All those weekend trips out to the cabin without Connie, getting hammered, getting blown—the lucky fucking dog.

But now *he* was the lucky dog, and he grabbed Buddy's head and fed him some Jim bone, wanting to feel the tickle of the boy's tonsils on the end of his dick. The boy gargled his own spit, trying to keep up with the pumping Jim was giving him. Dick tingling, he pulled out and pressed the spit-covered thing against Buddy's face. "Is this what you like, Buddy?" he asked. "You like this big fucking cock? Is it better than Dave's?" He leered down at the boy kneeling at his feet in the water. His hand dug into the front of his bike shorts, jacking away. He nodded up at Jim, who stroked the kid's cheek, putting his fingers into the boy's hungry mouth. Buddy sucked his fingers with as much sensuality as he did Jim's dick, and this made Jim crazy. He stabbed into Buddy's mouth again, pounding his meat against the back of Buddy's throat. He gritted his teeth and lifted up on his toes, trying to hold back the flood he felt welling up in his nuts.

"Aw, Christ," he shouted, releasing gush after gush of come into Buddy, who sucked it all down greedily. Buddy pushed his shorts down and shot a sputtering load. It glowed in the moonlight, as did his impressively large penis, thick and pulsing, still drooling.

"Oh, boy," Buddy said, getting up. He leaned against Jim, pressing his body against the older man's. "We're gonna be good friends, ain't we, Jim?"

"Oh, yeah," Jim said, holding the big boy close. He felt Buddy's lips on his throat, his big hard-on snuggling up to Jim's softening one. *Real good friends*, he thought.

Jim grew accustomed to Buddy and his mouth. Hiking with the boy, he'd feel a tug on his backpack and turn to see Buddy handling his enormous pecker and eyeing up the front of Jim's shorts, waiting for the inevitable spurt of growth. Swimming nude, they'd both be as hard and randy as teenagers, wrestling and humping underwater, scrambling to the rocks to empty their nuts on each other's wet and sun-browned bodies. Rest and relaxation had turned into sex, sex, sex, and Buddy was perpetually hard, perpetually horny. But he wouldn't do anything but blow Jim. Jim had tried once, not exactly gung ho on the idea, to reciprocate, and Buddy wouldn't let him. "Let me take care of you," he had said. "It's what I like."

And so Jim let the boy do what he liked, sitting up on the porch on a rickety old chair, Buddy between his thighs like a dog, lapping up the stiff prong that jutted from Jim's dark bush. Buddy's head bobbed, his tongue stiff on the sensitive underside of the Jim bone, his unshaved chin rough on the dangling balls. Jim stroked Buddy's hair, petting the boy, forcing more and more dick down his throat. He'd noticed he was being more and more free with the boy, taking liberties, using his mouth like a pussy. Most recently he liked pulling out and squirting thick ropes of come across the boy's face, watching it drip down his nose and into his gaping mouth. He did that earlier and then surprised him by getting down on his knees and licking the goo off, causing Buddy to spray Jim's crotch with hot spew.

They were at it again. Jim's naked legs were spread wide, the hair on them lightened from the sun. He felt like a new man. He put his hands behind his head, enjoying this leisurely blow job, listening to Buddy slurping and moaning, making more than enough noise to cover Dave Mazzeo's approach.

Neither the sucker nor the suckee realized that their privacy had been violated until Dave cleared his throat. Then both men jumped about ten feet, and the old rocker gave out under him on his way down. Dave busted out laughing, Buddy put a hand over his heart, and Jim picked himself up out of the rocking-chair rubble.

"You two are something, I'll tell you," Dave said, giggling still. "I've been watching for some time, and I am impressed."

"Hey, Dave," Buddy said, naked and bonerized.

"I see you've been treating Jim here neighborly, and I want to thank you," he said, holding out his hand to shake Buddy's. Buddy took the hand and let Dave pull him off the porch. Jim watched the two men embrace, kissing hungrily. Buddy pulled and tugged on Dave's clothes, unbuttoning his shirt, fumbling with the zipper of his jeans. Jim's erection, scared away by Dave's arrival, had returned, reinforced.

Buddy moved Dave to the porch, getting his pants down to his knees. Dave sat his white-briefed butt down and let the boy pull off his hiking boots and relieve him of his jeans and socks. The sight of the man's bare feet triggered the animal in Buddy, and he got down on all fours and licked Dave's wriggling toes. Dave looked over his shoulder at Jim, who stood stiff and transfixed, amazed at the spectacle.

"I could use one of these at home," he said, laughing. "But what would Connie say?"

"And you want to give this up?" Jim said, finding his voice finally. His throat was thick, and he had a hard time keeping his eyes off of the bunchy muscles of Dave's shoulders, his grapefruit-size deltoids, the deep drop to the waistband of his B.V.D.s, where black and curly hairs sprouted.

"Yeah, just to get her off my back. But I want you to take it. See what I mean?"

Jim thought he saw what Dave meant, but he also saw Buddy's tongue sliding up Dave's black-haired shin, sticking the hairs to the skin. A glistening drop of come welled up like a tear and fell from his dick head, a dewy string.

Dave stood.

"Buddy here's going to pull down my shorts and get to working on my knob, Jimbo, and I was wondering if you'd kindly lick my asshole while I'm enjoying a little trip down my pal's throat." He looked back at Jim, who could only blink. "If you were to lie yourself down, Jimbo, I could squat over your pretty face. You get it now?"

Jim wiped his face with his big hand, shaking his head. "I don't know," he said.

"You never ate asshole?" Dave said, incredulous. "Not even a girl's?"

"Never went with any girls like that," Jim offered lamely.

"And Buddy here didn't—"

Buddy's head snapped up. "You said I was to stay true!"

"Easy, boy," Dave said, tapping Buddy's cheek gently. "Get back to my legs—you're almost there." And then to Jim: "Just lie down and get your head close to the edge, Jimbo."

He put his head on the floorboards and looked up at Dave's white cotton butt. The briefs came down slowly, and Jim was presented with the Mazzeo moon, thick white glutes covered with hair. He gulped.

"Chow time!" Dave hollered, and he squatted over Jim's face, the dark crack opening, fat pink lips coming his way. They seemed to kiss Jim's chin, and then Dave readjusted his stance, and they landed smack on Jim's mouth. Jim kissed back and worked his tongue around and tried to keep his nostrils clear to breathe through. He felt Buddy's chin on the top of his head, making him hungry. He started eating Dave's butt, pretending it was pussy, but that didn't do too much for him; after a while it seemed that he'd always wanted to munch on Dave's hole. He stroked the man's broad back, reaching up and around, trying to grab his nipples, but they were lost to him in the thick mat of hair that covered Dave's chest.

"Damned if this ain't heaven," Dave said, and Jim agreed, his hair going spitty from Buddy's dripping drool. "Now, what do you say I turn around now and let you boys switch. Does that suit you both?"

Buddy nodded vigorously, still riding Dave's pecker. But Jim had some reservations. He'd been willing to do some work on Buddy, but Buddy was different and had earned a grudging tongue bath. Dave, on the other hand, was a slick-assed motherfucker, not to mention a coworker. He was also hotter than hell, and Jim had long been eyeing him up, following the older man around the garage in the beginning like an apprentice. He was only some five years older than Jim, and at 38 he was looking especially good, especially at that moment, the big, dripping dangle of his cock hovering over Jim's face. Its huge helmet was as red as a tomato and similarly shaped. He'd seen it soft in the men's room often and knew even that it was uncut—Dave tended to stand back from the urinal. The hair around it was thick and matted with Buddy's spit. The balls swung over Jim's forehead.

"All you gotta do is get it wet for Buddy's ass," Dave said.

The Jim bone hopped.

"Just do it, baby," Dave said, Buddy already getting to work on his ass.

Jim opened up, and it dropped in. As easy as that. He closed his lips around it and sucked. Easier still. Then Dave worked it in and out. A fucking breeze. Dave's huge, baggy balls covered his nose and stopped his breathing. Not bad, not bad at all.

"And now..." Dave said, bossy motherfucker. He pulled his plug out of Jim's salivating mouth, grabbed Buddy by the arm, and hauled him up.

"If you'll just lean yourself over right here, Buddy, I'll bet Jim wouldn't mind sucking you some while I'm fucking your ass," Dave said, spitting on his cock, getting it worked up.

"Hey, Jim," Buddy said, leaning over the supine man.

"Hey, Buddy," Jim said back.

"I could suck you some too," he said, and Jim nodded.

Dave stabbed into the boy, making him grunt. "Fuck!" Dave hollered. "This is what I've been missing!" He humped Buddy's ass with firm, even strokes, going deep and taking the boy's breath away. Jim got on his hands and knees and pushed his face into Buddy's crotch. The damn thing was as big as a tailpipe, and Jim had trouble getting past the head. Buddy pressed his face into Jim's back, his cheek smeared back and forth by Dave's thrusts, his tongue licking the sweat from Jim's shoulders. Jim grabbed the fat prick and jacked it, his mouth all over the head, crazy for the sweet leakage that spilled out every time Dave hit the kid's prostate. He heard the sharp slaps as Dave rode the boy, and his own pecker was aching from loneliness. He repositioned himself so that he was sitting before Buddy and all the boy had to do was bend over and take him into his mouth.

"Maybe the two of you could switch again," Dave said, grinning, sweat running into his eyes. He ran a hand over his forehead, his arm huge and flexed. He rode Buddy one-handed for a while, letting Jim enjoy the show, while Buddy gave Jim some inspired head. The boy's mouth was like a vacuum; he was drawing the come up from the well. Jim's nuts all but disappeared, and Buddy began to snort as Dave banged into the pliant ass. Jim fell back, hitting his head on the rocking chair, the pain minor compared with the pleasure he was getting from Buddy's mouth and roaming fingers. Buddy played with Jim's little hole, poking it gently, rubbing it with his thumb. It was slippery with spit from the boy's mouth, and the thumb slipped in easily, making Jim yip and tense up, but he soon relaxed and even wriggled his ass, trying to suck up more of the probing digit.

"Aw, shit, kids," Dave said. He got up on the porch, straddling Buddy, whose mouth he pulled off of Jim and filled with his own big rod. Jim watched with admiration as Buddy sucked the thick and veiny uncut monster, watching Dave's ass cheeks flex, the dark crack of his ass winking at him, making him dizzy. While Buddy caught the first blast of Dave's load, he jacked the Jim bone furiously, causing Jim to cry out and geyser his own hot cream all over Dave's knees. And Buddy, still stroking and sucking his two neighbors, brought himself off with a silent gush and a copious flow of juice that shot across Jim's smooth brown chest.

Back at Boyle Boys, Dave and Jim were sitting out behind the shop eating lunch. Naturally the events of that weekend at the cabin made them the best of friends these days.

"Connie's going to her mother's for the weekend," Dave said, waving his sandwich around. "Thought maybe you'd come by and play some cards. Or something."

Jim felt the tickle of his overalls against his hardening prick. He'd stopped wearing anything underneath them.

"I was thinking," Jim said, taking a bite of an apple, "that we could go to the cabin, see what Buddy's doing."

"Sounds like a plan," Dave said, the crotch of his overalls tenting already. "But Friday seems awfully far away. Why don't I come by tonight and try to talk you into buying the cabin again? Connie says I ain't working on you hard enough anyway."

"Well," Jim said, taking another bite of his apple, "Connie knows best, I guess."

On the Mound

Grinning over his beer at Nick's, Hank told me again that he had a plan, his ratty baseball hat turned backward, his head ducking close to mine. I liked him best like this—smiling and butting his forehead against mine, chewing on a swizzle stick in this corner bar that reeked of old beer and cigarettes. I looked at him, thinking I couldn't love him any more than I did right then. My eyes wandered over the edge of the bar, down over his lap to where he fingered the stringy ends of his cutoffs. His thighs were huge, busting out of the confines of his shorts. The rolling mound of Hank's crotch caught my eye as it always did; the denim there was white from wear.

"So, what's this plan?" I asked him.

Hank slapped a hairy hand on my back, shaking his head and grinning. "Buddy," he said as he touched his crotch and belched, "I gotta piss."

I followed him to the john with my eyes, watching his stick-stuck-up-his-ass strut and wishing it was my stick stuck up there, but that seemed as likely as our sadder-than-sad softball team winning the county finals next week. It didn't hurt thinking about it, though. Not much, anyway. After all, he was the unwitting inspiration for innumerable jack-off sessions that left my pud sore and my ball sac high and dry.

He wore construction boots, slack-topped socks that could no longer accommodate the girth of his calves, and a white T-shirt that had seen better days, ripped here and there and not providing much coverage. It was short in the front, and a good part of his muscle-rippled stomach showed, along with a spreading trail of sun-lightened hairs. Hank came back from the men's room, walking toward me with a big dark spot spreading across the front of his shorts.

He got back on his stool, eyeing the fresh round I'd just ordered. I'd already tried the get-him-drunk routine: I got him loaded at my place once and threw a porn tape into the VCR. It was a bi tape, and I hoped he'd get the subtle hint, but he passed out before the opening credits. I jacked off beside him, peeking into his shirt and sniffing at his crotch, wanting but not daring to lay hands on his body.

"What's this plan?" I asked again, my cock shifting.

"I ain't telling you," he said, sipping his beer and looking at himself in the mirror behind the bar. I looked too and saw what we'd heard a thousand times—that we looked like brothers. We both had short, straight brown hair and dark eyes, and our noses had been busted one way or another. Our shoulders were thick and broad, which was pretty much how it was for us all the way down to our oversized feet.

Hank looked at me in the mirror. "Can't tell you."

"Come on," I said. "You can't wait to tell me. It's all over your face."

"You'll think I'm goofy," he said, going red and looking down the other end of the bar.

"I know you are." I cuffed him on the side of his head.

"OK," he said. He tipped his head closer, and I felt his

breath on the side of my face. "Don't you laugh," he warned, his face all serious and mean-looking.

"I won't," I said. "I promise."

"Way I figure," he began, "it's a fucking miracle we made it to the finals at all, and we both know we ain't got a chance in hell of winning, the way practices have been going."

"No argument there," I said. I knew we sucked, and it was nothing but a strange sort of luck that had gotten us this far.

"So we're going to have to do something—anything—that might give us a little shine, you know?"

I nodded and let my gaze drop to his belly rising up, brown and hairy, from the waistband of his shorts. Lower, I saw the neat packing job he'd done in the john—dick to the left, balls on the right, both sides looking painfully cramped.

"Hey," he said, waving a hand in my face. "What's so interesting down there? Someone drop a nickel or something?"

"Sorry," I muttered, pissed at being caught. "Go on."

"You know Billy Barnes of the Pirates," he said. "Fucker's hitting like nobody taught him what a strike is. I also happen to know the guy's a queer, and it wouldn't surprise me if his whole team's a bunch of cocksuckers." Hank took a swig from his beer and squirmed in his seat. He had his grin back.

"So, what of it?" I said, sitting up on my stool.

"Whoa, buddy," Hank said. "I ain't suggesting a bash party or anything. You know I don't care what a guy does with his dick. Sometimes I think those guys got the right idea." He looked thoughtfully into the air over my shoulder.

My mouth went dry as I stared at him. This conversation was fucked-up; it occurred to me he might be putting me on. We'd talked about this before, back when I was fishing around, hoping for a bite. All I ever found out was that my best pal thought what a man did with his own dick was his own business. I figured he didn't care what I wanted to do with mine either.

"Your plan?" I reminded him.

Hank looked at me, blinking. He looked surprised to see me. "Plan," he said. "Plan. Yeah, right. Well, pal, my plan is to distract the shit out of Billy Barnes."

We left Nick's pretty smashed and walked back to my place, leaving Hank's pickup in the parking lot. Hank sang some song he made up as we went along, going on about how the Pirates use their dicks for baseball bats and Billy Barnes fucks the inside of his ball glove. Hank's shirt was off, and his chest hairs glistened with sweat. I liked his nipples all red and pointy, like they'd been worked on, and Hank was buzzed enough not to notice my staring or not to care. Either way, I was all but walking backward to get a good look at him.

At my place Hank kicked off his boots and hollered for beer. I got a couple and sat beside him on the couch. He tipped his head back and downed half the bottle, watching me through the dark fringe of his eyelashes, over the sun-reddened tops of his cheeks. He set the bottle down hard.

It was hard to look at him. Everything about him made me nuts—the swirling hairs on the insides of his thighs, the white skin at the crease of his elbows, the smell of his yellowy socks, even the belch he made. "S'cuse me," he said.

I said, "Want to watch a movie?" It was a long shot, but it made sense at the time. I was sitting there, and he was all spread out beside me, legs thrown wide, one hand behind my head on the back of the couch. Neither of us had a word to say just then, and the quiet was buzzing in my ears.

Hank cocked an eyebrow and looked at me sideways. "How about that bi flick you've got?" he said.

I fumbled around my tapes, surprised to my toes that he even remembered. I kept an eye on him all the same; I figured he'd either pass out immediately or was setting me up somehow. I popped in a tape and turned on the television.

I stood up to take my place on the couch, waiting for Hank to keel over or burst out laughing. I already had the beginnings of a boner that I didn't care to hide at this point. I watched Hank's face. His mouth was open, and he was staring at the screen. I looked too and saw four—make that five—guys fucking and sucking, and not a single female in sight.

Wrong tape. My mouth dried up, and my throat went tight. *Wrong fucking tape!* I screamed in my head.

Hank said something.

"What?" I said, my voice cracking.

"The sound," he said. "Can't hear a word they're saying."

They weren't actually saying anything because they all had something in their mouths. I turned up the volume, and there was the sound of deep moans and slurping. A dick popped out of someone's mouth, and the guy said, "Yeah," then got right back to work.

"Check that shit out," Hank said, watching a guy take a huge dick up his ass. "Fucker didn't even blink." Amazed, he wouldn't take his eyes off the screen. The guy in the film was loving every inch of the cock sliding up his hole. He opened his mouth to swallow another guy's healthy-looking meat.

"Fuck!" Hank said, shaking his head, grinning at me. I grinned back. "Buddy," he said, "you watching me or the flick?" He planted his heels on the coffee table and laced his fingers over the hump of his crotch.

I didn't know what to say. I waited for the punch line or just the punch, thinking maybe he'd hit me. *Shit*, I thought. *Let him try it—I'll knock his lights out and fuck his ass to boot.*

"Get on over here," he said, squinting at me. I saw a glint of something in his eye. I got myself to the couch, and Hank said, "This shit make you horny?" He pushed the heels of his hands against his fly. "It does me," he said, lifting his hands to show me the thick coil of cock he'd pressed into service, his shorts concealing it as well as a carpet would a fire hose. "Buddy," he said, smiling, "your chicken's choking." He was looking at my crotch, which was dotted with precome. My dick was cast in iron and dripping like a leaky pipe.

We unzipped and unbuttoned simultaneously. Hank's prick hopped up like a divining rod. Eight cut inches—a man with good-sized hands couldn't touch thumb to forefinger around its middle. Hank got a hold of it and shook it.

My own stick was poking around in my damp shorts, its head pulsating and getting restless. I peeled off my shorts and let the beast free.

We both said "Blow me" at the same time. We'd said it often enough, but never with any conviction, never with such big aching needs. Suddenly it seemed my buddy had the most beautiful cocksucking lips I had ever seen, and I became obsessed with seeing my seven slippery inches sliding into his mouth. I got up on my knees, wobbling on the couch cushions. "I…I don't think—" Hank started.

I steadied myself with a hand on his big shoulder. "You don't have to think," I said to him. I got up on my feet, planting one on either side of his butt, my dick waving stiffly over his head. He watched it warily.

"Just open up," I said, thumbing my prick downward, allowing him easy access. I stared down the barrel of it, aiming it at his half-open mouth.

The tough guy was gone. The man I straddled was like an overgrown kid—a cute, shy fucker with a thick pole sticking up and dripping with something like honey. I wanted to go down on him, eager to stretch my lips around his fat thing, but not until I'd had my dick in his mouth—not until he slobbered on my joint the way I planned to slobber on his. "C'mon," I said, swinging my bat inches from his lips. I could see the dark red inside of him, the white edges of his teeth.

He closed his eyes and stuck out his tongue, flicking the tip of my cock. His hands left his dick and grabbed hold of my thighs. He gripped me with sticky fingers and took the big end of my dick into his mouth. I sighed, feeling the slide of his teeth across the head. I tipped my pelvis to feed him more, and he choked and spit. I backed away, nearly falling off the couch. He held me fast in those big hands, slipping his nose just under my balls and taking a deep sniff. "You stink, pal," he said, lapping it up, slurping on my hairy nuts and licking up my shining shaft. He went down on it again and came up choking again.

"Damn," he said, drooling. "How do they do it?" He looked up at me, at my big arched dick, his hands busy again around the huge stalk he had sprouting from his beautiful bush of glossy pubes. I reached down and fingered one of his red nipples that poked up high from a swirl of hairs. I pinched it lightly and saw Hank's eyes widen.

"Man," he said, his voice low. "That drives me crazy." I saw the grip he had on his dick, the head all purple. He got up on my cock again, pressing his hard tits against my thighs.

He worked on me slowly, not taking much more than my tip in his mouth, but I didn't need any more than that. He was as hot as a fever, and his tongue had a stroke all its own. I gripped his ears and fed him cock until I was pressing against his teeth and teetering on the edge of something big. Something wicked was happening around my piss slit, a burning tingle that traveled down my shaft. I should have pulled out and let the feeling pass, but I was locked tight in a beautiful hump, fucking Hank's mouth with short strokes. My cock blew, and I blasted a week's worth of funky spew into Hank's slack-jawed gape. That was when he slapped hands on my ass cheeks and swallowed me whole, taking my come and a good length of my dick down his throat.

I was panting and a little rubbery at the knees, but I had not forgotten my buddy's throbbing member. I laid myself down on the couch and went to work. Hank's thighs turned to stone, and I saw his toes bend back. His nuts tightened hard, and I felt a rumbling. Hank held his breath, and I readied myself for the big one. I sucked him up, my lips going thin at his enormous base, and he threw an iron hand on the back of my neck, choking me with cock and come. I stayed on him, sucking the last drops out of him until he went soft.

"I sort of lost my head there, sport," Hank said after a spell of heavy breathing. He still had one of his nipples in the pinch of his thumb and forefinger.

I didn't know what to say. I was still swallowing slimy drops of his load. His limp prick slipped out of my mouth and nestled itself in its bush again, much like a tired puppy. I licked its red rim one last time before sitting up.

"We should hit the sack," Hank said. I watched him walk into the dark of my bedroom. "You coming or what?"

I walked into the cool darkness of Nick's a little blind from the glare outside. The long bar was to my left, small tables to my right, and booths butted up against the wall. I looked for a familiar back, the one I'd been thinking of all day, imagining myself holding on to it, pumping myself into the small pucker he had hidden in the hairy crack of his gorgeous ass.

Hank had called me that morning at the lumberyard where I work. "It's all set," he'd said, and I heard him giggle.

"What's all set?" I asked him.

"You just meet us at Nick's at 5."

"Us?"

"Me and Barnes!" he growled. "What's up with you?"

"Nothing," I said.

"You're still basking in the glow of last night, aren't you?"

"What the fuck are you talking about?" I snapped.

"Baby, you don't even know glow," he said. "I'm gonna set you on fire tonight. Don't forget Nick's." Then he hung up.

As my eyes adjusted now to the darkness of the bar, I scanned the booths, spotting Hank's turned-around baseball cap. I walked over to him and saw he wasn't alone; a sneakered foot was on the seat by his hand. Hank looked up.

"Hey, we were just talking about you," Hank said, smiling. I saw that the foot belonged to Billy Barnes, who sat up and put his feet on the floor, looking at me blankly. Empty glasses littered the table. Hank leaned back against the wall.

"Sit down, buddy," he said, throwing a glance at the other side of the booth. I squeezed in beside Barnes, who was staring at the glasses on the table. He lifted one that still had something in it and put it to his lips. Hank raised a hand and got the bartender's attention, twirling a finger over the table.

"I don't even like you guys," Barnes said suddenly.

"That's not what you were saying a little while ago," Hank said.

"Yeah, well, then I don't like *you*, Hank," he snorted. The bartender came over with three sets of shots and beers. "And I know you smoke-bombed our dugout last time we played."

"Now that's not fair, Billy," Hank said, smooth-voiced, reaching across the table to ruffle the yellow bangs that hung in the man's eyes. "I was out on the mound. How could I have managed to be in two places at once?"

Billy looked at me. "I don't know how he did it, but I know he's the one." I shrugged. "I like *you,* though," he said.

Hank nodded. "He does," he said. "He told me."

Billy raised his shot glass. "Here's to us, pal." He smiled, swinging his glass toward mine.

"Yeah, here's to you two," Hank said. Grimacing, we downed the most bitter whiskey ever. Nick's foul-smelling draft beer never tasted better.

Billy Barnes twisted in his seat to get a better look at me, and Hank leaned back to enjoy the show. I realized I was an integral part of his plan to undermine the Pirates' potency on the field by mining their star player's potency in bed.

I stared at Hank, lifting my chin as Barnes put a leg up against me. Hank slipped a hand inside his shirt, his fingers lingering over the red nipple I'd had in my grasp the night before. His lip curled in a smirk, and my pecker did a turn.

I didn't try to catch up with them drinkwise, figuring someone had to keep his head. While Barnes and Hank discussed highlights of the season, I tried to figure out what I needed to do. The game wasn't until next Saturday. I could see doing this the night before, but why now?

When Hank left to take a leak, I waited a beat and got up to join him, leaving Billy to his rotgut and beer. At the urinal beside Hank, I gazed at his streaming dick. I got mine out but couldn't pee, I was so hard. I shook it at him, and he looked over his shoulder at the stall—empty. He reached for my hard-on, taking it in a firm grip. I watched his prick rise and stand out from the toothed edges of his zipper.

"It's driving me crazy watching him watch you," he said to my cock. "I'm sitting there getting a little pissed off, as a matter of fact." He seemed to remember where he was and let go of me. He eased himself back into his jeans.

"What do you want me to do?" I asked him.

"Whatever you want, whatever you can," he said.

I jacked on my shaft because he was still watching it. He let out a big groan. The door opened. Hank flushed, and I did what I could to hide my stony prong. I went soft fast as a big guy with tattooed forearms stepped up to the urinal and unfurled a long piece. He peeled back a meaty hood of skin and splashed into the bowl. I zipped up and left.

Getting Barnes back to my place wasn't difficult; he was all for it. The three of us walked the couple of blocks, climbed the steps, and stood in my living room. Barnes ran a hand over his blond hair, fat lips closed tight over big white teeth. He looked to me like a farmer and had, in fact, grown up on a farm. He pushed up the sleeve of his T-shirt and rotated his throwing arm like I'd seen him do on the mound. He didn't seem to know what to do with himself.

"So, what are you doing tonight, Hank?" Barnes asked.

Hank sat down on the couch and hit the remote control, turning on the television. "Thought I'd crash here tonight, pal," he said. "Can't drive in this condition." He unlaced his big boots and kicked them off.

Billy looked at me, and I shrugged. "Sit down," I told him.

"Hot in here," Hank said, unbuttoning the few buttons he had bothered to do up on his shirt. He exposed his chest, and I stared. Billy couldn't help taking a few glances himself. "Ain't you hot, man?" Hank asked him.

"I could turn on the AC," I suggested.

"It ain't working," Hank said quickly.

"Oh, yeah," I said.

"Sure is hot," Hank repeated, his hand on his chest, a finger on his red nipple.

"Crash here often?" Barnes asked.

"Whenever I can," Hank told him. His hand moved slowly down his stomach to the waistband of his shorts.

Barnes looked from Hank to me. "What's he doing?" Hank undid the button and then the zipper.

"Taking off his pants," I said. Hank stripped down to the bright white B.V.D.'s he must have bought for the occasion.

"I thought we'd be alone," Barnes whispered. He put his face in close, his blue eyes digging into mine. He was near enough to kiss, so I put my mouth on his, pushing past his lips with my tongue. He made a noise and pressed himself against me, putting his arms around me, holding me as though he thought I'd try to escape.

I looked over his shoulder to see what Hank was doing and saw him already sleeping, his mouth open and drooling, his arms and legs thrown wide. *Fucker*, I thought. *Jealous, my ass.* I let Barnes push me toward the bedroom.

I fell back on the bed, and Barnes stood over me. "Where's the light?" he asked. I told him. He turned it on and closed the bedroom door. There was a chair in the corner of the room with a pile of dirty clothes on it. He knocked everything to the floor and sat down. He folded his arms across his chest. "Take off your clothes," he said.

"For real?" I said, smiling.

"Just do it," he said, and he was serious. He looked good sitting there, his forearms furred with golden hair, his face flushed and sweaty, his legs spread wide.

I pulled off my T-shirt slowly, beginning to enjoy myself. I balled the shirt up and threw it at him. He caught it with one hand, holding it to his face. "You smell good," he said. I sat down on the bed and bent over to undo my bootlaces.

"Do your shorts now," I heard him say, and I undid my fly. I stripped down to a pair of boxers I had not planned on being seen in, ratty ones that were stained and full of rips and tears. I was shy suddenly, stepping out of my shorts and not knowing what to do with my hands, wishing I had some pockets to put them in. I slipped them inside my boxers.

"Those too," Barnes ordered. I pushed them down over my hips, and my cock bobbed freely. I looked down at the little guy, wishing it were a bit more impressive. I petted it and heard Barnes say to leave it alone.

"Get over here," he demanded. I walked over to him. "Turn around," he said, and I did. I felt a finger on one of my ass cheeks. "What's this scar from?" he wanted to know.

"Sat down on a cigarette once," I told him, and I heard him laugh. He put his mouth on it, probing it with his tongue while his fingers crept between my legs, catching up the soft package of my dick and balls, squeezing purposefully. I felt his mouth move, slipping into my crack, his pointy tongue going south, lapping up my mossy butt, which I stuck out to allow him easier access.

The door opened quietly, and I saw Hank peering in. I put my hands on the hands that were on my erect cock. Barnes's tongue was on my hole, and I could feel him trying to get it in. I bent at the waist, feeling my cheeks spread. Barnes ate me out, and Hank came closer. I looked up and was struck by the beauty of him, big and bearlike, his thick dong bobbing hard and coming right for me. He came closer and closer, and all I had to do was open my mouth to take in his awesome cock.

"Switch?" I heard Barnes ask. I could not leave Hank's dick. I took as much as I could into my mouth, my jaw aching, threatening to dislocate. I dropped my ass down and squatted like a girl dog about to take a piss.

"Shut up and eat your dinner," Hank said, and I felt his voice in his pecker. He put his hands on my head, held on to my earlobes, and softly leaned into me. He pulled out, and his cock head thumped my nose and made my eyes water. I kissed his heavy ball sac and the sparse wiry hairs there, breathing in the funk of his crotch.

Billy managed somehow to worm his way under my squat, his face coming up under my own nuts. I felt the rasp of his stubbly chin first, then the heat of his breath over my balls. He reached up for my pecs, grabbing up two handfuls. He did some fine-tuning with his fingers, rolling my nipples between his thumbs and forefingers, pinching and pulling urgently. I felt his tongue on the ridges of my sphincter.

Meanwhile, Hank's dick was butting against my lips. I looked at him, and he said, "Let's get this show on the road."

We got Billy up on his feet so that he was standing between us. I pushed up his T-shirt, baring his stomach and a sandy-colored trail that thickened once it got past his navel, spreading out after that, covering his pecs and swirling around his small brown nipples. Hank reached around from behind and pushed Barnes's gray jersey shorts down. Barnes stood there with them around his ankles, his shirt up and over his tits, in a fraying yellowed jockstrap that could not hold all it was designed to hold. Billy's nuts leaked out of the pouch, and his prick strained upward, barely contained and leaking profusely. When I saw Hank drop to his knees behind Billy, I dropped my head and sucked hard on one of his firm, tiny paps. I nipped and chewed and licked across his chest, down the hairy trail into the navel, then farther down to the striped elastic of the athletic supporter.

The big wet head poked up out of the jock, dribbling ooze that I dipped into with my tongue. Billy slapped a hand on the back of my head and humped my mouth, roughing up my lips against the scratchy fabric of the strap. I sucked up his balls and felt something on my chin—Hank coming through from the other side of Barnes's crotch and licking under my lips. I released Barnes's nuts and gave Hank a kiss under the arch of Billy's groin, his works hanging over our heads like mistletoe, precome dripping onto my hair.

"Hey," Billy said. "What about me?"

We got back to business, working on Barnes from both sides, making the man writhe between us. I reached up for his nipples again, getting hold of both of them and pulling. Billy shoved his piece deep into my mouth. "Oh, baby," I heard him say, "take it all." I swallowed him down and kissed his bush, tickling him under his balls with my tongue for good measure, all the while listening to Hank's pleasant slurping on the other side.

"Well," I heard Hank say, "I think that's enough for now."

"What do you mean?" Billy stammered. "Man, I was just getting into it." He humped my mouth a few more times until Hank pushed me off the Pirate's prong.

"I said enough," Hank repeated, giving me a look I had a hard time deciphering. "He's ready," he added.

"Oh, man, am I," Barnes said, thumbing down his boner and jacking it. The tip went pearly.

"Get on the floor," Hank ordered. "On your knees."

Billy's face changed—his brow came forward and shaded his eyes. "I don't think so, my friend," he said. Hank took a step forward, his stiff cock bobbing.

"Floor," Hank said. "Now!"

The two were in each other's face, barely breathing. I sat on the floor looking up at them, playing with my hard-on, waiting for the first punch to be thrown. Barnes's ass cheeks were clenched tight and twitching, his hands balled into fists. Their cocks were having their own standoff—red-rimmed and glistening, they faced each other like fleshy swords.

Barnes finally backed off. "I thought I was going to fuck him," he mumbled, nodding my way.

"Well, he thought he was going to fuck you," Hank told Barnes, looking down at me. "Didn't you, pal?"

"Well, to tell you honestly, boys," I said, getting up slowly, "I kind of thought I was going to fuck the both of you."

We improvised that first night and had an impromptu circle jerk, the three of us standing close, pulling pud with one hand and groping one another with the other, dropping three big loads onto the rug. We got to fucking the next night and the next six, and by the end of the week, we had each fucked and been fucked twice. As for the big game, well, the Pirates whipped our butts, so I guess you could say Hank's plan backfired, but I have this feeling he got exactly what he wanted—in the end.

VANITY FARE

Billy Maguire looked in the mirror and made his pecs hard. There was a fine spray of hair across his chest that seemed to gather a bit at the center, the gully between his tits going dark with shadow when he flexed. His chin was dark with hair too—a halfhearted goatee/beard/5-o'clock shadow. He squatted and looked at the arch of his legs, which were heavy, like his arms, with muscle.

He was, on any given day, flawless.

He walked across the room. It was walled with windows on one side and flooded with sun, resembling a dance studio or an artist's atelier. This was where he lived. He fingered his crotch, just to the right of his balls where they rested or hung against his thigh, and then he sniffed his fingers, smelling somebody's spit. With that same hand he touched his left nipple and thought of the boy who played basketball for Tulane, lying face-down on the bed and begging for Billy's dribbling dick. Billy shook his head and touched his chin and did this thing he did sometimes, pretending he was in a shaving-cream commercial.

It was early morning, and he was just getting up or just coming home or both, depending on whom he spoke to.

About last night: It was true that he had had dinner with Matt, who had at one time worked for Calvin Klein as a pool boy and then as a model. Billy had had the Dover sole and something with chanterelles. The sole, alas, was more lively than the company, and he told Matt, perhaps indelicately, that he had a blood test appointment the next day and thus could not possibly go with him to the club. He then went to China Rose's and met up with a tall blond lad whose shoulders spoke of crew team and who swore his name was Roderigo Fernandez. He was presented with Roderigo's license as proof and his phone number as well, although he ended up with someone else.

The someone else: His name was Derek, "but everyone calls me Deke," he said. He was tall—tall enough to play basketball and young enough to be in college, and in fact he played ball for Tulane. He was wearing a white T-shirt and baggy jeans that did him no justice. He drank the beer Billy bought him and scanned the crowd, Billy thought, as if he was looking for something better to show up. Nothing better showed up, though, and Deke said toward the end of the evening, "I'm in New York to watch my brother's place. He's in Aruba or something. He's been broken into seven times, doesn't like to leave it alone, you know?"

His brother's place was basically one room with some large closets, each supposed to pass as another room. One closet contained the kitchen, another was masquerading as a bathroom, and the last one a bedroom. It barely contained the bed, let alone the 6 feet 5 inches of a boy named Deke.

Right away Deke set the rules: "I'm a top guy," he said, dropping his big-assed jeans. They fell a couple of stories down to the floor. "Just thought you ought to know."

Billy lay across Deke's brother's bed, his head propped up on his hand. "What a coincidence," he said. "Me too." The boy stood on two miles of legs; he towered over the bed. His limbs were long but thickly muscled. Billy could look up into Deke's blue striped shorts and see the big inert piece of flesh called Deke's dick, the dime-size opening of foreskin, the grim or perhaps just indifferent set of its piss slit. Billy put a hand on Deke's thigh, the hardness of the boy's quadriceps, and went quite hard himself.

"Suck my dick," Deke said, and Billy fought a smile.

"I'm kind of tired, man," he said. "And I was thinking you'd do the sucking and I'd do the fucking."

"Not fucking likely," Deke said, digging into his shorts and pulling hard on his pecker, the extra skin gathering over its head. Billy reached up and pinched the bunched-up end of flesh. Uncut dicks always reminded him of turtleneck sweaters. He pushed Deke's hand aside and took hold of the big dangle of cock. It was soft and warm and sizable. And the major difference between its flaccid and erect states, he was to learn, was the direction in which it pointed. It got not much bigger, though considerably harder, and stood at a 45-degree angle from his crotch.

"I bet you have a girlfriend, don't you?" Billy said, touching his chin.

"You bet right, my friend," the boy said, setting his hands on his hips and admiring the jut his dick made against his shorts.

"I bet you're a real stud on campus," Billy went on. "I bet you bone chicks right and left."

"You're a fucking psychic," Deke said, slipping his thumbs into the waistband of his boxers. Billy stood up and started undressing. He was slow with his shirt buttons, looking around the tiny room. Pulling his arms out of his shirt caused him to elbow Deke. It was a lot like trying to undress with someone in the john of an airplane—something not completely foreign to

Billy. Deke sat on the bed, making a little more room for Billy. The fly of his shorts fell open, and up popped Deke's dick. It was a squat yet noble monument to Deke's desire, and its excess foreskin created an architecturally interesting flourish at the top, a curling lip, a sort of ringed spout. Billy stepped out of his trousers and folded them. *But what to do with them?* he wondered. There was a chair out in the main room over which he hung his pants and his shirt. He walked back into the bedroom—it was so hard not to think of the word *bedroom* enclosed in quotation marks—in his shorts and socks. He sat himself down beside the boy.

"So," Billy said.

"So," Deke countered.

"What do you like?" Billy asked him. The boy sighed and leaned back on the bed on his elbows.

"I told you: I'm a top guy," Deke said with a hint of exasperation. *Poor Deke*, Billy thought. *Maybe this isn't going as easily as he had originally expected.* There had probably been no small number of men who had willingly fallen to their knees in the presence of such an example of straight-curious-fraternity-fucking-brother-basketball-player-from-Tulane. Of course, the very notion was of some enticement for Billy as well, who had the beginnings of a woody, which promised in short order to become a log.

"So," Billy said, leaning back too. "Let me get this straight: You get sucked or you fuck ass, is that correct?"

Deke nodded with a little satisfied smile.

"So tell me—you ever eat pussy?" Billy asked, putting a thumb into the space between his tits where the hair thickened. Deke's eyes followed Billy's thumb, but not his line of thought. After a moment he looked up as if from a trance and said, "That's different."

"Well, of course it's different. I mean, aside, even, from the obvious reasons. You know—pussy, pecker. But did you know that in a fetus, that you and me and your mom and the old lady who lives right downstairs, we all start out with the same genitalia. Did you know that?"

"I didn't *want* to know that," Deke said. "Dude, all this talk about fetuses and my mom is doing my dick some real damage." And indeed, it was no longer standing stiff with pride but had fallen. "Needs resuscitation," Deke said. "Know anything about that, Mr. Obste-fucking-trician?"

"I told you: I'm tired," Billy said, yawning in earnest.

"For Christ's sake," Deke said, and he rolled himself over and on top of Billy. He humped his hips a few times and made himself hard again, and Billy as well. Deke had his hands on either side of Billy's head, and he ducked his own head down and licked at the center of Billy's chest with an impossibly long tongue. He turned his head and swiped at one of Billy's dark nipples, and Billy brought his surprised hands up to Deke's waist, the warm skin there, and he pushed the shorts down off the boy's butt and saw its paleness shining over Deke's shoulders as the boy raised his hips high. He wiggled his ass, throwing his weight from one leg to the other and back again until he shimmied his boxers down to his ankles. He stepped out of them and brought his big feet up onto the mattress with the rest of him, so he was squatting over Billy. *This is nice*, Billy was thinking, putting his hands under Deke's ass hovering over Billy's thighs. He fingered the boy's split, the deep seam of his ass. It was smooth and hot. His thumb ran over the boy's pucker.

"Watch it," Deke said.

"Take your shirt off," Billy said back.

Deke got himself out of his shirt, putting his weight on Billy, his balls spread out over Billy's balls. It felt good—better than good. Billy rubbed the tops of Deke's thighs.

"You're cute," Billy said.

"Thank you," Deke said.

"I love fucking cute guys," Billy said. "In fact, I think that's the thing I like doing best in the whole world."

"You're cute too," Deke said, pressing his weight against Billy's crotch. "I don't know about this fucking stuff, though."

"But you're giving it some thought," Billy said, thumbing the boy's pecker, as tense as a diving board.

"Maybe you can fuck me," Deke said, closing his eyes and bringing his shoulders up to his ears. His thick-based prick did a hop or two, and Billy saw a pearl in the boy's piss slit.

"Maybe," Deke continued, "Maybe if you blow me, I'll let you fuck me?"

"Is that an offer?" Billy asked.

"It's sort of an idea," the boy said. "I was on TV last Sunday."

Billy brought his eyebrows together.

"We played Villanova," Deke half explained.

"You lost," Billy said, and the boy nodded. Deke moved himself a little bit forward, dragging his ass across Billy's genitalia. Billy winced, and Deke's face hovered over him. After Billy rearranged himself and was comfortable again, he put his hands on the boy's knees.

"You're the tallest boy I've ever fucked," he said.

"You haven't, though," Deke said.

"You've got a point there," Billy conceded.

"So do you," Deke said, reaching behind his ass and grabbing Billy's concrete erection. "You got something to wrap this thing up in?"

They started out slowly, tentatively. Deke made it clear that while he wasn't exactly a virgin "back there," he was by no means a bottom either. "We don't have to," Billy said—and almost meant it. He was liking the boy more and more. He was lying beside Billy with his hands behind his head, and Billy stroked the boy's chest, the small buttons of his nipples, the stray, straight hairs that surrounded them. He put his lips into the hollow of Deke's armpit, which was deep and thick with hair and tasty. Deke laughed and squirmed and locked his arms around Billy's head. Billy licked down Deke's side, his rippled rib cage, lateral obliques, iliac crest, down into the channel of his pelvis, into more hair and the straight, stiff peter, which was thick and meaty. Billy took it into his mouth, the whole of it, and bit gently into the base of it, getting hairs caught in his teeth. Deke took Billy's ear in his fingers, caressing the lobe.

"I can feel the hole," Deke said, and Billy tried to look up at the boy's face. "Where it was pierced, I can feel it," the boy said.

"Closed," Billy gurgled, the tapered head of Deke's dick head lying hotly on his tongue. It leaked a salty ooze that Billy savored. He went down the shaft again.

He sucked on the boy, bringing him close to coming several times, enjoying the tight bands of muscle that subdivided his stomach and the way the boy's huge feet curled, his toes waving like fingers. Each time, the boy grunted through clenched teeth and batted Billy's head back, his wiener dripping like a faucet a twist shy of shut. He nosed into Deke's nuts and dragged his tongue across the boy's pinched hole. He placed his hands on the backs of Billy's thighs and lifted his ass off the mattress. The butt crack split, and the sphincter relaxed, and Billy licked into it, making the boy sigh.

Deke wrapped his hand around his iron shaft, pressing it over his balls and against the top of Billy's head. Billy ate Deke's asshole, and the boy clamped his thighs over Billy's ears, flexing his ass cheeks, and Billy sucked up the butt funk. It made him dizzy and crazy and ready for jamming. He pulled his face out of the boy's crack and situated himself between Deke's yard-long thighs. Deke's legs hung over the hooks of Billy's arms. Billy's cock lay hot against the spit-shiny pucker.

"You want it?" Billy said, shoving a little with his hips, prodding the hole with the snaky head of his prick.

"Don't make me beg," Deke said.

"I want to hear you say you want it," Billy said, grinning slightly. Just humping over the boy's crack was giving him head rushes.

"I want it," Deke mumbled.

"Again," Billy ordered.

Deke jerked his legs, and Billy fell on top of him with all his weight, slamming Deke's legs into his chest, his own chest sweating against the back of Deke's thighs.

He put his face over Deke's, pressing his cheek against Deke's flushed cheek. He felt the tension of the boy's jaw and the obligatory struggle Deke made. His ass was a furnace, a red-hot sinkhole, a steaming bowl of creamy oatmeal, and Billy was dipping into it. He felt the fire of it at the tip of his dick.

"You want it," he whispered.

"I do," Deke said, giving up, and he hollered when Billy slipped in swiftly.

Billy went in to the pubes and pushed even farther.

"You're killing me," Deke breathed.

"I'm making love to you," Billy replied.

"Fuck me, you fucking faggot," Deke grunted, and Billy withdrew only to slam himself back in twice as hard. He watched the boy's lips curl back and his teeth clench together. Sweat moistened the skin above his lip. He pushed his head back into the pillow and exposed his throat for Billy to tongue and kiss and nip. Deke got his lips near Billy's ear and talked to him and got his arms around the man and fumbled for the bobbing ass. He slapped at Billy's cheeks and grabbed them, taking control of his own fucking. He pulled Billy into him with all his strength, breathing hotly into Billy's ear, begging.

"Is that all you got?" he grumbled. "Is that all of it? I need more, man. Give me more; I want more."

"You're a dirty little fucker," Billy panted, feeling his nuts knot up. A little earlier he had planned to put the boy through his paces, to try out a variety of positions. He had imagined Deke facedown, ankles in Billy's hands, being pushed into that position. Sweat dripped from Billy's chin. It wasn't likely he would finish this stroke without blowing, he was thinking, when Deke's ass began to rise up and suck Billy in. Deke's face was flushed. He sat up and pummeled his crotch, and the juice began to fly, the boy blowing air between clenched teeth. Billy's head dropped, and he pumped the boy's ass with fury while Deke hung on to his nipples. He shot and filled the reservoir tip of the rubber and then some. He pulled it off and held it like a stinking sock.

"Bathroom's around the corner," Deke said, his eyes closed dreamily.

When Billy padded back into the little bedroom, Deke said, "You ought to leave."

"Right," Billy said, turning around sharply and grabbing his clothes. He dressed quickly and was heading for the door. Deke walked behind him, wearing socks and the thick remains of a meaty erection. He unlocked the many locks and opened the door for Billy.

"That was, uh—" he said.

"It sure was," Billy said, nodding. He peeked again at the boy's swinging club and gave it a playful swat.

Oh, l'amour, Billy thought, taking the steps two at a time. He pushed the big glass door open. The night met him briskly. He could hear the far-off whine of sirens, and a whore singing a Madonna song walked past him, swinging her purse and her big hips. He checked his watch—it was just a little after 5 a.m. He wasn't far from the Darkroom.

The little after-hours club was jumping. The constant strobes cut into the colored smoke that hung heavy in the air with the sweat and beer and stink of men who had tried too hard all night long. Billy got himself up to the bar to get a glass of something, anything. He ordered a vodka on the rocks and, feeling someone pushing up behind him, turned around. It was Matt, the ex-pool boy.

"You must have gotten your studying done," he said, slurring.

"Studying?" Billy smiled, clueless. All he could think of was the Tulane b-ball boy.

"Your blood test?" Matt said.

"Oh," Billy said, looking around for the bartender.

"Oh," Matt echoed. He stared at Billy, and Billy stared back. Matt put his hand on the front of Billy's trousers and gave him a thorough groping. Billy's dick began to respond.

"I believe we are experiencing some mutual interest here," Matt said, and he looked down at his own crotch, which Billy saw was making itself apparent.

"Uh, yes, I've noticed that there does seem to be some chemistry here," Billy said.

"Between the two of us," Matt added.

"Well, yes."

"I want you to fuck my brains out," Matt said.

Somebody beat me to it, Billy thought, but it was hard saying no to someone who looked as good as Matt. Harder still to say no twice.

Billy leaned against him and slipped a hand into his shirt, feeling the boy's splendid hairless pecs and finding his pert nipple, then tweaking it.

"I've got a car," Matt said as a limousine pulled up to the curb.

Billy turned to Matt. "Yours?"

Matt nodded.

"Did you have this earlier?"

"You were in such a rush to leave," Matt said, shrugging.

"My loss," Billy mused.

"Is your gain," Matt added, fighting a grin.

The backseat was bigger than Deke's brother's bedroom. Matt wasted no time getting Billy undressed and ready for action. "Here?" Billy said, looking through the window that separated them from the driver.

"He likes to watch," Matt said. "And I save some money 'cause I don't have to give him a tip."

Billy sat back. He spread his legs, and his dick stuck straight up. "You see that all right?" he asked the driver.

"Yessir," came his response from the front.

Matt leaned over Billy's lap. He glanced up at the window. "You see this all right?" he asked again. "Let me know if you don't." He turned and put his mouth over Billy's big head.

He went all the way down, his lips stretched thin at the base. He stayed there a long time, swallowing and swallowing again. Then he came up for a breath of air.

"You taste like rubber," he said to Billy.

"That should make you feel fairly confident," Billy answered.

"It makes me horny," Matt said. "Who was it? Tell me all about it."

Billy laughed and leaned his head back along the plush seat. He saw a door set in between the two seats before him. "Hey, is that a bar?" he wanted to know.

Matt was unable to reply because his mouth was full. He tried to nod and scraped the top of Billy's shaft with his teeth. The driver answered for him: "It is, sir."

Billy opened the bar and poured himself a glass of vodka, amazed to find ice and even stirrers. He chewed on one while Matt blew him.

"So, what's your name?" Billy asked the driver.

"My name is Keith, sir," said the man. The limousine stopped at a red light. Billy peered into the dark hole, trying to make out Keith's features. All he could see was a strong jaw and longish sideburns and Keith's dark eyes lighting up in the rearview mirror, reflecting the wet streets before him. Billy looked down at Matt's head. It bobbed pleasantly, riding along the length of his rock-hard shaft.

Matt looked up and fumbled with the control panel behind him. A sunroof opened. Matt stood up, his pants came down, and Billy was suddenly face-to-face with Matt's perfectly shaped ass. Billy sniffed it, pushing his face between the flawless cheeks. He kissed the stubble of Matt's shaved puss and reached through his legs to palm the boy's balls. Matt arched his back, and his butt seemed to open like an abyss. Billy stroked himself while he ate out Matt's gaping hole—his pole was cued up and ready to go.

He stood behind Matt, enjoying the wind of the ride. His pecker bumped into the boy's greased slit when Keith hit a pothole. Matt grunted appreciatively. He took the dick all the way in and rubbed his butt against Billy's hipbones. Billy played with the boy's chest, his sculpted pecs, his cute pealike nipples. He did not notice the car pulling over and had no way of knowing that Keith had then leaned in through the window and taken Matt's cock into his mouth. Matt sighed heavily, and Billy took it as a compliment.

The street was rain-slicked and deserted, save for a whore up at the corner. Billy chewed on the back of Matt's neck and wiped his face across the boy's honey-blond hair. He felt a meaty finger probing his asshole, and he spread his legs a little, shifting around to accommodate the big hand he thought was Matt's. He fucked Matt a little harder, causing the model to beat dramatically on the roof of the limo with his hands.

Billy was closer to coming than he wanted to be, what with the finger pushing into him and helping him along toward shooting. It was ungentle and just what he needed. He pounded Matt ruthlessly, using the hole for his own pleasure, not caring much whether Matt was enjoying the ride. The finger fucking made him selfish, made him mean. He raped the boy's butt, their bodies slapping together. He stopped seeing his surroundings—the dark-faced buildings, the eerie light of the streetlamps, the lone prostitute not doing any business. He saw only the back of Matt's head and felt the pull of his pussy. He felt too the banging of his own heartbeat, thudding like a time bomb in his chest.

"It's going," he said, and he let it go, sloshing up Matt's eager butt with short shots of dick cream. He felt weak-kneed and sat down, leaving Matt to his own devices. He saw Matt's device, then the driver slurping over Matt's shaft. Billy pushed Matt's ass, giving Keith a mouthful.

"Yeah," Matt said into the cool morning air. "All right!" he shouted, and he unloaded with a great flourish into his driver's hungry mouth. Billy sipped his vodka and started dressing. A garbage truck rattled by, the men hanging off it staring at the bare-shouldered Matt. Billy checked his watch. He got out of the car. The streets were still dark, but the sky was light.

"We'll drive you," Matt said, panting.

Billy smiled at him and shook his head. "It's a nice morning. Think I'll walk." The smile stayed with him all the way home.

Hired Man

Jeremy slipped into the kitchen, where Mrs. Dooley was doing the breakfast dishes. "Late," she said without turning around. "Jacob's left already." She would never call him Jacob to his face, always Mr. Devereau, but alone with Jeremy she always tried to mark her territory in some way, as though they were competing for Devereau's attention. She turned, wiping her red hands on a dish towel, looking over Jeremy's head.

"You're still expecting breakfast?" she said.

"I am," Jeremy replied. He picked up the morning paper left by Jacob, giving himself something to look at besides the old bitch.

"Too indulgent, that Jacob," she muttered. Her iron hair, as thick and coarse as a horse's mane, was held back with two bobby pins. There was a clock on the wall over her head—it was just after 6.

Mrs. Dooley muttered and overcooked his eggs and left him alone to eat in peace.

Jeremy's father had worked for the Devereaus. He was gone now, dead at 42, just missing his son's high school graduation two years back. Jeremy's mother had been long gone, having run off with a seed salesman when Jeremy was 4, leaving father and son to fend for themselves. Sometimes, when he was drunk and maudlin, his father would get all weepy and ask God to bless the Devereaus. If it hadn't been for them…

Jacob was eight years Jeremy's senior and had command of the richest farmland in the county. The Devereaus weren't farmers, though, choosing to lease their lands, and they were one of the richest families in the state. Jacob's father had died not long after Jeremy's father, and a few days later Jacob's dark hair turned silver. He was a good and quiet man, and for that reason Jeremy had always considered him to be much older. He held himself like an older man, Jeremy thought—mature, intelligent, settled. He wasn't a tall man, but Jeremy was always surprised when they stood face-to-face and he was able to look Jacob in the eye, his leanness and quietude making him seem towering to Jeremy.

The west lawn was a five-minute drive and a half-hour walk. It wasn't yet hot, but the dew was off the grass already, making him feel all the more tardy. He half walked, half ran, getting a stitch in his side and cursing the hard soles of his boots. As he hurried he thought about the day's work ahead of him. There was an outbuilding Jacob wanted taken down and a rock boundary that needed mending. He stopped at the top of the hill that overlooked the west lawn, breathing hard. He could see Jacob standing by the shed he wanted dismantled. He was looking through the door as if something inside had caught his interest. He was wearing his straw hat, reminding Jeremy of van Gogh. He trotted downhill to join his boss.

"Didn't have to run," Jacob said, whispering.

"I was late," Jeremy answered, adding an apology.

Devereau stayed at the door, looking in. Jeremy looked too and couldn't see anything, until his eyes adjusted from the bright morning glare to the soft shade of the inside of the building. Then he could just make out the recumbent form of a man, stark naked.

"You want me to get rid of him?" Jeremy said quietly, ready to rouse the trespasser and send him on his way. He looked in again, taking in the whole expanse of the man's inert body: the dirty soles of his feet, his hair-covered legs, the ruddy droop of his ball sac and cock, his muscled gut, the twin peaks of his chest, his thick arms, one laid across his face, covering his eyes but not his bearded chin and half-open mouth. Jeremy felt a queer turn in his stomach, as though he recognized something frightening. The man lying there was unknown to him, but the feeling he got looking at his naked body was no stranger; he'd long been ignoring it—his whole life, he felt. He felt mortified, his cock rolling over, thumping to life. The sleeping man rolled over too, spreading his legs. Jeremy stared at the dark split of the man's ass, ashamed.

Devereau stepped back, taking care to keep quiet. He held his work gloves twisted in front of him.

"He's fixed it up nicely for himself," Devereau said with a half smile on his face.

"You said you saw smoke out this way the other night," Jeremy added.

Devereau turned to him. "Looks like we've got ourselves a tenant." He slapped his thigh with his gloves, looking back into the shed. Jeremy stole a glance at his boss's chambray work shirt, nearly all unbuttoned, showing the deep crevice between the thick slabs of his chest. The shirt was quick to come off when they worked out in the sun, and Jeremy had had ample opportunity to gaze upon and commit to memory the wide, dark areolae of Devereau's nipples as well as the wispy black hairs that grew around them.

"I'll tell you what," Devereau said. "Take the truck and run out to Fischer's and pick up that heating unit."

"Ride back?" Jeremy offered.

"No, believe I'll walk back. I can see the land better on foot." He turned his back to the cabin and looked out over the rolling pasture of the west lawn. Jeremy knew he was considering leasing it to Meyers Schwam for grazing land. Jeremy got himself into the truck, catching his ass on the cracked plastic seat, and then drove off, watching Jacob in the shaking rearview mirror. Before he topped the hill, he braked, seeing Devereau walking toward the cabin, stopping at the doorway, and then walking into the darkness.

There was a man at Fischer's who would look at Jeremy directly, making him uncomfortable. It wasn't the direct stare that was as unnerving as the man's good looks. The man's name was Mike Flowers, and his dark eyes would fix on Jeremy and stay on him, divining secrets. What he wanted, most likely, was not to harm Jeremy by revealing publicly what he had so easily figured out about the Devereaus' hired man but rather to share with Jeremy this secret and thereby get into his Wranglers. Jeremy, however, was still of the opinion that there was something wrong with himself, that he had something to be ashamed of, something that required all his will to ignore. No man, he figured—not Mike Flowers, not Jacob D.—would ever do what Jeremy wanted both men to do.

He walked into Fischer's, and Mike Flowers looked over Mr. Green's shoulder to see Jeremy standing there in his worn jeans and boots, his blue T-shirt washed and faded to sheerness in spots. Jeremy took off his Stetson and wiped the moisture from his brow with the crook of his arm, trying not to look back at the man. Mike Flowers was Jeremy's height and dark—he looked Italian but was actually German. His thick black hair was kept short, his face clean-shaven. The set of his mouth, Jeremy noticed long ago, was always in a sort of smile, as if there were always something amusing on his mind.

"That's fine with me," Mr. Green was saying, "but the missus said she wants this color. Do you have this color?"

"Well, not in stock, Mr. Green. This one's a special order. We're talking four to six weeks here," Mike said.

Jeremy walked down the fasteners aisle, wondering what Devereau had to say to the naked sleeping stranger. *Probably told him to clear out,* Jeremy decided. Devereau wasn't too fond of trespassers. Jeremy picked a bunch of nails from a bin and put them in his pocket. He could see clearly in his mind the man's form, his sprawl on the bedroll, and he could place himself between the hair-darkened thighs, pushing his face into that white moon, licking into the hair-choked split. He scooped up a small handful of carriage bolts and pocketed them, feeling with his fingertips the erection he'd developed. He put his hand over it, stroking himself.

He saw Mr. Green leave and heard Mike Flowers call from the counter: "You need any help, Jeremy?"

Shit, he thought. He untucked his shirt, but it did little to hide his erection. "I'm all right," he said, his voice sounding a little tight.

"That heating unit's in. You picking that up today?"

"Yup," Jeremy replied. He looked down at himself and was wondering how long it would take for his boner to deflate when Mike Flowers noiselessly rounded the corner. He saw it—Jeremy saw the man's eyes draw a bead on it like an eight-point buck—but he kept his mouth shut. He grabbed a plastic bag from a roll on the shelf and started filling it with finishing nails.

"Keith didn't show up this morning," Mike said quietly. "Probably went to the Darien last night."

Jeremy nodded absently, looking for something in particular on one of the lower racks.

Mike turned and faced Jeremy directly. He hefted the bag of nails casually on his palm, but a nervousness played over his lips and eyes.

"I suck dick too, you know," he said, his voice barely heard.

Jeremy kept his eyes on the rack the entire time. He nearly laughed when Mike caressed his behind, getting hold of a cheek and squeezing. Blood rushed to his face, and Mike squeezed again.

"I could suck yours," he said.

Jeremy kept quiet; not saying anything was not an admission of guilt, as far as he was concerned. The prospect of a blow job, however, filled his mind the way his dick had filled his pants. He'd long thought of a blow job from Mike Flowers, ever since he saw the man in bathing trunks on the lake trying to get up on water skis. There weren't many men in the town of Barley he fantasized about—there was Mike Flowers, of course; a couple of guys he went to high school with; Billy Barnes at the Texaco; and Travis in Westport with the red hair and green eyes.

And then there was Mr. Devereau. Jacob.

The thought of his boss gave Jeremy a start, and he stepped away from Mike Flowers, whose hand was making the rounds down between Jeremy's legs.

"Somebody's coming," Jeremy said in a sudden fit of clairvoyance, and Mike's hand flew from Jeremy's behind. Just then the door opened.

"Aren't you something?" Mike said, fixing himself. He too had gone hard, and he had a none-too-easy job concealing his excitement. He looked over his shoulder and waved easily at Eleanor Derby, Jeremy's first-grade schoolteacher. "Be right there," he said to her, smiling, looking back at Jeremy, his smile giving way to pain.

"What are you doing tonight?" He reached out and touched the front of Jeremy's jeans. A shudder passed through Jeremy's body, and his dick spat out gobs of come into the confines of his underpants. Mike seemed not to notice the convulsing and continued to stroke Jeremy until Jeremy shuddered and pulled away.

"I've got to go," Jeremy said, his shorts wet and uncomfortable.

"You want that heating unit?" Mike said, looking slightly disappointed.

"I'll be back later for it," Jeremy said, his boots clopping toward the door.

Jacob Devereau stood in the musty darkness of the cabin. Funny, he was thinking, that he'd come here intending to pull the place down and now it was inhabited by a naked sleeping man. A heavily sleeping man. There was an empty bottle of Four Roses beside him. Jacob stepped closer and closer, standing out of the way of the light that came through the door and fell over the body and its swarthy flesh. The man had changed position again and curled into himself, bringing a knee up to his chest, keeping the other leg straight. Jacob knelt by the man. He was strong-looking and long-bodied and smelled of whiskey mixed with sweat. Half of his face was covered with the crook of his arm. Jacob saw the small white scar on the man's left hip, the patch of hair that grew at the small of his back, spreading out thinly over his meaty buttocks, thickening again on his thighs. Between the press of his thighs lay his scrotum, mossed over with long, straight hairs.

He rolled over suddenly, his eyes still closed, but his breathing was less deep, less regular. Jacob ignored all of this for a closer look. The man's nose was long and hawkish. Thick lashes lay on the tops of his sunburned cheeks. His hair was brown and needed a cut. His lips were thin, and his chin was covered with beard. He had a rough beauty that was not lost on Jacob, who remembered all of this about him, the way he looked, because this was not the first time he had laid eyes on the man. He ran a finger down the furred thigh that covered the man's genitals. The leg moved easily, and his crotch was uncovered, and the cock fell into the widening V, thick with blood and the need to piss.

"I came back like I said," the man whispered.

Jacob nodded, unbuttoning his shirt. He threw it to the floor and wiped at the wide nipples that Jeremy was drawn to. Rather than fuss with his tight boots, he pushed his jeans down as far as they'd go. He put his hands on his bared hips, his cock a rocky jut from his groin. He closed his eyes when he felt the hand close around it, sliding the skin of it back. The head was kissed and licked; lips enclosed it, sucking the skin back into place.

The man blew Jacob until they were both breathless. He reached up and plucked at the rubbery nubs of Jacob's tits, snorting into the man's soap-smelling bush. A waterfall of spit spilled from the man's mouth and cascaded over Jacob's swinging nuts. Jacob took hold of the man's head and fucked it, looking down to see his heavy prick swallowed.

The man coaxed Jacob down onto the stinking bedroll. Getting between his thighs, he pushed his fingers into the thatch of hair that grew thickly under Jacob's balls, searching for the soft indentation. Jacob looked up at him with cool reserve, his fingers laced over his belly. He watched as the man spat on his own piece and hoisted it up, rolling a few fingers around Jacob's sensitive ditch, probing his insides. Jacob closed his eyes and waited for the fat cock to slide up into him, recalling the last time this same man had done this same thing to him and how good it had felt then.

It hurt at first, of course; it had been well over a year since the man had come around, and the only things to invade that region of his body since then were his thoughts and a finger every now and then, which did not compare with the solid hickory branch this man used. He composed himself, lifting his heels from the floor, his smooth thighs spread to accommodate the man's wide and bucking hips. He looked up to meet the man's wild eyes, bits of twig and leaves caught in his hair, blasts of his breath blowing down on his face, not foul but sweet, and Jacob reached up and hooked the man's neck, bringing his head down to his own to plunge his tongue into his lover's mouth, wanting to be fucked harder and deeper and faster. Grunting and spitting, the man rooted his bearded chin into Jacob's throat, biting and tonguing and leaving marks, pistoning into Jacob's hole the way they both wanted. The friction of the man's belly was just right against Jacob's burgeoning prick, and Jacob felt a surge in his groin, a singing in his nuts that signaled the beginning of the end. He got his hands full of the man's ass, digging his fingers into his crack, and forced all of him into his wide-open hole.

The man began to moan, his mouth just under Jacob's ear. His muscled gut, pressed against Jacob's crotch, was slicked with the seep that oozed from Jacob's cock. Jacob held his breath and tilted his head back. His toes cracked in his boots, and he felt a sweet release of come as he shot between them. He fingered into the man's hole and fiddled with the hardening there, and the man fell deep into Jacob and stayed there, gasping and filling him with a lava flow of semen.

They stayed together for a long time.

"How is it with your hired man?" the man asked. "I saw the two of you yesterday. He has a fine face."

"He's not like that," Jacob said with some regret.

Jeremy met Mike Flowers at the east end of the Devereau property. He'd been sitting in the truck an hour early, searching his soul, debating his conscience and lust. He fought with himself for an hour, trying to deny his true nature; then he saw the cockeyed beams of Mike's Bronco bouncing toward him. He breathed out hard, fighting the urge to shake. The Bronco pulled up beside him. Mike got out and came around to Jeremy's open window.

It was different with guys. There was no courtship, there were no preliminaries. Even with easy girls you might have to sit though a whole movie before you touched tit. Mike leaned in through the window and put his mouth on Jeremy's, reaching in and feeling up his crotch. He opened the truck door from the inside and opened Jeremy's jeans, took out his cock. Jeremy watched Mike's dark, bobbing head, feeling the intense, wet suck of the man's mouth riding the length of his shaft. He shifted, getting his legs out from under the steering wheel, hanging them out the door, leaning back on his elbows. He stopped thinking about things then. He was gripped by Mike's strong, callused hands, listening to the sucking noises Mike made, his senses activated. Mike took all of his cock into his mouth and swallowed, his throat constricting around Jeremy's blunt dick end. Jeremy let his head fall back, thinking, How easy.

Mike stopped abruptly, fumbling with his own pants. He took out his big pale hard-on that glowed ghostlike in the dark. "C'mon," he said urgently.

Jeremy got out of the truck clumsily, his knees shackled by his jeans. He bent at the waist and licked the white helmet of Mike's cock. It was already wet and tasted milky. He opened his mouth wide. He played with Mike's balls, heavy and big, much bigger than Jeremy's. He hefted them and twisted their loose, hairy sac and sucked the end of Mike's pecker. Mike grabbed Jeremy's head and fucked into his face, and Jeremy choked. He tasted more and more of Mike's precome and grew accustomed to the thrusts that came at him and did his best to accommodate the big-shafted slide it made into his mouth, to the back of his throat. He held on to Mike's hips for balance, urging the man to work harder. His own prick was fired up and ready; a countdown had started. Just having his mouth fucked was enough to bring him off. He touched himself every now and then, snorting into the curling hair that grew black and thick around Flowers's big cock.

"Good job," Mike was saying, his dick planted. "Real good." His thighs tensed, and his nuts jogged, and Jeremy was taking him all the way. Mike stood up on the running board, straightening Jeremy's back, and banged into the rough-edged hole. He went up on his toes and practically hollered when he came, and Jeremy, in concert, nearly wept as he let loose a hot load of come all over the crinkled legs of Mike Flowers's Dockers.

Mike wiped up his dick and licked his fingers. "That was sweet," he said thoughtfully, reaching out for Jeremy's arm and pulling his face up to be kissed. "Can we do it again?" he asked.

Jeremy pulled on his prick—it had yet to soften. "I suppose," he said. "If you want to."

"Not now," Mike laughed, cuffing his friend on the top of the head. "Some other time, though."

"Sure," Jeremy said, looking up at the starry sky. "Anytime."

He drove home, taking the long way. He could smell Mike Flowers's ass on his fingers. He did not feel released or unburdened—he didn't feel anything, except maybe that his dick had betrayed him. He never should have had anything to do with Mike Flowers, but he wondered when they'd get together again and grew hard thinking of the things they'd do. He was thinking he would like to fuck Mike Flowers, stand behind him with his hands on the man's hips and slam into him. His dick, hard, shifted and betrayed him again.

Jacob was up when Jeremy walked in the door. He sat in his chair in front of the television in his underclothes and an open bathrobe. A can of beer balanced on the chair arm. Jeremy stood in the middle of the room looking at the television. The news was on.

"You missed dinner," Jacob said. "You're a pain in Mrs. Dooley's ass."

"She's the ass pain. She hates my guts."

Jacob smiled.

Jeremy looked at him sitting on his threadbare throne, bare legs stretched out before him, blue broadcloth boxers tight at the thighs, gaping open at the crotch.

"Did you get rid of that guy?" he asked.

Jacob shook his head, keeping his eyes on the news. "I told him he could stay on awhile, give us a hand around here."

Awhile, Jeremy thought. *A hand.* He wondered if the guy had any clothes. He wondered if the guy was a cocksucker like Mike Flowers. *Like me.*

"You go to the movies again?" Devereau asked. He shifted in his chair, and his fly gaped more, catching Jeremy's eye.

He felt caught in the headlights of a truck speeding toward him. His mind went white, as blank as sheets, and he couldn't think of anything but the bouncing beams of Mike's Bronco's headlights. He stood there with his hands in his pockets, squirming like a worm on a hook, and Jacob seemed almost to smile.

Still Life With Dildo

Will Baines would have smoked, had he smoked. It seemed like a good idea, something to do with his hands. He was waiting in the lobby of the Drake, waiting to be sent up to Mr. Southworth's apartment—apartments, actually—at least that's what the concierge (or whatever he was called) said.

Will was in his first year at Columbia and was hard up for money. A buddy he worked out with told him about some of the modeling he had been doing for art classes at the Pratt and Parsons design schools. "Why not here on campus?" Will had asked.

His friend gave him a cockeyed look. "You think I want everyone here looking at my shit?" he said. Will had seen his friend's "shit" and thought it kind of nice, and he said to himself later, in the showers, that shit as nice as that should be seen all over the place. "Put a couple of signs up, man," the guy continued. "Put 'em up downtown. You'll get calls, I guarantee. And do yourself a favor—use a picture of yourself, something that shows off your body. Know what I mean?" He stepped into his jeans and shot a smile Will's way. "And put down that you're OK with private sessions. I got one now who'll pay twice what the profs can pay, and he's good for a couple of beers too. See you later."

Will could never remember this guy's name. Keith or Kyle or Karl, Will figured—some K name—but he wasn't sure. And lately he kept missing him at the gym.

"You may go up now," the man at the lobby desk said.

The elevator was a smooth, fast ride. The doors opened to a marbled entry hall, its walls hung with some impressive paintings of nudes. Will stepped up to a reclining female—the Southworth signature was small but decisive in the lower-right-hand corner.

No amateur, Will was thinking.

"Pardon me," a man's voice echoed in the hard and shiny room.

"Mr. Southworth," Will said, extending his hand and smiling at the handsome 40-ish man who stood in the doorway.

"I am Hartley, Mr. Baines," the man corrected. "I have been instructed to direct you to the studio where you will work with Mr. Southworth. Would you follow me, please?"

Will nodded and followed Hartley through a long and narrow hall, white and spotlighted and strangely without any doors opening off of it, except for the double doors he could see in the distance, at the end of the corridor. Hartley opened the doors and stepped back for Will to enter.

The room was huge and open to the sky through a bank of windows set in the ceiling, and it was bare, save for a screen, a chair, a table, and an easel beside another table that was set up with paper and supplies—sticks of charcoal, Conté crayons, graphite, and pastels—everything neat and orderly. Will sat down in the chair. It was draped with white muslin, and the screen was set up behind it. The table had a bowl of flowers on it. The skylights were also curtained with muslin, and the light filtered through cleanly. Will looked down at his ankles—tanned still from spring break in Fort Lauderdale—tapering down into the neon tops of his running shoes. He put his hand on his chest between his pecs, his pinkie brushing his nipple. It quickly went hard, and he calculated the number of weeks that had gone by since he last got laid—a disappointing roll on a dormitory mattress with a girl named Christy. His dick began to take a short, restricted stroll in the confines of his jeans. The door opened.

"Good day there," a man said.

Will tried again. "Mr. Southworth?" he asked, getting up and walking across the room, very much aware of the quite visible lump in his jeans.

Mr. Southworth wasn't nearly as old as Will had expected. He was a tall, well-built man who seemed to be in his late 30s, Will guessed. His hair was red and longish, curling at the back of his neck, and just beginning to recede. His face was tanned, freckled across the nose. He was unshaven, and a sandy shadow of red and gold fell across his cheeks and chin. He gripped Will's hand firmly and shook it three times. Brick-colored hairs curled at the man's throat, sprouting up from under a white T-shirt and a blue button-down shirt. He looked to Will as though he'd just stepped off a yacht.

"Nice to meet you, Will," Southworth said. "Your friend Kevin recommended you highly." His eyes dropped and toured, making a glancing appraisal, and Will tried to get used to the scrutiny. This was his first gig—he hadn't even gotten around to making his posters when Southworth gave him a call. He didn't even know how Kevin—*So that's his name*, he thought—had gotten his phone number.

"Let's get started," Southworth said. "You can undress behind the screen."

Will undressed quickly and stepped out from behind the screen. Southworth was busy with his setup. Without looking up, he said to Will, "Push that table away, would you? Maybe later for that."

Will settled into the chair, and Southworth got behind his easel, glancing at him and looking up at the light that poured in. "Get comfortable," he said, and Will found a posture that seemed enduring. "Yes, that's quite nice," Southworth said. Embarrassed and unsure of himself, Will did what he could to keep from smiling. He didn't even know what to look at.

"Chip," Southworth said.

"Beg your pardon?" Will said, raising his eyebrows high, afraid to move any other body part.

"My name is Chip," Southworth repeated. "Rather, that's what I'm called. Please call me Chip."

Will heard the scratch of charcoal against paper—that and Southworth murmuring to himself again and again, peering around the side of the easel. He moved around a great deal, stepping back to eye his work and lifting his arms over his head and stretching.

"You're good," he said after a while. "Kevin was right."

Will made a mental note to buy his lifting partner a beer sometime.

"Your legs are quite defined," Southworth said a bit later. "You must run."

And then, after what seemed like hours to Will's restless body, Southworth made a suggestion: "How about a break?"

Will got up from his pose and shook his limbs to revive them. The studio door opened, and Hartley carried in a tray with bottles and glasses. Will put his hands over his crotch, suddenly very much aware of his nakedness. Hartley seemed not to notice and went about pouring bottled water into the two glasses. He handed one to Southworth and carried Will's over to him. Will had to uncover himself with one hand to take the glass.

"You're doing a fine job," Southworth said when Hartley had left the room. He paused to take a drink. "I'm glad you're different from your friend—that your body types are different, I mean."

Will nodded. Kevin was a couple of inches shorter and packed with muscle across the chest, shoulders, and arms. His legs were squat and a little bowed and furry with dark hair. Will was leaner, with longer muscles, and smoother, save for his thick brown bush of pubes. He absently plucked at them with his free hand. "Would you rather sit?" he heard Southworth say.

"Actually, no," he answered.

Southworth got himself a stool. "So, tell me about yourself," Southworth said.

"Not much to tell," Will replied. "I'm from upstate, a little town near Syracuse. I'm going to school."

Southworth hooked his heels on the stool's lower rung, and his knees split wide. Will spotted a darkness in the crotch of the man's pants where a seam had come undone and was now filled, Will guessed, with a wiry growth of curly snatch hair. Southworth did not speak much—and certainly not about himself—but was very attentive, and he drew much out of Will: about his growing up, key events in high school, what made him decide to study literature. But all the while Will spoke, he could not keep his eyes from the magnetic hole in Southworth's chinos. And he could not shake the strangeness of the situation—telling his life story while standing naked before another man. He had had the usual experiences with nudity—communal showers in the high school locker room, an occasional skinny dip with his buddies, and, of course, physical examinations, to which this situation seemed most similar. All that was missing was the rough handling of his balls and Southworth's telling him to cough.

They got back to work. Southworth wanted a number of shorter poses, standing this time. Will's mind wandered, listening to the soft noise of Southworth's drawing. His thoughts were now drawn to the dark hole in Southworth's chinos, and he found himself wondering what it would be like to touch his finger there—to put his tongue there, even. He imagined Southworth up on the stool with his legs on Will's shoulders. To his horror his prick began a jerky rise. He thanked God that his back was turned to Southworth, and Will concentrated on the shadow of his body that fell across the floor until he noticed the prominent silhouette of his engorged pecker jutting out from his midsection.

"Now face me," Southworth said, "and put your arms up over your head."

"I, uh…" Will said haltingly. "I need to go to the bathroom, I think." He said this over his shoulder. Southworth came out from behind his easel, fingering a stick of charcoal. Will laughed nervously.

"Oh," Southworth said. "Happens all the time. Happened just the other day to your friend Kevin."

Will took a step toward the door, trying his best to conceal his hard-on.

"I'll ring for Hartley—" Southworth offered.

"N-no, I can find it," Will stammered, limping to the door, his dick vibrating stiffly.

"There's an old trick models have when this sort of thing arises," Southworth said, getting to the door before Will and stopping him there. He glanced at the strong, thick stump that constituted Will's erection, its big pale head sporting a gaping piss slit. Hartley stepped in then, as good as summoned, ready to take care of the matter at hand. He too looked at Will's cock, sizing him up. "It's almost more thick than long," Southworth observed.

"Sir," Hartley said, nodding in agreement.

"Hartley will take care of this for you, Will. Hartley was once a model himself, weren't you, Hartley? And a damn fine one too," Southworth continued, without waiting for a response. "My uncle hired him for me when I came home from studying at the Sorbonne. And he's been with me ever since." Southworth settled onto his stool again and spread his legs, exposing that dark hole. He wiped his charcoaled hands on this thighs. "Anyway," he said with a wave of his hand, "time is wasting, and there's only so much good light left."

"Please be seated," Hartley said, and Will sat down on the chair by the screen, his rod standing upright. Hartley pushed Will's knees apart and positioned himself on his knees between the boy's bare feet.

"I—" Will started.

"Oh, it works," Southworth assured the boy. "Works every time. You just sit back and relax, and Hartley will take care of you."

Will looked at the man at his feet. His hair was the color of steel, and his eyes were blue. His tongue slipped out and went over his lips as he bowed his head over the fat of Will's prick. Will felt the man's breath first, a warm rush of air. He looked over at Southworth, who sat watching with interest. He winked at Will, smiling coolly and nodding as Hartley closed his mouth around the pink flange of Will's cock head.

Hartley took the thing to the bone, his jaw seeming to dislocate to accommodate Will's clublike thickness. He felt Hartley's throat tighten around the end of his dick. *This is crazy,* he was thinking. He also thought of his gym pal, Kevin, sitting in this very chair and getting his knob worked over. *Would love to have been here for that,* he said to himself, leaning back and closing his eyes, feeling the warm liquid of Hartley's mouth sliding up and down his shaft, slipping off to nibble on Will's balls, sliding a tongue under them and lifting them. They rolled into his mouth, and he sucked hard on them. Will squirmed. He'd never been blown so excellently—he had yet to find a girl even willing to give him head, save for some chick he picked up once at the shore who blew him under the boardwalk. But that job paled in comparison to the one he was getting from Hartley, who went back to Will's throbbing stick and swallowed it again and again. Will grabbed the man's head and fucked his cock into that hot mouth, stretching Hartley's lips thin and tight, gagging him with the fat, hard stubby.

"You wanna eat my load, pal?" he said, oblivious now to Southworth, who was sitting still and rapt, his mouth opened slightly, a rage of hardness buckled up in his tight chinos.

"Yes," Will heard Southworth croak, his voice crumbling with lust. "Give it to him."

Will stared at Southworth and twisted his fingers into the grayed hairs of Hartley's head, blasting a mouth-filling load into him, cursing through clenched teeth, his whole body twitching as Hartley sucked out the last stringy remains from Will's hypersensitive piss hole.

"Very nice," Southworth said, getting up from his stool, his cock visible in outline. He went back to his easel, his hands from time to time pressing on the formidable lump that lay like pipe beneath the thin cloth of his pants. Hartley got himself to his feet, wiping his mouth with his fingers and pulling a handkerchief from his pocket, handing it to Will. Will looked at the white cloth, realizing he was to wipe himself with it.

"So," Southworth said casually, "if you'll just stand beside the chair and maybe lean against it, we'll see how that looks."

Getting back to work, Will found the time passing quickly. He glanced at Southworth, who came out from behind his easel to study something, some odd cast of light or problem with foreshortening, absently thumbing the fly of his trousers. He crossed his arms over his chest and smiled. "I see," he said, "that we're running into that problem again," as Will felt the beginnings of another erection, the slow, lumbering fill of blood as his pecker fattened and stood out from his body like a railroad spike.

"I'm really sorry," Will said, sure that his modeling days were over, at least with Chip Southworth.

"Not to worry," Southworth said. "I was just going to suggest we wrap up anyway." As he spoke he kept his gaze on Will's hard-on, and he had his hands on his belt, undoing it and then his pants, opening them up and letting them fall to his knees. He toed off his loafers and unbuttoned his shirt so that he was standing in his undershirt and nothing else, his long curving prick protruding like a saber. His thighs were muscled and freckled, and his crotch was dark with hair the color of brick and mud and clay. Will stood still, as if locked in a pose. Having just received his first blow job from a guy (which was fantastic enough), Will decided—since that's what he had been wanting ever since he was a teenager, when he fell in love with everyone from Mr. Tucker, his baseball coach, to the calculus teacher he had in 11th grade to his geeky but massively hung neighbor Freddie Schwartz, who didn't mind jacking off in front of Will—to have another shot at getting off, all in the same day and with another, even hotter, guy. It was almost too much. Almost.

"I've obviously overestimated Hartley's talents," Southworth said. "Or perhaps I've underestimated yours."

Southworth took a few steps toward Will, close enough to touch Will's belly with the pointed end of his prick. He put his hands on Will's chest, palming the boy's nipples, leaving the black dust of charcoal on them. He mauled the muscles and took Will's points between his thumb and forefinger, pulling hard and twisting. Will felt weak and enslaved; no one had ever touched him this way. His dick twitched heavily, its end greasy with ooze. Southworth let go of Will's tits and put his hands on the boy's shoulders. Will felt his knees go weak.

He had never had cause to think of himself as a cocksucker and had never really imagined it ever happening, but he found himself now with Southworth's worthy dick in his face. He looked up at Southworth's face, handsome as a movie star's, and swallowed hard. "I never—" he started, and he saw Southworth smile.

"It's easier than you think," the man said. Will looked at the cock, which seemed suddenly quite long. He opened his mouth and tasted the tip. He sniffed the shaft and pushed the man's balls with his tongue. Southworth held the thing down for him, and it slipped into Will's mouth easily. "Not too much at once," he heard above him. "This is best when eased into." The smooth head slipped over his tongue, in and then out, and stringy spit thick as honey fell onto Will's knees. The cock went back in—more of it this time—and Will felt himself fighting a gag. Southworth's hands dropped to Will's tits again, causing Will to grip his own dick, jacking the hot fistful. He heard Southworth make a noise—a moan, maybe, or a deep-rooted sigh—as Will took the man deeper into his throat.

Southworth put his hands under Will's armpits and pulled him up. He pushed the boy back until Will felt the edge of the table against his butt. Southworth removed the vase and told Will to sit up on the table. "Lie back," Southworth said, and

Will did, with his butt at the end and his legs hanging over, his toes not touching the floor. Southworth got in between his legs. "Put your heels up," he said, and Will did, feeling the first lick of tongue on his butt hole, causing him to yelp and tighten up convulsively. Southworth poked into the hole with his finger, and Will's mind swirled: *No way* gave way to *Maybe*.

"That's quite a grip you've got there," Southworth said.

"Thanks—I think," Will replied.

"Have you ever?" Southworth asked from Will's crotch.

"Not ever," Will said, looking up at the ceiling as Southworth moved his finger in and out of the boy's hole. It was not unpleasant, but Will worried about his personal hygiene. "Am I, uh…clean down there?" he wanted to know. "I could wash up or something."

"You're fine, just fine," Southworth said. As if to prove this, he lapped the hole with his velvety tongue, soaking the dark hairs that surrounded it, even pushing into Will's boy cunt, causing the boy to curl his toes and make throaty noises. He crossed his arms over his face, amazed at the strangeness of things, especially the fact that a man's head was between his legs, chowing on his bung hole. *Weird as hell*, he thought, *but not bad, not bad at all.* He felt himself opening up to Southworth's hungry mouth, his hole going soft and mushy.

"You wouldn't mind if I introduced a little toy, would you?" Southworth said, getting up. Will's asshole missed Southworth's gnawings immediately. Will watched the man walk over to the table and open a drawer. He saw Southworth pull out a dildo.

"You said 'little,' " Will said, propping himself up on his elbows. Southworth was wielding a fake pecker that was bigger than any other Will had ever seen—thick as his own, if not thicker, and a couple of inches longer than Southworth's. The man held it like a billy club, and it occurred to Will that he'd almost *rather* it were a billy club.

"Are you game?" the man said.

Will swallowed hard. It didn't seem possible, having that thing up inside him. Where, he wondered, would his displaced innards go?

"We'll get you started with something smaller," Southworth said, his tone warm and jocular. He rubbed his hands together as if he were going to give Will a rubdown. He licked his finger and pushed it into Will. He swirled it around, and Will squirmed but decided it wasn't all that bad. The second finger wasn't so hot at first—and he almost said "Forget it"—but that too began to feel all right after a while as Southworth worked them in and out and in again.

Will sat up to look at Southworth, who was intent on his work and staring at Will's pussy as if it were a work of art. Will's cock hovered hard over his belly. He petted it, and it bobbed and stiffened more. Without thinking, he smeared a finger on his piss slit and brought the gooey digit to his mouth to taste the dripping honey that was on it. Southworth noticed this, and Will felt for a moment as if he had been caught picking his nose. He held out the finger for Southworth to try.

Will soon asked for Southworth to insert a third finger into his hole, and a fourth followed shortly thereafter. Southworth was fucking him with half a hand, assuring Will that he was ready for the next step. Southworth stood up and thumbed his prick down until the head slipped into Will's gash.

"This is nice," Southworth said, running his hands along Will's smooth thighs, massaging the muscles cabled beneath the skin. The cock head slipped in easily, the hole already soft, wet, and heated up. Southworth pushed himself in all the way so that the curling hairs of Will's ass commingled with the wiry bush that surrounded the base of Southworth's shaft. The man bent over the boy and put his lips to Will's sternum, leaning to the right to slide over a beady nipple and take it gently in his teeth. Will squeezed his eyes shut; his nips were almost too sensitive, and the toothy pressure took his breath away. His cock squirmed, trapped between their bellies, and he bucked his hips for some friction, feeling the furry rasp of the hairs that covered Southworth's lower abs and spread up across his chest, nearly concealing his red nipples. Will sought those out with his fingers, got them in his grip, and hung on them, causing Southworth to moan and hump into Will with short jerky jabs.

This is kind of nice, Will was thinking. He lay on his back, legs in the air, held by the ankles in Southworth's firm grip. He got his hand on his dick and stroked himself to match the stroke of Southworth's boner deep inside him. He looked into the man's sky-blue eyes, and a familiar feeling washed over him, which was odd because he couldn't have found himself having an odder experience than the one he was having right now. He closed his eyes and saw a flash of something: a baseball falling from nowhere, out of the air like some fallen piece of sky. It hit him squarely between the eyes, knocking him on his ass. When he opened his eyes again—they would both be black the next day, his nose broken—he saw his coach's face, beard-rough, sunburned, openmouthed. "You OK?" Coach wanted to know. Will couldn't speak. A bag of ice found its way gently over his face, and Coach Tucker put his hand on Will's chest and kept it there. "Break it up and hit the track—five miles in a half hour, or you'll do it all over again till you get it right!" he shouted, and Will's teammates jogged away grumbling. Will tried to get up too. "No way, sport," Coach said, his hand centered strongly between the boy's tits, fingers rubbing over

Will's left nipple, making him feel bad and good all at once. "You stay put," Coach said, touching the boy's thigh firmly and sensually, so that Will found himself erect, his athletic cup filling with hard, bent dick, the cup rising, dislodging. "Enough of that, now," Tucker said, his hand glancing over the considerable bulge and patting the boy's stomach.

Southworth pulled out with a soft sucking noise, and he slapped Will's flank. "Down," he ordered, and Will got off the table. Southworth turned him around and bent him over the table, pushing his legs apart. He entered Will again, holding on to the boy's white ass cheeks. Will tilted his pelvis to get more of Southworth's dick, and he played with the dildo that lay on the table. He gripped the monster thing with both hands and looked at the rubber head. It appeared to be bigger than the circle Will could make with his mouth. The shaft filled his hands, and the head was a challenge in itself. "Lick it," he heard Southworth say. "Go ahead and taste it. That prick was up your buddy's ass just yesterday."

"You're full of shit," Will said, twisting around to look at the man fucking him.

"Honest," Southworth said, pumping a little more roughly, making the boy grunt and drop his head onto his folded arms. Southworth reached under and grabbed Will's fevered cock. He jacked the wrist-thick piece, and Will sniffed the dildo, catching a funky scent of something. He licked the tip with his tongue, tasting the salty-sweet flavor that remained. *Wouldn't mind reaming him myself,* Will thought, and his dick ached with the image of the sweaty, hairy fucker squatting down and taking Will's prick up the butt.

The image was so vivid that Will found himself sucking in earnest on the giant rubber cock and taking Southworth's thrusts with pleasure. The man's handling of his pecker was bringing him closer and closer, and something inside him—some button or knob—went hard from the knocking of Southworth's cock. Will felt some switch get triggered that made his dick stiffen even more and cannonball a series of gobs that emptied completely his big bag of balls. He shouted out with each burst, choking himself on the huge dildo and driving Southworth to distraction. The man pummeled into the boy's hole and brought himself just short of shooting when he pulled out and sprayed his cock lotion all over Will's sweaty, muscled back.

Will was hefting a pair of dumbbells when he spotted Kevin.

"What's up?" they said simultaneously.

"You see Southworth?" Kevin asked, pulling at the crotch of his cutoff sweats, filled excellently.

Will stared at the elastic waistband of jockstrap that showed. He nodded.

"I'm taking a drawing class this semester," Kevin added casually. His eyes seemed to stroll across Will's body. He looked up from whatever he was looking at and smiled, green eyes lighting up. "I could use a model myself," he said. "Some figure studies. You know."

WIll nodded, starting to smile himself.

"Do you, like, have a student rate?" Kevin asked. "Could you cut me some sort of break or something?"

Will did a few curls with the dumbbells. His biceps balled as big as grapefruits. He bent over, dropped the weights, and looked up at Kevin, his head at crotch level.

"Yeah," Will said, winking, "I think we can work something out."

The Fall of Richmond

"Dick." He ignored the nagging voice and rolled over. "Dick?" He pulled the covers over his head, pushing his face into the pillow. The dreams he'd been having were vague now, they were fleeting, and he tried to force his way back into them. He was following Richmond up the rickety metal ladder on the side of Moseby's water tower.

"*Dick!*" The last one was too firm, too punctuated, to be ignored.

"Earlene, for Christ's sake, it's Sunday," Dick growled. "What in Jesus' name could possibly be of such vital importance?" He threw off the covers to see his wife's pinched and unhappy face and wondered again what he'd ever seen in her to begin with. It was not that she was unlovely, but here was a woman whose looks had been overwhelmed by her mean-spiritedness.

"My car won't start," she hissed, all but spitting and trying like hell to hold her Sunday tongue. "I can't get the girls and me to church."

He got himself out of bed, ignoring the big poke of his piss hard-on, threw on whatever was handy, and stomped down the steep and narrow staircase and out the front door. He saw his daughters sitting prim and pretty in the backseat with their Barbie dolls. He waved hello and sneaked a peek crotchward to make sure his boner wasn't as obvious as it felt. He got in and tried to turn the engine over. Nothing. The battery was drained completely, and he noticed then that the interior light switch was turned on, probably since last night, when Earlene came home from bingo smelling of cigarette smoke and peach schnapps. He swore under his breath and looked into the rearview mirror to see his daughters' keen ears offended by their blasphemer of a father. Dick jumped the car's battery with his pickup, then stood waving in the cold as his fuming wife and spoiled kids sped off to church.

Back in bed Dick grabbed one of Earlene's pillows and shoved it down between his legs, luxuriating in the cool, starched plain of percale. His dick, still hard despite the morning chill and the long piss, made a channel for itself in the smoothness of the pillow—in and out, in and out—and he thought about what he always thought about and came easily, his cock smearing into the warm cream. He stripped Earlene's pillow and threw the soiled case toward the bathroom and settled down under the covers to fall asleep for another few hours.

When he awoke, the covers were gone, kicked to the floor, and Earlene's brother was standing in the doorway.

"What are you staring at, Richmond?" Dick mumbled, only half surprised to see his brother-in-law. He rolled over to hide his naked cock and gave Richmond a pleasant view of his hairy butt.

"You ain't put on no weight since high school, have you?" Richmond said, leaning against the doorjamb. He crossed his arms over his chest.

"Just losing my hair, is all," Dick said, wondering whether he should grab one of Earlene's pillows for cover. "It's only been…what, five years?"

"Earlene's over at Ma's," Richmond said, ignoring the last of what Dick said. He looked past Dick and out the window. Richmond still lived with his mother. He had his own diner, though, where he cooked breakfasts and lunches six days a week. He was probably half an inch taller than Dick, just shy of six feet, and was still fairly high-school trim himself. He had just the smallest beginnings of a gut, so far as Dick could tell.

"I suspect she'll be there all day," he said in a lazy way, just looking out the window with his dark-lashed green eyes. His right arm boasted a tattoo of a breaking heart that he got when they went to a tractor pull in McGraw not too long ago. He never bothered to explain its significance, but it seemed somehow fitting, Dick thought, what with Richmond being kind of somber and always looking like he lost something dear to him. "Darnell and her rats are coming up from Cato," he added.

Dick leaned on one elbow, his head on his hand. He kept one leg bent forward, covering his stuff. He liked his brother-in-law a lot, knew him before he knew Earlene, who wasn't out of junior high back then. He and Richmond were best buddies then, hanging out after vo-tech. Dick was in the auto-mechanics department, and Richmond was studying culinary arts. They spent their weekends together, not really mixing with the others in their class. They went hunting and fishing and tinkered with an old Mustang that Dick's dad kept in the garage.

The mention of Darnell seemed to make Richmond a little wistful, and Dick wondered if maybe his brother-in-law regretted their recent split-up. Darnell had been a waitress at the diner at one time. She had four kids already and claimed to have another one on the way with Richmond's name on it, but Dick wasn't so sure of that. Theirs was a short-lived hitch. Darnell couldn't stand the thought of being married to a short-order cook, even if he did own his own kitchen, and Richmond...well, Richmond just couldn't get used to the instant responsibilities he found himself facing. The divorce came as no surprise, especially to Dick, who knew all along that Richmond wasn't exactly what you'd call the marrying kind. He always seemed to Dick to be something of a man's man, with little time for the frivolities of women. Dick always admired Richmond's self-sufficiency; indeed, there was a little pedestal in his heart on which Richmond stood, shy and serious, a ripped flannel shirt and nothing else tied around his waist, his almost-black hair the way it used to be, grown long and curling like a girl's and just pretty. *Earlene should have such pretty hair*, Dick was thinking now.

Richmond pressed his arms up over his head and let out a loud yawn. His shirt rose, and Dick looked at his friend's belly. He hadn't seen Richmond in just his skin in a long time. Richmond put his arms down, and his stomach got covered again, and Dick felt himself thickening under the cover of his leg, his prick heating up and getting hard.

He got up quickly, turning his back on Richmond, looking for something to put on. He found his sweats on the floor by Richmond's feet. He stepped into them, staring at Richmond's blue Converse high-tops. The sweats did little to disguise his tumescent condition, but at least it was covered, and he actually liked the bobble of it. He straightened up and looked Richmond in the eye, feeling cocky and hellish. He pushed his shoulders back and stuck out his chest. He was close enough to smell Richmond's breath.

The doorbell rang.

Richmond sighed, a sad-sounding exhalation. Dick's shoulders dropped a little.

Dick swiped at his pecker as it bounced with him down the steps to the front door. He opened it and saw Timmy Green, his next-door neighbor's kid. Dick felt a blast of cold air and dismay.

"What's up?" he asked, adding, "I ain't alone," in hushed tones. He stared through the screen door at the skinny kid standing there shivering in a T-shirt and jeans. He had his hands jammed into his pockets, and his shoulders shook.

"I'm locked out," Timmy said.

Dick just stood there. As much as he wanted to, he couldn't bring himself to ask the kid in.

"I was wondering if you still had that spare key," the kid said, his teeth chattering.

"Not since that butt-lick brother of yours broke in and they had the locks changed."

Timmy made a face. "Well, can't I come in, then?" Timmy asked, shaking hard. Dick caved in and pushed open the screen door. The air tightened his skin and turned his nipples into little pink pebbles. He was just about to warn Timmy to keep his trap shut when the toilet flushed upstairs and Richmond came ambling down the steps, fumbling with the buttons of his fly.

"Hey, Timmy," Richmond said to the boy, then turned to Dick. "Ain't you got coffee?"

Dick made coffee—or a close approximation of the beverage—leaving his two houseguests in the living room. He kept glancing down the front of himself, past the twin slabs of his pecs and the wiry down that covered them to the bump his dick made in his sweats. He tried to rearrange the configuration of his cock and balls, but to no avail; they poked out noticeably.

He shrugged. What the hell; it wasn't as if either Richmond or Timmy hadn't seen it before, except that Timmy was probably the only one looking now. Dick had seen plenty of Richmond in the old days, and Richmond had plenty to be seen. He had a regular banger, Dick recalled, feeling almost nostalgic, and he could see the big swinging thing clearly, as if he'd seen it every day since then.

But he hadn't, although there was a part of him that wished he had. That part was small and deep, and he kept batting it down, boning the missus and the baby-sitter and the secretary in the finance department down at the Ford dealership...and, every once in a while, Timmy Green. Yet whenever he was alone and palming it—this a.m., for instance—he had in his mind an image of Richmond climbing the water tower, bare-assed and yelling at the top of his lungs: "Dick Winkler, I fuckin' love you, man!" It was amazing that the whole town hadn't heard him bellowing. Oh, sure, they were fucked-up, and sure, it was a Sunday and everyone was in church probably, except for these two, and sure, Richmond also turned around then and farted like an old man who'd eaten 90 years of beans, a sort of trumpet that heralded his declaration and rendered it, at least in Dick's mind, null and void. That he loved Richmond was his own little dirty secret, one that he decided then and there to keep forever to himself.

What he did with the Green boy was another dirty secret and a huge source of shame for Dick Winkler. The skinny kid didn't mind hanging out with Dick in his garage, tinkering with that old Mustang and shooting the shit and sucking Dick's dick every now and then. Timmy himself had a horse-size appendage he liked to show off, and Dick would be talking about something, his head under the hood, and turn to see Timmy spread out on the workbench with his jeans around his ankles and his big old joint flopping around in his grasp like half a boa constrictor frozen stiff. Dick would stand transfixed, staring at the huge, weepy thing, and would throw a rod himself that was no less instinctual, no less demanding, and he'd have to pull it out and whack off himself.

He wasn't too comfortable now, having the two of his secrets together like that in his living room, and he stood by the door to make sure Timmy kept to himself. He could see the boy sprawled in the chair by the wood stove, which was being stoked by Richmond. Dick saw Timmy's glory trapped in the tight confines of his left pant leg, as clear as day. *Kid ought to do something about that,* Dick thought before realizing that Timmy went without underwear more for Dick's sake than for any other reason.

Dick threw a glance at Richmond, who was crouched in front of the little wood stove. He could see the pale patch of skin left bare by the gap between Richmond's sweatshirt and jeans, and he could see that Richmond too went without drawers today. Dick's bothersome peter warmed up again. He stroked himself gently, ignoring present company, and found himself under the watchful eye of Timmy, who threw a hand over his own pants-bound snake.

It didn't seem a half-bad idea, having some kind of circle jerk with his first love and his latest suck buddy. Certainly his dick was all for it. He shook his head, and the crazy idea rattled around in there like a lone marble. *I'm going fuckin' nuts,* he said to himself. He made a mean face at Timmy that was supposed to say, *Cut it out.* He turned around and went back to the kitchen stove, where the coffee was boiling on a burner. It smelled about right, he decided, and he said out loud, "Good enough."

As he was pouring the coffee into mugs, he heard Richmond whistle and say, "Timmy Green, what in the world have you got there in your pants, for crying out loud?"

Dick quickly called out, "Hey, Richmond, your coffee's done, so come and get it."

"Dick, you got to see this. Boy, is that real?"

"Oh, Jesus," Dick muttered.

"Fuck right, it's real," Timmy said, and Dick closed his eyes to say a quick prayer to the good Lord above that Timmy would keep his mighty staff in his pants.

"Richmond," he barked. "Coffee's getting cold!"

"*Ho-o-oly,*" Richmond whistled. "That is something."

Dick loudly clanged a spoon around in his mug, wondering what the hell he was going to do about this. Just then he heard Richmond ask, "Don't it get any bigger? I'm just curious, is all."

"Sure it does," Timmy replied, and Dick shook his head, feeling forsaken.

Richmond joined Dick in the kitchen, fidgeting with the crotch of his jeans. "Boy," he said, his eyes wide and serious. "You should see that kid's equipment, Dicky. He has an abnormally large schwanker." He took the cup Dick held out for him.

"Like you don't give him no competition," Dick said sullenly, jealous of his little buddy's sudden notoriety. "Your dick's as fat as my fist. What you lack in length, you more'n double in width." He shot a glance at Richmond's crotch. "Looks like you're toting a fucking soup can in there."

Richmond's mouth fell open, and only the smallest air escaped. He looked at Dick as though he'd received an awful shock, a mess of bad news, and Dick was speechless himself with fear and embarrassment.

"Look," he said slowly. "I didn't mean..."

Richmond blinked his big green eyes.

And then, as if on some terrific cue, the Green boy came into the kitchen with his swaying dangle of boy meat hanging out of his open fly. It made at least an eight-inch drop, weighed down by a ponderous ovoid head. He stepped up behind Richmond and slid his hands up under his sweatshirt. Dick watched the hands under the gray fleece come around on either side of Richmond's torso and lay to rest near or on Richmond's pert little Hershey's Kiss nipples.

"*Ho-o-oly,*" Richmond whispered.

Made bold by Timmy's derring-do, Dick put his hands on Richmond's jeans, opening them. He uncovered a lot of black hair and the fat white sausage he hadn't seen in five years. He picked it up out of its pubic nest—it filled his hand as though he'd grabbed someone's ankle—and pulled on it, tugging gently. It fattened even more, going stiff under Dick's manipulations.

Richmond's hands held on to the coffee cup as though it were a lifeline. Timmy pinched and twisted on the man's nipples, causing him all sorts of pleasure, and Dick was doing a fine job jerking him off. *Did he ever know how much he'd been wanting this?* Dick wondered of his brother-in-law. He looked down and saw himself poking stiff and straight against the worn sweats, spotting himself with precome. He dropped to one knee and brought his face into the soft black hairs that grew in thick below Richmond's navel. The rest of his torso was smooth, milky-skinned. Timmy lifted the sweatshirt, and Dick put his mouth on Richmond's pointed tit.

Timmy took the coffee mug out of Richmond's hands, setting it on the counter. He pulled the sweatshirt all the way off and threw it behind him. Dick's mouth smeared down over his brother-in-law's belly into the thatch of hair and the big base of his fat silo of flesh. He tongued around the stiff prong, chinning the swinging balls. He sniffed Irish Spring and nuzzled the man's bristly nuts and laid hands on Richmond's hard, cool-skinned ass cheeks.

When he finally took the egg-shaped end of Richmond's dick into his mouth, they both made low, throaty noises. A hunger that had predated this moment by many years was finally being acknowledged, and a feast had begun. Dick slobbered over the beer-can pecker, taking as much into his mouth as he could, a small but satisfying portion that was nothing short of a mouthful. He felt the slight pump of Richmond's hips and saw briefly the slide of Richmond's jeans as they traveled to the floor. Timmy filled in wherever Dick couldn't and was soon snorting up Richmond's asshole like a pig going after truffles.

"*Ho-o-oly,*" Richmond said, laying his hands on Dick's short brown hair. Dick went down as far as he could and gagged. He backed off, and through his tears he saw his buddy looking back at him, his face a map of amazement. "I didn't know you were a cocksucker," he whispered.

Meanwhile, Timmy was like a gopher in his hole, gnawing on the tight knot of Richmond's hair-ringed asshole. Richmond flexed his cheeks hard and pinched the boy's spit-covered face. "What's he doing back there?"

Dick took a look. Timmy was prying at Richmond's butt cheeks and squirming, half of his head locked into Richmond's crack.

"Smothering, I think," Dick reported, and Richmond unclenched. Timmy fell back, breathing hard.

Timmy picked up his penis and stiffened it, looking up at the two men. "You ought to kiss," he told them.

"You ought to fuck off," Dick said.

"No way," Timmy said. "I started this. You ain't gonna hog it all yourself." He shuddered a little as his thumb cruised over his slippery cock head.

"We want to be alone," Dick said, pushing out his jaw. His cock was still in his sweats, throbbing. He left it there for the time being, opting instead to milk it through the sodden jersey from time to time, more and more early dew springing from the split head.

Richmond turned his back on Timmy once more. He put his hands on Dick's shoulders, signaling, Dick thought, his need for more cock sucking.

"No," Richmond breathed, stopping him. His hands drifted up the back of Dick's neck, his thumbs pressing behind his friend's ears. He stepped forward clumsily, his ankles manacled by his fallen jeans. He pulled Dick up. Their lips met.

"Oh, yeah," Timmy said.

It wasn't as strange as he'd imagined, Richmond said later. When Richmond opened his mouth, his tongue darted into Dick's. They were both especially pleased by the sensation of their bearded chins coming together, the firmness of flesh. Richmond's cock rolled over Dick's. He dropped his hands to Dick's waist and pushed the sweats out of the way so that their naked pricks could wrestle. Richmond drooled into Dick's mouth, tongue-fucking the hole and humping himself all over Dick's furry belly. He dropped his hips, and his dick slipped under his brother-in-law's wrinkled nut sac, the blunt head making its presence known against Dick's privy, making him juice even more.

Richmond broke the kiss, and his lips crawled over to Dick's ear. "You're a wet motherfucker," he said softly, his tongue caressing the lobe.

Timmy groaned, forgotten on the floor with his ten inches all in a frenzy. His legs suddenly went rigid.

"*Guh!*" he said by way of a warning.

"You gotta see this," Dick said, turning Richmond's head to witness Timmy's coming. "He's a fucking geyser."

Timmy's piss hole seemed to widen, and a thick spray of jizz blasted out like a creamy rocket. It flew high and landed thickly across the boy's ecstatic face. The next shot was no less impressive and covered Timmy's bony chest. The third and fourth and fifth puddled on the boy's stomach. He milked the rest out, grinning up at the stunned voyeurs.

It was Richmond's turn to go down on his knees and take Dick's cock into his mouth. He rolled his tongue over the head, lapping up the stickiness there, then swallowed the thing whole. Timmy, obviously a glutton for punishment, crawled, dripping, up to Richmond's behind and pushed his face once again into the crack. Dick dropped a hand down to his balls, concentrating on the pleasant rasp of Richmond's chin against his sac in an attempt to delay his own imminent ejaculation. But then he slammed into his brother-in-law's face, forfeiting his plans for a protracted session of sodomy.

"I'm gonna—" he started, his voice rising from his nuts.

"Uh-huh," Richmond breathed and nodded, staying the course and swallowing up the gush of come that Dick piped into him while he jacked his own cock, obviously enjoying the rimming he was now getting again from the Green boy. Richmond relieved Dick of every last drop and continued to suck on the bone so that Dick felt the growing possibility of a second orgasm. It electrified his body, curling his toes and making him sweat. His heart beat hard, his pulse thudding in his ears. Richmond's muffled moans built until he was snorting on Dick's joint and blowing gobs of hot come all over Dick's long, hairy-knuckled toes. Dick grabbed Richmond's head and dropped another load into him that weakened his heart and made his knees rubbery.

"Oh, man," Timmy said, his long, soft prick hanging down over his balls, the head resting on the linoleum. He looked up at the clock over the sink. "Bet the folks are home from church," he said. He tucked himself away and dabbed at the come on his face with a corner of his T-shirt.

After Timmy left, Richmond lingered in the kitchen. The smell of sex was strong, even over the odor of burned coffee. He stood by the counter with his pants still at his ankles, sipping from his cold mug. When Dick came back from a piss, he found his brother-in-law staring off into the air.

"I don't think..." Richmond started and stopped. He rubbed an eye, then scratched his ass. "I don't know," he said. He looked at Dick. "I don't think it can happen again."

Dick nodded, saying OK but hating to. What he really wanted was to kiss Richmond again. He watched him pull up his jeans and fasten them.

When he was dressed, Richmond lifted his hand to say good-bye. He looked as sad as ever, as sad as always.

"See you," Dick said.

That night, about midnight, the phone rang. Earlene answered it and handed the receiver to Dick. "Who is it?" he asked, but she'd fallen back to sleep.

"Hello?" he whispered, expecting bad news.

Richmond apologized for calling and rushed to assure Dick that he wasn't fucked-up or anything. "I just wanted to hear your voice," he said, sounding bold and sheepish all at the same time.

"I understand," Dick said.

There was a long pause during which he listened to Richmond's breathing. Then Richmond spoke.

"Can you meet me tomorrow?"

"I can," Dick said. "I will."

"At the water tower. You remember that, don't you? That water tower behind Moseby's Mill?"

"Yeah," Dick said, closing his eyes and seeing Richmond's ass flashing in the sun. "I think I do."

A Queer Turn

I'd told this one to stay away. I didn't want him coming around anymore. He stood by the door, naked, his cock erect, defiant.

"You shouldn't be here," I told him, ignoring the hard-on, gathering all my resolve. Truth was, I loved his dick, worshiped it, even. It had a fat beginning and slimmed a bit, topped with a little cherry of a head, this little bullet not much bigger than, say, my thumb to the first knuckle, long like that and snake-headed. He could slip that thing up my ass with a little spit and ingenuity, and I'd be none the wiser until he'd push in and surprise me with his sudden width. He could wrestle me around until he had me topped, skewering me with his backward baseball bat, swearing and sputtering over my chest. He wasn't much more than 5 foot 6, but he was a wiry little scrapper, and I did love the way he fucked me.

But no more. I had my reasons.

"Why you got to be this way?" he said with a smile, his voice soft from beer. He had his hands behind his back, one naked foot on top of the other, this little brown spray of hair at the center of his chest, nipples the color of dried blood. His torso was lean, white. I liked his hipbones, how they jutted out like a girl's. He made me feel like an old man, my soft beginnings of a beer gut, soft all over, it seemed, except down there. I saw him looking there. He liked that too, that he could do that to me. Simply watching him bend over to untie his boots could make me hard.

"Come away from the door like that," I told him, because it was open, and I didn't want anybody seeing him like that. Wasn't I in enough trouble already with this boy? He did not know the trouble he caused me, but he wouldn't have cared much even if he did.

He didn't move, so I turned off the lights. Then I went up to him and grabbed his arm and pulled him away from the door. I led him to one of the sofas and pushed him down onto it. I had a fire going and could see by the light of it his amusement at being pulled around.

"Why you got to act all mad? Tough guy," he said, tossing his chin my way, stretching himself out. He spread his legs so that I could see between them the little dark knot of his asshole, which he must have just shaved around, clearing the brush of curling dark hair that used to keep it hidden. His balls were tight, no slack-skinned low-hangers, and they were clean and pink. I'd never seen such hairy balls, and now it was all gone, and they were as bright and bare as billiard balls, his fingers playing over their new smoothness, stopping at a bit of stubble where he'd not gotten close enough.

"I told you to keep your mouth shut," I said, standing over him, my pecker making a sorry jut in my pants. I regretted my excitement and the control this boy had over me. Twenty years old, he hadn't any right to control me the way he did.

"Mike," he said. "Michael." His voice was smooth and easy; it wrapped around my prick and squeezed and pulled me to him. I fell over him, humping his crotch with my covered cock. I pushed at my jeans, freeing up my dick. I knew he liked the feel of it there, and I liked the drag of fuzz on his hard, channeled belly.

I got my hand down between us, feeling up that new baby skin, smearing his gut with my first batch of precome. He must have felt the wetness of it, because he pushed his hand between us too, then brought it back up to his mouth, licking his fingers noisily.

"More," he said when he was done, digging his hands into my armpits and trying to pull me up, wanting my leaking prick in his mouth. I straddled his head and felt his hands on my butt cheeks and let him suckle the fat end of my boner, siphoning the sticky self-lube my big bag of nuts produced, groaning with each salty taste of the stuff. I squeezed his face with the sides of my knees; I fucked into his mean little mouth. He started fingering my hole, getting all fidgety back there, and I turned to see him humping the air, his torpedo aimed for my ass crack. Slightly curved, the creamy white of old alabaster, its little arrowhead caused my butt hole to gape with want. I dragged my pecker out of his mouth, trailing a slimy line of spit and jizz down his chest until I felt the point of his banger just under my balls.

"You old pig," he said, his lips disappearing, his teeth showing. "Dirty old fucking pig."

I stopped dead, and he thrust into me.

"You fucking love my cock, don't you, Mike?" he said, grabbing the knobs of my nipples, twisting them. I sat back and felt the stretch my hole did, gobbling up the thick-based pole.

"I like it fine," I said, bouncing on it, feeling the pointed end going to work on my prostate. I tightened the grip I had on myself, the hard handful I was jacking. I stared at the fine hairs between his small, flat pecs. I put my hands there to steady myself and felt his chest give, and his face softened the way it always did when he was about to come. He'd get all clingy and push his face up into me and wrap his arms around me and tell me he loved me.

I was all set to gush on him and for him to get sweet on me, but neither happened. He whipped out of me and left my hole blowing smoke rings of wanting. He slipped out from under me, leaving me on wobbling knees. Suddenly he was in front of me, on his knees too, his little white ass in his hands as he spread his cheeks and showed me his newly bald cunt.

"You've had a change of heart," I said, the first thing that popped into my head.

"Shut up and pop me," he said, not looking back.

I got hold of his hips and pulled him back. My dick was wet enough to slip into his little pussy, but the rest was slow and painstaking, the boy gasping every now and then, grunting with every half inch. The light from the fire made our shadows flicker on the walls like dark flames, and the boy's back was wet, his knobby spine trail a little crooked, his shoulder blades jutting. I licked his back and listened to the sloppy handwork he did on himself as I pushed in and out of him with my man's dick, thick from bottom to top, as big around as a church candle, which was why he'd sworn off fucking with me and always wrestled for tops. "Horse dick," he'd said once. "Go find yourself another horse."

But now he was making amends. He straightened, pressing his back against my chest, his shoulder blades rubbing against my chewed-up nipples. I looked over his shoulder and watched my little man taking aim.

"Not on the slipcover!" I warned, sounding like the queen I never wanted to be.

"Oh, shit," he said, paying no attention to me. His little ass wriggled, impaled, as he worked his little butt button to hardness and jet-streamed an arc of come that cleared the sofa and landed with a splat on the floor. The next blasts lacked the force and speed of the first and fell in clotted clumps on the sofa's arm, and he slumped over the mess he'd made.

I pulled out and slid my hot, wet dick along the crack of his skinny ass, squeezing his little cheeks together for some friction. I lofted a shot of jizz that fell on the back of the boy's buzzed head, making him curse, and grunted the rest out on his wet, bony back.

I didn't see him for a while. His brother and his friends came around, though. I liked the quiet one, the one named Hal. There was something about the way he sat with his shoes off, his fingers woven between his toes, listening to his buddies' bullshit, staring at one and then another with a fascination that was not idle. He seemed to love them all: Kyle; cocky Bill Davis; the dark, mean-mouthed Tim. His light eyes would focus on Davis's brown ankles and then shift to the plaid hem of Kyle Briggs's showing boxers and then to Tim's hand going up under his shirt to scratch his muscled gut, his dark happy trail fanning out and spreading across his torso.

Now that it was getting colder, the boys started coming by more often, my little cabin becoming something of a clubhouse for them. I did not mind much, but it seemed to keep Kevin from coming over. Wasn't that what I wanted, though? Still, I could not say that I didn't miss his tapered boner and grunted curses.

His brother, Kyle, was looking at me and then at Hal and then at the fire. He lay back on the carpet, bending his legs at the knees. I could see into his shorts, dark with shadow. Tim raised his arms over his head, pulling up his T-shirt and baring his belly, its furred, hollow concavity. I'd seen him earlier in the summer wearing next to nothing and wanted to see him that way again. He grabbed another beer from the bag he kept between his feet. I'd offered to keep them in the refrigerator when he arrived. "Too far to walk," he'd said, half his mouth curling up with a grin. His eyes were chocolate-brown, dark-rimmed, with thick lashes. He was the least intelligent of the three but sometimes the most attractive.

He said: "You win all them trophies yourself, Mike?" He was referring to the table by the door to the kitchen, laden with trophies, men and boys with laurel-wreathed heads and upheld arms.

"It's decoration," Kyle said. "You wouldn't understand."

"And you do?" Tim laughed back.

"They look cool," Kyle said. The golden boys glistened as the real boys spoke, and I remembered a dream I had a couple of nights ago in which all these boys and Kevin too held me aloft in their arms, carrying me down to the lake and down the Briggs's long dock to throw me off at the end, only there wasn't any lake—it had gone dry, nothing but a huge gape of a hole lined with the stink of dead fish and seaweed, buzzing with flies. They counted off, bellowing like Marines: "One! Two! Three!" On three I felt their hands leave me, and I was airborne, falling, falling. I awoke before hitting bottom.

Tim stretched out his legs. He was wearing boots without any socks, reminding me of Kevin, and I wondered if Tim was the one Kevin told me about, the one he would go to whenever he needed to get sucked—the other sucker besides me, that is. I eyed the soft roll of denim that covered his crotch, worn white from touching, the way our pockets show the outlines of our wallets. His showed the 2-by-4 outline of his pecker. I was wondering when I was going to see the uncovered version.

When the beer was gone, the boys left. I went around blowing out candles, stoking the fire for the night, feeling a little heavy in the crotch. I stripped and turned on the shower. There was a knock on the door. I smiled to myself, thinking *Kevin.* I wrapped a towel around myself and went to the door.

"Mr. Polsen?" I heard through the screen.

It was Hal.

"I think I dropped my wallet here," he said, glancing over his shoulder. He looked as though he was afraid he'd be seen. I stepped back and let the boy in.

"I was sitting over here," he was saying, walking over to the front of the sofa he'd leaned against earlier, playing with his toes. The living room was dark save for the light of the fire; the wallet lay just under the dust ruffle, easily found. He put it back in his pocket and stayed where he was, waiting.

I walked up to him, standing close. I could hear the rush of his breathing, the fear he had in him. His hands moved slowly toward the knot of my towel, and it fell to the floor.

"Well," I said, unable to come up with anything more worthy.

There was then a knock at the door that made me jump. The boy said easily, "That's Kyle. Let him in."

I went to the door, naked and swinging.

"Hey, Mr. Polsen," he said, sounding nothing like his brother. He was looking past me at Hal, who was taking off his denim jacket and elbowing out of his T-shirt, standing in the firelight like some golden boy. Kyle stepped in, mesmerized. He walked slowly to one of the sofas and sat down hard as Hal unbuttoned his jeans and let them fall down his slim hips.

I found myself with a dripping boner as hard as a candle in a cold, empty church. Hal knelt on the carpet. Kyle looked away from his friend, at me, his hands still on his lap.

"He wants to watch," Hal said. "Come on, Kyle."

Hal was in command. I stepped up to him and felt his hot breath all over my prick, his snaky tongue flicking at the buttery head. He hummed, taking me into his mouth. "Shit," I heard the Briggs boy breathe, and I leaned into Hal, filling him with my horse dick. He coughed and swallowed, and spit spilled out of his mouth in shiny ropes that fell on the carpet, his thighs, and my feet. He tongued into my piss slit and then let his lips stretch wide as I pushed myself down his throat.

The Briggs boy hauled out his cock and was stroking it, watching us. Again and again he'd lick his palm and jack his tiny-headed prick, an exact replica of his brother's. Had either of them any idea they had twin boners? Seeing it made me miss the older Briggs, and my ass felt empty. I peeked at Hal's crotch; it looked like a perfect fit. I turned around then, offering the boy my ass. He paused as if unsure of what to do next, and then I felt a few tentative licks and then his rooting nose burrowing into the fur of my crack. I looked over my shoulder at Kyle, who was staring intently at his friend's behind, working his fingers along the underside of his own tapering shaft, tickling himself just under the head.

"My dick's all lonely, Kyle," I said. "You want to come over here and keep it company?"

Hal unplugged his face from my ass long enough to explain that Kyle wasn't queer.

"And you are?" I asked the hungry-mouthed boy over my shoulder. All he did was nod.

"And you just like to watch?" I asked Kyle. He nodded too before clearing his throat and saying, "Just checking shit out. Somebody taking a shower?"

"That was supposed to be me," I said, distracted by Hal's deft tongue.

I made Hal stand up, and I lowered my ass and invited him in. I felt his slippery knob bump around blindly between my legs. When he found a soft spot, he pushed in, and I let out a yell.

"Does it hurt?" he asked. "Am I too big?"

"You're a regular giant," I told him. "Just take it a little easy at first."

He slowed his manic thrustings, rising up on his toes and gripping my hips, attempting some technique. Kyle spread across the couch, opening his legs. I told him he ought to take off his jeans, and he paused to consider the suggestion.

"Nah," he said. "I'm fine."

I watched him work on his cock, palming the head. The kid behind me was all over my back and panting, licking me all over, his hands roaming up and down the front of me, never lighting anywhere for more than a few seconds. I could not say, though, that it was not pleasurable; I was as stiff as I get and wishing he'd pay more attention to my dick. He touched it lightly, playing with the greasy head and making it hop. I squatted a little more to help him hit the right spot, and when he did I had to hang my head. His pesky fingers found my nipples then and stayed there, bless him, and I found myself about to come without the aid of any manual manipulations. I tensed and spilled like a Brazilian in a Kristen Bjorn film.

"Whoa," Kyle breathed.

"Shit," I muttered.

Hal continued his assault on my asshole, and I grinned and took it until he squealed and pulled out, squirting my back with a hot spray.

"That was cool," Kyle said. He started shoving his boner back into his pants.

"Aren't you going to get off?" I asked.

He shook his head. "Hal already told you; I'm not a queer," he said.

I dreamed about Kevin. He was wearing my father's flannel bathrobe, nothing else. He walked around the house with a beer bottle, going from window to window, waiting for something, someone. It was raining, but there was sun too, and everything was golden, misty. Where was I? I don't even think I was there. It was like watching a movie. He stepped away from the window, swinging his beer bottle, his robe opening, coming untied, more and more of his beautiful skin being revealed, his little cock, thick and stubby save for that gumdrop head. He scratched beside his balls—they were still smooth, freshly shaved; I could smell the soap he used. *That's strange*, I thought.

He turned his back, and the robe fell off his shoulders. On his back, tattooed there, was a portrait of his brother. *That's kind of nice*, I decided, thinking that it was some kind of tribute to brotherly love. He turned around then, and he wasn't Kevin anymore but Tim, leering sexily. "I could use a rim job," he said, laughing. "I heard Polsen likes sucking ass."

Hal walked in, naked, laughing too. "He likes getting fucked too."

"Who doesn't?" Kyle said, peering up over the back of the sofa.

And then a woman's voice from upstairs: "You boys ought to be sleeping!"

The friends all shushed each other, giggling like schoolboys. Kyle laughed out loud.

"Don't make me send your father down!" the woman shrieked.

The young men giggled more. Tim made farting noises, and Hal hooted.

"That's it!" I heard the lady say, and then there were footfalls on the stairs. A naked man walked into the living room, his cock hard. He was big and hairy, pot-bellied. He carried a belt in one hand, a big dildo in the other. He turned his face into the light. It was my face. He was me.

I opened my eyes. It was still dark. I felt warm air, breath, and flinched.

"You snore," Kevin said.

"What are you doing here?" I said, catching my breath. He'd scared the shit out of me, but I'd be damned if I'd let him know it. I felt his hand slip under the bedclothes and rest on the center of my chest.

"Were you dreaming?" he asked. His face was very close to mine, and I smelled his chewing gum. He licked the corner of my mouth. "Have you ever dreamed of me?"

"I don't remember my dreams," I told him, opening my mouth. His tongue slipped in, long and snaky. I thought about his brother, how he'd sat on the sofa with his dick in his hand, the pink tip of his tongue sliding across his lips.

He started undressing. *This is becoming complicated*, I thought; I moved here because it was quiet and pretty. Things were getting to be mathematical all of a sudden, and there were too many equations, too many young men.

"This place is crazy," I said.

"This place sucks," Kevin said. He knelt on the soft mattress, and I rolled toward him. I found his cock with my mouth. It was hard and smelled already of spit. Had someone already sucked him off, or had he been jacking off? It hardly mattered. It was dark, and I was horny again, and dick was the great pacifier. I closed my eyes and sucked him to the back of my throat.

KARMA

Micah sipped his coffee; the heat of it hurt his tongue, which he'd apparently injured last night eating out Kelly's ass. He could see Kelly now, facedown, legs spread. Kelly had a smooth little fanny that appealed to Micah, a young man's rear end: blemish-free, peach-fuzzy. His balls spread out between his thighs like something spilled, easily slurped up and rolled about in Micah's mouth—but only one at a time because of the size of the things. Nothing boyish about them or his prick, with its horselike dimensions. Pink and straight, with a network of blue veins coursing under its surface, it had a downward point, a beautiful helmet.

"Mikey," Dick Jones barked, startling him and causing him to spill some coffee. Dick laughed; Micah didn't.

"You had this dreamy look on your face," Jones said. "You know how The Gland is about that."

"The Gland is playing golf with some Du Pont." A brown stain spread across a report Micah had just finished. This, oddly enough, wasn't his day. Despite the awesome ass-licking, butt-fucking time he'd had the night before, this day was shaping up miserably. It was pouring when he went out to start his car that morning, only to find it wouldn't.

"Not the wrestling lover, I hope," Jones said.

"She might like wrestling; I didn't receive a profile," Micah said.

"I didn't know you had a brother," Jones said, pulling tissues from a box on Micah's desk and floating them atop the spilled coffee.

"I don't have a brother," Micah muttered.

Dick's mouth squirmed to fight a greasy smile, his hand going inside his gray flannel vest. His white shirtsleeves were rolled to the middle of each forearm. He had the upper body of someone who crewed the Delaware. Micah glanced away from the oar-hardened wrists and sneezed.

"Getting a cold?" Jones said. "Out in the rain without your rubbers?"

Micah looked up, making his features dull, feigning incomprehension. Jones sighed.

"Oh, Mikey. No ear for irony."

"I told you about that 'Mikey' shit, didn't I?" Micah said, blotting up the rest of the coffee.

Jones rolled his eyes. They were that strange contact-lens blue, but natural, his own. He looked through glasses that looked borrowed from someone named Fritz. His blond hair was cut short to combat a natural kink and underplay a slightly receding hairline that Micah secretly found attractive.

"So, who was your celestial twin?" he wanted to know from Micah. "I seriously thought he looked like your brother."

"My ride this morning?" Micah said. "Friend of mine." He waved the report to dry it, giving himself the air of a coquette with a fan. Dick grabbed the fluttering papers.

"Sometimes I think I don't know you very well at all," he said. "Print up another copy of this, Micah, that's all you have to do."

"What do you mean?"

"I mean open up the appropriate file and click on the print icon, for Christ's sake."

"No, I mean about not knowing me very well."

Jones looked at his watch.

"I've got a lunch meeting in 15," he said. "What are you doing after work."

Fucking, I hope, Micah thought, his mind running through his good-excuses file and coming up with a wake for a dead aunt—why, he didn't know. Easier than explaining Kelly, he figured.

Jones regarded him drolly, looking very close to shaking his head admonishingly.

Micah had met Kelly at the gym. Kelly was the chiropractor's assistant on duty when Micah turned his head sharply to check out a wagging bob in someone's shorts. He was all but crippled immediately. *Instant karma,* he thought, carrying his head crookedly to the back of the gym. "Pinched nerve," he grimaced, pointing to the back of his neck.

Kelly jumped out of his swiveling office chair and bounded over to Micah like he was a code-blue emergency. He led Micah gently to one of the rooms in which the doctor manipulated bones.

"I'm not licensed to do anything but give you ice," Kelly said, his voice deep. He wore Lycra shorts and a cropped T-shirt—typical gym gear for someone in as good a shape as he was. *But can I trust him with ice?* Micah wondered, trying to check out the boy's basket. His damned nerve throbbed, preventing inspection.

"Dr. Glenn will be back soon," Kelly said. He wore a name tag that made his T-shirt swing, its sleeves long gone, his pesky, pert nipple popping into view every now and then. "Would you like to lie down?" Kelly asked. His red hair was combed back with gel, just long enough to flip up in back. There were freckles running across his arms, his shoulders. *Is his dick freckled too?* Micah wanted to learn.

"I've got two or three fused vertebrae," Micah said, pointing again to his neck. Kelly brought an ice pack and placed it with care on Micah's neck and came around, squatting before his patient.

"Does it help?" he wanted to know. His legs were spread, and the heavy wad in his skintight shorts became Micah's focal point.

Micah nodded as best he could.

He left the gym with the ice pack and Kelly's number, feeling like a smooth operator despite the odd tilt to his head and the shooting pain that made him see stars.

e dialed Dick's extension.

"Yallo," he answered.

"My car's not done yet."

"Can't your, um, friend drive you?"

"He's at work," Micah told him. "Never mind. I'll call a cab."

"What about your aunt's wake?"

"Canceled," Micah said.

"Canceled? They canceled a wake?"

"Hang up, I'm calling a cab," Micah said.

"Like hell you will."

There was an accident on 176, and traffic was stopped dead. Dick put the car in neutral and popped in the latest Dave Matthews CD. "This guy's gay, isn't he? I think he's gay."

"How the hell would I know?" Micah snapped. He hadn't any plans for his evening, but he never thought he'd be stuck in a car with Dick Jones. *He wouldn't be so obnoxious with his mouth closed,* Micah thought, *or biting a pillow.*

"So why'd you lie to me this morning?" Jones asked. "Don't you like me anymore?"

Micah looked at his hands in his lap. "Look, I'm sorry," he said, unable to come up with anything suitable to follow that up with.

Jones shrugged. "I'm callused, buddy, don't worry. No feelings to worry about since that nerve-ending removal. Hurt like hell for a little bit, then—nothing. Haven't felt a thing since. Ask my wife."

"How is Candace?" Micah asked, putting his shoulder to the window.

"Gone," Dick said, taking his hands off the wheel. He laughed. "Our first anniversary is next week."

"Jeez, I'm sorry," Micah said, feeling like an ass, and for some reason he remembered a dream he'd had that morning in which the roof of his house was gone and it was raining like hell. It started to rain in real life, drumming the roof of the car like anxious fingers. Jones switched on the wipers, but there was nowhere to go and nothing to see. He turned off the engine. "I'm low on fuel," he said, and then, "So, who's the guy?"

"This morning?" Micah stumbled. He was not comfortable talking about his personal life at work—those were two worlds he did not like to overlap.

"And last night," Dick said. "It's none of my business. I'm just interested lately in people who are enjoying a healthy sex life. I'm simply making idle conversation."

"We're no longer idling," Micah said.

"That is subject to debate," Dick said, then: "So, what's he like?"

"Are you sure you want to know? Why do you want to know? When did you suddenly become bi-curious?"

"I've always been curious. I watch The Learning Channel."

"His name's Kelly. He collects grenades."

"Hand grenades?"

Micah nodded. "They're nicely displayed, though."

"No doubt," Dick answered. He sat quietly for a while regarding the view through the rain-streaked window.

"What happened at home?" Micah asked.

"Are you sure you want to know?" Dick said, turning, fixing his blue eyes on the knot of Micah's tie. He shrugged. "The usual, I guess. Candace collects grudges. She remembers every shitty little thing anyone's ever done to her."

Micah said nothing, keeping his ill opinion of Jones's wife to himself. "You all right?"

"Oh, I am just fine," Dick answered him with a big fake smile.

They picked up a six-pack close to Micah's house."Just wasn't working," Dick said, scratching himself. His shoes were off, and his tie undone. Micah sat across from him trying to be a good listener, trying to maintain eye contact. His gaze tended to drop down the stretched-out length of the man before him, though, and he'd find himself unaware of what Dick had been saying.

"You know what I mean?" Dick said, breaking Micah's concentration.

Micah nodded slowly.

"You're a good friend," Dick said, leaning forward, obscuring his crotch.

No, I'm not, Micah thought, *I'm a fucking pig, so lean back again, because it makes your crotch look like a mountain in those trousers.*

Micah held up his empty bottle. "Another?" he asked.

Jones made an iffy face. "What about your plans?"

"No definite plans," Micah said. "I'll call him later. Anyway, he's working."

"What's he do?"

"He works," Micah said, wishing he could lie again, "in a gym."

Dick nodded. "I thought I saw deltoids this morning."

"He's a chiropractor's assistant."

"Is that anything like a dental hygienist?"

"He's really sweet," Micah said.

"Again, no doubt," Dick said, rolling his blue eyes.

Dick looked at his watch, then looked up at Micah. "Hungry?" he asked. Micah shook his head. "Me neither."

The beer was gone, and they opened a bottle of gin somebody gave Micah for Christmas. "Mixers?" Dick asked.

"Diet Coke?" Micah offered.

Dick shook his head.

Micah found some reconstituted lemon juice, so they drank the gin on ice with squirts from the plastic lemon.

"You should change," Dick said.

"I thought you liked me the way I am."

"Your clothes, I mean," he said. "I like you fine the way you are."

"I like you fine," Micah returned.

"You should get out of your work clothes, though. You look like you're at work."

"I wore these to work today," Micah said.

"Go change or something," Dick said.

"OK, all right," Micah said, getting up and making his way down the hall to his bedroom. He was feeling more than a little buzzed—he'd skipped lunch and now dinner, and the alcohol was feeding on him. He stripped down to his underwear, humming the Dave Matthews song he'd heard in the car. He stood in front of his bureau opening drawers and looking into them. He had no idea what to put on.

Dick was standing in the doorway. Micah saw him there and said, "I don't know what to wear."

"Have I ever seen your legs before?" Dick asked him. "You have big legs. Is that what your boyfriend is doing for you? Making your legs big? Lots of squats?"

"He's not my boyfriend. I don't even know his middle name."

"You know mine, though," Jones said, and Micah nodded. "And I know yours."

"You do?" Micah asked.

"Yup," he said.

They both stopped talking, but the voice in Micah's head was loud and rambling and wary. *Not a good thing*, it said. But look at him, his compact form there in the doorway, framed and backlit, the blond fuzz of his head, his 31-inch waist—each a siren song to Micah. *But he's married*, came the voice of reason, *and straight and a coworker. He's disconsolate and kind of drunk and probably just horny. To take advantage of him now would be like raping a paraplegic, wouldn't it?*

Micah blinked, and Jones was suddenly standing very close to him, his juniper-berried breath like cologne to Micah's nose.

"You're thinking way too much," Dick said. He put his big hands on Micah's chest; they were warm and moist through his T-shirt. "Jesus, you've got pecs too," he whispered.

"They were on sale."

Jones's left hand trailed down Micah's torso, stopping at his polka-dotted shorts. "I had you pegged for a white Calvins kind of guy," he said, swirling a finger into the fly.

"These were on sale too," Micah said. "Are you sure—" he started but stopped when he felt Jones's finger poking his soft prick into a doughy semierect state. Dick went to his knees, pushing his face against the front of Micah's shorts, mouthing the burgeoning head of Micah's prick.

"I'm not sure if this is a great idea," Micah continued, palming the back of Dick's head and forcing it harder against his groin. "I mean, what will we say to each other tomorrow? Are you going to talk to me at all?" Jones pushed up Micah's T-shirt, exposing his crunched abdominals, the smooth six-pack that was his glory—they were like leather-covered rock—and Jones exhumed his face from Micah's crotch.

"Jesus," he exclaimed. "You've been hiding all this!"

"I didn't think you'd be interested," Micah replied. His cock had become engorged and pressed itself insistently against the front of his boxers. Dick dragged the garish shorts down, unveiling the quivering rod. He stabbed his tongue at the hardened, goosefleshed conduit, licking up to the bulbous head that had always seemed to Micah a little odd, a little overboard, and so unlike all the other aerodynamic, arrowheaded cock heads he'd seen in his lifetime. He'd always felt strapped with a tom-tom. Odd or not, though, Jones was not averse to licking it up and down and handling it like a drumstick and sticking it all into his mouth.

"It's better than I thought it was going to be," Dick said.

"That's good to hear," Micah returned.

"I was always bugging Candace to buy bananas and zucchini and cucumbers. Was I sending some heavy subliminals, or what?" He unshouldered his suspenders and unknotted his tie. He looked up from what he was doing. "You OK? You look a little sick."

Micah nodded—he was feeling anything but sick. His cock tingled, needing to be touched more and more. He thought about the next day at the office. This was totally fucked-up, he decided, looking down at his shiny, rosy knob not eight inches from Dick Jones's mouth.

Dick talked as he undressed, about Candace, his lack of sex experience ("You know, with guys, I mean!"), even about some account they were working on. "Talked to Joe about that media plan for Westways. He thinks they're going to go with it." He got himself down to his T-shirt, trousers, and dark socks. He wasn't lean, and he wasn't fat, but he hovered somewhere in between, which was perfection as far as Micah was concerned. Jones wrinkled his brow, looking up at Micah, taking a deep breath. Standing, he unlatched his slacks. He himself was wearing the white Calvins, their pouch filled with a lot of flaccid dick. He gripped himself, pulling on his soft package.

"Guess I'm more nervous than I thought," he said, making a sheepish face. He let go of himself and grabbed hold of Micah. He got down on his knees again and took the man's prick into his mouth. He played his tongue along the underside when he went down and used it to lash the sensitive head when he drew back, his teeth lightly dragging and causing Micah to gasp. He was able, despite his inexperience, to bring Micah closer than he wanted to be to shooting. Micah pulled on Dick's meaty earlobes, pushing into his tight-lipped mouth and hitting the back of his throat, liking the muffled sounds the man made. His balls were bathed in drool that leaked from Dick's sucking mouth.

"Enough," Micah said, tugging on Dick's ears. Dick sat back, his fanny resting on his dark-socked heels. The pouch of his briefs had doubled in size. His plumped dick rode downward along his balls. His crotch was camera ready, picture-perfect. He had the look of an underwear ad.

"Take off the rest," Micah said, and Dick pulled off his T-shirt. He was covered with golden-brown hair. His pecs were fat and accented with small brown nipples that were pointed and widely spaced. He put his thumbs into his shorts.

"This is a pretty definitive moment," Dick said.

Micah laughed, his cock bobbing. "I think you had your definitive moment a while ago, pal, right before you started giving me head."

"Guess you're right," Dick said.

"We can stop here," Micah said. "We don't have to do anything else. We can forget this ever happened."

"No way," Dick said, shaking his head. "No fucking way."

The shorts came down.

Dick Jones had the kind of cock that Micah dreamed about: fat-shafted and topped with a tiny gumdrop of a head that pointed up and out.

"Jeez," Micah breathed.

They waltzed to the bed and wrestled across the mattress, kicking off pillows and bedsheets, seeking a flat and uncluttered surface on which to fuck. Micah had already decided that it would be a nice gesture to let Dick fuck him. He got himself down on all fours in front of the man and started licking the perfect pecker. Little pearls seeped out and were tongued away. He chewed on Dick's fuzzy bag, bringing the whole tight thing into his mouth, sucking and snorting like a pig at a buffet.

"Mikey," Dick said softly, touching the side of the man's face, and Micah came off the bag, dragging his mouth up the sweet, curving shaft, up to that little point of a head. He went down hard, swallowing Dick's dick and breathing hotly into his bush.

When Micah crawled up Dick's torso and sat down on his cock, Dick said, "No way."

"You don't want to?" Micah asked.

"No. I mean, yeah, I want to, I just can't believe it. I read my horoscope this morning, and it didn't say anything about fucking you."

"You want to, though?" Micah asked, wanting to be sure.

"Abso-fucking-lutely," Dick said, pushing up with his hips and stabbing into the hole. It was an easy slide in; the sweet, pointy prick was perfect for fucking, although it thickened quickly and felt like a fire plug once it was all the way in.

"Shit," Dick said, cupping Micah's ass. "This is nice, man."

Micah squatted on the cock, playing with the brown points of Dick's nipples. He maneuvered his rear end so that his prostate bore the brunt of Dick's sharp-headed cock. His own dick bobbed happily and untouched, tapping away on Dick's stomach and leaving sticky dots.

"Am I doing it right?" Dick asked, and Micah laughed. "It doesn't take a rocket scientist, I guess," Dick said. "But are you enjoying yourself? Does it hurt? Am I equipped with a monster cock that is eviscerating you as I speak?"

"I'm in fucking heaven," Micah said.

"You look like an angel, man," Dick said, thrusting up sharply, making Micah gasp. He reached up and grabbed the back of Micah's head, pulling him down for a full kiss that made Micah's head swirl. He felt compelled suddenly to reach down between their bellies and start pulling on his cock.

"Shit," Dick whispered, his mouth full of Micah's tongue. "I'm—" He struggled to unpin himself, but Micah rode him out, taking the full blast of Dick's load up his ass. Then he sat up straight, his hand on his bone, and aimed for his coworker's face.

When it was all over, Micah unseated himself and stretched out beside Dick.

"I'm sorry, man," Dick said.

"What for?"

"Coming early."

"You were right on time, as far as I'm concerned."

"It's just that I haven't had sex in 32 days."

"Not at all? Not even jacking off?"

Dick turned to look at Micah. "You consider that having sex?"

"Well, yeah. Kind of. It's pretty much the same, isn't it? The end result, I mean."

"Well, then, I haven't had sex, according to your standards, since this morning in the men's room at work after I left your office," Dick said.

"That's so sweet," Micah said, putting his head close to Dick's.

"Yeah," he said. "So, tell me, buddy, do you really know my middle name?"

Micah made a face. "Sure, I do. Sure," he said, trying to think of it. He was sure he'd seen it somewhere, on some interdepartmental mail or something. It began with a J or an M, he thought, or maybe an S.

"It's John," he said.

"Nope."

"Jacob."

"Jacob?"

"Not Jacob," Micah said. "So, what's mine, then, smart-ass?"

"Jacob?"

"Nice try, asshole," Micah said.

"Steven," Dick tried.

"Close enough," Micah said, licking a running drip of come from Dick's chin.

BOYSTOWN

Maybe we weren't getting a lot of studying done; maybe we were always this close to academic probation. "But maybe ass really is more important than the social structure of England in the 16th century," McFeeley said in all earnestness, burning his fingers on what was left of a big, fat joint.

McFeeley and I got together at orientation. We were standing in line to register for freshman comp. He stood behind me. I'd seen him all weekend—he looked like a man to me and not at all like some prefrosh 18-year-old. He'd worn the same clothes all weekend: a scruffy yellow Polo button-down oxford-cloth shirt and a pair of chinos with a tear in the ass that hung open like a toothless grin, exposing a variety of boxers throughout the three days. On this particular day I noticed tattersall, which tugged at me somewhere inside, becoming meaningful for no apparent reason. I had, I guessed, a tattersall fetish.

I straightened my shoulders and pushed out my chest when he came up behind me. I glanced back casually—you know, checking out the lines and shit, and mumbled a "How ya doin'?" He smiled, his green eyes on me, and nodded. He chewed gum, his dimples working in his cheeks.

It was a slow-moving line, inching up a little at a time. McFeeley was moving a little faster, though, and I felt the wind of his spearminty breath against the top of my head. I was afraid to move—I didn't want to turn and bump into him, and I didn't want to get any closer to the girl in front of me, and I didn't want to stop feeling the heat his body generated radiating toward me.

I got up to the table to register, my hands shaking, my cock just about hard. After a few moments of floundering, I found a class that sort of fit my schedule. I put the pencil down and turned, McFeeley having pressed up against me the whole time I was bent over the table.

"Wait for me," he said uncoyly. I nodded, a sudden slave to his whim and my boner.

I went with him to his room. His roommate for the weekend, an Asian he called Duck Soup, was at the getting-to-know-you party in the quad. McFeeley unbuttoned his shirt, his chest thick with hair and muscle.

"You gonna wrestle?" he asked, stretching out on the bed, his chinos going taut over his crotch and accentuating the McFeeley log.

"Now?" I asked. "Oh, for school." I shrugged, feeling more than stupid. "Thinking of it, I guess."

"Me too," he said, his hand going behind the curtain of his shirt.

I still don't remember exactly how he got me on his lap. I recall his scratching an itch on his back, having taken off his shirt. "Is this a fleabite?" he asked me, wanting me to come closer for a look. The next thing I knew, his big black-haired chest was tickling my ear, and his hand rumbled over my hard-on.

"You suck dick?" he asked. "You've got pretty lips. Pretty eyes too. Don't look like a cocksucker, that's why I didn't bust a move the first night at that asshole dance." We'd pissed together at the dance, wordlessly, shyly. I didn't look at him or anything. A feat in itself, I thought at the time.

His voice lulled me but not my cock. He played with it to distraction.

He had me stand for him, undoing my pants. My dick poked up stiffly in my briefs. He slid them down. My pointer vibrated as he regarded the pouting snout of my foreskin. "Cool," he said, leaning forward and taking the frilly end into his mouth, teething on it, pulling it, tonguing into the turtleneck of it. His hands circled my waist, fingers resting in the crack of my behind. He pressed his cheek against my prong, inviting me to hump his face, and I did for a while, but I had to pull back. "I'll shoot," I said, and he looked up at me, his face all serious.

"Oh, no," he said. "Don't do that yet."

He had me sit down to watch him strip off his pants. He was solid, already a man, and I felt so fucking pubescent looking up at him, with my boner all sticky between my thighs. He stood before me in his tattersall boxers, the front dotted with leakage. He was prickly with hair, his legs carved columns, slightly bowed. His toes lay on the linoleum like fingers, his feet wide and white.

He stepped up to me, pushing me backward, crawling over me, straddling my middle. He bent over and pushed his mouth against mine, the stubble of his face burning mine. He licked around my lips and into each nostril and then across my eyelids. I could feel the big press of him against my chest, still wrapped in tattersall. I wanted to haul it out and feel its hot skin and slimy leak; I wanted to taste it.

"Never sucked dick?" He pulled my arms up over my head, tipping his hips forward, butting the soft underside of my chin with his cock. I shook my head slowly to feel the head of it down there.

"You picked a roommate yet?" I had: Kevin Stein, bright and innocuous and unattractive—but only because he asked me.

"You wanna room with me?"

I nodded slowly, his huge dick restricting the full movement of my head. "OK," I said quietly, my spit thick and making it hard to speak. I wanted him fiercely, pointedly. All the things I'd ever wanted to do rushed through my head like a porn flick on fast-forward as his cock rested against my throat.

He rolled off and lay beside me.

"Go to it," he said.

McFeeley's log was thick and long and straight. It did not taper to a point like mine; instead, it stayed the same circumference from base to head, a frigging telephone pole of a dick. I held it in my fist, impressed with its being there. I'd always wanted to suck dick, forever and ever—I just hadn't had the opportunity. There had been a couple of close calls, I guess—jacking off with a buddy, trying to pretend it was a matter of course, meaningless. Cases like that, you just jack, come, and act like nothing ever happened.

But this time there was no pretending, no need to pretend. It pulsed in my hand, wanting my mouth. I pressed my lips against its flat red-rimmed head. I took it into my mouth and tried to swirl my tongue around it. His fingers played over my shoulders, and I laid a hand on his thigh, stroking the fur on it. His nuts, two racquetballs in a bushy bag, bobbed as I ran my bottom teeth along the tender front of his cock. There was no way I could take half of it in my mouth, but I was satisfied, and

I think he was too. I used my hand to take care of the rest, a firm sliding grip that banged against his pubes.

"Oh, my God," McFeeley said, an arm slung over his face. "That's a sweet fucking mouth."

He rolled me over, his dick planted in my mouth, and began to fuck me that way. He screwed my face gently, taking care not to choke me. I gripped his fleecy ass, fingering into his crack, loving the feel of him in my hands. His bung hole pushed out like lips waiting to be kissed. I poked around it, the hairs there coarse, thick. "Touch it," I heard him say, and I fingered the plushness, the wrinkled, winking gash turning hard and tight. I pushed in and found him wet as a whore. He fed me a little more dick. He throbbed on my flattened, useless tongue; he throbbed into the aching cave of my throat. He stopped breathing, and his whole body tightened. He brought his fanny down hard on my finger.

"Oh, fuck," he whispered as his cock chugged in and out of my mouth, its split opening and hosing my tonsils with the warm pudding from his balls. His thighs tensed against my cheeks, and he pulled out to finish the job by hand, gushing sweetly over my lips and chin.

He turned around and grabbed my pecker. "Never played with one like this before," he said, fisting it, exposing the swollen head. I shot up into the air between us, splashing us both.

"Jesus," McFeeley said, wiping his eyes. "You could have warned me."

McFeeley liked games. His favorite was "I'll Get Him First." I guess he made it up. I mean, it doesn't exactly sound like the kind of game you'd play in the backseat of a car, your miserable parents up front trying to get you to Disney World.

When we moved off campus from the room we shared in Boynton Hall—*Boystown* Hall, we used to call it—we realized the freedoms we just didn't have on campus. McFeeley liked loud sex, a lot of loud sex—something that living in the dorms didn't foster. And I liked screwing the swim team, but discretion made up a small part of their valor, and smuggling the breaststroker Dickerson into my twin bed (with McFeeley feigning some pretty awesome snoring and drunken mumblings, all the while jacking off and watching us have at it) was no small feat. "No more mower sheds for us!" we rejoiced, toasting ourselves with shots of beer our first night, trying to get a quick buzz before Dickerson came by to our private housewarming party.

There was this new guy, Val Palmer, a transfer from the Midwest. Mack and I spotted him at the student union."Mine," I said, as though calling him first would give me dibs on this blondie with the falling-down socks and big, switching ass, his homemade tank top riding his little pink nipples into some kind of hardness.

"To the victor go the spoils," McFeeley said with some smugness, and a week later I came home from biology and walked in on the two of them, McFeeley naked on his knees, his big dick disappearing into the fat-lipped mouth of Mr. Palmer, who lay spread-legged on the floor, his little flopper hanging out of his undone jeans.

I stayed where I was. Mack liked an audience anyway, although he didn't see me at first. He was too busy staring lovingly at Palmer's widened mouth. Val hummed and kissed the red end of McFeeley's joint and licked the thick shaft and slack-skinned balls that swung mid-thigh. He took them into his mouth, and McFeeley lowered himself onto Val's face. He unbuttoned the boy's shirt, uncovering those now-famous—with me, at least—nipples, firmly puckered, like his lips.

His chest was free of hair except for a pretty feathering of the stuff narrowing up from the big blond bush that surrounded his impossibly white, nicely thick, and strangely soft cock. He moaned under the touch of Mack's fingers.

Mack was a big-ass monster. His beefed-up arms were leglike in their girth, and he was more interested in the gym than the gridiron for a couple of fairly obvious reasons I don't feel it necessary to go into. But he didn't mind making the occasional tackle, throwing himself headlong at one of those big, sweating guards from Penn State.

Unlike Palmer, McFeeley was all haired-up with black curlies, but under it all his skin was as white as a salt lick. He was as pretty as a picture—to me, at least—his face nicely sculpted, his cheek and chin always carrying a shadow of beard no matter when or how often he'd shave, his mouth full and always smiling, reminding me of kissing. His green eyes were closed as he squatted himself on Val's face.

The boy under him squirmed and scrambled, his hands impotent weapons against McFeeley's sequoia thighs and boulderlike glutes. I noticed Val's prick twitching to life.

It was then that I also noticed that I had been noticed, McFeeley blinking up at me with a shit-eating grin. He reached down and swung Palmer's little bat at me. "You snooze, you lose," he said.

"Hmm?" Val mumbled with a mouthful.

I gave Mack the finger.

"Feels awesome, baby," he said, his voice dripping with sex. "C'mon, buddy, clean me up."

I left them alone, myself in some sore need of attention. I drove fast to the bookstore on Route 222, where'd I'd stop every now and then after class. I walked sheepishly past the attendant, trying to look like I wasn't here for a blow job. My dick felt as obvious as a shoe in my pants, though. I got some quarters and roamed the place—it was a big room lined with stalls, featured movies posted outside each door. My peers today were familiar faces: two old men sucking Luckys and giving me the glad eye. "Cold enough for you?" they both asked as I walked past.

Out of a booth fell a thin boy wearing sad bicycle pants, wiping his lips with the edge of his T-shirt. He looked up at me like I was his next meal. From the same booth exited Monty Viceroy, patting the wet spots on his crotch and checking his zipper, his car keys already in hand. He saw me and glanced away quickly, but he knew he was busted, so he gave me a little nod. I'd seen him here before and in the library john at school, so I was not surprised to see the president of the student council looking so postcoital. He ducked his red head and did some fancy stepping around his trick and the two smoking fogies.

Present company did not present any likely or likable suck candidates save for Viceroy, him only for the sheer pleasure of doing someone in politics. I viewed some video sex and yanked on my pud. McFeeley and Val were probably covered with goo and in each other's arms right now, I was thinking. McFeeley had probably already turned on *Mighty Morphin Power Rangers*, which he never missed, his dick soft and heavy and sticky and reeking of Palmer's ass.

I sighed, feeling lonely. I heard someone getting change and checked my watch. The screen went blank. My Sambas smacked on the sticky floor, sounding as though I'd walked in wet paint. I wondered why there weren't any good fuck films about hockey players. I tucked my rock away, the stubby, flat-ended thing with its frill of skin. I sniffed my fingers.

Standing to the left of my door, wearing a tank top and warm-ups and startling me when I emerged, was someone who looked vaguely familiar. I was pretty sure I hadn't boothed it with him before, though. His hair was flattopped, and he had the long, stretched-out muscles of a basketball player. He looked at me, then away, his hands restless in his pockets—I could hear them rustling in the nylon. What I could see of his chest was free of hair; there was a russet peek of titty when he worked his shoulders into a purposeless shrug.

I left him standing there. As eager as I was to see him with his filmy pants about his ankles, he didn't seem the type to suck or be sucked. There were a lot of players who just liked to garner some attention, showing off their tent poles before secreting themselves and their cocks away in a video closet and adding to the sticky mess on the floor, going home chaste to the wife or girlfriend. I walked away from this one, trusting my judgment.

Sometimes I'm wrong, though, and so when this one turned and followed me, staying a few doors behind me, I figured I was going to have to reconsider my initial impression.

He mumbled a greeting, and I said hey, and he leaned toward me and said he felt here the same way he felt in church when he was a boy. "You know—a lot of whispering and thinking bad thoughts when you're supposed to be praying." He had long white teeth and was clean-shaven. He looked to be about 30.

"You go to Kutztown," he said, and I looked at him a little more closely, wondering if I should know him. Had we already boothed it?

"I was coaching tennis there," he said. "Name's Nicholson. I remember seeing you around. You're what's-his-name's roommate."

And Nicholson was the one what's-his-name told me about, the coach let go when rumors of sexual impropriety started circulating. "He was probably screwing Velakos," McFeeley speculated. "But fucking Velakos is fucking with fate, man, 'cause the fucker's nuts. Probably went to the dean with a butt full of the coach's come." McFeeley had a good eye for such things—Palmer, for instance, who was probably walking back to his dormitory room with a butt full of McFeeley's man juice. Good fucking eye, Mack.

I didn't feel right about this one, though, not trusting my own eye. He was nice to look at—very nice—with his short brown hair and his heavy brow and his pants rustling like a flag in the wind. I caught sight then of someone familiar, a black man whose dick never seemed fully engaged, who took a long time to come. We nodded—it was nice to be remembered. The huge vegetablelike curve of his dick was apparent through his zebra-stripe workout pants. I looked over at Nicholson. He scratched his bared tit.

The two old guys shuffled off, giving us whippersnappers dirty looks, and Bicycle Shorts left, miffed at being so completely ignored. It was just the three of us then, circling the outer walls, every now and then popping individually into a booth to refreshen our tumescences.

There was an alcove out of sight of the security cameras, which hovered and flashed little red lights over our heads. It was a favorite resting area for me when I felt like loitering outside a booth, and it was also a handy place to gather a small group of daring pud-pullers. I'd seen as many as seven guys in the tight little space doing all sorts of shit. I stood and waited. It was a proving ground—I figured if Coach came around and stopped too, it was a done deal.

He came around, parking himself in a doorway, gripping the front of his pants. He stepped into the booth and looked at me, but I stayed where I was. I fingered the outline of my dick, making it hard. He kneaded himself through the blue nylon, producing a sizable erection. He pulled it out and shook it at me, the second time I'd been wagged at like that today. Second time's the charm, I told myself and undid my jeans. My cock hit the air running, thrusting up with a snap. I did not have the coach's length or girth, but I made up for it with a wealth of foreskin. I could see his lips wet with drool, and I figured I knew what his favorite food was.

I pinched the end of my pecker and twirled it around for him like a bag of Shake 'n Bake. I skinned the head back and fingered the hard bluish head. I pushed my jeans down my hard-muscled quads and lifted my shirt. My chest and stomach were covered with a fine stubble of see-through hairs. I pinched my right tit and rolled it under my thumb, circling it, feeling the rasp of mowed-down hairs all around it.

Nicholson's prick was monolithic. His grip failed to cover half of it, and his fingers could not close around it. It was by far the longest johnson I'd ever seen. He worked it in his fist and squeezed out a ladle's worth of juice, leaking as much as I ejaculate. He wiped his sticky hand on his stomach as though the stuff were offensive, while I was thirsty for some of that.

There was the sound of someone getting change, $5 in quarters falling and reminding me of Atlantic City. Nicholson's cock was gone in a flash. I peered around the corner. Another old shuffler, probably a retired trucker, got himself into a booth and stayed there.

I gave Coach the all-clear. I still had mine out; it was buzzing in my hand. I watched the slow unveiling of Nicholson's member and decided then and there to bend at the waist and have a taste. I was not normally inclined to the act, though certainly no stranger to it. The fat gusher appealed to me—its fat knob, the trim and taut shaft that looked suntanned, a brown ring running around the middle of it, marking the beginning of the deep end.

"We could watch a movie," he said.

"I'm claustrophobic," I told him. "It's all right here; nobody can see." I liked it outside the narrow, coffinlike cubbies. I liked the chance of an audience, the dangerous thrill of being caught by the club-armed attendant.

The black guy pulled up like a shadow, soundlessly. Nicholson quickly turned shy, but I kept playing with mine. The man stepped into the alcove with us, between the coach and me, his back against the wall, and let out his hose. It was similar to Nicholson's in size and shape, and it was the color, almost, of an eggplant. He kept his eyes on my prong, which seemed hardy and useful and insistently hard. His head was shaved, and he wore a Tommy Hilfiger T-shirt through which he rubbed his rubbery tits. Coach eyed us both, shrugging his shoulders and dropping his pants, and we were all unimpeded. I reached out and plucked at one of Coach's rusty nipples—it shrank up and pointed at me. I twisted until I heard him sigh.

I wanted them side by side, their similar, contrasting bangers swinging toward my mouth. Tommy's curved downward as though tugged by gravity and its heavy purple knob. He smacked it against his thigh until it left wet marks. Coach's cock was bone-hard and ruler-straight. I decided then and there to blow them both. I wasn't much of a cocksucker—not much!—but when would this ebony-and-ivory opportunity present itself again? I went to my knees in the alcove between them, and they both stepped up.

I licked Tommy's salty tip and held on to Coach's staff, jacking the rocky thing as I nosed under the plummy hang of Tommy's balls. I looked up to see the two of them fiddling with one another's pecs, their hands pawing, their faces coming closer and closer. I switched to the concrete head of Nicholson's dick, forcing it to the back of my throat. I heard his sigh and the smack of lips, and I squinted up to see Tommy's snaking tongue bathing the stubble of Nicholson's chin. I felt my own leaky piece twitch. Tommy thrust his dick in my face, and someone's fingers tangled in my hair.

I sucked one and then the other, switching back and forth. I was pretty pleased with my performance, and my cock was feeling as though the head would come off in a gooey blast. I pulled on it until I felt my nuts suck up into my insides, and my pecker vibrated over and over again.

Coach was close too, I could tell, but there was no telling when Tommy would get off. I decided to concentrate on Nicholson's sticky knob, using my hand to get to where my mouth couldn't. His hands cradled my head, holding it still, and he fucked into me, and I swallowed an amazing amount of dick. He made a noise, something between a moan and a growl, and he pulled out, swearing and panting, looking down at his pipe. He aimed for my mouth, his own gaping, and shot five or six blasts into me, thick and stringy.

Tommy grunted with approval and lust and turned my head with a finger and added his own deposit of come, adding to my already sizable postnasal drip.

"Ah, shit," I said, feeling like a cat stretching in the sun. I tossed a big load onto the gray linoleum, getting a little on Tommy's Filas.

I got home after dark, and McFeeley was on the couch watching *The Ren & Stimpy Show*. He was wearing a pair of boxers and some dark-heeled socks. He lifted his hand in greeting.

His boxers were the tattersall ones, my favorites, and I found myself wishing I hadn't just wasted my time and come back at the 222 Adulte Shoppe. I could see the warm, soft, fuzzy sac that leaked out of the leg of Mack's shorts. I felt a little wistful.

I went into the bathroom, ready for a shower. Mack followed me. I turned on the water and started undressing. Mack sat on the lidded toilet watching me. "What?" I said, getting down to my shorts and finding my dick glued to the inside of my briefs. I gave a little yank and felt as though I had ripped off a chunk of skin. I checked for bleeding. McFeeley snorted.

"Where were you?" he asked, smirking. "Who was sucking your dick?"

"Sex, sex, sex, McFeeley—is that all you think of?" I said, my cock pulsing upward.

Long Way Home

Billy Tompkins was going home on leave. He was hitchhiking up from Fort Stubbs, riding first with a trucker and a traveling salesman and then with a couple of college jocks who got him stoned on some killer weed. When asked what his plans were, he'd say, "I got myself some catching up to do," and he'd notice the twang he'd managed to pick up in a few short months from bunking with some good old boys from Arkansas and Georgia. One of them, a boy named Hachett, had blown him in a supplies room at the PX where they were both working the day before he left. "I really miss my fiancée," Hachett had said, wiping come off his chin with the back of his hand. His load lay on the floor between Tompkins's shiny black leather boots.

"Why?" Billy'd asked. "Does your fiancée have a dick?" He smirked, wiping off the wet end of his pecker and shoving it back into his shorts.

"I'm making do," the soldier had explained. "And I'm being faithful to my Kathy—she said to stay clear of pussy, or she'd cut my business off." Hachett took a hankie from his pocket and cleaned up the floor. "Look," he'd said, getting up off his knees, "I ain't queer or nothing, but if you bring a rubber next time, you can fuck me up my ass."

"I'll keep that in mind," Billy'd said.

He was thinking about that in the car with the college kids. The air was thick with pot smoke, and one of them cracked a window. The fresh air smelled sweet to Billy. He had his hands folded over the crotch of his pants, applying steady, even pressure on the ridge of his bone. Dope made him horny and then sleepy—he was enjoying the horny part of this buzz and looking forward to the heavy nap that would come later. The boys talked about school, some fraternity on campus.

"They're a bunch of fags," the one driving said. Billy couldn't remember what his name was. He had dark hair that was cut short like Billy's so that his scalp showed white—hair like a 5-o'clock shadow. They both had good sets of shoulders, Billy observed, and the other kid—his name was Todd—had some nice definition in his arms, visible when one was slung over the back of the seat. Billy had noticed when they first stopped for him that they were both wearing shorts, even though it was cold.

"But you pledged that house anyway, didn't you?" Todd said.

"Fuck you," the other one shot back.

Was his name Travis? Billy wondered.

"No way; it hurt too much the last time," Todd said, laughing. "Keep that big thing away!"

Travis, or whatever his name was, looked in the rearview mirror and caught Billy staring. "You OK back there, soldier?" he asked.

Billy nodded. "I forgot my name," he said.

"I told you that shit was good," Todd said, twisting in his seat and hanging over the back of it.

"No," Billy said, laughing at himself and going red in the

face. "I mean *his* name." He pushed playfully at the driver's head with his fingers.

"He's Taylor, and I'm—"

"I remember you," Billy said. "You're Todd. I got a cousin named Todd."

"Small world," Taylor said.

"Ain't it?" Todd said, looking long at Billy, then looking away, out the window on Billy's left. He laid his chin on the headrest. The boy had dirty-blond hair and eyes that were greenish blue. His skin was pale, and his lips were full, half smiling. He twisted his fingers, making his knuckles crack.

"Maybe you want to get in the fucking backseat," Taylor said, elbowing Todd's side.

"Fuck you," Todd said back.

"Maybe I want him back here," Billy said. "That all right with you, Taylor?"

Their eyes met in the rearview mirror. "I don't give a fuck," Taylor said.

"Taylor hates sex," Todd said. "Sex with other people, that is."

"Eat me," Taylor retorted.

"You're real demanding tonight," Todd replied dryly.

Billy unbuttoned his jeans. He lifted his butt off the seat and pushed his pants down to his knees. Todd seemed to be staring at the white glow of Billy's briefs, but it was getting dark and hard to tell what the boy was looking at. Billy put his hands on the mound of his crotch and kneaded the thickening lump of cock and balls. He grabbed himself and gave a good squeeze, feeling his dick stiffen. He pushed down on his balls so that they pressed against his moist butt hole. He looked to see the boy's head in silhouette, dark shadows where his eyes were, the sky the color of fire through the windshield. Taylor plugged a tape into the stereo, and bass throbbed around Billy's head while his cock throbbed under the heel of his hand. Having freed his knees from his jeans, he put his arms behind his head and spread his legs as wide as they would go. The boy's fingertips went to Billy's thigh, swirling in the dense hair that covered his powerful quads. Todd pushed himself forward, and Billy put his hands out to help him over. Taylor glanced at his buddy and then returned his gaze to the road before him.

"What the fuck are you doing, Ganzer?" he said quietly, barely audible above the loud music.

"I don't know yet," Todd answered, his face close to Billy's in the twilight.

"First," Billy said, "he's going to suck my dick. Is that all right with you, Taylor?" He saw Taylor shrug. "Is that all right?" he repeated.

"Sure," Taylor shot back loudly. "And just what is it that I get to do?"

"You get to listen to your buddy slurping up my cock while you jack yourself off, I guess," Billy said.

Todd's hands slipped under Billy's denim jacket and massaged his pecs roughly. Billy lifted his shirt and grabbed Todd by the neck, guiding his mouth to one of Billy's soft, sensitive nipples. The boy's tongue swirled around it, lapping around the flat brown areola and teasing the fleshy pea-size tit with his teeth. Billy put his hand down the back of the boy's shirt, stroking his spine and the big flat muscles of his back. Todd's mouth slipped off the nip and into the dip of Billy's sternum where an errant patch of hair grew. It was a nice drop down over muscled ridges, following a route of smooth, straight hairs to Billy's soft bush that crept out from under his B.V.D.s. He felt the boy's mouth there, his tongue trying to push under the elastic waistband. He got a hand down between them and helped him out, thumbing down his briefs and baring his pubes for Todd to bury his nose in and the base of his rigid cock for the boy to flick his tongue at. The boy put his hands on Billy's crotch, fingers encircling the handful of genitalia, holding it all tightly and making Billy's erection throb. He got it all out and uncovered and went to work on the big smooth end of it. They both moaned.

Taylor adjusted the rearview mirror in an attempt to check out the action. All he could see, Billy figured, were the dark bob of his buddy's head and the pale contrast of Billy's skin.

Billy managed somehow to get his feet up on the seat in front of him, making a circle with his legs so Todd could get through from below. Billy lifted his ass and allowed Todd access to some dark snatch. "Kiss my hole, buddy," he said. He moved one of his feet over to Taylor's shoulder, and Taylor leaned against it. He felt Taylor fumbling one-handed with the laces of Billy's sneakers, loosening them and trying to work them off. They fell to the front seat. Taylor struggled with the socks next, while his buddy tongue-kissed Billy's pucker and jacked his hard-on.

"You're doing a fine job," he said to Todd, and Taylor tugged on Billy's sock one last time, baring the foot and dropping the sock onto his lap. He put his face close to Billy's foot, resting his cheek along the warm arch, and Billy wriggled his toes against Taylor's bristled scalp. He had to push Todd's hand off his prick—too close, too quick. Taylor's tongue was a surprise on Billy's instep; he licked upward and took Billy's big toe into his mouth. His driving by now had become a little reckless. He pulled over fast and hard, coming to a skidding stop, and surrendered himself to the worship of Billy's left foot, slobbering over it, licking it from ankle to toenail.

Billy played with himself while Todd experimented with fingers. One was easy, two made Billy squirm a bit, but three drove him crazy, and he rode those fingers and jacked himself, using his free hand to play with his tits. Todd began to chew on Billy's inner thigh, and it was over for the soldier. He launched a high-flying gob. It was a come bullet with Todd's name on it, and it hit the boy right between the eyes. Billy could feel Taylor snorting on his ankles with his face pinched tight and guessed the kid was creaming on the front seat.

Todd got out of the car. "Open the trunk," he told Taylor.

"What for?"

"Man, I've got to change my clothes," Todd said.

"Why, you shit yourself back there?" Taylor asked, lighting up a cigarette.

"Something like that," Todd said, grinning in the dark.

Taylor got back on the turnpike after dropping Billy off. Todd sank down in his seat.

"You all right?" Taylor asked, though he didn't really care. He was getting tired of Todd's playing around. They weren't exactly lovers or anything—at least not by Todd's definition. Todd was Taylor's only sexual outlet, though, and Todd's winning ways with other men offered Taylor vicarious experiences he otherwise would have missed.

Todd sighed hard and put his bare feet up on the dash. "He was cute," the boy said after a while, and Taylor silently agreed and wished he'd had the opportunity to suck on more than Billy's feet.

They were still hours away from Massachusetts. Todd nodded off to sleep. Taylor pulled off into a rest stop when he had to pee. He got out of the car and went into the men's room. He was followed in by someone he noticed sitting in a parked van when they pulled in. The two stood a few urinals away from each other and stared at the wall. Neither one of them was pissing yet.

"Kind of cold for shorts, ain't it?" Taylor heard, and he turned to look at the young man beside him. He stood all cocky at the urinal, in tight jeans and cowboy boots caked with mud, aiming with one hand, the other hand on his hip keeping the front of his untucked flannel shirt from getting pissed on. Taylor tried not to glance at the man's crotch.

"Supposed to snow," the man said. Taylor nodded. The man looked at Taylor's legs. Taylor could hear the unsteady flow of piss start from the man's dick. He faced the wall again and started himself.

"Where you headed?" the man asked, turning a little Taylor's way.

Taylor saw the head of the man's cock and the flow that came from it. It stopped, and he gave the thing a shake, and Taylor saw more and more of the cock as it grew in the man's hand. Taylor stiffened up too, and he did his best to keep that fact hidden from the man, but he jumped back when his cock head touched the icy porcelain of the urinal.

"Looks like we got ourselves a couple of problems," the man said, pulling on his dick and smiling.

Taylor's head was spinning. He wished Todd were here; he'd know what to do. He tucked his hard-on away and started to leave, but the man caught him by the arm and held him fast. He guided Taylor's hand to his engorged cock. It was hot and hard as a baseball bat in the sun.

"What's your hurry?" the man said. He was better-looking than Taylor had first thought, with blue eyes and curling brown hair that was thinning over his forehead. He was wide at the shoulders and taller than Taylor by a couple of inches. He smiled in the boy's face, gripped his arm, and rubbed his cock against Taylor's hand, which opened to take hold of the thing.

"Here?" Taylor said, hardly able to speak. *The door could open any minute*, Taylor thought, *and who knows who might walk in. Maybe a cop, for Christ's sake.* He let go of the man and tried to step back, but he was held fast.

"In a stall," the man ordered, and he pushed Taylor along. They squeezed into the last stall, and the man put his hands down Taylor's shorts, cupping the boy's cock and balls, applying gentle pressure. He put his face against Taylor's neck. "You're a cute fucker," Taylor heard him say. Taylor went red and put his hands on the man's shirt, feeling the geography of muscle that covered him.

"What's your name?" the man asked.

"Taylor."

"I'm Nick," the man replied tersely. "I'd, uh, shake your hand, but—"

"No problem," Taylor said. "But what if somebody comes in? They'll see our feet."

"I've got a van," Nick said.

"Let's go," Taylor whispered.

"What about your friend?"

"I'll leave him a note," Taylor said.

Once they reached the van and slid the side door shut, Nick leaned back and watched Taylor go to work. He gripped Nick's long dong and smeared its head against his lips, the juicy tip slicking up his mouth like lip gloss. He tongued the head and heard Nick moan, feeling the muscles of his thighs tense. He ran his free hand up Nick's leg until his fingers were caught up in the hairy thatch of his asshole. Probing the tight ringed lips, he took half of Nick's leaky prick into his mouth, and the head hit the back of Taylor's throat.

Not getting to the bottom of this one, Taylor thought, looking cross-eyed at the rest of the dick he was holding. He breathed in the sweet-and-sour stench of the man's crotch, closing his eyes and lifting his head, beginning to give Nick a proper blow job. He tried to remember everything Todd had taught him this past semester in their dorm room, when they should have been writing papers and reading Kant. He worked his mouth up and down, pursing his lips at the knob and letting them stretch wide when he sucked down the mile-long shaft. Every now and then he'd notice a fresh seepage of precome that would set his mouth watering, and big glistening strands of spit would drool off his chin and down onto Nick's hairy balls.

"Damn," Nick said appreciatively.

Taylor grunted in reply. He could tell by all the usual signs that the guy was just a few bobs of the head away from blasting off. He backed off and let Nick regroup, which involved pushing Taylor down on the carpeted floor of the van and pulling off his shorts. Taylor's rod stood in the chill, a nice fist-filler around which Nick couldn't close his hand. He stared at the fat, pale head and then kissed it. Taylor bucked his hips and butted the end of his dick against Nick's lips.

Nick looked down at the boy. "That's a lot of cock," he said appreciatively.

Taylor blushed, and he made his dick dance in Nick's hand, silently begging for the heat of Nick's mouth. He got it soon enough, and it was hotter than he had imagined. He put his hands in Nick's hair and forced the man down to the pubes. Nick gagged and came up for air. "Yeah, I like that," he said, going down on Taylor again. He flattened his nose against the boy's bush, and Taylor kept him there. Nick gobbled up prick and stretched his jaw, snorting into Taylor's wiry hairs. He came up again and said, "Let's fuck."

"Not with that," Taylor said, pointing at the long, jutting pole between Nick's legs.

"Well, I can't have this in me," Nick said. "My ass won't open that wide."

"Sure it will," Taylor said.

Nick stared at the boy's twitching cock, shaking his head. "No fucking way," Nick said, jacking on the thick club and bringing a shine to the piss slit. "You could hump my butt crack, though."

Taylor shrugged. *Close enough*, he thought, as Nick got on his hands and knees and proffered Taylor the beautiful vista of his hair-choked cleavage. He grabbed the man by the hips, planted his shaft in the ditch of Nick's behind, and started rutting him that way. He pushed Nick's shirt up, baring the man's back and raking it with his fingernails. He slipped his hands underneath his muscled torso, finding the pointed tips of Nick's nipples and taking hold of them, pinching and pulling.

Nick's crack was rough, and the hair there was wiry and raspy. Taylor was having the time of his life. He humped Nick squint-eyed, wishing all along that he could slip and plunge deep into the hot man's ass. He'd never fucked anyone ever—Todd wouldn't let him. Being this close to the real thing was making Taylor sweat. He let go of Nick's tits and moved his hands across the man's stomach, grabbing his rigid pipe and shaking off drops of ooze.

"Does it feel good?" Nick asked as Taylor plowed along the furrow of the man's butt. "I can feel your balls against my hole, man; it's making me crazy."

The underside of Taylor's prick was on fire, and he pulled on Nick's, evening their strokes. "I'm close, buddy," Nick whispered. The van was rocking now with Taylor's humping, and Nick started heaving and tossing his head around and swearing through gritted teeth. Taylor wondered what noises Nick would have made had he been plugged with cock. He gripped the man's endless shaft, smashed his face into Nick's back, and shot up suddenly, hosing over Nick's tight rosebud and creaming his sucked-up balls. Nick straightened up and pushed Taylor's hand away as he milked himself a thick puddle that lay steaming on the van's carpeting. Taylor's cock stuck tight between Nick's legs.

Nick drove home with his radio turned up loud, listening to his favorite country-music station. When Garth Brooks came on, he turned the volume up even more and drummed his fingers on the steering wheel. He'd had recurring sex dreams about the country singer. He gave his crotch a squeeze—it was a little tired—but if Garth had sung a little and drawled "Get it on up, boy," Nick would have popped a boner toot-sweet.

When he got home he checked his answering machine, and the light was flashing. He knew who it was. It was Willy Hachett, his little soldier boy down in Fort Stubbs. Nick felt a small flash of guilt. Willy was calling to check up on him and let him know that he was saving himself for his next leave.

"Oh, Kathy," Hachett's recorded voice said. "I can't wait to get home and feel your pussy deep inside me." Nick laughed at his paranoid buddy's mistake—Willy was sure his army buddies were listening in on his conversations. *Oh, well,* Nick thought, slipping a hand in his pants and giving his cock a tug. "Oh, Willy," he said out loud, wrapping his hand tightly around his long, hard shaft. He wouldn't mind if Hachett were here right now, on his hands and knees. He wouldn't mind slipping his "pussy" deep inside Willy's butt and hearing his soldier sigh, "Oh, Kathy."

"I got your Kathy right here," Nick said, swinging his prick like a bullwhip. He got up again and pulled up his jeans. He grabbed the van keys, left the house, and got back on the road again, wondering how long it would take him to drive to Fort Stubbs.

Trick, the Butcher's Apprentice, and the Half Brothers Bermder

Up on a hill overlooking Hardcastle was a decrepit trailer resting in a field of automobile carcasses and rusted metal barrels filled to bursting. There were a number of dogs on the property—wild curs attracted to the field by its owners' habit of tossing garbage out the windows and scraping dirty dishes just outside the door.

Lester Bermder stepped out of the trailer. The pack of dogs scattered automatically. He surveyed his vast land-holdings with pleasure—everything was his as far as his eye could see, thanks to his great-granddaddy's prudent investing and robber-baron tendencies, not to mention a hint of pyromania. A loud groan came from inside the trailer, making Lester wince and reminding him that all he saw was not his and his alone but shared grudgingly with his half brother, Lester Paul.

Lester scratched his belly, made hard with hundreds of sit-ups every day. He dug a hand into his underwear—all he had on—and did some more scratching. His hair was wild across his head, big waves of yellow to be tamed only with pomade and a hot comb. His face was angled, dimpled, full-lipped, and furred, and his nose would have been pretty if it hadn't been busted so many times. He was big, big and hard, and he caught the eye of many a shopgirl in town—not to mention a few glances from certain menfolk as well. "If only he wasn't a Bermder," the girls would sigh.

The Bermder name was none too popular in these parts, thanks to Lester's great-grandfather, Lester Marie Bermder, who purposely and maliciously blew up the wool mill—which had been the mainstay of the economic community—wreaking financial hardship on nearly every citizen of Hardcastle. And then, to add insult to injury, Lester Marie Bermder bought up virtually every inch of land from the suddenly destitute citizens of the town, and he also bought the interest in the mill and had it rebuilt, restoring the town's commerce. So even today there wasn't a father who would stand to have his daughter hitched to a Bermder. Few have tried and remain an example for future generations. One unfortunate girl found herself tarred and feathered and run out of town, and her hapless husband, the late Elijah Lester Bermder, unwilling to have a wife who looked like a chicken and smelled like roofing material, let her go. This was the double threat of being connected to the Bermder clan—that the town would turn its back on you and the Bermders would too. And, of course, one had to consider as well the genetic implication of bringing another Bermder into the world.

And so stood the last of the long line of Bermders, Lester Bermder, while his bastard half brother, Lester Paul, jiggled the trailer and made a general ruckus. Lester beat on the side of the trailer, denting its aluminum siding.

"I told you I'd let you know when I was done, you big stupid butt fuck," came Lester Paul's reply, shouted through the wall with much vehemence.

"Hurry the fuck up then, for crying out loud, you dumb cunt," Lester shouted back and was heard clearly by Lester

Paul and by much of the community of Hardcastle, on their way to Sunday service. Lester heard then the chugging and puffing of Lester Paul, striving toward release.

"Don't get none on my pillow this time, dick lick," Lester added, and Lester Paul began his hooting and hollering, and Lester put his hand in his undershorts again, gripping his thickening prick. He pulled it out and took a short piss into the weeds that grew by the steps. He heard his half brother's heavy breathing. Lester Paul stood in the doorway, filling it. Broad and dark, he leaned against the doorjamb with his big arms folded across his chest. He was profusely tattooed. His belly was covered with curly black hairs, and some were caked with a creamy white smear of fresh come.

"Damn," Lester said, looking away from the stuff and the front of Lester Paul's underwear, which was dotted with piss stains and more fresh jizz and packed full with Lester Paul's fat goddamned dong and boccie-ball testicles. He thought, the way he always would think, seeing Lester Paul's massive artillery, that it was cruel justice that his bastard half brother ended up with the bigger set of jewels. Lester had himself his formidable version of a whopper now and pushed his brother aside.

"My turn," he said, and Lester Paul stepped out on the landing, thumbing open his shorts to stick his prick out the leg hole and take a sputtering leak.

Lester had his dick out before he hit the bed. The sheets were cold and smelled like his ass, and he pushed his face into them as if they were a bouquet of daisies. He humped his mattress silly, pushing a pile of pillows down to his crotch, wadding them around his throbbing billy club, creating for himself a pleasant burrow. His hands twisted in the sheets, and he arched his back, driving himself deep into the pussy pillow. He squeezed his eyes shut and flared his nostrils and held his breath. Images ran through his mind: pictures of boys just out of high school, boys who worked at supermarkets, boys in red-striped boxer shorts, boys in gym socks, boys in naked embrace. He had a crush now on just such a boy, the boy who was the butcher's apprentice at the Shop-Ease. Lester threw his head back and grunted through the gnashing of his teeth while his dick spat out gobs of semen, making a soggy fucking mess of his pillows.

They skipped a shower and headed into town for breakfast. Lester was already thinking about stopping in at the Shop-Ease for a tenderloin or something. "Tender loins," he muttered and began to giggle at his own funny. He sat behind the wheel of the old Dodge pickup, bouncing in his seat and not quite seeing the road before him.

"Jesus Christ, Lester," Lester Paul said, doing some of the steering himself, keeping them from running off the road and into a row of mailboxes. Lester Paul took a look at himself in the rearview mirror when Lester could be trusted to drive unattended. He slicked back his hair with his hand. It was chestnut-brown and had a mind of its own. He pulled a comb from the glove box and spit across the teeth and ran that through his hair. He was every bit as good-looking as his half brother, and it was a damn shame, he was thinking, that he had to leave the county to get pussy. He pulled his hands inside his overalls and touched his warm crotch. He tried to remember how long it had been since he'd had any. He scratched his dick hairs to help himself think.

"Lester, when we get laid last?" he asked finally.

Lester fingered the hairs on his chin.

"Can't say," he said. Lester had come close, he remembered, the one time he drove to Drexlerville for that alternator and stopped in a public pisser for a spell on the crapper.

"Damn," Lester Paul said, rubbing himself hard.

" 'Nough of that," Lester said.

Up ahead a boy was standing with his thumb cocked. Lester Paul spotted him first and told Lester to stop.

"There ain't no room up here, and he can't go in the back with all them dead chickens, you know," Lester said. He slowed up, though, and was going about ten miles an hour when he passed the boy.

"Plenty of room up here," Lester Paul said, sliding over close to his half brother. The boy ran up to the old Dodge and leaned in the window. He was probably close to 20, Lester reckoned, scrutinizing the boy's face while Lester Paul asked him where he was going.

"Don't matter," the boy said. "Wherever."

He got in, and Lester Paul moved over a little and a little more, until it seemed to Lester that he had nearly half

the front seat to himself again.

"We're heading for some eats, me and my half brother here," Lester Paul offered. "We got ourselves a diner in town since we don't cook ourselves."

"You bought a diner," the boy said incredulously, "because you don't cook at home?" He laughed, showing straight white teeth. His hair was blond and strangely cut, Lester thought—shaved all around the bottom and left to grow on top. The boy had an earring and a tattoo of a scorpion on the arm he rested along the back of the seat. He wasn't as big as the Bermder brothers, but he had a decent build—at least so far as Lester could tell, what with Lester Paul hogging the view.

"You're not from around here," Lester Paul said. "We're the Bermders. Ever hear of us?"

The boy shook his head. The brothers shared a look at each other.

"I'm Lester Paul. This is my half brother, Lester."

"Seriously?" the kid said, bending forward to look at Lester's face. Lester smiled and nodded. "Nice to meet you," the boy said, raising his hand off the seat.

Lester looked at him, and so did Lester Paul.

"It sure is nice to meet you too," Lester said, leaning over his half brother to see the boy directly. His shirt was opened and revealed a chest pleated with muscle. "Hey," he said, "are you a model?"

Lester Paul elbowed him good in the bread box.

"Lester, you best keep your eyes to the road since you just about ran over Thelma Goodly, Mr. Rubberneck."

Lester elbowed his half brother back twice as hard, but with little to no effect. Lester Paul turned in his seat and faced the boy, who seemed to take all this in with some amusement.

"Hey," Lester Paul said, "you sure are pretty."

"What's that smell?" the boy wanted to know.

Lester and Lester Paul ducked their heads simultaneously to sniff their armpits. Then Lester said, "Probably them dead chickens."

"Got to get them to the dump," Lester Paul said. "I thought I told you, Lester, to get them to the dump. Boy, you never listen."

"*You* told *me*? Goddamn it, Lester Paul, it was *me* telling *you*." Lester leaned over his half brother again to smile at the boy and look at his crotch.

They were sitting at their table with their milk shakes while the boy was in the bathroom. Lester Paul was fuming because the boy had opted to sit beside Lester. "You keep your hands to yourself," he said now through gritted teeth, "else you want them broke."

"Lester Paul, you don't scare me none, and I can't help it if I have magnetism," he said charmingly, daring even to blush.

"You got a boy," Lester Paul insisted. "And I saw this one first."

"It's up to the boy," Lester said, "and here he comes."

The kid was just shy of six feet and probably considered himself good-sized, but he must have felt downright waifish beside the Bermders. He slid next to Lester and ducked his head down to his coffee cup to take a sip. Breakfast came—six eggs to a plate, a stack of pancakes about a foot high, and about 50 strips of bacon.

The Bermders were dainty eaters with flawless table manners. Their meal took them quite a while, and the boy sat back, positively stuffed, as the brothers slowly and meticulously cleaned their plates over and over again.

With the food out of the way, Lester Paul once again made eyes at the boy. "I'm just traveling around, going wherever, you know?" the boy said. "Did you ever read *On the Road*?"

"Can't say that I have," Lester Paul said.

"He don't know how to read," Lester said and felt a size-12 boot crack against his shinbone, which he suffered silently, slitting his eyes at his half brother. "Excuse me," he said to the boy, putting a hand on his thigh. "I think I'll head on over to the Shop-Ease now." He slid out of the booth and stood beside the boy. "I don't believe I caught your name," he said graciously.

"Trick," the blond said.

"Well, Rick," Lester started, and the boy rushed to correct him: "It's Trick, like magic trick, you know?"

"Like trick or treat," Lester Paul added, nodding and grinning like a fool.

"Well, it sure was nice meeting you, Trick," Lester said, shaking the boy's hand excessively.

Lester stood in the cold-cuts line until his number was called. He stepped up to the high counter and smiled over it. "Hey," he said softly, and Danny Waxford looked back at him blankly. The paper hat he wore was cocked, riding the short, slicked-up bristles of his hair.

"May I help you, sir?" the butcher's apprentice asked.

Lester scowled. "Don't you love me no more?" he whispered, pushing his head over the counter. He saw the kid's eyes dart left and right.

"You're going to get me fired," he said without moving his lips. "You have to order something."

"I'll have some of that headcheese," Lester said grandly, adding as an aside, "whyn't you come by the trailer after your shift, and we can have some fun." He winked then, and Danny winked back. He handed Lester a wrapped package of headcheese and let his fingers trail over the man's big hands.

"There you go, sir," Danny said. "My dick's hard, dude."

"So's mine," Lester said, and he backed away from the counter to show the boy, treading on some old lady's feet. He turned and caught hold of Thelma Goodly, whose face was screwed up in pain. He picked her up and sat her down on some canned goods and got himself through the checkout line and out of the store as quickly as possible, the big club of his desire banging up against the front of his overalls.

Lester Paul, meanwhile, was having no trouble getting into Trick's pants. While they waited in the truck for Lester, Lester Paul simply grabbed the boy and pulled him across the seat, positioning himself over the shocked boy. And somehow, like Houdini, Lester Paul managed to get Trick's jeans undone and down to his knees. "Are you crazy?" the boy asked, his voice muffled against Lester Paul's hard chest. He knew that somewhere over him, behind his assailant, there was a windshield and a parking lot filling up with people just out of church.

"Crazy for you," Lester Paul said, digging into his overalls and grabbing his big aching need. "You got me all worked up." Trick felt the hardness of it through his clothes and Lester Paul's clothes—it felt as though someone had shoved the thick end of a baseball bat in between the two of them.

The truck door swung open.

"Damn it all, Lester Paul, I saw you from the checkout line," Lester shouted. "What in the good goddamn are you doing in here?" Lester Paul got up reluctantly, and Trick unbent himself and sat up as straight as he could, leaving his pants where they were. His prick had slipped up out of his briefs, its head hot against the hairy trail that meandered up the boy's belly. "Oh, my, that's a fat one," Lester Paul hummed.

"Now *you're* driving," Lester said, getting in beside Trick. Lester Paul positioned himself behind the steering wheel and pressed mightily on his crotch so that there was an audible crack that made Trick wince. Suddenly Lester Paul swung over Trick and put his finger in Lester's face.

"Don't you make no moves, you dirty son of a bitch," he said menacingly. He started the truck and slammed it into gear, and they were on their way, and before they were out of the lot, Trick had his hand on Lester Paul's humongous thigh, rubbing it up and down and generally causing a wet ruckus in Lester Paul's shorts. Lester Paul kept both hands on the wheel to make up for the fact that he wasn't really watching where they were going; instead, he eyed the boy's white cotton crotch.

"Lester Paul, you're going to kill us all dead, and you won't even have gotten your end wet with this one," Lester said calmly, hanging his arm out the window, and the truck careened over Hailey Capshaw's petunia bed. He said to Trick, "I'm sorry, boy, but you're going to have to cover up them pretty freckled thighs of yours as they're driving my brother here to distraction. Unless, of course, you're wanting to die in a fiery automobile accident."

Trick pulled up his pants, and Lester Paul's driving improved, but not much.

Lester either tried or pretended to watch television while Lester Paul and Trick romped in the back of the trailer. "Would you look at all these tattoos!" he heard Lester Paul bragging. He kept his eye on the clock, waiting for his boy's shift to be over. Come 5 o'clock, Lester was pacing, worried that the boy was standing him up. Meanwhile, the two in the back were carrying on like sailors on leave. There was much moaning and groaning and sucking noises and fucking noises. Lester could see their shadows on the curtain that separated the sleeping quarters from the rest of the trailer, and their bodies came together before his very eyes in a strange configuration Lester thought he'd never live to see—Lester Paul squatting over to get it up the ass. Lester marched up to the curtain and yanked it open.

"Just what in the hell do you think you're doing, Lester Paul?" Lester demanded. "I'd really like to know."

Lester Paul looked up. Trick was practically riding him piggyback; he held onto Lester Paul by the shoulders, although his dick insertion assured him sufficient foothold, so to speak.

"You just never mind—and shut that curtain, Nosy Rosie," Lester Paul said, squatting and allowing Trick to put his feet back on the floor.

"Now, you know a Bermder don't ever do that kind of thing, Lester Paul. What would Daddy say?" And Lester gave his half brother a swift kick to the nuts. Lester Paul clutched his privates and howled like a wounded dog. He straightened up so fast, he threw the boy off. Lester heard them uncouple with a pop, and Trick hit the back wall of the trailer with a thud.

"I think you just killed your new husband," Lester said. Just then there was a knock on the door. Lester put his hand inside his T-shirt and touched a nipple. He shut the curtain and opened the trailer door. Danny stood out on the stoop, peering in.

"Well, come in," Lester said, grabbing the boy's arm.

"I thought there was some sort of rumble going on," Danny said.

"Boy, are you all right?" Lester Paul was saying behind the curtain. "Speak to me, boy, speak to me." Danny and Lester heard Trick's low moan.

"Everything's going to be all right," Lester said. He pulled the curtain open again. "OK, lovebirds, hit the pike. It's me and my buddy's turn."

"I didn't even come yet, you son of a bitch," Lester Paul said. "And besides, I think Trick's neck is busted and he ain't ought to be moved. Hey there, guy," he said to Danny, waving, before turning his attentions again to Trick, who was lying twisted on the bed.

Lester turned to Danny and caught him staring at Lester Paul's naked body. "That one there is a picture of his mama," Lester said, pointing out a particular tattoo. "Ain't she the ugliest white woman you ever saw?"

"She's your mama, too, ain't she?" Danny said.

"I told you," Lester said patiently, "my mama's the true Mrs. Bermder. Christ only knows who that old whore is." And he pointed at the not-so-pretty ink drawing of Lester Paul's mother.

"Leavc us be," Lester Paul said. Trick seemed to be reviving; leastwise, he had a fresh erection, and Lester Paul was already getting up on the mattress, planting his big feet on either side of the boy's hips. Trick's dick was pointing straight up at Lester Paul's chute.

"Don't do it, Lester Paul!" Lester shouted as his half brother dropped his ass down and impaled himself on Trick's beefy prick. "Bermders don't ever take it up the giggy." Danny gulped audibly, and Lester turned away as if it were too much to bear. Lester Paul commenced to riding the sausage. The sight of the huge man, his back marked up with tats, was impressive, especially when he lifted himself all the way off Trick's sizable pole and slammed himself down onto it again without so much as a whimper. Lester saw his little buddy grope himself. He slipped a hand down the back of Danny's pants and found the boy was without underwear. As Lester Paul bounced himself against Trick's hips, Lester poked with his finger against the bung hole of the butcher's apprentice.

"Are you in the mood for some loving?" Lester whispered in Danny's ear. The boy nodded his head. He stepped sideways, and Lester saw the big impression of Danny's great curving cock against the tight, worn front of his pants.

Lester Paul's back was slicked over with sweat. Lester could easily ignore his half brother's shiny bobbing ass, but Danny seemed to be mesmerized by the sight. He stood staring while Lester plied his ass with big mauling hands, fingering the boy roughly. He got Danny's pants undone and pushed them down to his knees. He himself went down to his knees, pressing his face against Danny's piss-smelling privates. He stuck his nose in the boy's pubic bush and breathed deeply. He rooted around under his buddy's nut sac, lapping each hanging orb with the flat pad of his tongue.

Danny touched Lester's head absently. "I want to do that," he said.

Lester pulled his head from between Danny's thighs.

"Now you're talking, little buddy," Lester said, getting up from his position on the floor. "Whyn't you just bend over, and I'll get you greased up." He licked back some drool that was beginning to seep from the corners of his mouth.

"Lester," Lester Paul grunted.

"Huh?" Lester said, staring at his buddy's jewels.

"Come here, would you," Lester Paul said breathlessly. Lester eyed his half brother.

"Why?" he said slowly.

"I want you to check if Trick here is still breathing. He ain't moved since he hit the wall," Lester Paul said, still riding on the unconscious boy. Lester leaned over the boy's face, trying to ignore the big swings of Lester Paul's cock and balls—he was loath to admit Lester Paul's size advantage. Trick's eyes did some fluttering then, and he let out a low moan.

Lester straightened up and said, "He's all right," and he couldn't help feeling admiration for a boy with a stand-up dick even when he himself wasn't able to stand. He gave Trick a long look, from the top of his head to underneath Lester Paul's bouncing butt. He touched his own granite member; the old pole was ready for sticking.

Lester got himself back to his boy, feeling all heated up and ready to give the boy a nasty ride. He towered over Danny Waxford and was breathing hard already. He wanted to engulf the boy, ride him from behind, cover him with his whole body, which was less than difficult—he was about 6 foot 5, and Danny was maybe 5 foot 8 with his sneakers on. He wanted to hunker down over the boy right there on the trailer floor, just a few feet away from his half brother, who was riding the unconscious Trick. He put his arms around the boy, turning him around so that Lester's pants-bound throbber was hard between Danny's shoulder blades.

"Oh, no, Lester," Danny said, twisting fast in the hulk's grasp. "This ain't what I had in mind."

"Well, what in hell were you referring to, then?" Lester said, looking down at Danny's bristled head.

"I thought it would be me doing the driving, if you know what I mean," Waxford said, winking up at Lester.

Lester winked back. "So, you want to go for a ride, do you? Well, why didn't you say so?"

He grabbed his coat and turned to the door.

"No, no, no," Danny said, shaking his head. "That ain't what I mean."

"He wants to fuck you," Lester Paul said. He twisted himself around so that he was facing his half brother and the butcher's apprentice. They could see clearly now the slide of Trick's sewer pipe in and out of the stretched hole of Lester Paul's butt.

Lester gaped. "Don't it hurt?" he cried.

"Dumb shit, does it look like it hurts?" Lester Paul said, balancing with one hand and tugging on a tit with the other. "Feels like I died and went to heaven."

Danny nudged Lester with his dick. It was long and strong and made a right-hand turn that Lester found charming.

"Don't you love me, Lester?" Danny said, making his eyes big and puppylike.

"It's just that it's always been a Bermder tradition to be the man when it comes to men," Lester said with some hesitation.

"You don't know what you're missing," Lester Paul said, filling his butt with juicy boy cock. Trick moaned again, less in pain this time and more in pleasure. Though still unconscious, there was an enormous amount of stimulation for him to process. He rolled his hurt head from side to side, seeming to enjoy the working-over his pecker was receiving.

"This is certainly a dilemma for me," Lester said, scratching his head and then digging into his pants, bypassing his engorged cock to scratch his nuts. The fastener of his pants burst, and what with all the nuts and bolts and lottery tickets in his pockets, Lester's pants dropped to the floor as if his legs had been greased. Meanwhile, Danny sucked on a finger, getting it nice and slick, and he arched around Lester and dug into the man's hairy ass crack. The wet finger slipped up inside, and Lester gasped like a girl slipping on cold panties.

"You could've warned me," he said, squirming on Waxford's digit, which felt impossibly thick and knobby. How, he wondered, would he endure Danny's curving club?

"Not so bad, is it?" Danny said, licking at Lester's chest, the big smooth muscle of it, dotted with a tiny hard nipple. Lester blushed.

Danny shrugged off his shirt so that he was standing nearly naked beside the huge man. He was thin and wiry, almost hairless. Lester ate him up with his eyes—he was stymied by the sight of the boy's naked rib cage. He was ready to suck on the boy like a juicy chicken bone. Lester glanced at his half brother. The thick staff between Lester Paul's legs hopped stiffly while his ass gobbled up Trick's massiveness.

"Bend over," he heard Danny say. He put his hands on the dirty mattress, close to Trick's bare feet. He felt Danny's hands on his ass cheeks, spreading them, and then he felt the boy's hot breath run across his pucker.

"Yikes!" Lester bleated, and he pinched out a little fart, like a sulfurous kiss. Danny backed off, resting on his haunches, and made another assault, this time plunging into the knot of

Lester's fanny. The knot loosened almost immediately, and Danny was munching butt with great finesse. Lester leaned on his elbows, Trick's toes just inches from his face. Lester could smell their sneaker funk. He eyed the bouncing Lester Paul, who eyed him back. Lester stuck his tongue out and touched the tip of it to Trick's bony big toe. Danny put his tongue into Lester, who sighed sweetly while sucking on Trick's feet, licking between the boy's toes, his tongue action corresponding to Danny's.

"I think you're ready," Danny said, getting up and bucking the knob of his prick against Lester's balls. Lester gnawed on Trick's sole, nodding. Danny blew a wad of spit onto his dick and smoothed it around. Lester felt the tip of it press against his sphincter. Danny's head was diamond-shaped—not a big, flat, featureless mushroom cap like Lester's. Lester's cock head looked like the flat end of a good-size ball peen hammer. Danny probed gently, putting more and more of himself into Lester's steaming cavity until he was jammed in to the hilt between the big guy's stony cheeks. He stroked Lester's back.

"You OK?" Danny asked.

Lester tried to answer, but he had half of Trick's foot in his mouth. He did his best to nod. Danny commenced to fucking with long, slow strokes. Lester stopped sucking. The sensation in his rectum was like nothing he'd ever experienced, save for a couple of memorable and healthy shits he'd taken. He relaxed totally and even pressed himself against the oncoming prong. Danny tried to reach around the man and play with his tits, but his arms weren't long enough, so he contented himself with the hanging pendulum of Lester's balls.

Lester Paul by now was on a low boil. He was humming, with his eyes turned heavenward, his fist beating fast on his meat, scattering drops of precome and sweat. He began to pant and bring himself down so hard on the boy that the trailer shook. Lester Paul stopped breathing, and his dick exploded. Lester caught most of it in the face; his half brother's goo clung to his lips.

"Oh, goodness," Lester said, his tongue slipping out to clean his mouth. He arched his back and asked the boy to slam him. He dipped down a little, and the kid was right there, right on it, banging on something up Lester's butt that buzzed through the big man's body.

"Yeah," Lester growled. "Yeah, baby, yeah." He shook his head and sprayed everyone with sweat. He growled and beat his fists on the mattress. Lester Paul could see his brother's fat and stubby prick pulsing.

"You're ready," Lester Paul grinned, nodding his head. Danny let out a little squeal, doing his best to keep it together, but he looked as if his banana was about to split with pleasure.

"I can't…hold it…any…longer," he said haltingly, like a boy gripping the side of a cliff. His eyes rolled back just as Lester held his breath and banged out wad after wad of cream.

"Yahoo!" Lester Paul shouted, and from underneath the darker Bermder came the muffled groan of the slowly reviving Trick.

"Oh, my," Lester Paul said, standing up as the boy beneath him shot a copious load that covered the insides of Lester Paul's thighs, making a general mess of him.

"I sure am hungry," Lester Paul said, rubbing his naked belly. All four men were sprawled together, legs entwined.

"There are them chickens I saw in the back of your truck," Danny said, eager to test his butchering skills.

"I say we get on down to your diner," Trick said; he was obviously feeling much better. "I saw a meat loaf special on the menu."

"Do you like meat loaf?" Lester Paul asked.

"Love it," Trick answered.

"It's my favorite too," Lester Paul said, snuggling up to his new boyfriend.

Danny turned to Lester. "I got a tenderloin test tomorrow I've got to study for," he said sorrowfully.

"That's all right, little buddy," Lester said.

The foursome broke up into pairs, one couple per vehicle—Lester Paul driving the pickup with Trick, Danny driving his car with Lester. They were all holding hands, both drivers being distracted by soulful, closed-eye smooching. One wonders how they made it to the diner in one piece—but then those Bermder boys were always kind of lucky that way.

FEVER

He grabbed me when I was walking by, saying, "Where you been, Carson?" I ain't small, but he is fast and strong, the strongest man I know of, and he got my arm twisted up behind my back. I thought he would bust it off, only I acted as though I didn't feel a thing. But he knew. He always knows.

He was stripped down to his shorts, and I could see he was getting uppity. He had a horse piece that he could swing around like an elephant's trunk, a circus piece, the hurting kind, and I watched it climb the front of his shorts and could see some of it through the fly along with the bunch of black hair he had down there. I heard him laugh at me for looking or for the dumb look on my face, maybe, or maybe because he was a little embarrassed, but I heard him laugh, and I looked up at him.

"Hey, pussy boy," he said, giving me that pickax grin, showing off his gap by sticking his tongue into it for me.

I got myself out from under him; I could do that much, but I didn't know what to do next. He stood there waiting, nostrils flaring, looking peeved. His hair shot off his forehead in a spiky rooster tail greased up with pomade, the same pomade I'd used as dick grease to dick Exton last month. He'd kill me if he ever found out, both about Exton and about using his pomade for fucking.

"Darvis," I said to him, but nothing else came, no other words, just his stupid name, and he looked at me, disarmed, and I grabbed his forearm—thighlike—and somehow got him into a jury-rigged half nelson, hopping around with him. He kept trying to throw me, but we were locked together like lovers, and I wanted to stay that way forever.

Finally he slicked his way out, and we stood facing each other again. I could see his pride, the way it stood so stiffly in his shorts, and I wondered what he had in mind for us to do this time. The last time, I got my hair all cut down to silvery little bristles, and he held me down and dragged his bare ass across my scalp, rasping his bung against my skull and squeezing out his goo all over me. He looked at me now as though he wanted me dead.

Swatting my head with his big hands, he called me "pussy boy" again and again. I held my tongue and watched his eyes and shoulders, which seemed to signal everything a split second before it happened, every movement of his arms, every hand lunge. I stayed back, playing him, watching him. I dreamed about him straddling the stick shift of the Mustang he said he used to have, the blunt, dull-angled head of it buried deep inside his ass. Crazy stuff. What was I to do? I watched his eyes and shoulders for the quick darts that muscles about to be moved make. He'd dance on the end of a pin with a billion other angels—rough-mouthed, dirty-handed.

"Carson," he said.

"It's Dow," I said, disappointment pulling at my mouth; he didn't even know my name. "Carson's gone."

"I know that," he barked, his hands coming at me. He'd throw me to the ground if he could, I knew. I felt the concrete under my bare feet, cold and smooth, waxed by me or Exton Jones or Muhammed. Never Darvis, though. Darvis waxes nothing but bananas, we all said. Never so he could hear us, though.

Darvis was getting peevish, and his initial interest was waning. I could see by the floppy swing in his shorts, the soft head peeking out the hem. His eyes went dull, lids dropping, and his hands unclenched, and he straightened his body, his torso a mosaic of muscle, veins coursing down his arms. I saw him breathe and took a breath myself, and it was over, it wasn't fun anymore, there wasn't any more sport to it. He pulled on the front of his shorts, glancing downward at my crotch. I had yet to lose my interest, my excitement. I was still ready. I stepped up, suddenly unchallenged. It wasn't that he wouldn't whip my ass; I could get him to beat me to death—that's the easy thing for Darvis. I wanted to confuse him, and I could see that I had. His eyes shifted; he looked away and back again and said something, reminding me of a little boy.

I put a hand inside my shirt and touched my chest, the hard dot of a nipple, teasing him. He wanted none of it now, not if he couldn't feel as though he was stealing or hurting. He went back to his corner, to his lumpy cot and faded girlies.

Exton and Muhammed were outside recreating. They'd be back in an hour or so, depending on the weather. It was Sunday, and we didn't have to do anything. Monday through Saturday we were up and cutting down trees, part of the deforestation crew. Darvis laid himself down and covered his eyes with his big arm. Strange to see someone here without any body art, no inky homemade tats—no girls' names, no swastikas, no burning demons.

"You all right?" I asked, because he'd been sick, although he'd never said. I could tell, saw the headache reshape his eyes, heard his teeth chattering at night when we were all sweating hot. "Did you take your quinine?" I asked him.

"Ain't none left," he replied, his lips barely moving.

"I got some still," I told him. "You can have it."

"Keep it," he said. "I'm all right."

His knees were up and bent, legs falling to the sides, and I could see everything falling out. He didn't care; he liked the way we looked at him, mouths open like baby birds. He'd fed us all at one time or another. He had a girl's name for each of us: I was his Connie, Muhammed was Keisha, and Exton was Baby Girl on account of his pouty mouth and blond hair. I'd seen him mouth-fuck Exton, holding him by his golden ponytail. And I'd seen Muhammed spread his ass cheeks and offer his black hole to Darvis and his horse piece and regret it later on.

Darvis wasn't so rough-and-ready now. His limp dick leaked out of his shorts and touched the mattress, so much thick cable, sleek, like an anaconda or whatever the hell kind of snake we saw just this past week hanging from a tree branch, tongue flickering. Exton had pointed to it and said, "Hey, Darvis, put it back in your pants," and we all laughed, even Darvis, who axed the snake's head off as it swung to lick Muhammed's ear.

"I thank you for that," Muhammed said to Darvis, his eyes wide, a bulging artery in his throat throbbing with pulse.

I could feel my own heart beating now up around my ears. The front of my pants showed where I'd leaked, a big wet spot. I pushed the ball of my hand against the hardheaded poke and shuddered. I sat on the edge of his cot, causing him to lift his arm and squint at me. He looked at me for a while, his eyes glassy. I touched his shin, his skin greasy with sweat. He covered his eyes again, granting permission, legs going wider, offering me his piece. I picked it up with my fingers, leaning down between his thighs, elbows making room on the thin mattress. His crotch stank of sweat and three days without a bath, making my mouth water. It was Thanksgiving Day for me, and I was about to eat a turkey dinner. I licked the salty tip of him, wishing he still had his skin like Muhammed did, a soft, sliding sheath for my tongue to play with. I filled my mouth with him easily, snorting through my nostrils. I swallowed what I could, feeling the soft slide down my throat, rubbery, pliable. Hard, it was like swallowing a stick. I liked him best like this—flaccid. I tickled his nuts, pulling the long hairs, and twisted the bag, making him moan a little. I drew my head back, using my teeth to scrape the underside of his shaft, wanting to excite him, to make him hard, but he stayed the way he was. I used my hand, tonguing the fat opening, rubbing my lips hard around the outer edge of his head. There wasn't anything I could do, though, to bring him up, to arouse him. I dug around in my own pants then and brought out my cock. Dribbling pre-come, it was slicked enough to jack, making wet, sticky noises. Darvis's foot moved and came to rest on my exposed balls, and I pushed my pants down, wanting him to put his foot between my legs, to bugger his toe up my ass, which I'd seen him do to Exton once. He kept his toes on my nuts, though, playing against the taut skin.

I groaned on his piece, taking as much as I could into my mouth, stopping my throat and my breath, and I felt the fiery rumble of orgasm on the edge of my palm. I said something unintelligible, that I loved him, and he pressed the ball of his foot firmly just under my balls, and I lost my head, screaming silently, hosing his ankle with my streaming juices.

"Dow," he said, and I dropped his pecker, all sticky with saliva, thicker now, harder. He said I had to clean him up, so I went to get a rag to wipe my spunk from his ankle. I was wetting it when he came up behind me. His piece was all up now, redheaded. I hadn't pulled up my pants yet, and my ass was there for him to take. He spit in the general direction of my hole, missing wide, and slapped my cheeks. He pinched out some of his leakage, smearing it over the head, lubing himself up for my tightness.

His first stab tore me open, it seemed, and he pinned my screaming head against the dirty porcelain of the sink. He fucked my ass with long, deep strokes, his hips slapping my behind, his big, swinging balls knocking against mine. He fucked me as though he had two feet of cock, and that's what it felt like rooting around in my insides. His thickness stretched my anus, his rocky shaft burning my ass lips. I squeezed out tears, trying not to cry. I wanted him like this, always did, wanted to be his bitch, his hole, and I told him so as he ripped me up, racing in and out of me, setting my cunt on fire.

He started calling me Connie, gripping my shoulders and forcing me back against his hips. "Connie, Connie, Connie," he whispered, breathing hard, spittle raining on my back. I wanted him to flip me over so I could see him, his wet chest and little red nipples, the hair on him in smooth, straight lines. I wanted to see the converging lines on either side of his muscled gut meet at his crotch, and I wanted to see his piece, the fat end of it pulling out my guts and pouring buckets of hot come all over my stomach. This wasn't for my benefit, though, and he was doing me his way, ruthlessly skewering me, pleasuring himself angrily, hollering at me for going loose on him, pounding my back and stinging my ass with sharp slaps until he couldn't keep it back any longer and threw himself all the way into me. It felt like he was trying to take a step inside of me, one foot and then the other, putting me on like a pair of pants, and I felt his cheek on my back, then his drool, and he whimpered, trying to hold still as his piece erupted, planting his seed in the hot, spaceless gullet he'd made inside me.

He let me up and said, "I'm ready," and he turned and walked over to where the shower was. I joined him, turning on the water, rubbing my face, waiting for the hot water to come, and he stood beside me, his piece still big, still stiff, stinking of my ass.

I saw him with Exton Jones, pulling on his work pants, making a nuisance of himself. He didn't seem to me to be as mean with Exton as he was with me, but Exton was smaller. He was wiry, scrappy, but he didn't have the muscle or the power. We were all three giants compared to him, and maybe that's why he got it so much, but we were all of us kind to him, even Darvis, and I was always making sure he was taken care of. Whenever I fucked him I fucked him on his back and played with his pecker, bringing him off, and once I sucked him off, but only once, maybe twice, and he said, "Dow, I like you best," but you can't ever believe anything you hear here. Nothing is ever the truth.

We were in the jungle working on a tree as big as a building. Taking it down would bring down four or five other trees as well, we figured, depending on the direction it decided to take. It would take the four of us to do it, all working together. Darvis and Muhammed worked the saws, and Exton and I roped the tree to guide it down the way we wanted. It was a crapshoot, though, and we all knew it, and at midday the tree was still standing and Darvis called for a break, staring at Exton, who was holding the thick rope in his gloveless hands. I wanted to be the one catching Darvis's favor. I always had a 25% chance, I figured—it was myself or Exton Jones or Muhammed or Darvis by himself—but the odds were against me this day, and he winked at Exton, and they went off together into the jungle. I looked at Muhammed, who didn't care; he wasn't really like me or Exton, didn't relish the thought of Darvis's rough hands on him the way we did, didn't crave his big piece or his bad mouth, his hands or his hard fuckings. He whistled up at a queer-colored bird in the tree overhead and said to it, "Sing while you can. You're losing your home soon."

I went into the jungle, following them. I wanted to watch them. I wanted to see what Exton Jones was willing to do for him and see how I could outdistance him, better him. It was crazy, I guess, but I had decided ever since that day we were together that I was in love with him, and I wanted him to be in love with me.

We shaved once a week—Sundays—and all had beards come Fridays save for Exton, who couldn't grow one. With his blond hair, long and silky, he was most like a girl, I guess, and maybe that's what made Darvis so crazy for him. I wasn't much interested in having a girl of my own or in being Darvis's girl either, but I would have been his man in a heartbeat. "You're my man" is what I wanted to hear from him, beating on my chest like a drum, thumping on the thick pad of muscle I had there from secret push-ups. I wanted him to roll over grudgingly, saying something like, "OK, but this ain't going to become a habit." I wanted him to reach back behind himself and pull open those fleshy globes, open those great muscled doors and show me his other door, the one he'd kept hidden, his little pink portal. Oh, man, can you imagine that? Him looking over his shoulder, saying, "Come on in, Dow. Dip your stick, buddy."

What I liked about Exton Jones—what I suspect we all liked from him—was his accommodating manner. He'd do whatever you told him, like he was simple or you had a gun to his head. I liked him because I could say my ass needed cleaning and he'd take my ankles and lift them high and get in between my butt cheeks and lick me clean. I loved to hear him snort around down there, loved the drag of his tongue across my bung, and I'd play with myself, bringing myself up to the very edge of coming, then stopping, over and over until all it would take was a long lick up my shaft and a finger tickling my cunt to make my dick explode. And then I'd say, "Bring it here, Exton," and he'd bring me his cock, his short, thick plug, sticking it in my mouth, and I'd get him to fuck me that way until he'd start whimpering and touching my face and telling me how I was his favorite, his jizz jettisoning down my gulping throat.

I stayed behind them a good distance, not wanting to inhibit them—not that you could, not Darvis. I could see that they'd stopped, and Exton was already on his knees. I could see the thick tube of flesh he was trying to swallow, and I was reminded of snakes and how they'll eat something so much larger than themselves. My throat ached for days last time I blew Darvis. I saw that Exton could put a good amount of it away. He was getting better—*Practice makes perfect,* I said to myself—his head bobbing back and forth, going sideways, loving the shaft with his tongue and teeth. Watching them gave me a hard-on, and I pulled it out to play with, kneeling on the jungle floor like Exton, wishing my mouth was as full as his. I closed my eyes and pictured the man's ass and my mouth kissing it, his balls draped over my face, each orb resting in one of my eyes, the big thing smothering me, making me hungry, hungry enough to take big, toothy bites of his cheeks and tongue-fuck his muddy run. I opened my eyes again. Exton's shirt was off, and he looked so boyish kneeling in front of Darvis. His pants were undone, and I could see his white behind and wondered how long it would be before Darvis was standing behind him and pile-driving our little Billy Budd.

I felt the weight of it, but it didn't register right away, not until it shifted and continued to slide over my calves, and I was paralyzed. It turned the corner of my knee and wound itself around my thighs, going between my legs, moving sensually, dragging itself around me like a lover, its tongue flickering against my balls. It brought more and more of itself around me, tightening its embrace. It coiled around the base of my cock, hiding most of it, squeezing it tightly, keeping it engorged. Its undulations made my cock quiver and leak. It looked to me like I was going to die, but I was going to come first.

"Looks like you've found the dreaded faggot snake," Darvis said, his voice nearly causing my heart to stop.

"Do something, Darvis," Exton whispered like a girl, his belly, I noted, awash with glistening come.

Darvis laughed, and I felt tears come to rest in the corners of my eyes. The snake courted with the head of my dick, which had turned a sickly purple. Its tongue licked me. I looked up at Darvis, begging him softly.

"You're always on your knees begging me for something, ain't you, Dow?" he said. And then he grabbed the snake's head, his hand moving like lightning, getting it just behind the jaws. Its body contorted, flexing its wrap around my cock and torso and legs. It tightened, and I saw stars, feeling as though my middle would bust, and Darvis unsheathed his knife and cut the head off with a simple flick of his wrist. The rest of the snake stayed around me, but it slackened its hold little by little, and I was able to breathe, and it uncoiled off my dick, which was no longer hard but very small and very soft. I stood and pushed the snake body off of me and got my dick back in my pants.

"Thanks," I said to Darvis, eyeing Exton too to make sure I didn't see any smirks, because I would have pounded his face off in a second. I went back to our still-standing tree and wiped my face on a wet rag, and we got together again, Muhammed and Darvis with the saw and me and Exton with the ropes, and we brought down the fucker by nightfall but lost Muhammed doing it.

They sent us another one who wasn't anything like Muhammed. He wasn't much impressed with Darvis's antics and seemed very unlikely to ever join in on the showers we took together, Darvis telling Exton and me what to do to each other, then doing to us whatever he had in mind, calling out to the new one, "Hey, Mr. High-'n'-Mighty, you don't know what you're missing!" dipping into me and then into Exton, telling the two of us to kiss or suck each other.

Mr. High-'n'-Mighty's name was Deloff, first name Christopher, and he looked as mean as Darvis. He could take down trees single-handed and could clear an acre in half the time it took Exton and me. He worked and worked and ignored us for the most part, but sometimes he watched us, a look of distilled disgust on his face.

There was one Saturday night, though, when we were all wiped out from the day's work but itching to drink some of the grain they sent us as appeasement for lack of decent food. Alcohol tended not to spoil or attract vermin, and they sent us plenty. We all sat around on our beds with our bottles, Darvis setting up a good array of empties beside his cot. We talked about the dreaded faggot snake and good old Muhammed, and I noticed Darvis and Deloff glancing at each other with much less malice than usual. Darvis was stripped to his shorts, his legs spread wide, enticing. Deloff had taken off his shirt, the grime of the day browning his skin. We hadn't any of us seen him with his trousers off. Exton and me had been discussing this fact earlier that day when we'd slipped off together to swallow each other's come. (I'd convinced him the protein of it kept the mosquitoes off us.) Despite getting off already that day, I was ready for another dose of medicine, and I could see that Exton was too, looking at all of us and putting his hands down his pants to squeeze his stuff.

"Exton," Darvis laughed, "you feeling randy again, boy?"

Exton went red on his cot and gave Darvis the finger, but you could see his boner plain as day. It seemed to catch Deloff's eye, I noticed.

Darvis lifted his hips and pushed his shorts off. His mighty pecker rose like one of the trees we hacked at all day long. "Here's something for you," he said nicely, and Exton eased himself off his cot and joined Darvis on his and started lapping the fat red head of the man's horselike piece.

Whenever Darvis was like this, Deloff was gone—he'd leave the bunkhouse without so much as a word. He stayed put this time, scrutinizing the coupled men. His hands went between his legs, touching the crotch of his trousers.

I remember Muhammed saying to me once, his big black cock pumping between my legs, "You do what you can out here. Pleasure so simple can't be no sin. It's like having a sweet every once in a while or drinking a beer on a hot Sabbath day. Jesus turns his head, I bet. Maybe he don't even do that. Maybe he watches." Seeing Deloff stand up and drop his trousers reminded me of that. His prick was fat and came to a point. It almost looked like a beet, the way it was shaped. He fingered the pointed end, the sleeve of skin there, and bared his white little head. His balls were large and covered with kinky fuzz, his thighs packed and cut with muscle. He was a little unsteady, a little drunk, and mesmerized by Darvis and Exton going at it, Darvis sticking his fingers into Exton's behind, causing Exton to suck faster and harder.

I wasn't sure what was going to happen. It looked to me like I was about to witness a threesome, the way he stared at them with such longing, but he turned his look my way, his other hand going to his right nipple. A huge, snaking vein pulsed across his biceps, and I felt pulled to him, only I wasn't moving. He came to me, though, offering his crotch to me, and I accepted it, tonguing the little head. I took it in my hand, and it filled my palm like a grenade, and I slurped my tongue over it and made him bigger and harder, and he groaned over me, undoing my pants.

It seemed almost to become a contest then, Darvis and Deloff competing to see which one was going to fuck his partner first, then to see who was going to fuck his partner hardest, then who was going to make his partner scream the loudest, come the hardest, come the most. He plugged my hole with his thing, stretching me, hitting up inside me just right and taking my breath away. He pushed my face against the dirty mattress and beat my ass with his pecker, knocking against my prostate and giving me the shakes. I heard Exton wail, and I felt my heart in my throat, and I begged for his cock. I begged good and hard for him to fuck my ass and make me his bitch, his pussy, and he slapped my fanny and called me a whore, and I heard Darvis growl and looked up to see him watching us, his lips wet with spit as he hurried his huge tree trunk into poor Exton's rear end.

I couldn't say who came first. I think we all came together or just seconds apart, all connected to one another by our cocks and our gazes. When he was finished Deloff wiped himself on my sheets and touched my shoulders sweetly, and I leaned back against his hot, wet cock. Darvis collapsed on his fuck, and they cuddled like brothers.

We drank some more, Deloff and I, and watched the flickering shadows the moonlit trees made outside our window. He told me he had a wife in Florida. "We all got wives," I told him, and he nodded, and I said to him what Muhammed said to me, that nothing could be bad about a pleasure so simple, and he nodded again and touched the lip of his bottle against mine, our bottles making a ringing kiss.

FROSH

We were splitting another pitcher at Digger's, a bar on Main Street frequented mostly by the guys on the university's swim team. Bishop and I were measly frosh, easily ignored but completely awestruck by these guys and the prodigious drinking they were doing. We were doing some drinking ourselves, but there was no way we could have matched drinks with any of them. Bishop and I were roommates, thrown together by the Fates, and I was thinking so far that we were a pretty good match. We were both on the quiet side and not terribly outgoing. We liked the same music, kept the same hours, and had even registered for some of the same classes. It seemed to me that we were on our way to becoming fast friends.

It felt a little strange to be sharing such close quarters with another guy. My home was filled with girls—I have seven sisters, and my father seems to be gone most of the time. So I was pretty thrown the first time Bishop stripped in front of me, and I still wasn't too comfortable with his habit of lounging around in a pair of ratty old briefs. He had an enviable build, though, from weight lifting and swimming. He was shorter than I was and thick with muscle from head to toe. His hair was blond and cut short, and his skin was brown from a summer of lifeguarding. To me he seemed to have everything going for him—looks, brawn, even brains—only he didn't know it.

But I knew it—and that was a bigger problem, as far as I was concerned.

So I was uncomfortable having Bishop lying around undressed, going unhurried and uncovered to the john with his morning erection poking up high in his briefs. I was uncomfortable with the late-night sounds I wasn't supposed to be hearing that came from his bed—the noise of his quickened breath, of his toes cracking as they curled, and of the soundlessness that came when he did, his breathing stopped for the moment and his hand clutched tightly around his pulsing shaft.

In my bed on the other side of our room, I saw him in my mind from above, as if I hovered over him, and his skin was a silvery white in the light of the moon that came in through the uncurtained windows. His white sheets were blue, and I could see the glistening blast of come that shot from his cock and the silvered gobs that spilled over his hand and seeped into his dark bush. His head was turned, his lips were parted, and his eyes were on my bed. He brought his smeared hand to his mouth and licked it clean, and he touched his chest where there was more of it and licked his fingers again.

Yes, I was uncomfortable, all right—uncomfortable with the boner I had nearly every time I was with him. And we had only been sharing the same room for three weeks. I was sure that something was going to happen to my dick by midterms. *If this thing keeps up,* I was thinking, *maybe I'll use up my lifetime allotment of erections in a month and a half or my balls will suck themselves up into my stomach and never come down again.*

I watched the bob of his Adam's apple as he drank his beer. He set his glass down and looked over at the bar, where most of the swim team had gathered. They had pushed away the stools and were standing, leaning against the bar in a row of cocked butts, long hairless legs, tapered ankles, and bare feet stuck in stinky sneakers. They all had the hair shaved off the sides of their heads, but the tops were deliberately left long, to be cut off the night before their big meet. They were all standing close together, shoulders touching shoulders, legs touching legs, arms touching arms, attached to one another like Siamese twins.

"I was thinking of joining the swim team," Bishop said.

"Cool," I replied, but I felt a small stab of jealousy. In my mind we were already best friends, and I had this mental picture of us hanging out all the time, the way we had over the past three weeks, Bishop studying on his bed in his underwear and me on my bed, wondering if he could see the boner I was sporting. Dinners at the dining hall, movies Saturday night at the student center—we'd even talked about joining the hiking club, but this swim-team thing...

It would take him away, I told myself. The swim team was insular and fraternal. It was an us-and-them kind of group. I gathered that much right away; they were a close-knit bunch of guys who lived, ate, drank, and swam together. I imagined Bishop getting sucked in, pulled away from me by the undertow of eight great-looking guys in nothing but Speedos. I looked down into my beer.

"Maybe next semester," Bishop said, and I felt a little better. At least now I had a few months to make myself as indispensable as humanly possible—or if not, a few months to find someone as hot as Bishop to live with.

Bishop didn't come home after his evening lit course. I sat with a book on my lap, eyeing the clock and looking at the same sentence over and over again, wondering where he was. Then the phone rang, and I answered it.

"Pete?" It was Bishop's voice.

"Yeah," I said.

"Yeah, I'm hanging with Jeffries, and we're probably going down to Digger's." His voice was low. I could hear some Guns N' Roses in the background and the sounds of guys talking and laughing.

"Who's Jeffries?" I asked.

"A guy in my lit class," Bishop replied.

"Cool," I said. "See ya."

"I'll see you—" I heard as I was hanging up the phone.

I tossed the book. *Fuck it*, I thought. *Fuck him.* The book fell open on Bishop's unmade bed. His sneakers were on the floor where his sheets had spilled down, as were his once-white socks that I could smell from here—a pleasant stink I hated to admit liking.

I stretched out across my bed and arched my back, putting my hands on my chest. Working out with Bish was really working out—I could feel my pecs growing bigger and harder. I thought about how Bishop looked heaving under a barbell loaded up with cast-iron plates, me spotting him and urging him on, and it was easy then for me to imagine him heaving under me as I told him, "Take that dick, buddy. Take all of my cock, pal." My hands slipped down over the hard bands of muscle across my stomach, down to the quickened pulse of my bone, stiff and loose in my oversize boxers. I got a good hold of myself with my left hand; I usually used my right, but the left one felt different enough to be someone else's hand, and I pretended it was my roommate's. With my free hand I plucked at my nipples through my T-shirt. I had Bishop kneeling beside me on my bed, stripped to his briefs, playing with my pecker and tits.

I opened my mouth to accept his imaginary cock, wetting my palm with a lick of my tongue and using the slicked-up surface to yank on my dick. "I love your cock, Bishop," I said out loud, and saying it made my crank quiver. "I want that big fucking cock," I whispered.

"You want it?" he asked me.

"Oh, yeah," I said.

"Where?" he said, and I could see him smiling down at me. "Tell me where you want it."

"You know where," I replied, feeling my face redden.

"Say it," he said. He pushed his cock down against my lips for me to kiss it.

Suddenly the door of my room swung open, and Bishop stood there with a couple of guys behind him peering over his shoulder. "Dude," Bishop was saying, "why don't you come with us—" They had been talking and laughing, but the sight of me on my bed with my legs spread, hard-on in hand, shut them up. I froze, unable to make a move to cover up. A pearly drop of precome spilled from my piss hole. "Whoops," somebody said. Bishop himself looked pale and couldn't back out fast enough. "Sorry," he said. "I'm sorry, man."

I had a lecture class the next day—sociology. I sat in the middle of a huge auditorium with about 120 other kids, ready to be bored for an hour and a half by the doddering old professor, who stood behind the podium as if he needed it to hold himself up. I settled in, opened my notebook, and started doodling, waiting for the old guy to get himself started. Somebody sat next to me, a guy wearing a baseball cap turned around and a T-shirt with the words COED NAKED TWISTER on the front. He fell into his seat and put his feet up on the back of the seat in front of him. He wore baggy shorts, and his legs were pale and hairy.

I glanced at his face and saw that he was looking at me. I nodded, and he said, "What's up," which was just like nodding these days, nothing one needs to answer. "This guy's gonna die up there one of these days," he said to me as the professor cleared his throat again and again.

I glanced over at him again. He had his hands over his crotch, moving his fingers every once in a while to scratch his balls. He had no books, no notebook—not even a backpack. His thighs looked as though he'd just finished a marathon, they were so big and well-defined. And, as if he knew what I was looking at, he pulled his hands off the package in his shorts and ran them over his legs. And then he put one of those hands in front of me. "Name's Mark," he said, his voice a whisper.

I shook his hand and told him my name.

"You're Bishop's roommate," he said. I nodded.

"I went to high school with him," Mark told me.

The lecture had begun, and the old man was spewing forth a ton of information on which we'd no doubt be tested. I bent over my notebook and began to scribble furiously. Every once in a while, I would glance over at Mark, who just sat beside me chewing his cuticle or fiddling with the hem of his shorts. When the lecture was over, I gathered my things, and Mark stood up and did a long, luxurious stretch. His shirt lifted and revealed a thick happy trail climbing up and out of his shorts. His ass jutted out: two nicely defined cheeks that begged for attention. In fact, all of Mark seemed to beg for attention.

He lingered, looking around. "You going to lunch?" he asked me.

"I've got another class," I told him.

"Right," he said.

"What?" I asked.

"I said, 'Right,' as in, 'I'll catch you later, then.' See ya." And then he was gone.

The room was empty when I came home from classes. Usually Bish was waiting for me, and we'd go to the gym or run or something. His bed was unmade, as always, and I sat down on it. I picked up his pillow and held it to my nose. It smelled like him, of course, but so much so that it surprised me. I pushed my face into the softness of it, smothering myself with the smell of Bishop, and my heart began to pound in my chest. My pecker stiffened and pounded in my pants. For a second I seriously contemplated taking off my jeans and humping the shit out of the pillow, but I regained my senses.

What the fuck is up with me? I thought, getting up and throwing Bishop's pillow away as if it were radioactive. I stood up and paced as much as one can pace in a dorm room: six steps one way, six steps another. I boiled some water in the microwave for some instant coffee and put on my favorite CD of the moment. I stood by the window that looked out over the quad, waiting to see Bishop. It was getting late, and I hadn't eaten. I ran to the dining hall right before it closed and ate spaghetti by myself, not tasting anything. I felt odd in my stomach and immeasurably sad. I hadn't felt so low since my parents had put the family dog to sleep. It didn't make any sense to me. *Snap out of it*, I told myself. *Put it out of your mind.*

I left the dining hall, and I saw that Mark guy sitting next to a football on a low wall outside the doors. He got up when he saw me. "Hey," he said, smiling.

"Hey," I said back, puzzled by his sudden appearance and feeling as though he had been waiting for me.

"Uh, do you play football?" he asked me, stepping up to me and matching my pace because I didn't stop to talk.

"Nope," I said.

"But you can throw one, right? And catch one?"

I stopped short and gave him a look. He was a head taller than me, and he had straight dark hair. The sleeves were torn from his madras shirt, and he wore cutoffs that were high on the thigh. I took the ball from under his arm. He smiled, showing white teeth that were slightly crooked, his canines pronounced and wolflike.

"I know a place," he said.

We started walking, down past the pond edged with willows, through a mowed, narrow field to another field with soccer goals set up, marked still with faded boundary lines. We started throwing the ball around.

"How's Bish doing?" Mark asked.

I could feel my face tighten. "Fine, I guess," I said. "Haven't seen him much lately."

"He's always reminded me of a cat," Mark said, pitching a perfect spiral I had to make a running leap to catch. I picked myself up off the ground and threw a wild pass back. I told him I always had dogs.

"You know what I mean, though?" he was saying. "I mean, he comes around when he wants to be fed or when he wants his head scratched. He was like that in high school, calling me up after a month of ignoring me and wanting to know if I had any weed or if he could come over and hang out on a Friday night, and I'd drop everything for him." He threw the ball.

I wasn't following him, really. I still had this vision of Bishop coming up to me, wanting his head scratched. It was a pleasant thought. I fingered the laces of the ball. It was getting dark. I couldn't make out Mark's features anymore, just his general shape. The ball disappeared in the air, and I heard the slap it made in his hands. "Nice throw," he said.

"He's all right," I said, my voice sounding funny to me. We suddenly seemed far away from everything. I heard him make a little grunt as he tossed the ball my way. I couldn't see a thing. It thudded hard to my left and bounced and rolled.

"Sure he is," Mark said. I could hear him coming closer. I went after the ball. The grass had become wet with dew. He was standing beside me when I bent over to pick up the football, and I felt the heat that came off him. I was waiting for him to touch me—my shoulder, my arm, some kind of contact. I heard his breathing and the chirping of the crickets in the tall grass. He took the ball from my hands.

"I could use a beer," he said.

"I have a sixer in my room," I offered.

"Let's go," he said, and we started walking.

We didn't talk again until we got to the doors of my dormitory. I looked up and saw the light on in my room. "Bishop must be home," I said.

"What time is it?" Mark asked. I told him, noticing the watch he had on his wrist.

"Shit," he said. "I have a study group to lead in five minutes. Maybe I can catch up with you later, man." He lifted a hand in a gesture of good-bye, and then, turning, he broke into a jog. I watched him as he ran away.

I shrugged Mark off, more interested now in getting upstairs and seeing Bishop. I took the steps two at a time and raced down the hall to my room. Some of the guys had their doors open, studying or listening to music or watching TV. "Hey, Bricker," I heard again and again, announcing my arrival.

I got to my door. It was covered with tabloid headlines that Bish and I had thought were particularly fucked-up and hilarious. I tried the door, but it was locked. I fumbled for my key and couldn't find it. I knocked and waited. I could hear music.

I wondered where my key was. Bishop didn't answer. I pounded on the door. "Hey, it's me," I said. "C'mon. Let me in."

I heard the click of the lock, and the door opened. Bishop stood there in a pair of shorts that seemed a little tented, but that could have been my imagination. There was some blond-haired guy on my bed. The smell of pot and incense hung heavily in the air. Bishop's eyes were red and maybe a little too wide. I had the distinct impression that I was interrupting something, and that pissed me off.

"This is Jeffries," Bishop said. The blond got up from my bed, holding out his hand. I shook it hard, sizing him up. His body was trim, and I could see the power of his shoulders, the decent spread of his lats when he turned and walked over to the window. He leaned on the sill, and his shoulders bunched up. He looked familiar to me, and I said so.

"Jeffries is on the swim team," Bishop said.

"I kind of met you last night," Jeffries said from the window without turning.

"Oh," I said. I picked up some books from my desk. I saw a bong on Bishop's desk.

He must have seen me spot it. "You want some?" he asked. "It's pretty excellent."

"I can see that," I said, feeling suddenly like somebody's aunt. "No thanks. I've got a ton of shit to do," I added, trying to ease up.

"Want us to leave?" Bishop said quickly.

I shook my head. "There's somebody at the library I want to catch up with anyway," I said. "Hey, you know this guy—his name's Mark. He told me he went to high school with you."

"Mark," Bishop said, looking down at the floor. "Mark...Mark..." He shook his head, but then something dawned on him, and his eyes widened, suddenly clear.

"You mean Mark *Fuller*?" he said.

I shrugged my shoulders. "I guess so."

Bishop seemed to compose himself. He picked at a callus on his palm. "So what's he got to say?"

"Not much," I replied, sensing something—an edge—that clipped Bishop's words. "Well, I'll see you." I pulled a punch at his shoulder that he didn't dodge. "Nice meeting you," I said to Jeffries. He was still looking out the window. His butt was cocked, and his long legs were hairless. He turned quickly, and I was caught with my eyes below his belt, catching a glimpse of the outline of his big dick in the silky mesh basketball shorts he was wearing.

"See you," he said, smirking, and his eyes dropped down the front of me, focusing, I thought, on my crotch.

I was nearly out the door when Bishop grabbed my arm. He held it hard, staring into my eyes. "He's a real bullshitter, man," he whispered. "I'm serious. Don't believe a fucking word he says."

I pulled my arm free. "Who is?" I asked. "Him?" I said, nodding into the room.

"Fuller," Bishop said, making a face. "Stay away from him. He's fucked-up."

I searched the library for Mark but didn't find him. I looked in the local directory and found him there, listed at an apartment off campus. I thought about calling, but I didn't know what to say, and I was afraid he would put me off. I didn't want to be put off. I walked to College Avenue and stood in front of the house. The first floor was dark, but the lights were on upstairs, and I saw Mark walk past an open window.

"Fuller!" I called, my voice ridiculously deep. I felt as though everything had slipped up into my throat: my heart, my stomach—even my dick. Mark came back to the window and looked out. I saw him in silhouette but could tell he was shirtless, seeing the light on his shoulders. I stepped under a streetlight. "It's me," I said.

"It is, isn't it?" he called back from his window. I could almost hear him smiling. He squatted down then and rested his chin on his folded arms.

"How do I get up?" I said. A breeze stirred the leaves.

"Are you drunk?" he wanted to know.

"No," I said.

"Come around the back," he said. "I'll put the light on."

He was at the top of the stairs, waiting. I saw him in silhouette again, and I lost my nerve. I wasn't sure what had brought me here until now, seeing him half-dressed and dark-faced. I slowed on the steps. He had his hands on the door frame, and I could see the cut of his triceps and the flex of his deltoids. I stopped. I put my hand on the banister.

"You OK?" he asked. I didn't answer. I wasn't sure. He started down the stairs. I felt his hand on my forearm. It was one thing to want something, another thing altogether to get it. Until now, wanting didn't mean anything—nothing had changed for me. But now something was about to happen—or maybe it was happening already.

Mark stood one step up from me and put his other hand on the back of my neck. Everything swirled around in my head: images of Bishop wet from the shower, padding down the hall naked because he forgot his towel; the look on his face when he and his friends found me spread out and jacking off; and now Mark's face coming in close to mine.

I pulled back. He let go of me and sat down. "Why'd you come here?" he asked me. I didn't answer.

"Maybe you want to go home now," he said. I shook my head. He stood again and started up the stairs. I followed him.

He walked through the foyer and into a darkened room. I stood in the doorway. My eyes slowly adjusted to the dark. I could see him sitting on his bed. He leaned over and turned on a bedside light. He stretched out on the bed and looked at me. I tried to meet his gaze, but my eyes slipped down, taking him in. His chest was muscled and hairless, with wide brown nipples. His stomach was ribbed, dark with hair below his navel.

At the crotch of his shorts was a mound, a small mountain of dick and balls that rose above his huge thighs. He bent his legs, bringing his heels close to his butt, and the crotch disappeared. His arms crossed behind his head. I could study him a little more closely now. His eyes were dark, his nose long and straight. His lips, like his nipples, were almost red, framed with the black shadow of a beard. His nipples poked up high, casting shadows and seeming to invite any kind of finger play.

My feet felt nailed to the floor, and my eyes felt glued to the expanse of Mark's skin.

"You're nothing like Bishop," he said finally.

"What do you mean?" I asked him.

Mark got up on one elbow, resting his head on his hand. "This is something Bish would do," Mark said, looking down at himself. "He would spread himself all out and wait for me to make the first move. I always had to make the first move with him—it always had to be me seducing him, even though it was clearly the other way around." He smiled. "In the beginning, anyway."

"That's what you're doing now?" I said, my voice cracking a bit. I felt a shot of red color my face.

"I'm not doing too good, am I?" he said, smiling again. He sat up. "Come here."

I took some steps closer. I got myself within his reach, and he caught my arms in his hands and pulled me closer. He pressed his face into the front of my shirt. I felt his hot breath seep through the fabric, warming my stomach. I put my hands on his head and scratched it with the blunt ends of my fingers. I moved down his neck and across his wide back, fingering the edges of his lats, seeing an odd triangle of tiny golden hairs growing just over his ass, half covered by the waistband of his shorts.

"Wait a minute," I said. "What was that about Bishop? You two—" I felt him nod his head. "No way," I said.

Mark leaned back. "He'd make me beg for it," he said. "He'd hold out and hold out, and then he'd be like, 'OK, you can blow me'—like he's doing me this big favor. He's a cute fucker, but a monster tease. Are you telling me you two aren't screwing around?"

"What?" I said, almost laughing.

"I thought you two were...close," he said.

"Not like that," I said.

Mark smiled. "But you wouldn't mind getting closer, right?"

"To tell you the truth, I really don't care much about Bishop right now," I told him. I figured I had Bishop just about figured out. All that walking around half dressed and half hard—I was just too naive to realize what was going on. I didn't care anymore. Besides, it seemed pretty obvious that Bish was boffing Jeffries now, anyway.

"Are you going to blow me or what?" I said to Mark, and he did.

He pulled down my shorts easily, and my pecker knocked him on the chin. I felt his breath all over my crotch as he sniffed at me like a dog, and then his tongue poked at my balls. My fingers twisted around his slick black hair, and my cock rested alongside his nose, its tip hidden in his bangs. He sucked my nuts into his hot mouth and mushed them around in there. He made noises deep in his throat. I made some noises myself. Humping his forehead was nice, but I was ready for my first blow job. (I wasn't exactly a virgin; I let a guy jack me off once at church camp when I was 17.)

I poked at his head with my forefinger, pushing him back and aiming my dick right at his pretty mouth. Mark's head came close to my crotch, and I saw my cock slide into his head. I felt his mouth around my cock and his nose butting against my pubic bone. My knees felt like rubber, my face flushed hot, and my palms slicked over with sweat. My dick felt like steel, and I poked it into him, riding the crest of his tongue and scraping along the edges of his teeth.

I pulled out to batter his lips with my spit-soaked cock head. Mark moaned and opened wide again, and I fucked his mouth, holding on to his ears, pulling on them. I felt a sweet tingle somewhere in my nuts that turned into a roiling boil, and Mark got a taste of what was to come when I started leaking. He grunted and swallowed and dug his fingers into my ass cheeks, clawing his way up my back and under my soaked pits to come down hard on my nipples.

When he clamped on my pinks, I started slamming into him, spewing a load of sperm into his mouth. Mark gulped and snorted, sucking out the last drops, and I saw him working his own rod, sliding his foreskin back and forth over the huge red knob of his cock. He went all the way down on me one last time, choking himself, and I saw a blast of white fly from his dick. He emptied himself on the floor and fell back against the bed, breathing hard, his lips shining, looking up at me.

"I've got to go," I said abruptly. I was freaking out, and my dick was still wet with his spit, doing a sorry jut from my groin. I had the feeling I could go either way down there—up or down—and I wanted to believe it had nothing to do with me, that it was out of my hands. I wanted to believe that this didn't mean anything.

"Sure," Mark said, putting his own half-hard dick away. "Whatever."

I pulled up my shorts and headed for the door. "I'll see you," I said without turning to look at him. I took the dark stairs three at a time. I got to the door and was fumbling for the knob when Mark appeared at the top of the stairs.

"Hey, give Bishop my best," he said.

The dorm room was empty and stinking of pot smoke. I opened the windows. The phone rang.

"You alone?" It was Mark. "I'm coming over, but I have to say something first. I thought I was getting one over on Bishop by putting the moves on you. I mean, that's what I started out thinking. I was pretty much just interested in making Bishop's life a little miserable. But you—you're a nice guy, and I get the feeling this stuff is kind of new for you or whatever. Am I right? Hey, are you there?"

My voice cracked when I tried to speak, and I didn't know what to say. "Uh, yeah," I managed.

"So, I'm coming over now. As soon as I hang up. I'm running all the way. Is that OK?"

"I think so," I said. "I think it's OK. I'll know for sure when you get here."

"It's just that I wanted to kiss you," I heard him say. "I want to kiss you now."

"Hang up," I said. I put the phone down and sat down on the bed, waiting to be kissed..

Coffee Talk

Glenn dialed Pete's number.

"Uh...hello?" the gravelly voice on the other line said. It was late.

"It's me," Glenn said. He could hear his friend breathing into the telephone. "You awake?"

"No," Pete said.

"You alone?"

"Mmm," Pete rasped. "Think so."

Glenn leaned back on the sofa and looked at his ceiling. He felt better already, just hearing Pete's voice. *Bad sign*, he thought, running a hand absentmindedly across his chest, his fingertips brushing his nipples through his T-shirt. His dick stirred. *Shit*, he thought. *Another bad sign.* "Um," Pete said slowly. "Does my clock really say 3:15? Can that be the correct time, Glenn?"

Glenn looked at his watch. "Uh, yeah, that's right."

"So what the fuck do you want?"

Good question, Glenn thought. What the fuck do I want? He had wanted Corinne, but now that she had dumped him, he was glad to be rid of her. "You've forced me to do this," she had told him earlier that night. "I mean, I want to love you, but you don't seem to want to be loved. Not by me, anyway."

Glenn looked up at the ceiling again; it flickered blue from the television. He imagined Pete up on one elbow, eyes closed, twisted up in a sheet. He stretched himself out on the couch, spreading his bare legs here and there, his free hand creeping down to the waistband of his boxers, Pete's breath in his ear. He told him about Corinne.

"Sucks, man," Pete said. "Tell me about it over breakfast. Your treat. Good-bye."

"See you," Glenn said, hanging up and digging his hands into his shorts. He closed his eyes and could see Pete again, half covered, spreading himself across the bed. He had by now memorized every detail of his buddy's body; he had seen enough of it at the gym and the beach and around their apartments, half dressed, undressed, soaking wet, covered in oil, pumped up, half hard. He'd even seen Pete's dick completely hard, the morning after they'd shared a bed and Pete woke up in a hurry, his big cock up-and-at-'em and poking out through the slot of his boxers.

Glenn pushed his shorts down to his knees and gripped his stiff dick in one hand, his balls in the other. He pulled and squeezed, letting his imagination take over. He could see Pete, his longish dark hair swaying as he hopped into the bathroom with his prong bobbing up and down; he could see Pete coming in out of the ocean in shorts that went nearly transparent in the surf, his black pubes shining through the wet white fabric; Pete stepping up to the urinal next to Glenn's and unloading his prick to take a long piss; Pete too drunk to drive home, stripping down to his shorts, getting ready for bed in Glenn's living room.

Glenn spit in his hand and stroked it over his cock. He used not to allow himself to think of his friend when he jacked off.

That's what Corinne was for. But she hadn't worked—at least not the way he had hoped. The only way he could fuck her was by thinking of Pete. He mentally replaced her pussy with Pete's tight, hot (he imagined) butt hole. Her mouth was Pete's. Her hands, though, were what he had the most trouble with. They were soft and dainty, and he simply could not pretend they were Pete's big, clumsy, hairy-knuckled, calloused, dirty-nailed paws. He discovered that he did not want anything to do with delicacy in bed; he wanted heavy hands, rough hands. Pete's hands.

His toes curled, his feet arched, and he tensed every muscle in his legs. He had quickly worked himself up to popping. He pictured himself with Pete, imagined Pete's hand on his cock instead of his own, and he tightened his grip, slamming his fist into his wiry nest of pubes, pumping the shaft and bothering the sensitive head. His ball sac stiffened, and he let out a little holler as he spewed out another load with Pete's name on it. "Oh, sweet," he said over and over again, squeezing out every thick white drop.

Pete was sitting in their booth, the one they sat in almost every Saturday. Patti the waitress raised her eyebrows when she saw Glenn walk in. "What's this?" she said, bringing him a cup of coffee. "Emergency summit meeting? Not used to seeing you guys in the middle of the week. Now I'm going to keep thinking tomorrow's Sunday."

"Breakfast," Pete said.

Glenn reached for a menu.

"Honey," Patti said. "Nothing's changed in there."

"Oh," Glenn said. "Right."

"The usual?" she said.

"The usual," the two men said together.

"You look like shit," Pete said once Patti had gone.

"Thanks," Glenn said.

"Didn't you sleep?"

"Couldn't," Glenn said, stirring sugar into his coffee. He did what he could to avoid looking at Pete: studying the empty sugar pack, patting his jacket pocket for his truck keys, pretending to give some chick the once-over. He breathed hard, almost sighing, and put his hands on his lap. He glanced at Pete, who was staring at him.

"What?" Glenn said.

"Man, are you OK?"

"Fine. Why?"

"You seem wrecked or something," Pete said. "I didn't think you cared too much one way or the other about her."

"What gave you that idea?"

The door opened behind Glenn's back, and Pete looked over his friend's shoulder. Glenn turned around to look too. A big guy walked in wearing tight jeans and a flannel shirt. His sleeves were rolled up, showing off powerful-looking forearms.

"Hey, good-lookin'," Patti called from behind the counter, causing the man to grin and go red.

"You know him?" Pete said.

"No," Glenn answered.

Pete seemed to be staring at Glenn, into him. *Don't look too close*, Glenn thought. *You might not like what you see.*

They ate their breakfast in silence, Glenn listening and sometimes turning to watch Patti flirt with her man at the counter. His flannel-shirted back was wide and solid, tapering narrowly at the waist and disappearing into well-worn jeans. His brown, slightly curly hair was buzzed to the bone around his head and left a little long on the top. There was something about this man's exposed scalp that seemed to cause a little trouble in Glenn's sweats. He felt his prick nosing around, wanting attention. He fussed with the paper napkin over his lap, fingering his hardening shaft secretly.

Pete put his feet up on the bench beside Glenn, startling him. He looked up red-faced, feeling guilty. Pete pushed his plate to the side, pulled a toothpick out of his shirt pocket, and twirled it around in his mouth. "So, you don't want to talk about it. That's cool," he said.

"See ya, Chuckie," Patti called out, and Pete and Glenn both watched the big man walk out the door. Patti came over to clear their plates.

"That your boyfriend?" Pete said.

"Why, I thought you were," Patti said, putting a hand on Pete's arm.

"No," Pete said, winking at Glenn. "I'm Glenn's man, and don't you forget it."

Patti smiled conspiratorially. "You know," she said softly, "I had a feeling. Now, my brother's gay, and we have the best relationship—he is such a riot."

"Hey," Pete said, looking around. "It was a joke. I was joking."

Patti gave Glenn a look and pursed her lips. "Pulling my leg again?" she said. "Never know with you guys. Never know anything anymore." She glanced at the door, the open/closed sign still swinging back and forth. She slipped the check onto the table. "More coffee?"

They walked out to their cars. "That was fucking weird," Pete said, pulling his hair away from his face. He had a wide jaw, a less-than-perfect nose—a little crooked from a bad wrestling move in high school—and brown eyes that resembled polished mahogany. He was wearing a T-shirt, and his nipples were hard in the chill morning air. He hugged himself, and his biceps, big to begin with, seemed to triple in size. He rocked in his sneakers from his heels to his toes. "What are you going to do?" he wanted to know.

Glenn exhaled loudly, shaking his head. He didn't care that he was dumped. He was actually glad Corinne had done his dirty work, but it was this other thing that was getting him down, that he did not know how to deal with. He felt like he was going insane, out of control. "It's my dick," he wanted to say. "I'm having trouble with my dick. And you."

"Hey, I don't mean the big picture, man," Pete said. "I just want to know what you're doing today. Like, do you have any plans? I was thinking of going to the shore to hang."

"I can do that," Glenn said. He dug his hands into his jacket pockets.

"Follow me to my house. I'll get a sweatshirt and some money. Take your truck?" Pete said.

"Sure," Glenn said, trying hard not to stare at the ever-present bulge in Pete's jeans.

It wasn't a long drive, but Pete fell asleep right away. He managed to spread himself across the seat of Glenn's pickup, strapped in at Glenn's insistence, the black webbing untucking Pete's T-shirt and baring his stomach, lined with dark hair. He was solid there, ribbed with muscle. The waistband of his jeans showed a dark, thin passage with room enough to slip a hand down, which Pete did often, scratching now and then or just touching. Suddenly he went hard, his dick growing straight up along his hairy stomach, up and out of the jeans, its pointed head resting over the dip of his belly button.

"Fuck," Glenn whispered, gripping the wheel with both hands. "Fuck, fuck, fuck." Pete's knee touched Glenn's thigh and stayed there. Glenn pushed hard on his own prick, grinding it, causing pleasure and pain. Pete snored, slack-mouthed and drooling. Glenn pushed on the accelerator, picking up speed. He glanced at his friend, his friend's dick. Touch it, he thought. Go ahead and touch it!

Pete sat up suddenly, blinking in the glare of daylight. He pushed his dick back into his pants. "Pull up over here," he said. Glenn looked at him. "Got to piss," Pete said, looking out through the windshield.

Pete got out and went into the brush. Glenn watched him disappear. Glenn thought it was odd, since Pete was never bashful about pissing. He had even taken a leak into a beer bottle one night when he and Glenn were driving home from a concert in a downpour.

Now Glenn waited for him to return. Five minutes passed. He beeped the horn. Nothing. He peered into the brush but could see no sign of his friend. He got himself out of the truck and yelled. "Come on, asshole!" he hollered. "Pete?"

He stepped into the bushes, into the woods. *Some joke,* he thought, but at the same time he began to get a little scared. *What if something's happened? Is there a deep ravine here somewhere that Pete could have fallen into?* He called Pete's name again. Nothing.

He walked deeper into the brush, looking for something that indicated Pete had been through here. The sky was a dull gray, and the woods were bleak. He stood still and listened, hearing his own breathing and heartbeat.

"Pete?"

"Over here," Glenn heard, turning around to find Pete leaning against a tree.

"What the fuck, man?" Glenn said, pissed off and ready to cuff the bastard for fucking with him like that. He got up to Pete, breathing hard, fists clenched. He stared at Pete's eyes. Pete stared back. It was cold enough for their breath to form foggy clouds between them.

"What's going on?" Glenn said, not comfortable with Pete's smile.

"Is anything going on?" Pete said.

"What are you talking about?"

Pete blew out a puff of air. "Can't stop thinking about what Patti said. About you and me."

Glenn looked at him for a moment. "You said it first," he said, almost mumbling.

"I know."

Pete touched the front of his jeans. He fingered his fly. Glenn could only watch, could not keep himself from watching as Pete undid the buttons of his jeans one at a time. The jeans opened to reveal a V of skin trailing down to his dark-colored pubes and the pale flesh of his fat, soft cock.

"I think it's time one of us had some balls and both of us faced facts," he said quietly.

Glenn stared at the nestling prick, the head hidden, the shaft smooth and pink, thick. *Facts*, he thought.

Pete put his hands under Glenn's jacket. Both men seemed to sigh. Pete's hands gripped Glenn's pecs, and he thumbed his nipples through his shirt. He looked up at the sky as Pete's hands slid down his torso, touching the top of Glenn's sweats. He slipped his hands down inside, and his cool fingers scooped up Glenn's cock and balls, warm and loose.

Pete stepped closer, pushing Glenn's sweats down, baring his ass and the rest of him. He pressed himself against Glenn, arms going around, hands grabbing ass cheeks. Glenn did not know what to do with his hands, had no idea where to put them. He tried Pete's shoulders, and Pete went down on his knees.

Glenn felt wet heat, a soft lap of tongue. Pete made a noise, taking all of Glenn's cock into his mouth, but Glenn wasn't quite hard, despite Pete's hungry mouth pulling and sucking, fingers digging into the crack of his ass, pressing gently on the soft spot. He touched Pete's hair for the first time, gathering it up in his fingers.

"Turn around," Pete said, and Glenn turned. "Bend over now," he heard his friend say.

He did as he was told, hands on his knees, and Pete got his face up in the crack, lapping up the hairy knot, slipping his tongue in, out, in again, deeper this time, pushing into the tight ring of his sphincter. Glenn's prick hardened into a curved obelisk, an aching wooden arc that seemed to burn into the crisp air.

"I want you, man," Pete said, pulling his tongue out.

"I want you too," Glenn whispered, his eyes shut. The lips of his hole pouted. Pete poked into it with his finger. He reached between Glenn's legs and grabbed his steely dick, jacking it, smearing the sticky jeweled tip. He pushed his nose into Glenn's crack again, making his prick hop.

Pete got to his feet and pressed himself against Glenn, pressed his big hard cock against the split of the man's ass cheeks. "Can I?" he whispered into Glenn's ear.

"You can try," he answered.

It wasn't as easy as it looked in the few movies Glenn had seen. And he wasn't prepared for the sheer size of it, the length and width, its fat hardness. Or for the slip of lips on his neck, the roughness of Pete's stubbled chin, the hard grip of fingers on his hips. Or Pete's hot whisper: "It's fucking incredible, man. You wouldn't believe."

Then the hurt gave way to something else that felt almost good and then very good. He felt the long slide of Pete's cock, the bang of its pointed head on his insides, catching on a spot that made his dick twitch. He grabbed his own pecker and caressed the fat shaft, slicking himself up with some precome.

"Give it to me!" he said loudly, his voice echoing through the woods. "Give me that big cock, Pete. Give it to me!"

Pete let out a wail, slamming himself up into Glenn's ass, making the man wince and dribble a gooey string of precome. "That's it, buddy," Pete said. "Take the load, buddy. Take my fucking load." He came deep inside Glenn's feverish ass, hitting that spot again and again, making Glenn's cock shoot a heavy white spurt across the forest floor.

They turned around and went home, making the drive in silence, neither of them knowing what to say. Glenn wondered what was supposed to happen next. He knew how he felt about Pete, knew that he loved him. He wanted desperately to say to Pete, "I've been in love with you for so fucking long." Instead he stared at the road, gripping the wheel, aware of his asshole and its wonderful new usefulness. He glanced over at Pete, who was looking out his window. "What are you doing for dinner?" he asked him.

Pete cleared his throat. Looked at his fingernails. "Actually," he said, "I have a date tonight."

Girl or guy? Glenn thought.

"Some chick from work," Pete said, as if Glenn had spoken aloud.

Glenn turned the radio on and cracked his window a bit. Pete folded his hands over his crotch. *I think things are going to be very different from here on in*, Glenn thought, biting the inside of his lip.

Things were different. Pete seemed to disappear with excuses of having no spare time, of being busy with this and that. Glenn left messages on his answering machine—terse recorded notes with long silent gaps. He felt as though he had lost something; he wasn't sure what, though.

He lay awake at night, unable to sleep, touching himself everywhere Pete had touched him. He pushed his fingers up inside himself, pushed anything cocklike up there: a beer bottle, a brush handle, a cucumber. He finally broke down and went to a shop that sold dildos and bought one that seemed Pete-sized. He felt lost and alone, a little crazy. He even contemplated calling Corinne just to have some company, but realized the mistake that would be.

He went to the diner alone Saturday morning. Patti brought the coffeepot and poured him a cup and was about to pour one for Pete.

"I'm alone," he said, feeling pathetic. Patti looked at him and put the coffeepot down on the table. She sat on the bench across from him.

"Are you OK?" she said.

"I guess so." He stirred his coffee, staring into it as if there were answers there. He stirred and stirred. Nothing. He looked up at her. She looked concerned, safe. "Tell me about your brother," he said finally, feeling some heaviness leave him.

Patti spoke to him quietly, discreetly, for nearly two hours, pausing to serve breakfasts and work the cash register. He was pushing his own uneaten eggs around with the corner of some toast when the door opened. He looked up, hoping to see Pete. It was Patti's friend, the guy who looked like a big lumberjack. Glenn looked back down at his messy plate.

When he looked up again, he saw that Patti was bringing the man over to him. He smiled and held out a huge hand. Glenn took it. "Glenn. Chuckie," Patti said. "Sit down, and I'll bring by some coffee, honey. Clean up that plate, Glenn."

Chuck sat down across from Glenn. "She's a trip," he said, thumbing at Patti, who was hugging an old lady at the counter. "Name's Chuck. I think I saw you here earlier this week."

Glenn nodded. "Saw you too."

Patti came up with her coffeepot. "Do you have anything in common yet?" she wanted to know. Both men went red-faced. "There you go," she said. "You both blush." They looked at each other across the table, starting to laugh. "And you both like to laugh. So what are your plans tonight, Glenn? Chuckie?"

Chuck looked at Glenn. "Are you doing anything?" he asked.

"I don't know," Glenn answered.

"Give him your phone number," Patti said, handing Chuck one of her guest checks.

"I can handle it from here," Chuck said, "if you'll let me borrow your pen."

Glenn put Chuck's phone number on his dresser and left it there for a week. He looked at it from time to time, even picked it up and carried it to the phone, but he couldn't bring himself to make the call. He was waiting for Pete. Pete, who was just confused, Glenn was hoping. Pete, who was going to realize that he was in love with Glenn.

He picked up the receiver and tried calling his best friend. Pete answered on the first ring.

"Man, I thought you were dead or something. Why didn't you return my calls?" Glenn said, smiling into the phone.

"Glenn," Pete said. He sounded surprised. There was an awkward silence.

"I'm coming over," Glenn blurted out suddenly. "Can I come over? I'll pick up some beer, a movie, some Chinese food. Have you eaten yet?"

"Glenn," Pete said. "I"m sort of engaged."

"Engaged? For the evening?"

"Engaged," Pete said, "like almost married, man."

Glenn felt the air all around him go cold. He stared at the mirror, feeling like the floor was about to fall away beneath him.

"W-w-well...that's, uh...great," Glenn stammered. "Congratulations, bud. That's really, uh...great. Look, I gotta go. There's someone at my door, I think. See you."

He hung up the phone. He reached for the piece of paper on the dresser—Chuck's number.

He had a couple of beers while waiting for Chuck to come over. He checked himself in the mirror; he was himself again and nervous as hell. He paced the living room, wondering if he should change his shirt. He thought about having another beer, and then the doorbell rang.

Chuck filled the doorway. He was holding a bunch of flowers clumsily. "Patti's idea," he said, blushing.

They did not go out that night, not like they had planned. They sat at opposite ends of the couch. Chuck leaned back and spread his legs, holding his beer bottle at his crotch and talking about his job as a contractor. Glenn looked into the open V of the man's shirt where a thin patch of red-brown hair lay. The urge to undo the rest of the buttons was strong, and Glenn put down his beer to free up his hands. It was fast, maybe too fast, and maybe he had had one too many. But he was not drunk, just impetuous, randy, and a little reckless. He thought he had caught Chuck glancing at his crotch once or twice, but he wasn't sure.

Both men shifted in their seats. Glenn put out a hand on the empty middle cushion of the couch, the no-man's land there. There was some music playing, but Glenn couldn't remember putting anything on the stereo. He looked at Chuck, and Chuck looked back at him, putting a hand close to Glenn's.

And then they were kissing.

Glenn put his hands on the front of Chuck's shirt, fingering the buttons there, sucking up the man's mouth. Chuck made a soft noise, opening his eyes, pulling Glenn onto him, his big hands all over Glenn's tight butt, gripping the denim-covered cheeks, slipping into the split of his thighs. He broke the kiss.

"Is this kind of fast?" Chuck asked, lips wet with spit.

"I guess," Glenn answered. He was wondering what he was going to do with the uncomfortable boner he had trapped in his jeans. He also wondered how Chuck would deal with his own erection. Glenn could feel it under him, a big and straight club that had wedged itself between them. He pressed himself against it, and Chuck let out a groan.

"Not fast enough," Chuck said, flipping Glenn over onto the floor. He opened all of Glenn's clothes, pulled at his shirt, tugged off his jeans. He stripped Glenn down to his socks and shorts. He stopped to look over what he had uncovered. Glenn's dick hopped against the front of his boxers.

Chuck pointed at Glenn's nipples, putting his fingers on them, fiddling with them, swirling around them. He kissed the hollow of Glenn's throat, licking down to the center of his chest, down and down, wetting the hairs that trailed up and out of his shorts. He licked over the waistband, over the head and shaft, sucking on the balls through the thin boxers, pushing his nose between Glenn's legs, sniffing around the pinched-up hole. He snaked a tongue around the crotch of the boxers and swiped at Glenn's tightened snatch.

Chuck looked up from what he was doing, looking a little frustrated. "May I?" he said, out of breath. He gripped the crotch of the shorts and tore them easily, like ripping paper.

"Oh, shit," Glenn breathed, feeling his cock go stony. "Please take off your clothes."

Chuck stood and slowly unbuttoned his shirt, revealing his massive hair-covered pecs and their wide nipples. He smoothed his hand over his stomach, dipping into his jeans, coming up with a few short copper-colored hairs between his fingers. He unbuttoned his pants and pushed them down. Glenn was staring up a mile of big muscled legs into the dark crack of Chuck's ass.

"Suck my cock?" Chuck asked, hands on his hips. Glenn climbed up those legs, getting his mouth close to Chuck's pale-skinned dick. It hung thick and heavy, almost stiff—not long but a mouthful nonetheless. Glenn choked himself on it right away, eager to get it all into his mouth. He tongued the head and played with the soft ball sac, sucking up the weighty dangle of smooth skin. He heard Chuck groan and felt his prick thicken, letting it ride into his throat. Chuck grabbed his ears, bucking his hips and fucking Glenn's mouth, stretching out his lips.

He got himself off the man's fat cock and looked up at him. The big club swayed by his face, dripping with spit. "Put it in me," he said.

Chuck got down between Glenn's legs and lifted them, putting Glenn's feet on his chest. He spit down into his hand and slicked up his dick, pushing it against Glenn's hole. *That's a lot of cock*, Glenn thought as Chuck pushed it in—not quite gently—and Glenn squinted against the pain. He pushed against Chuck with his feet.

"Sorry, man," Chuck said, taking it easy, fucking Glenn with a smooth long stroke that felt better than anything Glenn had ever experienced. Chuck grabbed Glenn's ankles and spread his legs wide. He tipped Glenn's ass up, staring hard into his eyes. "You're feeling very good," Chuck said. He put his face close to Glenn's and kissed him. Glenn hugged the man's waist with his legs, getting and keeping all of Chuck's thick dong inside his ass.

"Oh, boy," Chuck said, rolling his eyes. He began to chug and pump into Glenn, turning Glenn's ass to mush, fucking it with abandon. He held on to Glenn's hips and pounded into him, grunting through gritted teeth. Glenn grabbed Chuck's tits, pulling on them.

"That's it," Chuck said. "Oh, shit, that's it." He pulled Glenn onto his fat prick and bounced him up and down on it, unloading into the slippery hole while Glenn's spew gushed between them in thick spurts, covering them both with gluey clots.

Glenn kissed Chuck good-bye at the door. "That was a very strange first date," Chuck said. "Can't wait to see what the next one's like. Will there be a next one?"

"Probably," Glenn said.

The phone started ringing. "I'll see you," Chuck said. "I'll call you tomorrow."

Glenn ran to the phone. "Hello?"

"Hey." It was Pete. "I was wondering," he said, hesitating.

"Yeah?" Glenn said, looking at himself in the mirror.

"You alone?" Pete said.

"I am," Glenn answered.

"Me too," Pete said.

"Where's the fiancée?"

"Don't know."

"Don't care?" Glenn said.

"Don't care," Pete answered. "I was wondering—"

"So I heard."

"Well?"

"Come on over," Glenn said, smiling at himself, thinking that his crazy first date just got crazier.

Walk Across Texas

He tipped back in his chair, scratching himself. His pants, tightly hugging his crotch, were hiked up, laying bare his shins, the skin shining under dark hairs. He yawned then and stretched his arms up over his head.

"I should go," the other man said, having looked Harlan Weeks over good and long. He stopped by two or three times a week to do this, to stop and stare, to sit awhile with Harlan and not have much to say. "It's getting late," he said.

There wasn't anything to do but stand up and get on with it, the long walk home. It was dark, but there might be enough moon to see by. Harlan had a car—it sat in the yard on cinder blocks, the grass growing under it, a home for rabbits now.

Harlan was a quiet one, Benjamin thought as he got up out of the chair he'd been planted in ever since he'd arrived. What had they talked about?

"Supposed to snow," said Harlan.

"It's snowing now," Benjamin said, looking out the window, seeing Harlan in the mirror of it.

"You ought to stay, I guess," Harlan said.

"Ought I?"

Harlan's cottage was small and all on one floor. He didn't own a couch to curl up on, only the two chairs they'd been in all evening, which pretty much belonged to the two dogs laid out like rugs by the fire. There was nowhere to go but the bedroom off the kitchen. Benjamin had often glimpsed the iron headboard, its paint coming off, and had on occasion sniffed the smell of sleep on Harlan, stirring up a cup of instant at the kitchen table, shirt done up wrong, socks nowhere to be found. *Listen to him piss; take him down to the lake for a swim without suits; bare-assed grab-ass*—his mind wandered. He pressed his forehead to the cold glass, glad to be staying, and felt himself through his pocket lining, his burgeoning, dissatisfied tool, a pants-bound uprising.

He had pictured Harlan often enough, stripped down to underclothes—old filmy boxers threadbare in the crotch, an unbuttoned henley gone yellow under the arms, sleeves pushed up, socks fallen about his ankles. Benjamin pictured him on the edge of his bed, elbows on knees, toes of one foot fingering the sideways sole of the other, looking up with his fat lip out, dark eyes suddenly saying more than the man ever had.

There used to be women. Harlan had been living with an ex-Mennonite woman, wild for being pent-up most of her life. The removal of her little white cap—her sin strainer—uncapped a she-devil, and she fucked her way down to Florida to wear a thong and dance on a bar, bare breasts flying. She sent Harlan a picture of herself, unrecognizably naked and devoid of the lush bush that Harlan once confessed was her best feature.

And there'd been a girl for Benjamin, one he very nearly married, but she'd backed out at the last minute with vague misgivings. "An odd feeling," she'd said, suddenly clairvoyant. He wasn't as broken up by the event as everyone thought. He didn't feel he deserved the attention he'd received and was actually disturbed by all the pies and casseroles sent to him by other single girls expressing their sympathies, as though someone had died. Benjamin felt he'd been given a second chance, if not granted a whole new life. He'd stayed clear of women since then, using the excuse "Once bitten, twice shy." Still, he was adored by homely girls in his parish, whom he'd visit on rare occasions. But most of his time he spent alone or with Harlan Weeks, another bitten, shy man.

He had not wanted to because it felt like cheating, but he climbed up into the cab of the truck anyway. The driver, a young man of no more than 20, turned in his seat, bringing a leg up, spreading his legs and showing off the hole just under his zipper, his stuff held fast in the waffled fabric of long johns.

"You can call me Tige," the young man said with a loopy, lopsided grin, "though my name is something else." He relaxed expansively across the seat and played with the hairs that curled up and out over the frayed neck of his T-shirt.

The ashtray filled to overflowing, and a bottle was passed and swigged surreptitiously, although there was no one around to see them.

The sun was just going down, and they were parked on a long-abandoned service road that had a reputation for this sort of thing—men parked in cars, quick walks in the woods, no names. Benjamin was eager to have things over with, to ride home with damp shorts and a temporarily dampened desire—until he'd see Harlan again, which always seemed to fire him up something awful.

"I live in Macungie," Tige said. "My dad owns this produce company. I've got an old lady too, and a kid." He spoke quietly, quickly, smoke leaking out of his mouth and nostrils, getting rid of a lot of truths as though they were burdens. Benjamin rolled his window down to get rid of his cigarette. His car and Tige's truck, one behind the other, were alone. He could hear trucks rumbling by on the interstate. He touched Tige's leg to start things off. He rubbed the thigh and inched up toward that hole, the patch of cream-colored thermal that seemed almost to glow. Tige sighed and stretched out more.

"I wish I could see you," Tige said. He opened his fly and lifted his ass, straightening his legs, pushing himself out of his jeans. His cock sprang up, white against the dark plaid of his shirt. "Wish there was more light." The cab light would have drawn more attention than either man wanted, would have illuminated them like stage actors, two men about to undress one another on a cold autumn night.

Benjamin leaned over to taste the cock—they were all different, the way they felt and tasted. He thought about his dad's fishing buddy, years ago, and the guy who came to fix the water heater, and the lawyer from Pittsburgh, and Dwayne Lutz from high school, the night before graduation.

This one tasted good, smelled clean, was hard and long, if not very thick. Benjamin put his hands on the warm skin of Tige's belly, enjoying its hard flatness and downy fur. He elbowed his way between Tige's knees and wished for more light himself, wanting to see this one laid bare: his pink, knotted bung hole; the mossy droop of his balls; the long lines of his thighs. He touched Tige like a blind man dying to read, touched him everywhere—his moist underarms, his alarmed little nipples, the hairy declivity of his sternum, the musky stink behind his nuts.

"Yeah," Tige was saying, "yeah...yeah." He touched Benjamin's head, feeling the shaved hairs at the top of the scalp, soft as down. Benjamin played with Tige's balls, pulling and twisting, grazing the now-taut sac with his unshaved chin.

They did what they could on the narrow front seat, their pants down to their ankles. Benjamin lay across the supine truck driver and breathed into his mouth, humping his prick across the man's hairy belly. Tige's cock worked its way upward between Benjamin's ass cheeks to rub against his asshole. Benjamin put his face on Tige's, smelling his hair, the smoke and shampoo of it, licking his smooth cheek. Their lips came together again, and Tige slipped a wild tongue into Benjamin's mouth, surprising him with its crazy undulations. Tige moaned beneath him, and Benjamin squeezed his legs together, catching the man's prick in a tight grasp. His own cock head, dragging across Tige's silky abdomen, sputtered and tracked slick lines of precome.

"I'm gone," Tige whispered, gushing a fountain of hot sauce all over Benjamin's behind. He made his stomach taut like a drum, a sounding board for Benjamin's rutting pecker. Benjamin, all too aware of Tige's juices gathering in his ass crack and running up and down the channel over Benjamin's pinched slit, felt his nuts rise gutward and shoot gobs of semen between the two hairy bellies.

"We're a mess," Benjamin said a little later.

"We're bad," Tige said, dabbing at his stomach once they'd separated, and Benjamin thought of Harlan.

He watched him stoke the fire and replace the screen. A piece of green wood spit and popped, and the dogs each opened an eye to regard the noisemaker. Harlan grabbed them both by their lazy heads and petted them with rough affection, saying, "How are my boys? Ain't you my boys?" and Benjamin said "Yes, I am," only not so Harlan could hear, and then Harlan got up and looked at him.

"Ready?" Benjamin wanted to know.

"Gotta be in East Texas in the morning," Harlan said, and Benjamin looked at him, getting this crazy thought in his head: *I'd walk across Texas for you, Harlan Weeks.*

He followed Harlan to the bedroom, stopping for a piss with the door half closed. When he came out of the john and walked into the bedroom, Harlan was sitting on the edge of the bed. His pants lay on the floor, his pale thighs thick with muscle, reflecting the glow of the lamp, boxers taut as drawn skin across his crotch. His gaze seemed to be on his feet, still in socks, one on its side. Then he looked up at Benjamin.

"I'm in my head," he said, almost smiling.

Benjamin nodded. He went around to the other side of the bed (*My side*, he was thinking), undid the long line of shirt and jeans buttons, and stripped down to the union suit he wished he hadn't worn. He couldn't very well take that off too and slide in bare-assed beside his buddy, as much as he wanted to. He stepped on the toe of one sock to get it off and did the same with the other. He got into bed.

Harlan was still sitting up, although his shirt had gone to the floor with his pants. His bare back was winged from hard work, tapered at his waist, where dark hairs grew. He turned suddenly and brought his legs up and lay back but didn't get under the covers, even though it was cold in the room. He didn't turn off the light either but lay there for what seemed like a long time, giving Benjamin an opportunity to look his friend over from head to toe. Harlan had a long torso covered with dark curling hairs, little overlapping O's all over his chest and stomach. He lay a big hand on his belly, nearly covering his crotch, and Benjamin looked at his nipples, how they jutted up and cast shadows across his chest.

Benjamin found himself aching with hardness. Lying flat like Harlan, he could see the impression of his desire visible under the pile of blankets.

"Ben," Harlan said, some frog coming to rest in his throat.

"What?" Benjamin asked.

"Good night, Benjamin."

In the middle of the night, with the moon throwing a rectangle of pale light across the bed, Harlan and Benjamin lay side by side, a good foot of mattress between them until Harlan rolled wide in his sleep and fetched up against Benjamin, who hadn't been sleeping. Harlan threw his arm over his bedmate and held him fast, his hand twitching against Benjamin's breast. Benjamin didn't dare move, didn't care to move. He felt Harlan's breath on his neck, making his mouth wet, and he swallowed hard. Harlan moved in closer, seeking more warmth, Benjamin guessed, until his hand slipped down Benjamin's body and into the fly of his union suit. He grabbed up Benjamin's erection, his palm rough against the shaft, and jerked it a little. *He's sleepwalking*, Benjamin thought, terrified his friend would awaken and find himself compromised. Harlan continued to masturbate Benjamin, who was suddenly breathless and dripping. *He is sleeping, isn't he?*

Harlan moved them so that they were on their sides. He sighed deeply, pushing his groin against Benjamin's behind. Benjamin stayed still and tried not to come. Harlan started humping himself against Benjamin's ass, his dick slipping into the rear flap that up until now had been nothing but a nuisance for Benjamin. Harlan gripped Benjamin's prick and stuck his sandy chin between his friend's shoulder blades. Harlan's hot pole burrowed between Benjamin's cool cheeks, finding a groove. Benjamin tried to stay still, tried not to enjoy himself. He was certain that there was going to be hell to pay sooner or later, that Harlan would awaken and feel double-crossed. Still, he could not stop the flow of early dew that sprang from his cock end, lubricating the shaft and Harlan's callused palm.

But how could he be asleep? His every movement was so precise, the way he pulled on Benjamin's prick, the way he pushed his own against Benjamin's little hole. He'd leaked enough himself to oil up the tip of his dick, so that it slid into the tight wedge of Benjamin's ass cheeks and right into him.

Benjamin grunted, feeling stabbed, even though Harlan worked slowly. Harlan rolled them over, Benjamin going onto his stomach with Harlan on top of him. The magic connection of Harlan's hand on his prick was broken, but the position allowed for a deeper penetration that was more satisfying than any hand job. Benjamin had never felt so deeply planted, so fully entered. Harlan brought his hands up under Benjamin's arms and clasped them at the back of his neck, a full nelson, and he hammered himself into his friend's rear end. Benjamin's legs spread—he wanted cock, more cock, sliding in and out of him. He lifted his ass to meet Harlan's hips, and they slapped together, and he felt Harlan's short, hot breaths on his back, and his drool and tongue. He got a hand beneath himself to pull on his prick. He wanted to be fucked forever, wanted to feel Harlan's cock filling him up always, but Harlan, with quiet moans and lips smeared against Benjamin's shoulder blade, was about to bring the fucking to an end. He screwed Benjamin fiercely, his breath whistling through clenched teeth, and he twitched and stifled a holler when he shot, his dick head somewhere in Benjamin's middle, spitting out a prodigious amount of spunk that ran out with each of Harlan's last strokes.

It was over then, and Harlan rolled off him, curling into his side of the bed, his back to Benjamin. Benjamin's ass was raw, his cock aching. He sat up and got out of bed carefully, not wanting to believe his friend had used him so completely and without so much as a word. He walked around the bed, seeing Harlan's closed eyes and parted lips, and he contemplated sticking his prick to those lips and letting loose the flow of jizz he was holding back now by a thread. "Harlan," he said softly.

Harlan didn't stir, but his lips closed, and Benjamin went into the bathroom to rid himself of his and Harlan's loads.

They never talked about that night. Never, although Benjamin relived it again and again, alone in his room, beating off. He hated himself for not having the courage to broach the subject, to say to Harlan, "That night you fucked me was the happiest night of my life." What was it about Harlan and his demeanor that discouraged such frankness? What was it about Benjamin that made him regard that night as some sort of shameful event? He watched Harlan and waited.

Spring came, and they went fishing. He stared at his friend's behind, the way his pants showed off his meaty package, the sweet, curling hairs at his throat, until he had to look away at something else and will away the boner he'd aroused. He looked at the trees. Their new buds reminded Benjamin of that deserted service road. The bare trees of winter, through which his car could be viewed from the interstate, bore leaves now, and he could park hidden.

He'd given his number out just that one time to Tige, but Tige didn't call until it was almost summer. His own house was stifling, he said from a phone booth somewhere. He sounded like a cowboy, his diction possessing the twang of country music stations. Benjamin gave him directions to his home, sheltered by elms and maples and firs and cool on this particular evening. He showered and waited, wondering what they would do, where they would do it.

Tige rapped on the screened door, peering through it, and Benjamin rose up from his chair, his palms itching.

"Good to see you," Tige said.

"Likewise," Benjamin replied, and he offered the man a seat and a beer.

They sat across from one another, making small talk about the weather. "My dad and me used to fish on that lake up there," Tige said, pointing in the general direction of Cross Lake, a mile or so up the road. Benjamin nodded, saying, "Had a boat docked there myself awhile but lost it in that big storm two years ago." Tige nodded.

They went out back where the shade was dark, the evening sky obscured by the leaves and branches overhead, and Benjamin looked Tige over, liking his height and his pointy boots and the top six undone buttons of his shirt. He was thicker than Benjamin remembered, having added some winter weight. He wore it well, and his jeans too. He filled his clothes nicely.

There were chairs back here too, but they both remained on their feet, and after a while each realized he didn't have to guard his glances and could stare outright, and they both did. Benjamin felt himself hardening under Tige's scrutiny and wanted to be touched where Tige was looking. He held his bottle down by his crotch and stared at Tige's and waited until he couldn't wait any more. He stepped up to the man, dropping his beer, and put his hands on Tige's chest, his fingers going into the opened vee and spreading across his pecs. He opened the shirt and slid it back off Tige's shoulders and put his mouth on one of his flat pink nipples, tonguing it up to a hard dot of flesh, and then moved over and did the same with its twin. He undid the big shining buckle of Tige's belt—a flat metal replica of a car battery, apparently—and bared Tige's Skivvies, boxers emblazoned with the Jetsons—George and Jane, his boy, Elroy, daughter Judy. His interest lay less in the pattern than in what Tige's boxers had no power to conceal. The front of his shorts threatened to bust and was soaked with the early leakings of his excited, drippy prick. Benjamin uncovered it, remembering it, tasting it again, taking all of it into his mouth with a big swallow. He slapped away a mosquito and sucked hard on the tapered end of Tige's cock. He felt the man's hands on his head, on his shoulders, slipping down the neck of his T-shirt and scratching just under the shoulder blades, coaxing more and more of his dick into him, taking the T-shirt up in his fists and pulling it up over Benjamin's head, breaking their connection for only a second or two, and then Benjamin was back at the sticky prong, lapping up its honeyed juices, forcing it down his throat. He heard his name being called from somewhere far away, and Tige slapped the top of his head.

"Someone's here," he whispered, getting himself back into his shorts and trying to pull up his pants.

It was Harlan Weeks—who else would be coming by to see Benjamin uninvited? (Not that he wasn't welcome, as always.) Tige and Benjamin separated, Tige taking a walk over to the side of the yard, trying to zip up. Benjamin batted at his boner. He looked over at Tige, who seemed fairly composed, and called out to Harlan, "Back here," straightening his pecker so that it stood behind the zipper of his shorts, nearly obscured.

Harlan stood at the back door.

Tige drank down his beer, glancing at Benjamin.

Harlan wore an odd pair of shorts, odd because Benjamin had never seen him in shorts before—always pants, blue work ones or an old pair of jeans worn white and two sizes too big. His unsunned legs were darkened by the mesh of hairs that covered them. His knees looked raw and knobby. He was holding a beer already.

He stepped out onto the grass, his feet sockless in old work shoes. He nodded at Tige, reaching out to shake his hand.

"Harlan, meet Tige," Benjamin said.

It was Tige who misread the situation, perhaps thinking Harlan had come in on some cue. He smirked then and grabbed the front of his jeans and gave Harlan a raw look. The gesture was not wasted on Harlan, whose gaze dropped to the bulge in Tige's grip.

"What are you two up to this fine evening?" Harlan asked unnecessarily.

"This and that," Tige said.

They stood together awkwardly—Benjamin felt awkward, at least. The other two seemed perfectly at ease with the buzzing tension that hung in the air like humidity, coating them, making them sticky.

Harlan took off his shirt and had a seat in one of the chairs, an odd set to his lips. His brown hair was all the more kinky this evening, and the hairs of his chest looked wet. The top button of his shorts was gone, and his belly, although hard and flat, doubled there at the stressed zipper. His crotch—as always—was well-packaged, wrapped in the confines of his shorts.

"It would be nice to take a dip in the lake," Harlan said. "Pity you ain't got that boat anymore, Ben."

Ben nodded, chewing his lip.

"You look familiar to me," Harlan said to Tige, who laughed out loud.

"I ought to," he said, giggling.

"I was afraid of that," Harlan said.

"You remember me?"

Benjamin, disturbed and off-balance, felt the need for another beer. He had poise enough to offer another round to his two friends, but when he came back with the cold bottles, he found Tige and Harlan stripped and rolling in the grass, white poles flashing in the light from the back porch.

Who is this man come here as Harlan Weeks? Benjamin wanted to know. He stood with his hands full, enraptured by the show the two made, all mouths and hands and shining pricks, hard and combatant, struggling for purchase and the upper hand. *Where do I fit in all this?*

He found his place between them, his clothes tugged off, hungry mouths sliding over his skin. He opened his mouth for Tige's cock and spread his legs for Harlan's hips. He was not fucked, not yet, but fingered brusquely, causing his pecker to bob and secrete a syrupy ooze across his belly. Tige sat on his face, offering his snatch to Benjamin while he played with Harlan's nipples. Benjamin lapped it up and was lapped up himself, his prong tongue-bathed by someone or other—who knew? He closed his eyes and stuck his tongue up Tige's tight hole and figured Harlan Weeks was possessed, some sort of sexual werewolf, prone to this sort of thing on account of the moon.

"Fuck him," he heard, reduced to ears, dick, and hole.

"You first."

"No, you, because I want to fuck you while you're doing it."

They got into position, and Benjamin, on his hands and knees, felt the first aching jabs of Tige's slender prick. It seemed longer and sharper and probed into him like some kind of tool. Tige held his shoulders and cursed Harlan's girth as he was slammed into Benjamin.

"Fuck," Harlan muttered. "Fuck, oh, fuck."

Benjamin turned around to see Harlan pull out of Tige's hole and spill out a load across the man's back.

"Looks like it's just you and me," Tige said, fucking Benjamin harder, making him grunt. They turned around, and Benjamin sank onto his back, the grass cool and damp beneath him. He kicked up his legs, and Harlan held his feet while his cock dribbled sweetly onto Benjamin's forehead. Benjamin thought he would go crazy looking up at Harlan's crack, at the big and heavy half-hard swinging, and when Harlan squatted, his club dropping into Benjamin's wide-open mouth, Benjamin thought he was going to die a happy man: his breath stopped, his cock throbbing, his hole pounded into again and again, his prostate in a state of delirium. He closed his eyes and smiled, his insides tickled, and then he heard Harlan say, "Move over."

How long had it been since that first night? Harlan's fat cock felt as familiar as Benjamin's own three fingers. Harlan held him, his arms underneath him, and banged himself up into his friend's bung hole, grass-staining Benjamin's shoulder blades. Tige stood watching, pulling on his dick and wagging it in Harlan's face.

"Close," he said, and Harlan turned toward the prick and opened his mouth, accepting the spurting flow of come that shot out of Tige's tiny-headed cock.

"Oh," Benjamin said, his prick filling his hand, Harlan filling his ass. He dug his toes into the grass and lifted his hips to meet each thrust. He tried to stall his own orgasm with willpower, but he was a slave to Harlan, helpless. He showered himself with a warm spray of white. It splashed his face and chest, clinging to his eyelashes and the hairs that grew around his nipples. Harlan leaned over and licked him clean while continuing to batter Benjamin's insides. When he worked himself up to another blast, he pulled out, crawled up to Benjamin's mouth, inserted the pole, and emptied his nuts of another prodigious load.

Winter came around again. Harlan tipped back in his chair. The dogs each opened an eye. Benjamin, on his knees in front of Harlan, opened his mouth wider to accommodate the thick base of Harlan's dick. Harlan played with his hair, his pecker stiffening all the more. "It's snowing," he said. "Looks like you'll be spending the night again."

Benjamin nodded as best he could.

Tuesdays We Read Baudelaire

Mr. Gerard said he was going to Paris. Luke and I nodded. "Paris is cool," Luke said. How he'd know, I didn't know. Maybe he saw something on MTV about it. I was wishing I had worn some other kind of underwear, because I knew Luke was going to tell me to take off my jeans any minute. The briefs I was wearing were my brother's—too big and not at all sexy except to me. I watched Luke playing with the buttons of his jeans. I could see his dick under the denim, the way it moved slyly down his thigh. Luke had a big one. Mr. Gerard pretended not to notice, but I knew he could see it, liked seeing it. He sat on his chair with a cup of tea on his knee. He was tall and thin, wearing wire-rimmed glasses. His hair was combed back with some gel. There was a volume of Baudelaire on the table beside him—that's what he called it; it wasn't a book, it was a "volume."

Luke and I were drinking beers. Luke said, "Could I have another?" and I said, "Me too." I'd finished mine a while ago but didn't want to ask for more. Luke was good at asking for more. That's what I liked about him.

"Of course," Mr. Gerard said, and he started to get up, but I said I'd get them. I liked walking through his house. The hallway to the kitchen was lined with pictures of men. The walls were painted a mossy green, and the trim was red, and it always reminded me of being inside a Christmas box.

The kitchen's ceiling was higher than the hall's, and there was a hanging fixture that looked like a streetlight. It had a soft shine, though, and everything looked neat and clean, the way it always looked. There was a box of cookies on the counter that wasn't opened, so I didn't take one, but I did look into a cupboard to see what was there. There wasn't anything but food. I don't know what I expected to find.

I got the beers and went back to where we were sitting. Mr. Gerard called it the sitting room. It was a living room and his bedroom all together, though. The bed was against the wall and piled with pillows, looking like a couch, kind of, and he had a couple of chairs that were huge and comfortable, roomy enough for Luke and me together, and a big table covered with things, mainly books and magazines. In this room the walls were red and the trim was green, and it wasn't like being in a box at all. It was more like some foreign country, what with the hanging silk-covered lamps, the odd drawings of chairs that hung on one wall, and a big gold-framed mirror. Luke liked standing in front of the mirror when he undressed. He was working out and was in love with his body, which seemed to change every day. I liked the mirror because it was like seeing a big picture of all of us together.

Luke and I worked together at Good Buys. He worked in the electronics department, and I was a cashier, mostly. We graduated from school together but didn't really know each other until we started working together; then it was like, "Hey, I know you," and we started hanging out together. He took me up to the top of the hill that overlooked Reading and pointed out where he lived now. He shared an apartment near the outlets with Kenny Farrell, who was turning out, Luke said, to be a real asshole. I didn't know it at the time, but the hill was real cruisy, and I noticed all the guys pulling up to us and sitting in their cars doing nothing, waiting for something to happen. Some of them waved at Luke. (One of them, it turned out, was Mr. Gerard. I didn't know it until later, though.) I didn't say anything because I still hadn't put two and two together, so Luke said, "Guys come up here to get their rocks off." He looked at me, and I could make out his face in the darkness but not what he was driving at. It must have shown on my face, though, the blankness, the "duh," because he laughed and said, "With other guys. In their cars or in the woods there, or you go home with them."

I said, "Oh," and he laughed again, harder this time, and I laughed too because I felt stupid, and he put his hand on my leg. It stayed there, and I got a boner. I was glad he started it, because I never, ever would have, even though I liked him so much that I dreamed about him and pretended he was in bed with me at night, one of his hands on my hard-on, the other farther down between my legs, fingering my butt. I would stare at him from across the sales floor when I could, and he'd catch me and make a stupid face or a jack-off hand sign, like "I'm so fucking bored," and I'd nod, loving him.

He leaned over me that night and started licking my face like a dog. I wasn't expecting that, but it wasn't so bad, and when he started on my neck, it made me crazy with wanting him, and I put my arms around him, getting my hands into the back of his jeans, finding him without underwear. I pulled him onto me, but his legs were stuck between the seat and the steering wheel. His ass cheeks felt smooth, like river rocks. I squeezed them hard. "Take it easy, he-man," he said, undoing the buttons of his jeans. His fanny felt cold in my hands, and I rubbed his cheeks to warm them. My fingers touched into the rough of his crack—he was hot there and a little sweaty. The smell of his butt was going to stay on my fingers for hours that night since I refused to wash it off, sniffing them through the night and making myself come two, three times.

What he did to me that night was rub his big cock against my stomach. He lifted my shirt and played with my nipples and pushed his groin against my gut and humped me that way. His balls rubbed against the waistband of my jeans, and I wanted to take them down, my jeans, to get my dick out too, but Luke held my hands up over my head, his elbows dug into my armpits. I squirmed under him, seeing the bars of headlights cutting through the night air all around us, Luke's hot breath falling down on me in blasts, some stupid song I hated on the radio. I pushed up with my crotch, my dick harder than steel, right up against his fanny. I'd never fucked anyone before, but I was sure that was what I wanted to do. He kept gut-fucking me, though, holding my hands and licking the insides of my arms, making these little noises that really turned me on, little grunts or something that made me think he was really getting into what he was doing. And then he said, "OK," and lifted himself, and I felt the spray of his come hit my face and the front of my shirt. He sat up, right on my crotch, and moved his butt around. Everyone could see him and knew what he was doing, even if they couldn't see me. He touched my nipples, just put his thumbs over them, finding them right away through my semen-spotted T-shirt, and I sauced in my jeans.

It was only a week or so later when he came up to me in the break room, touching the back of my neck even though there was a camera in the room up in the corner by the ceiling. (I think they even had them in the toilets.) He said that we were going to visit a friend of his and that he brought a joint for the ride.

"Where does this guy live?" I asked.

"Just in Flying Hills, man," Luke said. He sat at the table with me and got one of his shoes off and put his foot up in my crotch, and I got a hard-on that lasted all fucking day.

He tried to explain it to me in the car on the way to Mr. Gerard's, but the dope made me stupid and lame, and I just wanted to put my hands in his jeans and touch his cock. "He likes watching," Luke said, unbuttoning his jeans to let me into the warm confines of his underpants. "You sit and have tea with him, and he reads a couple of poems, and then we fuck around."

"Does he fuck around too?" I asked.

Luke shook his head. It was dark now, and his cock glowed green under the dashboard. I had it in my mouth and was sucking on it, lapping up the sweet seepage that leaked out. "Shit," he said. "That feels awesome, Billy." He put a hand on the top of my head, forcing my mouth down into his pubes, and I swallowed him. I did some serious head bobbing, riding his veiny shaft and leaving a pool of my spit in the hairy hollow where his belly and dick met. He slipped his hand inside my shirt and fingered one of my nipples and made me feel wild, unable to get enough of him into my mouth. I wanted to eat him up. I growled and moaned, and he pinched my tit hard, and I had to stop because I was close enough to make a mess of myself, humping the seat piggishly.

"You're a fucking animal, man," Luke said, pulling off to the side of the road. "We're here." He got out of the car, putting away his wet and sticky boner, and got himself ready to introduce me to his friend Mr. Gerard.

I had expected someone older, I think, someone less attractive. Mr. Gerard—I never learned his first name—looked to me like someone who was really hot trying to look like a total dweeb, like Clark Kent or something. He shook my hand, with this prissy smile on his face, and led us into the sitting room, asking Luke how he'd been, going on about how long it had been since he'd seen him even though Luke told me they'd gotten together the previous week. There was a tray on an ottoman set up for tea: the pot on top of some little burner, three cups all ready for us. The room flickered with candles.

Mr. Gerard didn't talk; he chatted. Every third word out of his mouth was "delightful," and every fourth was "fascinating" as he sat cross-legged in a chair going on and on about this and that, his eyes flicking between Luke and me.

And then he said, getting up, "I need to make a phone call. Would you excuse me?"

When he left the room, Luke nudged me. He unzipped his jeans, and his prong poked out from his shorts. "C'mon," he said, "get undressed."

"What for?" I asked.

"It's time to frolic," Luke said, looking at me with a little smile. "He'll be back to watch."

I stood up and took my pants down. Luke told me to leave my socks on. "Next time you have to wear tighty-whiteys like me." Luke left his briefs on, his dick sticking out through the pee hole. He looked very sexy to me, and I lunged at him, but he dodged me. I fell across the pillow-covered daybed, my rear end swatted. He fell on top of me, his cock going hotly between my butt cheeks. We hadn't fucked yet, but I was hoping we would sometime and liked letting him know I thought the idea was pretty awesome. He burrowed his dog into the channel of my crack, licking my back. I rolled over, flipping us so that I was on top, his cock still trapped between my cheeks. I wriggled my fanny, feeling the sudden ooze of slickness that had leaked out of his fat-tipped bone. He put his hands on my hips and slid me up and down against his shaft. He covered my belly, putting a finger into my belly button, rubbing me there, and then his hands moved up the ribbed cage of my middle to the chocolate kisses of my nipples. I had my eyes closed, my head tilted back. I could smell his hair, I could feel his lips against the back of my neck, and I heard him say, "Pretend you don't see him," and I looked up, and there was Mr. Gerard across the room with a gigantic hard-on sticking out of his pants. He was rubbing the end of it, peering at us like a museum exhibit. Candlelight reflected off the lenses of his glasses. "Suck my cock, man," Luke prompted, and I slowly got off him, feeling the loss of his burning prick against my rear. I turned so that my butt was pointing at Mr. Gerard, and I made my little hole wink and purse, but Luke moved me with a finger, allowing a clear view of his dick sliding into my mouth. I sensed movement in Mr. Gerard's corner and glanced over to see him edging closer, getting himself behind one of his enormous chairs, hiding his fat pecker and the jacking he was doing. I was thinking it would have been more fun if he joined in. From the corner of my eye, he looked awesome, his black hair like one of those British movie stars who play pirates and Shakespeare, long and wavy like that.

Luke spread his legs, and I played with the taut cotton that covered his balls, giving them a good squeeze. I petted his thighs, which were all feathery with hair and hard with muscle from playing soccer or whatever he did when he was in school. I chugged down on his boner, feeling my throat constrict around the head, feeling him throb alongside my tonsils, and he put his hands on my head and did some pretty impressive moaning, saying my name, rolling his head from side to side like I was taking him to the edge of ecstasy or something. I lifted my head to look him in the eye, a drippy string of drool and precome connecting us.

"Bring it here," he said.

Up until now Luke hadn't really gone near my cock. He might have licked it once or twice while we were locked in a sixty-nine and his prick was rooting around in my esophagus, but I couldn't have said he ever really sucked it. It didn't make much difference to me up until then, but the thought of it happening made my dick ache with wanting to feel his lips around it. I crawled up the bed on my knees, sinking into the pillows, bringing him my cock. When I got it close enough for him to kiss the end, he looked up at me and said, "Take it easy." He took hold of my prick like it was a finger sandwich and stuck out his tongue at it. I steadied myself with one hand on the wall behind Luke's head. Mr. Gerard had moved again, getting a better view. I could see his great penis, pale and huge, with its rolling skin and bright red head. He held it with both hands and still couldn't cover all of its shaft. He pulled on his trouser snake, pinching out a flood of leakage, baring and covering the bulbous head. But I forgot about Mr. Gerard when I felt the first heat of Luke's mouth and the slide of my dick head over his flattened tongue.

I did my best to keep still, but I couldn't help myself and had to fuck that soft wetness. It was better than anything I'd ever felt, better than the cool and slippery slide of the percale pillowcase I'd been fucking ever since I could remember, better than the space between Eric Moser's hairless thighs, better even than the spitty cup of my hand. I loved the friction of his chin on my balls and the terror of his slight underbite when his bottom teeth caught on the sensitive underside of my cock head. Together the sensations combined and doubled, tripled;

I was practically shaking but banging into his mouth with a vengeance. I started breathing hard, and Luke was tapping my thighs, then hitting my stomach, choking on me. I pulled out, out of control, and creamed across his face, practically bawling, and I felt the warm squirt of jizz on the backs of my thighs as Luke unloaded.

"That wasn't so bad," Luke said later in the car. "Was it?"

I shrugged. Actually it was the single most awesome experience of my life. I'd just had an orgasm that was like an explosion, and it was witnessed by a man wanking on a monster dick, watching me like television. "Not bad," I agreed.

I was surprised one day when I saw Mr. Gerard in the CD department of Good Buys. "I'm looking for a Puccini disc," he said when I came up to him. He looked different to me this day—his hair wasn't so gelled, his clothes not all black and woolly. He looked very much like a normal guy. "Luke is busy tonight, but I was wondering if you'd care to drop by."

I told him I didn't drive.

"I'd be happy to pick you up. Shall I? After work?"

I waited outside the store for half an hour and was just about ready to give up when he pulled up in a little black Jag. He apologized for being late. "I was at the gym," he said, and I noticed under his jacket that he wasn't wearing a shirt and tie but a stringy tank top. There was a dark brush of hair between his pecs, straight and shining. He had on a pair of sweats, old gray ones with a rip in one knee. He looked more normal than ever. I sank into the leather seat with a sort of awe. He hadn't shaved, and he was wearing, I thought, contacts. It was like being with another person altogether.

He kept quiet. Apparently he liked the song on the radio. He hummed bits and pieces of it, his eyes intent on the road.

Mr. Gerard excused himself to go to the bathroom once we arrived, and he took a long time. I sat and leafed through some boring magazines. *Where's the porn?* I wondered and figured he was taking a bath or something. He came out the same way he went in, though, and sat down beside me on the bed made up as a couch.

"Take off your clothes for me," he said casually, as though he'd just asked me to get him a glass of water. I stood up, feeling a little shy, and moved away so he'd have a good view. I started stripping.

"Take your time," he said, leaning back on some pillows. The crotch of his sweats was prominent, a mountain of a molehill. I unbuttoned my shirt slowly, getting down to my T-shirt. I still had shoes and socks and jeans and briefs to go, figuring it would be a long show, not really thinking about how fast clothes come off. I went for the shoes next, untying them, bent over, feeling the blood rush to my face. I saw his hand run over the lump in his sweats.

The shoes came off quicker than I'd expected. I straightened up and wondered what to take off next—shirt, socks, or pants. I did some mental head scratching and decided the socks would go next, but I was going to need some help. I stepped close to Mr. Gerard and put my foot on the cushion between his legs. He caught on quickly and didn't seem put off by the idea. He grasped my foot and gently peeled the sock off, rubbing the sole with his thumb, his other hand on my ankle and creeping higher. When I gave him the other foot to unsock, he pulled me onto him.

"You're better at this than you let on," he said, his mouth close to my ear. His hands went all over my backside, and it was becoming apparent that my cherry little behind wasn't meant for Luke after all. He ran his thumb along the seam of the ass of my jeans, applying pressure at my hole and again where my balls were flattened between my legs. His mouth worked all over mine, his tongue darting and stabbing, flat and slobbering, then hard and pointed, and he stuck it into my mouth so that it nearly went to the back of my throat, taking my breath away. He let me up for air once, rolling us around so that he was on top, and his sweats were gone, and he was humping me with his humongous tool. His legs were covered with fine black hairs. I could put my hands on the backs of his thighs and cup his ass cheeks, which were smooth and firm with muscle. He sighed when I put my fingers into his crack, and he pawed at my briefs, rolling them off my hips and pushing them down my thighs, and they turned into tight ropes around my knees. His cock rolled over mine, dwarfing it, leaking a sticky goo that made it slick between us. His balls dangled down in the V of my legs, banging against my little chestnuts, slapping against my pinched-up little hole.

He got up and stood over me. "Get on your hands and knees," he said quietly. He had his great prong in his hand, palming it, getting his juices flowing. I looked at the gigantic head and wondered how he was going to get it into me without splitting me open. "Don't worry," he added. "I wouldn't dream of hurting you."

He got behind me and started eating out my butt. I could feel the ring of my anus flutter under the stroke of his tongue. He licked up and down my ditch, wild hairs springing up all over the place. He bit my ass cheeks and chinned my balls. He handled my prick gently, tugging on the end of it, his fingers smearing in the grease. I heard him say, "Ready?" and I thought, *I'll never be ready for that thing.*

He didn't fuck me, though—not with his cock, anyway. He fingered me with his left hand and jacked off with his right, and he told me to turn over. I think he was afraid I'd jizz up his bedspread; I'd already gotten plenty of dick drool on it. On my back I lifted my legs and put my feet on his chest. His finger poked at that spot I'd recently found on my own, and it was driving me crazy. Mr. Gerard looked down at me with this glazed look on his face, his eyes slitted. He licked his beautiful lips, working another finger in. He tapped my thigh with the heavy head of his dick, leaving wet marks.

"Jerk yourself off," he said, because I wasn't touching myself—I didn't need to, really. I was sure he was going to make me come, working his fingertips over that hardening ball up my ass. "I want to see you come," he said, and I said, "OK," and it just happened. I started squirting all over myself, clotty streams of white flying all over, landing on my face and in my hair and on the pillows behind me, which might have pissed him off if he hadn't been so horny.

Mr. Gerard bent over and started lapping up my come like a cat over spilled milk. I could feel his fisted cock between my legs, then the hot spray of jizz as his prick spit out all over my cock and bush and balls.

He fell back on the bed with a huge sigh, his stiffer looking like a candle dripping wax. I wanted to lick it off. He looked at me with sleepy eyes. I was fascinated by his cock, the enormity of it, the way it started falling, a tree in slow motion, big and white, across his thigh, slime still coming out of the fat head.

"You want to do it again, don't you?" he said to me, and I nodded.

"Dinner first," he said. "We'll go to Joe's. And when we come back you can fuck my brains out. How does that sound?"

I shrugged. "OK, I guess," I said, though inside I was starting to boil. My dick was still hard, and I imagined what it would be like to be up inside that muscular ass and very nearly had a little accident.

Mr. Gerard got up and took my hand, pulling me up and leading me to the bathroom. He turned on the water and started filling the tub, pouring in this and that, turning the water a pretty green that smelled like limes and oranges and roses all together. He touched the pointed prong that wouldn't go away.

"Insistent," he said thoughtfully.

We got into the hot water, and he pulled me to him, getting me between his legs as though we were tobogganing, and he put his lips against my head.

"Have you read any Kaváfis?" he asked me, and I carefully shook my head no.

"Oh, you must," he said. "You must."